SECRET OF THE OMBAX

FLAGSHIP OF THE AUTOMATED EMPIRE
BOOK ONE

DENNIS M. MYERS

**Flagship of the Automated Empire
Volume One**

Secret of the Ombax

Dennis M. Myers

Dewstar Media
www.dewstarmedia.com

ISBN 978-1-969950-99-5 (eBook)

ISBN 978-1-969950-15-5 (Paperback)

1st Edition, 2025

This story is dedicated to my uncle,

Lynn Elton Baker

A
True artist
One who creates art
Because it is what he lives for
That is all there is to it
He is one of the inspirations in my life
Instead of choosing the easy and more profitable path,
He chose to follow the path of true creativity that he loves.
A man
of faith
And
Family.

(Hey look, I drew a TREE!)

POUCH-BROTHERS

Mas'eeng Bayfod, First Seven, Late

Daksey's tail hurt as he walked. Lush green vegetation rose on both sides of the path, shading them from the sun. He shifted his pack a little higher to keep the bottom further from the wounded appendage. The top of the pack pressed down on the lowest quill of his crest, but that was only a minor annoyance. He followed Bongeex through the forest. Brilliant sunlight splashed the ground in spots as it fought through the leaves. The pack on his pouch-brother's back bulged larger than his own. He would claim it meant he was the better hunter. Daksey thought differently.

His pouch-brother glanced over his shoulder and huffed. "You should try harder targets. You'll bring home more meat."

"You should take less risk. You'll bring home meat more often."

Bongeex chut-chutted with laughter. They continued for a while in silence. Then he stopped and turned to Daksey. "I think you and I bring home the same number of meals. I bring more from a single hunt but sometimes miss my prey. You rarely miss your prey, but it's smaller. Less risk. I think it balances out."

Daksey snorted. "You believe your way is better?"

Bongeex tilted his head. "I don't know." He shifted his pack. "But it feels better when we get home, and the crowd gathers."

Daksey chut-chutted. "Bring home something big enough, maybe you'll be a pouch-husband before your next molt."

Bongeex undulated his neck in agreement. "Or very soon after, pouch-brother. Very soon after."

"Has an egg-mother approached you, already?"

Bongeex swayed. "I've caught glances. But only egg-mothers of Botham, and none have approached, yet." He turned and started through the trees again. "It's not much further, now."

"I know." Daskey snorted. "I'm not lost."

Bongeex chut-chutted. "You are quick to anger, today."

Daksey felt himself start to sway, but held his neck still. "All is well. You are annoying." He arched his shoulders forward, pulling the pack off his thick tail, again.

They topped the next rise and started down into their familiar valley. The foliage thinned, and the tall Koyosek trees of their village came into view. Daksey could see the three pennants streaming from the watch platform at the top of the tallest tower. White in the middle, dark blue on each side. That was home for the brothers.

As they approached the central clearing, the top rooms of several homes came into view. High pitched hoots of joy sounded out as the first children spotted them.

As more of the hand-crafted tree homes came into view, the ruckus grew. By the time the lowest structures came into view, the children had already gathered, waiting for the hunters.

Daksey reached into the small bag strapped to his right thigh and grabbed a handful of koyo nuts. The children gathered close, eyes darting, tails held high, their downy crests swayed every which way as they moved. He started tossing them, one by one over their heads. Some leapt, some reached, and others turned and scurried to get the sweet treats, all while they hooted with glee.

Home to the brothers, the central tower loomed overhead. With rooms shaped like giant leaves connected by massive vines wrapped around a central spire. The swooping curves and sharp points made a spectacular contrast.

The aroma of Espay's kitchen delighted Daksey. His meals were always the best. His other pouch-father, Soyok, sometimes cooked, and it tasted good, but Espay had a way with the spices that Daksey preferred.

The massive, curved door at the base of the tower swung open. The large frame of their egg-mother greeted them with a deep throated approving warble. Daksey smiled as he spotted his little sister, Moya'se, peeking out from behind. She had recently had her second molt, no longer the little tailbiter Daksey remembered. The quills of her crest were clean and sharp, like an adult's. Already half as tall as her brothers, by the time her adulthood molt came, she would be nearly as tall as the egg-mother she hid behind. Bongeex and Daksey stopped, shoulder to shoulder before their mother. They knelt and bowed deeply.

"Botham Kempok," Bongeex said. "Great Egg-Mother, and tribe leader. We bring meat for the family. We bring honor for you."

Kempok took a long breath, and undulated her neck, letting out a soft, deep hoot of joy, mixed with a touch of approving warble. "Botham Kempok Bongeex, Botham Kempok Daksey. I am honored to have such good hunters in my house." She started chut-chutting. Even as the tribe leader, she thought traditional greetings were a bit overblown.

Daksey and Bongeex chut-chutted as well, then followed her inside. Moya'se scrambled backwards and leapt over Kempok's tail as she swung around.

"Foondek and Deytham are already home with Masax. The sun is nearly down. Did something delay you?"

"It took me longer to catch my prey, today," Bongeex said. "I didn't want to return with an empty net."

"And you, Daksey?"

"Bongeex waited for the larger beast. He brought home more meat. It's a good thing."

"Sometimes. Put the meat down in the cold room. Then go clean yourselves. Dinner will be ready soon."

Bongeex headed to the passage leading to the lower levels.

Daksey shifted his pack on his shoulders, lifting the burden from his tail again, then turned to follow his brother.

"What's that on your tail?" Kempok asked.

Daksey turned back. "A bite. It's small. It will heal."

"Are you in pain?"

"A little."

Kempok reached up to a high shelf, well out of Daksey's reach, and took down a long wooden spoon. "Take off your pack."

He complied, setting the meat on the ground, then turned his back to her.

Kempok used her long, slender fingers to locate a very specific spot in the middle of Daksey's back. "You should have had Bongeex do this for you." She began tapping the spoon on the spot.

At first, the tapping was uncomfortable. Kempok always used too much force. But soon, his little brain woke to the danger and flooded his system with relief. The pain went away, and he felt much better. He gave a soft hoot of quiet joy.

"Half the males in Botham have a slow hindbrain, Daksey. You don't need to suffer. Just ask someone to help."

Daksey shrunk. "Yes, Kempok. I will try. Still, Bongeex likes to call it out more than I like. It's not a bother, but sometimes I would rather bear the pain."

Kempok snorted. "Siblings. There should be more trust between you. Now go. You smell like dirt."

When he finally reached the cold room below the main level, he found Bongeex sprawled in the middle of the floor on a pile of spice leaves. His face buried in them as he breathed deeply.

"I see you have found your marriage prospect. Good for you, pouch-brother."

Bongeex rolled and chut-chutted. "Caught me."

"I take it the leaves are fresh."

"Espay must have brought them in while we were hunting. Very fresh."

"They were fresh. Now they smell like Bongeex."

"They haven't been washed yet, anyway. No harm." He grabbed a fistful of leaves and held them toward Daksey's snout. "Try."

Daksey tilted his head and sniffed. He undulated very slightly. "Yes. Very nice. Now we should go clean ourselves."

They headed to the adjacent room, which contained a basin set in the floor filled with warm water, large enough for several family members. Light drifted in from high, ground level windows on one side. A small fountain at one side of the basin added fresh warm water. At the other side, a dip in the rim allowed a small stream to flow into a drain hole at the base of the wall.

Bongeex pushed past his brother and splashed into the basin. Water ran over the floor, and flooded the drain. He chut-chutted, spun around, and slapped the water with his tail, drenching Daksey.

Daksey snorted. "Leave some water for me." He climbed into the basin, taking care not to splash. The water he displaced flowed swiftly along the floor and into the drain hole. The expected sting on his tail never came. It must already be healing. He gave a thought of silent gratitude to Kempok and her handy spoon.

He reached up and took one of the stiff brushes from the wall and went to work on the thickest parts of his skin.

Bongeex grabbed a stick with a sponge on the end. He dipped it into a bowl of soap and scrubbed his back. Lather soon formed and spread into the basin. When he finished, he dipped the sponge again, and held it out to Daksey.

Daksey traded his brush for the sponge and began to scrub himself again. "Where did the other sponge get to?"

Bongeex snorted. "Ask our sister."

KEMPOK'S deep voice echoed up the passage. "Daksey, come down and eat with us. We have a guest."

Daksey turned the page in the large book he read. "I will be there soon." He placed an ornate ribbon onto the page and folded the book closed. His room had several handcrafted shelves filled with great tomes, along with various carved figures and game pieces. He placed the book alongside others of the same series.

When he reached the eating room he found both Kempok and his little sister Moya'se already seated. Bongeex and Espay were busy bringing in trays of food. Soyok could be heard rummaging in the kitchen.

A stranger sat at the table. One with dark gray, almost black skin, and golden stripes.

"This is Depek," Kempok said. "He is on okdeyok to the western sea and back."

"By your stripes I see you are from Kadayax. It is an amazing city."

"You've been?" Depek asked.

"Bongeex and I went with Espay when we were young. He showed us where the river flows into the sea. It was very nice. Your city is so clean."

"Thank you, yes. We take great pride in it."

"Where are you going?"

"I'm heading to Saxfoth on the north coast. From there, I'll ride a ship to the west. Then come back around through the desert. I'll visit the southern settlements on my way home."

"You'll still have to come through the pass at Bamthapeem on the way back. Will you visit us again as well?"

"Here," Depek said, "or if it's still early in the day, perhaps I will make it to Ko'dex. They seemed very nice, but I didn't stop on my way here."

"Are you staying long? Maybe you could help lay the floors."

"Daksey, that's not polite. A guest isn't required to do work."

"I wanted to be sure he knew he could offer help if he liked. A guest can offer help wherever needed. I didn't mean he had to."

Depek chut-chutted. "I'll be climbing the steps to Bamthapeem tomorrow. After resting for a few days, it's on down the other side of the mountain. I'm afraid I won't be able to help with the floors this time."

"Not to worry," Bongeex said. "Daksey and I make a great team."

Daksey undulated. "And we'll have Foondek and Deytham. It's their home, after all."

DAKSEY AND BONGEEX sat on the watch platform, the highest level of their home, well above nearby trees. Moonlight from Ma'pox, the closer moon, their only illumination as they gazed at the stars.

Daksey pointed to the sky where a small star caught his attention. "See, there. That one moves fast."

"Why is that important? It's probably a space rock coming close. It will be gone soon."

He shrugged. "You don't understand. I've seen it before. It goes past, and then it passes again. It happens often, and I think it's regular intervals."

Bongeex tilted his head. "What does that mean?"

"Do you remember last year, the Desok Bofoy'bo?"

"Oh, the book about the planets and the stars? Do you think that's a planet?"

"No," Daksey said. "I think it's something going around our world. Big enough to reflect light, but not so big that it looks like a moon."

"Maybe it will hit Ma'feng and be gone."

"It comes too often. Much closer than Ma'feng. I'm certain it's closer than even Ma'pox. It moves faster in the sky than either moon."

Bongeex snorted. "Why can't it be a rock?"

"Yes, it could be a rock. Maybe. But remember our lessons on orbits?"

"Orbits? The lines things make?"

"The paths they travel. If it were a rock, it would most likely come in at an angle, loop around, maybe fall into an elliptical orbit."

Bongeex tilted his head. "And?"

"And this one looks to me like it has a round orbit."

"So?"

"What if it's a spaceship?" Daksey hooted wistfully.

"Spaceship? Like the Dapkasamok? The ancient mythical beings from another star?"

"Yes. Like that. What if they have returned?"

Bongeex chut-chutted. "Oh. Sure. And the dust of Kempok's egg-mother is rising up tonight to meet them."

"Stop. I mean it."

"It's silly. Those are just stories. None of it is real."

Daksey snorted. "Why are you so sure? Do you think we are being lied to?"

"I think they are only parables. Stories to tell us how to act, and how to be good Ombax. You can't take them seriously."

"Maybe. You used to believe in those things. Remember when you used to sneak the Ofkey'bo Athmo'tham out of the classroom at night so you could read ahead?"

"I was young. I've molted twice since then." Bongeex stood and stretched. "I'm going down." He jumped to the next lower platform and began climbing down.

Daksey stayed behind and watched the stars, waiting for the spaceship to appear again.

TRANSITION

Tuesday, July 9, 3297, 14:07

In a star system designated by humans as Wold 2384, an empty patch of nothingness near the inner gas giant twitched. In a blue flash and a belch of radiation, a ship appeared beyond the farthest moon. Flashes of brilliant lightning quickly faded, leaving behind the *ADF Pang Yu*, a long, tapered cylinder with a wider section aft of the missile compartment and a ring mounted around the forward compartment that slowly rotated. Beyond the missile compartment, a stout, winged landing craft hugged the hull. A large cargo bay door filled the opposite side.

In the control center, the lights remained dim. Display panels lit the faces of the crew as they bent to their tasks.

"Conn Nav, normal space detected," said Master Lieutenant Patrick Dugan. "Jump transition complete."

"Jump transition complete, Conn aye," said Commander Betsy Alvarez, captain of the *Pang Yu*. "Engineering Conn, rig for dissipation." Her station was the conn. Mounted in the center of the command space, she was tethered in place by several sturdy straps.

The voice of Sub-Commander Brenna Dotseth, her chief engineer, surrounded her. "Rig for dissipation, Engineering aye."

The ship shuddered as radiator fins extended to dissipate a week of accumulated heat.

"Conn Engineering, fins extended, heat dissipating. Heat sink is at four nine nine and falling."

"Conn aye," Betsy said. "Ops, report all contacts."

"Report all contacts, Ops aye," said Sub-Lieutenant Aretta Hodges. She swiped her display, then zoomed in. Text appeared, and she grinned. "Con Ops, we have one contact. Bearing zero zero two by five eight." She grinned. "Contact is confirmed as the *AEX Endurance.* She's in orbit around a Terran-size planet. Two small moons." She paused. "Wow. Lots of green and blue, Captain."

"Excellent," Betsy said. "All hands, secure from the transition watch, set the freefall watch, section one." She paused for a moment. "We've sighted the *Endurance.* As soon as we bleed off enough heat, we'll jump to their location." She closed the circuit and turned to her first officer, Lieutenant Commander Jason Gannon. "Notify *Endurance* of our arrival. Give them our location, vector, and full status report. Be sure to establish a connection with their network."

Jason nodded. "Aye. I have the conn. AutoGov, notify *Endurance* of our arrival. Give them our location, vector, and full status report. Request recommended jump coordinates."

"Notify *Endurance* of our arrival, aye," AutoGov said. "Location, vector, and full status report have been transmitted. Coordinates requested."

Betsy pushed herself out of the way to make room for him, then twisted and floated herself toward the aft of the control center. She angled her feet forward, toward the outer hull, then floated into the transfer deck. The slide tube let the spin gravity drop her onto her feet in the rotating ring of the ship. A new addition to the *Pang Yu,* the fifteen-meter wide ring contained crew quarters, fitness training equipment, the crew lounge and galley, and several other amenities that were easier performed with gravity.

Betsy stopped on the small platform skimming above the central corridor. She waited for the right moment, and stepped off at the entrance to the galley.

Retty smiled as she entered. "I already dialed in a mocha sweet for you, Captain."

"Thank you. One more jump and we can take some time off."

•• ———————————— ••●•• ———————————— ••

MORE THAN 500 million kilometers away, the *AEX Endurance*, a large spinning ring with jump engines mounted along her axel, orbited a green and lush planet. One side of the ring, dubbed "forward" contained the Mission Control Center on a small part of the upper level.

"Dropship reports separation, Skip," said Communications Supervisor Kai Tono. "All systems go for planetary landing."

"Aye." Administrator Skip Onada glanced up at the larger display. "Anything on that burst out near the gas giant?"

"No sir. Not yet."

"Keep monitoring. It looked too much like some kind of jump drive for my comfort. If it's alien, I want as much notice as–"

Kai interrupted. "Sir, we have an incoming message from the *ADF Pang Yu*. They confirm inbound jump and have provided a status report. They are requesting recommended jump coordinates."

Skip grinned. "*Pang Yu*? Send them our orbital parameters. Reserve an area for them and send them the data."

"Aye, sir."

"And ask what kind of jump drive that was."

Skip reviewed the main screen. The shuttle had started reentry and headed for the surface.

"Sir, their status report calls it the Shin drive. Isn't that the one they were testing before we left?"

Skip nodded. "Probably. Send them the keys to the network in our response and ask for an ETA. Oh, did they list who the captain is these days."

"Captain Elizabeth Alvarez."

Skip smiled. "Betsy?"

"Sir?"

"Seven years ago, she was the captain of a Mercorps destroyer. *Conqueror*. Her friends call her Betsy. If she's here on the *Pang Yu*, she must have left Mercorps and joined our side. Give her access to anything she wants, but have an alert sent to me for any level two access and above, just in case, then send the response."

"Aye, sir." Kai turned to her task. "And sir, the report says they left Earth on August 17. Less than a year ago."

•• —————————— ••●•• —————————— ••

THE ENGINEERING SPACES of the *Pang Yu* were a brightly lit, well-organized confusion of equipment, pipes and cables, all color coded and decorated with various symbols.

"Reactor is running at full," Brenna said, "heat sink is cooling normally, power banks are recharging. Do you need anything, Wayne?"

"Nope. I have the watch. I grabbed a bite to eat before we started, and that jump came real early."

"I know. I'm glad on the one hand. A twelve-hour window is huge, but on the other hand, less than a half hour into the window is pretty close to a miss."

"Are you worried about our next jump?"

Brenna shook her head. "Not really. It's a short jump. But be prepared to start the engine overhaul as soon as we dock. I want this thing fully retuned and ready to jump again as soon as possible."

"Are you planning on us leaving early?"

Brenna shook her head. "I'm planning on there being a major issue that we won't discover until we're deep inside the engine. I expect it'll be far more complicated than we ever wanted, and that we'll have to work extra-long and hard to launch on time if we don't find it quickly."

Wayne's jaw dropped. "Seriously?"

"Or if we get in there and don't find any issues at all, we complete the overhaul rapidly. Then we maximize time off before we begin another year-long voyage."

Wayne grinned. "Okay, that I can get behind."

Brenna floated forward from engineering through the over-sized engine room and beyond to the machinery spaces, and finally joined Jason at the conn. "What's it look like, XO?"

"The world looks habitable. *Endurance* sent us their status and the key to their network. Everything looks nominal. As soon as we bleed off enough heat and recharge power, we can jump again."

"Did you tell them I want access to their chief engineer? I want to get started right away with the upgrades."

"I'll send that in the next update," Jason said. He glanced sideways at Brenna with a smile. "They did send his contact information, along with the rest of the command staff. Tell me, did you ever look over the crew manifest before we launched?"

"I knew Skip Onada and his family were on board. And I knew Jake went with them. Jake Tory. He served on the *Pang Yu* when I reported for my first tour onboard."

"Did you know the chief engineer, Robert Quesada? I mean, I never met him personally, but I can't forget that name. The man who threw his career away to save your life."

Brenna froze. "I... I knew. Yes. So, shoot me. I knew it was him. That's not why I came. You know that."

Jason chuckled. "I'm not doubting your motives, Brenna. Just be sure to get the job done. What you do in your free time is none of my business."

Brenna tried to laugh but her chest tightened. This was really it. He was there. She had no idea what would happen next. It had been seven years. Had it been too long?

She made her way to the transition tube, installed where the old crew's lounge used to be, and slid out to the ring section. The long duration of the journey would have had debilitating effects on the crew if they had to spend the entire time weightless. The ring was the most recent addition to the ship. It housed the crew quarters, a workout facility, crews mess, and a lounge. The one third normal gravity gave the body an up and down.

"Hey Brenna," Patrick said. "Want some coffee? I'm making a fresh batch."

"You bringing some up to the XO?"

He nodded. "Maybe we can watch a show when I get back."

Brenna chuckled. "Not this time. I'm going to get some rack time before we jump again. I should have about six hours before the charge is complete."

His face fell. "Okay. No worries."

She headed to her stateroom. The forlorn look on his face, the heavy sigh, echoed through her head like a warning claxon. Under her breath she said, "Tread lightly there. Need to let that crush fade."

THE TIPSY RAVEN

Thursday, July 11, 3297, 7:57

Radinka Stormbringer threw open the door into the rustic tavern and strode inside. She looked at the randomly generated crowd and scoffed. A medieval serving wench with curly pink hair carrying a tray of drinks and food smiled at her as she slid by, "Welcome to the Tipsy Raven. Find a seat, I'll be right over."

Radinka grabbed the wench's arm and leaned toward her ear. In a hoarse whisper she demanded, "The back room. Where is it?"

The wench cringed, backed away, and tilted her head to the rear of the tavern, to the left of the massive fireplace a large stack of wood stood out. "Go to the left of the woodpile. All the way back, then look right. The door is hidden behind the firewood."

Radinka sighed. "A tavern with a hidden door. This is stupid." She walked to where the wench had directed her, found the door, and entered the room, closing the door behind her.

A tall, thin man with wild black hair and a sharp goatee wearing a dark purple robe turned to greet her. A glowing white wand floated above his head. "About time you showed up. Set this as your entry point so you don't have to go through the crowd again. Just in case someone real pops into the game."

"Isn't it restricted?"

"No. That might draw attention, but the description sounds awful, the preview is sloppy and dumb, and the gameplay, once you are inside, is repetitive and boring. Casual gamers ignore us, and the good ones never bother."

"And what about the game master?"

He shrugged. "The GM handles everything. Always remember that. We can play our game, as long as we stick to the rules."

"The rules?"

"Good lord, woman, weren't you briefed?"

The other occupant of the room, an elven thief, short, slight of build, but distinctly female with yellow, unnaturally wild hair, stood from her seat at the table. Above her head, a glowing pink unicorn. "She's a late addition. Be nice, Ferdinand." She extended her hand to Radinka. "I'm Briana of the Vale. As he said, the GM runs this *automated* simulation, so all we have to do is pay attention to the rules that *govern* this place. The scenario is simple. We are all agents of the King sent to an outpost of the Evil Duchess to cause damage, so that loyal forces, which could arrive at any time, will be able to move in and take control with ease."

"Yes," Ferdinand said, "we are to thwart all efforts of Duchy forces to establish good relations with the local population. Get it? The local population?"

Radinka sighed. "I'm not stupid, Ferdinand. I'm following along just fine. What I don't understand is why they sent you. Couldn't find anyone with a brain?"

Ferdinand grinned. "In this scenario, I'm a wizard. Master Ferdinand Agazax, if you will. I'm able to conjure up magic items, spells, and such. Do you understand that?"

A wisp of Radinka's wild green hair fell in front of her eyes. She tossed it back. "I'm Xavier's replacement. The enemy compromised him shortly before departure. As of now, I'm the commander of this mission. Do you understand that?"

"What? That's not possible. I'm the next senior–"

"This wasn't done by seniority, it was based on a certain skill set. The King himself made the decree. If you are not happy with it, file a complaint."

Briana laughed. "I'll fetch a pigeon."

Radinka smiled. "What is the current status of the game?"

"Look at this, she shows up, announces her takeover and starts giving orders. Just like that? How do we know you are who you say you are?"

"How else would she know to come to this simulation, go all the way to the furthest corner of the map and find this particular tavern, then look for a back room?"

"I understand it's abrupt from your point of view. However, consider this, you are protesting an order given over seven years ago by a now dead King."

Ferdinand grunted. "But why?"

"Remember the late change in leadership? How they killed the King, and his son took the throne?"

"Yes, but–"

"But nothing. The son sent me. Simple as that. He had an additional mission in mind. Remember, he still needed to secure a position on the ship for me."

"Additional?"

"Yes. I have a mission separate from yours. I'll oversee your activities, but always with an eye for my own goals. Understood?"

Ferdinand and Briana looked at each other. The elf shrugged.

"Now, give me the updates."

Ferdinand crossed his arms. "There have been multiple attempts by the forces of the Baron who runs this outpost to speak with the locals. They are apparently a savage bunch, because all of the people they met were killed."

"That sounds nasty. Do we need to do anything? Sounds like it's not going well even without our help."

"It isn't. On that front, I think we are fine. But we'll need to weaken their fortifications, and make the outpost ready for invasion."

"Ah, now that gets a little tricky. What options have you considered?"

"I'm working on a new magic spell that might give us an advantage in a pinch. It's based on an outdated way to make people invisible. They have a counterspell for that old one, but I think I can create a new one with the magical implements I have at hand. I need to find the proper, shall we say, ingredients. Eye of Newt and all that. I'm calling the magic item the Amber Eye. I also considered the Alpha Eye."

Radinka raised a finger. "I like Amber Eye. It sounds more intelligent. Invisibility is good."

Ferdinand smiled. "Yes, we'll need the Amber Eye to be very intelligent. So glad you understand."

"I may have some magic items that will help. A gift from the King. I'll see about bringing them to our next meeting."

"How often should we meet up?"

"I'm thinking we can start off coming together twice a week or so. Maybe every third day. Give us all a chance to think over our next moves."

"Fine. Then we meet back here at the Tipsy Raven in three days. Together, we will thwart the goals of the Baron."

Radinka smirked. "Didn't you give the Baron a name too?"

"We just call him the Baron," Briana said.

"I suggested Baron Blackheart," Ferdinand said, "but she didn't like it."

Radinka chuckled. "That's a little bit on the evil side, don't you think? I'm sure he's a good man, in the wrong corporation. Baron will do. It's only a game, after all."

"There is also the problem of reinforcements."

"Reinforcements?"

"Yes. An enemy ship has been spotted on the horizon. She'll be in port in a few days. We should make plans to sink it, make sure it isn't seaworthy. Disrupting the flow of information back to their homeland seems like a good idea."

"One last thing," Radinka said, "one of my coworkers doesn't seem like the type who approves of role playing games. How can I be sure my activities here won't become known to him? That Radinka Stormbringer won't be exposed, as it were."

Ferdinand smiled and raised his wand. "I've cast a spell upon the great tome of indexing. Anyone who attempts to open the book without the counterspell will cause the pages to go blank. Permanently."

OLD FRIENDS

Tuesday, July 16, 3297, 9:09

A brightly lit space filled with displays, Mission Control Center, the control hub of *Endurance* was formerly the bridge. Even in the bright lights, the display near Kai easily caught her attention. She turned to Skip. "Sir, the *Pang Yu* has entered normal space. Right on schedule, and on their mark."

"Did you get how much radiation she bled off?" Skip asked.

"Yes sir. A big splash. Mostly infrared but a big spike of gamma, too. They were right to pick a spot so far off. Much closer and we would have had to bleed off extra heat, and that gamma... that's almost enough to be a weapon."

"We haven't asked them about their range yet."

SKIP BOBBLED in the near weightlessness of the docking ring.

The hatch finally slid aside and Betsy floated forward. Two more officers followed closely.

He grinned. "Captain Alvarez, good to see you again. How was your trip?"

"Shorter than yours," Betsy said, "but still too damn long." She glanced to each side. "Any reason for the formality, Administrator Onada?"

The other officers floated behind her. A young man with an eager grin gripped a railing, and another woman, a Sub-Commander, with a familiar face, free floating in the still air.

Skip grinned. "No. Just trying to be polite, Betsy. It's been a long time."

She shook her head. "Couple of decades. Not worth noticing."

"That radiation blast we saw. Seemed kind of dangerous. Same engine the *Pang Yu* was playing with before we left?"

Betsy smirked. "It's a new design entirely. It keeps the radiation on the outside of the bubble. We're fine inside."

Skip smiled at Brenna. "I almost didn't recognize you with hair."

Brenna touched her hair. "It grew back too fine, so I cut it short."

"And so as to not be impolite," Betsy said, "this is Junior Lieutenant Wayne Chispas. He works for her."

Wayne saluted then extended his hand to Skip, while grinning at Brenna.

Brenna rolled her eyes. "We have a lot of material to go over with your engineering team."

"I'm sure you can see to it in a day or two. You've had a long trip. I would like to extend the full hospitality of *Endurance* to you and your crew. Get some downtime. Go for a long walk. We have a park, and there is a farm on the lower level."

Betsy crossed her arms. "Sub-Commander Dotseth is allergic to time off."

"Makes her cranky," Wayne said.

Brenna frowned. "There are several courses I want to get people started on, so we can have question and answer sessions before the lectures begin."

"The courses won't be enough?" Skip asked.

"For engineers?" She chuckled. "Never. There are always plenty of things engineers like to discuss."

"I see. Just get with Quesada and set up a schedule. He's the head of engineering."

Brenna nodded curtly. "I'll get in touch with him."

Skip smiled at Betsy. "She's still as intense as I remember her."

Betsy laughed.

"It's good to see you again, Brenna."

Brenna sighed, stepped forward and wrapped her arms around the old man. "Same here, Skip. Same here."

"Jake and Malee will be glad to see you too."

"I know. I'll make time. I want to get started. This is a major overhaul, and it's going to involve all of your engineers."

Skip gave her a nod. "Go on, then. Get to work." He smiled as she turned and left with Wayne in tow, almost at a run.

"So," Betsy said, "do you think it's just the work, or should I warn Quesada she's coming?"

"Oh, you're no fun. Let it be a surprise. Are you hungry?"

Betsy smiled.

"I have to admit," Skip said, "I was a little surprised when I heard Captain Alvarez commanded the *Pang Yu*."

"Tong's so busy building the Allied fleet, he doesn't have a lot of time for anything else, and Kip's deeply involved in building the training side of the house. He wasn't too keen on the idea, but she and I go back a long way. She didn't trust anyone else to take the ship. Besides, with the new engine, this didn't seem like such a long commitment."

Skip nodded. "I understand. Once you become attached, you care about who takes command. I would have thought you had your choice, though."

"Sure. But the new ships are being built so fast, there aren't enough qualified commanders to go around. Nobody wanted this old tug."

"Old tug? I still remember hundreds of people crammed together when Tong and his crew saved our lives. Most of my family were on board. None of us would have survived if they hadn't shown up."

"And now look at you. Captain of the *Endurance*. The first exploration ship seeking a new civilization and all that."

Skip motioned for her to proceed toward the drop tube. "I haven't gone by 'Captain' in a few years. We adopted civilian titles. It will make the transition easier, now that we are transforming into a colony."

"Transforming?"

Skip sighed. "Some of the scientists are agitating for elections. It's almost time for me to step aside and let them figure things out."

"Anything wrong?"

"We had expected an advanced civilization. We had expected to be handed an enormous amount of alien data. We have a considerable data team and a lot of computing power. We expected to be digging through thousands of years of stored imagery and entertainment. We expected to see... anything.

"Now, our data teams have absolutely nothing to do. Most of them are still in cryo. Instead of an advanced civilization, we've found a bunch of primitives. I've got three people looking at their damned smoke signals, and over in the east there's a drum network. Got a couple of people on that. Instead of trying to decrypt data, we've enough idle computing power to simulate a good sized chunk of reality."

She paused at the opening leading to the lower decks. "No signs of technology?"

"Two moon bases, and a large ring shaped structure in a stable orbit between the moons. We've sent drones to the bases, and are considering sending a team out at the ring. No radio signals, no indication of laser communications. We found one spot on the planet with an electrical field and maybe a few internal combustion engines."

"Industrialization?"

"Nope. If they have them, they must make them by hand. Or flipper or whatever."

"Anything useful on the moon bases?"

"Empty relics. No atmosphere, naturally. We've identified a great deal of equipment, but nothing particularly advanced. All of it has been sitting, exposed to vacuum, for four thousand years."

"Damn. Like Proximus?"

"Exactly. Except, given the shape of the hatches, we don't think they were the same creatures."

"Environmental suits?"

"Piles of dust where we think they hung. Mostly organic."

Kai's voice interrupted them. "Skip to the bridge, please. The landing team is on final approach."

"On my way." He turned to Betsy. "Are you seriously hungry or would you like to join us? We are attempting contact again." He motioned toward the opening.

She chuckled, then stepped into the drop tube. "My XO is handling everything aboard the ship. I have time."

•• —————————— ••●•• —————————— ••

WAYNE FOLLOWED Brenna like a puppy dog might follow a bouncing ball. She didn't mind, His eagerness reminded her of herself at a younger age. The thought made her flush. Best to get this over with. She swiped her display and brought up a map of the *Endurance*. Another poke and the icon she needed to find appeared – the man she would need to talk to about her plans to upgrade the engines of the *Endurance*. It would give her greater range, and even allow her to return to Earth, if she chose, in far less time than it had taken them to get out here.

"What are you thinking about?"

Brenna glanced at the young man. "Nothing. He's this way." The icon on her display approached the intersection ahead. Just before it crossed her path, she jumped out and smiled. "Hello Quesada. How have you been?"

"Ah," Robert stopped mid step. "Sneak attack. You've changed your methods." He eyed Brenna's rank insignia. "Sub-Commander? After seven years?"

She shrugged with a half-smile. "I spent five of them working on the new engine. I rejoined, and the promotions followed."

Robert laughed. "Of course they did. It's good to see they value brilliance at Allied."

Brenna smirked. "Is that some sort of pickup line?"

"Pickup line? If I wanted to kiss you I would have handed you a tranq patch."

Brenna rolled her eyes. "For the ten billionth time, I'm sorry about that."

"Wait, what happened?" Wayne asked.

"She didn't tell you? A year-long trip, and you never mentioned how you tranqed your superior officer?"

Brenna smirked. "Oddly enough, it never came up."

Robert gave Wayne a quick nod. "When they stole the *Pang Yu* and saved hundreds of people from the Halo."

"The Halo?" Wayne asked.

"Endurance Halo. The habitat this ship is named after. It was destroyed before the war. Before the fight at Proximus."

Brenna hitched her thumb at Robert. "And then this guy abandoned his post during the standoff over Proximus in order to save my life." She took a deep breath.

Robert shrugged. "Seemed like a good idea at the time."

"Wow," Wayne said. "You guys have some history."

Brenna laughed. "I wouldn't call it history like that."

"Why not?" Robert asked. "We kissed."

Brenna took a deep breath and exhaled slowly. "My head was filled with drugs."

"Is that why you never followed up?"

Brenna shrugged. "I don't know. Things got complicated really fast after Proximus."

"I heard they transferred you to *Wu Gu Hu*?"

She shook her head. "I ended up out at Europa. Jump engine development center."

"I never heard of that."

"It's famous now," Wayne said.

"They put me on the design team for the new engine," Brenna said. "The radiation problem held the whole project back. The solution I cobbled together on the way to Proximus was... well, it hadn't been tried before. It took a long time to get all the aspects worked out, but we were finally able to arrange all the parts so the jump bubble forms outside the ship. No event horizon passing through the crew as it expands."

"It still throws off a lot of radiation," Wayne said.

"You made a horrific inbound splash," Robert said. "Reminds me of a tactical nuke."

Brenna waved her hand. "We managed to shunt it all outward, but it's not going to be stealth tech, that's for sure."

"What about inside?"

"Inside levels spike during transition, but not very high. Pretty tame, really."

Robert crossed his arms. "Do we replace the engines we have with the new design?"

Brenna laughed. "Yeah, that's step one. Of about five thousand."

"Oh?"

"We have to set emitters all around the hull, and get them to sync up, be in tune with each other."

"How many emitters?" Robert asked.

"According to my design specs, you're going to need several hundred for *Endurance*."

"So, weekend project?"

Brenna laughed. "Depends on your mining capabilities. Available resources, and such. We estimated that the worst case scenario would be about five years."

"Five years?"

"Worst case. I'm sure if you concentrate on building out the automation first, you can cut that way down."

Robert glanced at the time. "I need to go on watch in a few minutes. We should sit down and go over the details."

Brenna grinned. "Oh goody, a date."

Wayne chuckled.

Robert flushed.

Brenna scoffed. "Oh, settle down, Romeo. I was kidding."

Robert frowned. "Right. Sure. Let's agree to someplace where we can talk. After my watch?"

"When is that?"

"In about six hours, of course."

"I suppose you'll be hungry," Brenna said.

"Naturally. There's a place I like to go. Salads and such. Mild intoxicants."

"Mild... wait, are we back to a date?"

Robert shrugged. "A date to discuss engineering specs. I wasn't suggesting you become intoxicated. Just pointing out the options."

Brenna nodded and tilted her head. "Sounds good. Meanwhile, I need to go run some simulations. Oh, and I'll need to find medical. They have tranquilizer patches right?" She winked at him, spun about, and walked into Wayne.

Wayne backed up. "Sorry, ma'am."

She laughed. "Follow me."

"I take it I'm not invited for dinner."

"I don't think you would learn anything."

"No ma'am."

"Haven't I told you before to drop the ma'am shit?"

He nodded sheepishly.

She spun and led him back the way they had come.

"We sent drones down first to conduct biological studies. Their biology is incompatible with ours. They have things that are similar to bacteria and viruses. The biologists named them things like ungefähr-bacteria and hodo-virus." He swiped his display to share an annotated list. "They feed off of the local version of DNA, and are incapable of working with ours. Now, I know what you are thinking, life finds a way. We understood that from the start. We identified the virus to hodo-virus connection as the most probable pathway to a merged biology. It's probably a fujin-fungal species that will pose a problem."

"Sounds like your biologists are having fun with dictionaries."

"We have a diverse group. They all take turns honoring their ancestors." He stepped out of the landing chamber with Betsy close behind and heard down the passageway. "We determined that the virus changes required are so massive that the intermediary life forms are not viable. That doesn't mean it will never happen, but it gives us some breathing room. That also doesn't mean that some enterprising fujin-fungus or pochti-mold might not set up shop. We developed disinfectants for those eventualities before we even considered face to face contact. We didn't even bring our drones back. Digital samples work just as well. What? What's that look?"

Betsy shook her head. "Nothing. You tend to talk a lot when you get nervous. Are you worried?"

Skip motioned for her to follow him into the Mission Control Center. "This is our third attempt."

"What happened to the other teams?"

Skip pointed to the chart display on the view table. "We sent the first team to an outpost in this desert. Every indication is that this site has the highest level of technology on the planet. There's a primitive oil refinery of sorts. We spotted electrical lighting, although we think they are trying to hide it. The atmospheric readings make us think they might be using internal combustion engines. Compression ignition if we got the gas mix right. No signs of industrialization, so their vehicles have to be handmade. Shortly after attracting the attention of the inhabitants, the team confirmed the existence of gunpowder. They were all taken out by cannon fire. The ship was struck and rendered unretrievable."

"That doesn't bode well. Do you think they are smart enough to reverse engineer it?"

"Probably. Maybe I should have started with the moon."

"These aliens went to their moons and then somehow reverted?"

"Looks like it."

"Great. So, what happened to the second team?"

Skip swiped the display and scrolled to a new spot on the map. "They were sent to a town near the eastern edge of that same desert. Structural surveys showed evidence of ruins in the surrounding areas. We had hoped to be able to explore them. As the team approached the town from the hills, a fog rolled in. We think a group of children were caught by surprise by their headlights. They reacted violently. Then the whole village came running. We lost the team to what looked like farm implements and torches."

"Oh, good lord. It's like right out of an old horror movie."

"Except we're the scary aliens this time. Luckily we were able to recall the shuttle."

"How many people have you lost so far?"

"Eight. Four people on each team. I'm only sending three this time."

"They're the ones about to land?"

Skip pointed to the map in the wall display. "This time we picked a location further to the southeast. There is a tribe living on this plateau near the forest. From what we've seen, they are a crossroads between the forest tribes and the villages to the north."

"Skip," Kai said. "Message from the dropship."

"Go ahead."

"*Endurance*, this is Davis. We hit some real bad turbulence coming over that last mountain. Landed hard. Hit a couple of trees."

"Are you going to be able to return in that shuttle?"

"Affirmative. Looks like we lost one of the external camera mounts and dented a fairing. All other systems are nominal. I'm recommending we proceed with the mission."

"Acknowledged. Proceed with your mission."

"Aye."

The view shifted to the individual cameras each team member wore. The images jumped as they moved, while over the view table a layout was being built, adding detail to the topography they already knew.

•• —————— ••●•• —————— ••

"This is wonderful." Brenna smiled at her salad laden fork. "I haven't had fresh greens in so long it's silly." She felt the crispness of the lettuce as she bit down. She took a moment to enjoy the creamy goodness of the dressing.

"Glad I could help," Robert said. "There are strawberries too. For dessert."

Brenna grinned. "I'm liking this place already."

"I figured. It's a long trip out here. Fresh food is always a relief after a long haul."

"How about you guys? Did you have fresh food while you were coming out?"

"Oh sure. We had the farm up and running before we left

home. Skip was adamant that we avoid the preserved food stores. He wants to keep them in case of an emergency."

"That sounds like a good plan."

"Where's your friend?"

"Friend?"

"That shy Junior Lieutenant you had with you earlier."

Brenna chuckled. "I have him taking measurements of the outer hull of your ship. We'll need to be sure our data is correct. No big deal. How's Jake? He married Skip's daughter before they left. How are they doing?"

"They seem to work well together. Skip's lucky to have such a close family."

"How about you?" Brenna asked. "Any family?"

"No one close. We drifted apart after my mother died."

"Sorry about your mother."

Robert nodded. "And you?"

"I grew up in a factory habitat. Excelled in school, got sent to an advanced education center, so I didn't end up being close to my family."

"What corporation?"

"Masters and Billings. Once I was old enough, I put in for Mercorps. Made it my first try. Then came more school, and then *Pang Yu*." She shrugged. "Not much there, really."

"Says the first Allied Admiral and the hero of the Battle of Proximus."

Brenna blushed. "Admiral is only a title. And all those ships were just hulls with drones. No crew."

"Still, you nearly died getting them into the fight."

"It would have been a spectacular death."

Robert smirked. "Gee, sorry I ruined it for you."

"Damn right you did. I would have been legendary."

"Indeed. They would be calling you the Ghost of Proximus by now. Complete with all the glowy melty bits."

Brenna giggled.

MAKSIM BORODIN SPOKE louder than usual. "Kamalov, come quickly. They have landed and are already exiting the shuttle."

"I'll be out in a moment," said Gadzhimurat Kamalov.

Maksim fidgeted in his seat, sliding to the edge as he caught sight of Yelena Shestakova. "Yelena has climbed out of the shuttle, and they've launched the drones. You are missing some spectacular views."

"Some things cannot be rushed, Maksim. You of all people should know this."

"Such a beautiful world."

"I've seen it before. This is the third attempt, remember? That little village was fascinating, right until those pitchforks came out."

"Don't remind me. I'm worried enough as it is."

"And then that nice city in the desert. Big oasis settlement, walled city, almost medieval looking."

Maksim shook his head. "Complete with cannons, yes. I know. But this time will be different. It has to be."

"Why?" Kamalov entered the room. "Because Yelena went this time?"

Maksim looked at his friend, his eyes begging. "Yes. It has to go well, because she is there."

Kamalov took a seat. "They did the research. This settlement is high in the mountains and appears to be a different culture from either of the previous two. They are on a trade route that runs through the mountains all the way to the sea in one direction, and that city in the mountains across the desert. If anyone should welcome visitors, it would be them."

Maksim sighed. "Exactly. Look, they have started up the path. There are steps carved into the slope."

"Yes, I saw the geological survey. There are three paths. West, to the village and beyond, south into the forest, and east to the sea settlements. They appear to have been carved centuries ago. Maybe longer."

The drone footage showed their climb from several angles. The path was clear of debris, well-marked.

Kamalov pointed into the display. "There is the first rest stop. Five hundred twelve steps from the bottom, and the same number to the next platform. Then another four hundred ninety three to the top."

"I wonder why that is."

"We were talking about that yesterday. We think the top set of steps is short because that's how many steps were left over. The five hundred twelve in the sections below are the repeated number. It points to perhaps an octal numbering system."

"How so?"

"Five hundred twelve steps is one thousand in octal. A nice big round number."

Maksim nodded slowly. "I see."

One of the drones was already at the top, high above the plateau. Neat rows of stone structures lined the path, joining to a second path from the south, leading to the west. Near the junction stood a tall platform. Pillars lined each of three sides.

"That's the structure we think is a temple of some sort."

"You think these creatures believe in God?"

"It is speculation, but would it surprise you if they did, and it was the same one?"

"A little. You know I'm not a believer."

Kamalov chuckled. "I know. I find it an intriguing idea, all the same."

As the group of humans neared the top, one of the natives spotted them, and called out to alert others.

Maksim nodded. "As expected. They are giving them a long look. No sudden moves, this time."

"No fog, either." Kamalov shook his head. "Perhaps we look frightful to them."

Maksim shrugged. "Have you seen their teeth?"

"I mean when that fog came up, and our people turned on their headlamps. Perhaps it was frightful to them to see that."

"I hope you are right. I would rather it was something like that, rather than finding they are xenophobic. But the cannon fire came without the fog."

Kamalov shrugged. "I wish we had all the answers, already. They were the site with the electromagnetic signature. We know they are generating electricity. We know that four thousand years ago, they were walking on their moons. Why open fire on us?"

"It makes no sense. If it were up to me, I would have stopped trying for a lot longer than we did."

"You objected to Yelena going down, didn't you?"

Maksim shrunk into his seat. "Is it that obvious? I think it's too big a risk. Two parties have been killed. Eight people. Now we send these three down. Why? And why did it have to be her who volunteered?"

"Maybe she thinks she can do it better."

"Of course she does. She's been like that as long as I've known her. When she was twelve she decided to climb the bridge all the way to Pluto."

"Is that far?"

"Over eight hundred kilometers from the station."

Kamalov laughed. "How far did she get?"

"They wouldn't let her out of the habitat. She was furious. Her father had to come get her and drag her home."

"Was that the end of it?"

"Of course not. We made the hike when she turned seventeen. Parents' permission, of course. Much better planning as well. Except for the adjustment to zero gravity, we did well."

"You were in love so early."

Maksim sighed slowly. "I don't remember a time when I didn't love Yelena Shestakova."

"They're nearly to the top. Quite a welcoming committee waiting for them."

"I know."

They watched silently as the team neared the top. The creatures backed away to give them room. When they arrived at the last step, they swung off their packs, and sat on them. Then waited.

One of the smaller natives offered them a bowl. Yelena took it, and tilted it slightly. She tipped it to her mouth and drank.

"That must be water," Maksim said. "She wouldn't drink anything else."

Yelena passed the bowl to one of the other men.

"That's Danzis, isn't it?" Kamalov asked.

"Yes. They wanted a geologist in the mountains. He's also a decent linguist, so they could cut the team down to three. Bill Hanley is the Archeologist."

"Look, they're sitting down too."

Maksim smiled. "Good. That's a good sign."

Yelena brought out a handheld screen. It lit up, and the crowd jumped back. The seated natives leapt to their feet, the quills on their necks stood up. A black and gold native shrieked and leapt onto Yelena. Several of the others jumped onto the human team.

Maxim stood. "No." He watched as one crushed Yelena's head. "No!" He fell to his knees.

"Dear God," Kamalov said.

Some of the natives were piling wood inside a stone circle. Maksim's heart fell. A fire pit. As the fire blazed, others stripped and gutted their kills. They skewered them, and set the bodies above the flames. Maksim could take no more, but he couldn't stop the display as those horrible creatures proceeded to cook his Yelena. Only when the feed from MCC ended did he finally sink into his chair and weep.

Kamalov tried to comfort him, but Maksim was lost in grief and anger.

"How could they do this?" Maksim moaned. "Those are not sentient beings. Not people. They are animals. Beasts. Evil creatures. Yelena. No. Those *monstry!*"

SKIP TOOK IN A DEEP BREATH, letting out a long slow shudder. "Keep recording, but stop the feed here. I don't think we need to watch this. Make sure the drones stay well above them."

The screens went blank, the silence in the room broken by the sounds of gentle sobbing.

"AutoGov, write up the next of kin notifications. I'll review them later."

"Acknowledged."

"I hope we're poisonous to them," Kai said.

"That's enough of that. We're the uninvited guests here. We've no idea why they did what they did. We're going to have to back up and leave contact for another time."

"But sir..."

"No buts. We've lost too many people already. This isn't what we expected. We weren't prepared for primitives. That unpreparedness has been laid bare. Three times. I'm not about to risk more."

A RUNNER FROM BAMTHAPEEM

Mas'eeng Bayfod, Second Four, Setting

Foondek and his pouch-husband, Deytham, were busy setting up the drums for the gathering. A circle of trees had been trained together, their upper branches woven to provide a large canopy over a central wooden platform. A communal gathering area for the entire village. Once every eight days they gathered to share food, and dance to the music. Deytham was very good at the low, steady beat. They made a good team. Foondek set up several of the small drums he used for the high tones.

"I think Masax has been holding an egg," Deytham said. "I think she's going to let it out tonight."

Foondek stopped and turned to his pouch-husband. "Tonight? If she did that, it would be a public display."

Deytham undulated with a soft hoot. "It would be very public, yes. If she gives it to you, I would be happy. But perhaps, if it were me, I would be happier. Does this make you angry?"

Foondek chut-chutted. "Don't be stupid. We all get an egg sooner or later. You were her first pouch-husband. The honor has always been yours. You are a season older than I am. The careful, dutiful one. I think she'll want to wait to be sure I'm mature enough before trusting me with an egg. No, pouch-husband, I'm already filled with joy, even with your pouch still empty. When it is filled, we'll both dance."

Deytham huffed. "Dancing with an egg? Don't be foolish. I would take far better care of it than that."

Foondek chut-chutted. "I only pulled your tail, no need to be defensive."

Deytham gave a tentative chut. "If you say so."

"When she decides to give you an egg, I'll be there with you the entire time it's in your pouch. I'll be there when the egg hatches, and I'll be there for you whenever you need me." He leaned in and pushed his snout into Deytham's shoulder.

Deytham relaxed. "I know. And I will be there for you. We'll raise a wonderful family for Masax. Now get back to your drums. I see five mid-tones laying in the reeds. They will need your attention, while I go make new cudgels for the hanging drums. The old ones have started to split."

"You should remember to oil the wood before you put them away. It has been hot this summer."

"Lack of moisture isn't the problem, Foondek. They become damaged when we play the Faadangmek. You know how much I love that one. I'm afraid my arms are stronger than the wood."

Foondek chut-chutted and undulated. "At least you keep the beat steady. The music makes my heart race ahead. Your steady percussion keeps me in time."

Deytham nodded his gratitude. "I will return."

Foondek tilted his head and went to dig those mid-tones out of the reeds.

As USUAL, the pouch-husbands had given it their all. Foondek still panted after their grand finish. The Faadangmek was an exhilarating composition. There were nine of them in the band, but only Deytham and Foondek were fully spent. The two pay'ak players sat on their haunches while plucking their long strings producing deeply moving tones. Three fepa'key tappers created intricate melodic harmonies with their tiny hammers. The two large egg-mothers who were the vocalists swayed and clapped while harmonizing their deep tones to the music.

Foondek's chest thumped with each beat. When he and his pouch-husband played together, the world became a joy, and everything felt good and beautiful.

When the song ended and the hoots of the crowd died away, Masax stepped forward. She lifted her head high, turning it sharply down to look at them. "Botham Kempok Deytham, come to me. Everyone, I want all to see."

Deytham tried very hard to hide his joy, but Foondek could still see it. He nearly tripped over his own tail. The crowd chut-chutted gently. They knew what was coming. He centered himself on her much larger mass, and knelt. "I am here, Botham Masax."

Masax sat back on her tail, placed one hand on each thigh, took a deep breath, and started to push. She moaned, inhaled again, and pushed harder. Deytham leaned forward with his hands outstretched, and caught the leathery egg with both hands as it emerged from between her legs. He brought it to his chest and cradled it, then slipped it inside his pouch.

The entire village broke into a cacophony of warbling, hooting and chut-chutting. The public display of the first egg of a family being given to a pouch-husband was a great honor, one that Deytham well deserved. Foondek felt the joy for his pouch-husband deep in his chest. Masax was a good wife. An egg-mother of great compassion and intelligence. He joined them on the dance floor and gathered them into an embrace.

"Koox." Kempok raised her voice above the crowd. "Daksey,

Bongeex, go fetch the koox. It's time to celebrate your brother's good fortune."

    •• —————————— ••●•• —————————— ••

"DEYTHAM IS CERTAINLY LUCKY," Daksey said. "Masax is going to be a great egg-mother."

"Yes, I suppose she is," Bongeex said.

"You sound unsure. Is something wrong?"

"I don't think that life is what will make me happy. I mean, raising a family, sure. But living in the same tree, planted into the ground like a vine, it doesn't have any appeal for me."

Daksey hooted softly. "To me it sounds like a great, peaceful life. So much better than living in a city, don't you think?"

"I don't know. I think I would rather have a grand adventure and explore the world. Did you know that Afothameex has more people than nearly all the other cities combined? They are also the second highest in elevation. First, if you count the observatory."

"Indeed, the scholars live far above all others."

"They have their snouts in the clouds." Bongeex chut-chutted with his brother.

The immense platter of koox covered most of the central table in the eating room. The brothers each took a side and carefully navigated the door back outside.

As they neared the pavilion, someone called out to have people make a path. The brothers set the large platter onto a pedestal near one end of the open area, opposite the music stage. Three of the larger egg-mothers started to direct traffic, making an orderly line.

Daksey and Bongeex stepped back so as to join the end of the line, allowing everyone else to have a share of the sweet treat.

"Someone is coming from the west," said one of the pouch-husbands.

"Clear a path. It's a runner," said an egg-mother.

The runner slowed to a walk, as he entered the pavilion. He was panting hard.

Kempok slid a stool in front of him. He sat on the stool, his breath still quick and sharp.

"Bring him water," Kempok said. "Let him rest for a moment."

The runner nodded in gratitude and attempted to speak. He choked, and tried to slow his panting. A bucket of water appeared.

"Daksey, pour some on his back. Make sure his neck is cooled."

"Yes, Kempok." Daksey took the bucket and slowly poured the water where it would do the most good.

Soon, the runner's breathing slowed. "Botham Kempok, Bamthapeem Mokfey invokes thay'kopfoy, as is her right."

Kempok huffed. "It's her right but only in great need. What has happened?"

"There is an illness. Many of our people have been struck down. Your skill as a healer is requested at once."

"For Mokfey to make such a request is unusual. Why are your own healers not caring for your sick?"

"They are all incapacitated," said the runner. "Only a few of us are unaffected."

Kempok raised her voice for all to hear. "Such a thing is rare. But thay'kopfoy is not to be ignored lightly. I will leave in the morning. By sunrise. Daksey and Bongeex will come, of course. I feel I should bring more of the tribe. Perhaps there are others who will join me."

Masax stepped forward. "I will be at your side, as will my pouch-husbands."

Akfoy stepped aside Masax. "I shall join you as well. My pouch-husband, Fethax, shall remain behind and care for our young ones. He could care for your youngest as well, Kempok. But pouch-husband Faykong shall accompany us."

Kempok undulated. "You do us all a service, Masax and Akfoy. We shall all meet here at sunrise."

Daksey turned to the runner. "Come with me. I'll take you to our home. You can wash yourself and rest."

The runner tilted his head. "I smell koox. It smells wonderful. You must have a very skilled cook in your village, to create such a treat." He sniffed the air loudly.

Kempok chut-chutted. "Bongeex, get the runner some koox before he starts kissing my tail."

RESTRAINT ISSUES

Wednesday, July 17, 3297, 10:22

The compartment of the *Pang Yu* directly aft of Operations had been fitted with cold sleep pods. The old medical center, repurposed for reanimation, was as busy as it would ever be. All ten bays were filled with patients.

Ted Becker, one of the first to be brought back, waited for his wife to awaken.

"I don't understand why you and your wife didn't arrange to come out of cold sleep simultaneously," said Dr. Puttkammer.

Ted balanced his weightless mass with one hand, and pointed to the straps holding Debra in place. "She has... restraint issues. We've done this before. It's better this way."

She shrugged. "I can't imagine why. Those are to keep her from floating around in zero gravity. She's not a prisoner."

"Just trust me. When she wakes up, still groggy and mostly blind, her arms try to move. When they can't, her response is very... assertive. I'm here to mitigate the effects."

She furled her eyebrows. "If you say so. She'll be awake any time–"

Debra's sudden thrashing caught her off guard. One of the

straps snapped. Her free arm went for the other restraint, eyes wide, racing back and forth.

"Debra, this is Ted. You are coming out of cold sleep. You are safe. I'm here."

Debra stopped moving, her eyes searching, trying to focus. Her head leaned toward the doctor. "Who's that?"

"That is Dr. Puttkammer. You know her. Chief Medical Officer of the *Pang Yu*. She put us into cold sleep. She came with us."

"Hello Debra," the doctor said. "Please relax. You're driving the monitor a little nuts. Can you release your grip?"

Ted looked down at his wife's hand. Her knuckles were white, as she gripped the remaining strap. "Darling, you did much better this time. Almost no damage at all."

Debra's eyebrows furled as her eyes began to focus on his face. She chuckled and released her grip. "I told you this would work."

Ted laughed and offered her a bulb of water. "Here. Sip slowly."

Dr. Puttkammer smiled. "It looks like you are in good hands. Stay where you are, and I'll check back in a few minutes and release you." She grabbed a handhold and smoothly floated to the next patient.

Debra pulled the bulb to her lips and sipped cautiously. "Did you go look?"

Ted shook his head. "No time. I scanned the headlines, and was immediately confronted with the reality that there are none. Nothing new for the last nine months. And we won't get anything new until the next ship arrives."

"What did you expect? The sudden discovery of faster than light communication?"

Ted smiled. "That's just it. I didn't expect anything. I looked out of habit."

"Can you imagine what the people of *Endurance* think? It's been seven years for them."

Ted frowned. "Yeah, about that. I'm wondering how they'll react. The war had only started heating up when they left."

"What do you mean? These are our people. We won. Stop worrying." She smirked. "You are always worrying too much."

Ted tilted his head. "Probably has a lot to do with who I married, wife."

She stuck her tongue out at him. When he pulled himself in to kiss it, she grabbed his shirt and pulled him into a closer encounter.

"A-hem."

Ted looked up and grinned as his face grew warm. "Hi, Doc."

"How are you feeling, Debra? Any nausea? Headache? Blurred vision?"

Debra smiled. "Nope. Just a slightly elevated heart rate and a bit of a flush."

Dr. Puttkammer laughed. "Fine. Get out of here. Be sure you eat before you try anything too strenuous, all right? Clothes are in the locker above your head. Oh, wait. Last thing on the list, you need your nutrient shakes. Replenish that microbiome. We have mint, chocolate and fish. Pick one."

"Fish?"

Ted laughed. "I'll take fish."

Debra frowned. "Should I even ask?"

"It's a bit like the garlic. Your taste buds aren't quite right, and it tastes way better than you think. But yes, fish. Or go with the chocolate."

Debra shook her head. "Mint."

The doctor smiled. "Mrs. Becker is feeling a bit obstinate."

Ted smiled. "The best commanders gather all available information and then make their choice." He shrugged. "She might make a bad choice, but that's going into her mouth, not mine."

Debra stuck her tongue out.

The doctor laughed and passed Ted the shakes. "Word of advice, keep the nearest fresher in your displays. Your digestive system will flush itself clean in a day or so." She grabbed a handrail and pulled herself to the passageway.

Shakes in hand, Ted helped Debra into the dark blue jumpsuit she had chosen all those months ago – standard military issue without any rank or station patches same as his. When she was nearly suited up, he rotated her so her feet were near his face, and slipped on a pair of zero gee slippers.

"This should give you some traction until we climb down to the habitat ring."

"Climb down? No elevator?"

Ted shrugged as he guided her around to face him. "Climb, ride, drop, slide, whatever. Let's get moving."

"Yessir. Right away, sir."

Ted rolled his eyes. "Are you pretending we are still in the military, or are you going to be some sort of extra dutiful wife?"

Debra grinned. "Extra dutiful. Just long enough for you to let your guard down."

"In that case, you still outrank me." He motioned toward the passageway. "That way. Up to the forward hatch."

She angled her body and thrust herself in the direction indicated. He followed close behind. Once out of the ship they followed the signage to an opening with a net stretched over. Two young women were drifting toward it.

Ted hesitated. "Drop tube."

Debra greeted the other passengers. "Hi Valerie, Amida."

They smiled and waved politely, then took hands and pushed themselves feet first down the drop tube.

Ted frowned. "These things make me nervous." He took a long drink of his microbial shake.

"Oh stop. You've done more dangerous things than drop down a tube with an automated air cushion waiting for you."

Ted shook his head. "I'm used to someone being on the other side, making sure nothing goes wrong."

Debra shrugged. She broke the seal on her shake and took a sip.

Ted laughed at her reaction. "Your face told me everything I need to know."

"Oh, shut up."

"I hear, and I obey. But the mint still sucks."

She carefully closed the drink and slid it into her pocket, then grabbed her husband, curled her feet up to his chest, and thrust him at the drop tube. He chuckled, as he twisted and turned feet first for the descent.

NEWS FROM THE HOMELAND

Wednesday, July 17, 3297, 13:00

Radinka materialized inside the empty back room of the virtual tavern. She sat in her usual chair and rapped her fingers on the simulated wood. She waved her hand and opened a display showing the tavern's main hall. The simulated patrons all milled about pointlessly. Within moments she had identified the loops. Each character had their own loop and coded interactions with others. Varied times meant things only occurred the same when loops intersected at the same time.

The elf, Briana, flashed into existence with sparkles and glitter. A moment later Ferdinand appeared in a puff of black smoke with a dramatic flourish of his cape. The two nodded at each other, and took their seats.

Radinka waved off her display. "We've a lot to discuss."

Ferdinand scoffed. He crossed his arms and leaned back into his chair. "What are we even doing here? This is pointless."

"Stay in character," Radinka said. "Just because circumstances may have changed doesn't mean we should... stop playing the game. We may have to shift our goals a little."

"Not to put too fine a point on it, but the king is dead, and the kingdom has fallen. Whatever is left back home doesn't even remotely resemble what we left. Who do we serve? And most importantly, without our Kingdom, who do we bill for our services?"

"The rumpled one has a point," Briana said. "We're a long way from home, and if those reports are accurate, home burned to the ground. Whoever we worked for doesn't exist anymore."

Radinka frowned. "I think you may have hit the crux of the problem. If the reports are accurate. What if the reports are nothing more than self-serving propaganda the Evil Duchess sent to keep her minions in line."

Ferdinand shook his head. "It wouldn't have been the Duchess, according to the news. Or did you miss that part?"

"I saw it," Radinka said. "And you are right, but remember she was kind of a stickler for honesty. With her dead we don't know anything about the people running the show. Nothing we can trust, anyway."

Briana threw her arms wide. "What are we supposed to do now? Just abandon our mission and pretend to be friendly forces come to visit the locals?"

"Maybe," Radinka said.

"Hardly," Ferdinand said. "I had friends back home. I can't imagine the pain and suffering they are going through right now. I say we exact some revenge."

"Exacting revenge might prevent us from ever getting home," Radinka said.

"You expected to go home when you signed up for this?" Briana asked.

"No, but now that things have changed so much, I do find myself with that urge. I want to see what kind of mess those loonies have made of things. Maybe throw a wrench into their plans. They can't last long. Maybe we could help build a new power base from the ashes of our old friends."

Ferdinand scoffed. "Resurrect a power structure that was rendered inert? Not likely. No, we are here, and I say we do something in the name of our King, and our friends, who may or may not have lost their kingdom."

Radinka shook her head. "I don't know. What if we are trading our one chance to be free of all this for revenge and no one cares? Would you have us sacrifice our lives simply to, what is it, mess up the chance of a good relationship with the locals?"

"Do you have a better idea?" Briana asked.

Radinka pointed at the wizard. "He wants to go home, he just won't admit it. I do too. The fastest way home lies with that nice, very fast ship that is now in port. We should figure out a way to be on that ship when it heads home."

"Capture one of their most prized ships?" Briana furled her eyebrows. "Return in the name of the kingdom with a fully armed vessel and wreak havoc?"

Ferdinand shrugged. "Or to plant the seeds of rebellion and resurrection."

Radinka sat down and leaned forward, clasping her hands. "How would we take control of a ship like that?"

Ferdinand smiled. "I can think of a few ideas. Let's adjourn for a day. Come back tomorrow. I'll mock up a scenario and we can talk it over."

"Here?" Briana asked.

Ferdinand shook his head. "The docks are down the hill to the left when you walk out the front of the tavern. Not far. I'll alter the simulation to suit our needs." He glanced around the room. "Maybe I'll pattern it after a real ship. Make it more interesting."

Radinka nodded. "Good enough. See you two tomorrow."

REPORTING FOR DUTY

Wednesday, July 17, 3297, 7:12

Skip's office, directly across the passageway from MCC, had a wide window that looked out to the balcony. The view of the park beyond was obscured by the drop tube from the central docking ring.

"Excuse me, Administrator Onada?" Ted entered the office through the open door.

"Just call me Skip." He motioned him toward a chair. "You're Becker. How was the trip?"

"We were in cold sleep the whole time. So... uneventful?"

Skip chuckled. "Wish I could say that. Seven years of jumping, with nearly every stop a big empty spot in the vast lonely universe."

"Uneventful?"

Skip frowned. "I'll send you the details, but we had a bit of a mishap. Lost two officers and one crewmember is still under repair. Brain damage."

"Sorry to hear that."

"According to your paperwork you were a marine. One of Mercorps finest."

Ted nodded.

"Then you became a bodyguard?"

Ted shrugged. "Seemed like a good idea at the time."

"Then you married the woman you were assigned to protect."

Ted smiled. "Sometimes the most unexpected things happen, and you just have to deal with it."

"And she's here to set up and maintain a new restaurant?" Skip shrugged. "That fits with our current schedule. We are waking up the second tranche of the crew over the next few weeks. We'll need more variety. But you're supposed to be our new head of physical security." Skip shook his head. "Look, I appreciate you folks coming here, and I owe your sister-in-law a huge debt, but we don't have a great deal of need for physical security. I'm not all that sure where to assign you."

"I have to admit," Ted said, "it's all they could think of. They were very happy to send Debra on her way. She had become too much of a target back home."

Skip frowned. "Target?"

"Did you read the part about how Monarch died?"

"Briefly. A well trained tactical strike team, mostly former Mercorps Marines with specialty contractors?"

Ted smirked. "That is what they called her in the newscasts, but a lot of people knew what she did, and who she was. Even after she changed her name." Ted shook his head. "There was this constant bombardment of threats and aggravation from people who thought of her as a murderer. Then there were the people on our side, who thought she might try to trade on her sister's name and move into a position of power."

"People were against that?"

"Some. Some for. She didn't want that, and the real annoyance was the folks that said she had to. Every election someone would try to nominate her."

ORIENTATION

Thursday, July 18, 3297, 8:32

Skip entered the quarters he shared with his sons to find Nando comfortably reclined in the living area. It was an all too familiar sight.

"Nando?"

Nothing. His eyes were closed, unresponsive to the outside world.

Skip kicked his foot. "Nando. Come back to reality."

Skip watched as the emotions played over Nando's face. He looked confused, but his eyes remained shut.

"AutoGov, bring Nando Onada out of the simulation."

"Bring Nando Onada out of the simulation, aye," AutoGov said.

Nando's eyes sprung open. His hands gripped the chair.

"Nando Onada is now out of the simulation."

"No shit." Nando blinked his eyes and looked at his father. "What the hell?"

"Aren't you supposed to be at work by now?"

"What? Oh crap. I forgot to set the alarm."

"Did you even sleep last night?"

"I slept online," Nando said. "You should try it, sometime."

"What's wrong with sleeping in reality?"

"Look, some of us younger people like sleeping in beautiful gardens surrounded by elves."

"Naked female elves?" Skip's eyebrows rose.

Nando grinned lopsidedly as he reached for his shoes.

"Go shower, first. I'll ping the cargo bay and let them know you're running late."

"Thanks, Dad." He headed toward the fresher. "Those elves are really soft, you know. Perfect night's sleep."

Skip shook his head as he entered his room. He slid the clothes in his closet far to one side, reaching deep for his dress uniform. The sounds of running water erupted. The gentle hush of water hitting the walls of the fresher, interrupted occasionally by the occupant.

Nando's voice was a bit muffled, but could still be heard through the thin walls. "And it wasn't imaginary elves. I have a girlfriend there. A real one."

"A real girl, in virtual reality? What happened to Shea? Aren't you seeing her?"

"No. We... we broke it off."

"And you have a new one already?"

"Yeah. We met in the Halo. She loves polka."

Skip shook his head with a chuckle. "Good lord, marry her." He fastened the top of his uniform, snugging it under his chin. He swiped his personal display and sent a ping to Lenny.

"I might."

Skip headed to the kitchen area. "Bring her to dinner sometime. Introduce her to the family."

The water cut off, followed by the low rumble of the air dryers.

Skip sat down and sent a message to the cargo bay. He heard Nando in his room, grabbing clean clothes.

He emerged smoothing the fabric with his hands. "Okay, I'm off."

"Did you hear what I said about dinner?"

"I heard." Nando shrugged. "Maybe eventually. She's kind of shy."

Skip tilted his head. "Shy?"

"She doesn't want to meet in real life yet. She wants to give it time."

"I see. Any reason?"

Nando took a deep breath and exhaled. "She said she had a couple of bad experiences. Wants to avoid the drama."

"She prefers to spend her time in a virtual drama, instead of dealing with a real one?"

"Exactly."

Skip frowned. "Do you know what the term 'red flag' means?"

"Stop, Dad. I can handle it. Worst case scenario, it's an older woman with age issues."

"As long as you're happy. Just don't lose track of time. We need you here in the real world on a tight schedule. *Pang Yu* started offloading already."

"Yeah, yeah," Nando said. "Have you talked to Lenny yet?"

"About what?"

"As soon as that ship showed up, he started packing."

"Oh, that again." Skip shook his head. "I hoped he would outgrow it."

"He's still dead set on going back to Earth."

"I know. It's just that there isn't anything there for him. All his family is here."

"Yeah," Nando said, "but maybe you guys should have recruited people with kids his age. He was twelve. Seven years, those seven years, with no peers, and no girls. I understand why he wants to go."

Skip sighed. "I know. Now stop talking and get on your way. I'm meeting Lenny in a few minutes. He's helping with the orientation."

"Okay. Just don't push him. When I was that age, pushing me only made me more determined, even if I knew it was a bad idea."

"Which is exactly why I haven't said a word about you breaking up with Shea and how much of a bad idea I think that is."

Nando rolled his eyes. "Bye, Dad." He ran out the door and down the hall.

LENNY NODDED to his father as Skip approached the clearing. The park was a large open area almost two hundred meters long, two stories high, and nearly the full width of the ring. There were trees, water features, and a park for children to play. The perfect place to greet the three dozen new arrivals. Two dozen women, one dozen men, and only three married couples in the group. They were all listed as colonists.

Skip stepped onto the small circular platform in the center of the clearing. Looking over the new faces, he was glad he decided against the military uniform. "Hello everyone. Gather around if you will, please. I am Skip Onada, Administrator of *Endurance*. I wanted to welcome you here. Some of you are staying, and some of you are here for a visit. Either way, we've prepared an orientation simulation so that you can get to know the ship. There is also a section that will help to familiarize you with the second habitat. We are in the final planning stage, and should be ready to schedule construction soon. My son, Lenny, will give you all a virtual tour of the ship. Even areas off limits to visitors are accurately represented, so all your questions can be answered."

Two young women in the front row were smiling at Skip. One of them elbowed the other and whispered something.

"I maintain an open door policy. If you need anything, let me know. I or my executive assistant, Jake. For minor issues or random trivia questions, there is always someone on watch in the control center." He motioned for Lenny to join him. "This is my son, Lenny Onada. He's the one who designed the virtual tour."

"Thanks Administrator Dad," Lenny said. A chuckle ran through the crowd.

The two young ladies seemed to be even more excited.

"For those of you that would like to wander the simulation on your own, I've sent you all the link. It's a permanent program. Just be sure you remember where you are in the real world. Everyone who would like the guided tour, grab a seat, sit back, and join me."

Skip smiled. "Enjoy yourselves. There will be refreshments at the other end of the park by the time you are done."

The two young ladies raced each other to grab spots next to Lenny. Skip shook his head. *What are they up to?*

THE STAIRS TO BAMTHAPEEM

Mas'eeng Bayfod, Second Five, Early

Daksey shifted the pack to make it sit more comfortably. His tail had healed, but the pack seemed heavier this morning. Bongeex was at his side as they slowly climbed the endless winding stairs up the south side of the mountain. Foondek and Deytham were directly in front of them. The sun, peaking above the mountains to the east, warmed the side of his face during every break in the trees.

"Do you think the stone builders carved these steps before they moved to the mountaintop?" Bongeex asked. "Or do you think they settled in up there, and then thought, hey, let's make some steps for people to come see us."

Daksey chut-chutted. "You would think they might have gotten halfway up and thought, 'Maybe this is high enough.'"

Foondek snorted. "Are you complaining, little Daksey?"

Daksey huffed. "Just joking with my pouch-brother. It's more entertaining than counting the steps."

Bongeex chut-chutted. "How many steps have we climbed, Foondek?"

Foondek snorted and turned to face forward again.

Deytham flicked his tail. "We are less than 320 steps away from the next rest platform. You can already hear the waterfall."

Daksey undulated. "Thank you, brother. That is good to know."

Bongeex chut-chutted. "See? It's not Foondek who counts."

Deytham flicked his tail again. "I count the steps like I would count the beats of the drum. You have to know the rhythm, or you will lose the song."

"Drumming is a good skill to have," Kempok said from behind Daksey and Bongeex. "I hope one of my younger sons develops such a useful ability."

Foondek chut-chutted.

Bongeex lunged forward and snapped at his tail.

Daksey tilted his head. "Bongeex has an excellent skill, egg-mother. He can produce a gas from beneath his tail that kills insects for a keyk'eed in every direction."

Bongeex snorted. "And Daksey is becoming very adept at tying knots. See how well his little pack is fastened?"

Daksey chut-chutted, and his brothers joined in.

"You may joke," Kempok said, "but hunting is only one skill. A Botham should have many skills to help the village."

As they neared the rest platform, a foul stench assaulted their noses. Kempok waved them away from the water. "From the smell of it, there is a sickness awaiting us. Stay away from the water."

"Are you certain it's safe for us to go there?" Bongeex asked.

"They asked for our help," Kempok said. "We'll do the best we can, but keep clear of any who seem ill until we know what it is."

"I'm thirsty," Foondek said. "Are you sure we should avoid the water?"

"Avoid it," Kempok said. "We do not know what is causing their illness. There is a spring not far from the next platform. You can wait until then."

As the sun sank beneath the mountains to the west, they reached the top of the stairs and approached the bridge. On the other side of the stream, stone buildings formed a small village on the plateau amidst towering peaks of rock.

They were greeted by a young gray- and black-striped Ombax with a headdress and a spear. His tail twitched nervously. "Welcome Botham. Bamthapeem Mokfey, egg-mother of our tribe, will be back soon. She... she..."

Kempok huffed. "Spit it out, child. What are you trying to say?"

"She ran to the river to lift her tail, again. Many Bamthapeem have been lifting their tails in agony since yesterday."

"Yes, we could smell the results at the waterfall. I'll go to her. The rest of you stay here. I'll see if I can determine the cause."

"Oh, we know the cause, Botham Kempok. They ate something they shouldn't have."

"That is good news for us, then. Everyone, spread out, help anyone you can. Give them one leaf of o'saf to chew on. In Daksey's pack, green bag with the purple ribbon. Then be sure to have them drink plenty of clean water. We need to keep them hydrated."

Daksey set his pack on the ground and passed out handfuls of o'saf leaves, then headed into the village. Whenever he encountered a Bamthapeem with a pained look, he offered the herbal remedy. A few villagers looked at him with skepticism, but they took the aid when offered. A few others refused, saying they felt fine. Not everyone ate the meal in question.

Later that evening when the worst had been tended to, and most of the easier cases were resting, Bamthapeem Mokfey and a few others, along with the Botham, gathered around the great fire pit in the center of the village.

"We saw them climbing the eastern stairs," Mokfey said. "They had thin, straight legs, no tails, little round heads. They looked like some sort of large insect. One of the tree climbers. They were covered in cloth, and carried packs on their backs. Such a strange sight. They climbed slowly, and knew we saw them, so we didn't think they posed a threat. Still, we took precautions."

"You were armed?"

"Knives in pouches. A sound choice. No sooner had we begun to sit for a discussion, they pulled out a forbidden thing. It glowed, and pictures moved in the air. They showed us their disregard. They had stolen the lightning and trapped it. It startled all of us. The attack started before I gave the command. The black and gold on okdeyok. He jumped very quickly with an ear splitting shriek. It set off many of the other pouch-husbands and brothers."

Kempok undulated. "It is wrong to catch the lightning."

Several others took up the recital. "Thunder warns the people."

Everyone present echoed the last line. "Electric power is lightning"

Daksey looked around. Nearly every quill had risen at the mention of their most sacred law.

"You did the right thing," Kempok said. "Perhaps eating them, as is your tradition, was..."

"Not a tradition to always follow," Mokfey said.

Kempok chut-chutted. "Probably not. But what were these creatures?"

Daksey flicked his tail. "There is a new star in the sky. It passes very fast in the sky."

Bongeex snorted. "Not this again."

"It passes above our heads several times each night. All we have to do is look up after the sun goes down. You will see it too."

"What does a fast star mean?" Mokfey asked.

Daksey leaned forward. "Do you remember the stories about the sky people? The Dapkasamok?"

"Those are stories," Foondek said. "Nothing more."

Deytham raised his hand. "Hear him out, pouch-husband. Daksey is not stupid."

Daksey nodded. "Thank you, brother. The speed it travels in the sky means that it's close. In orbit over our world. From what you describe, they are not Dapkasamok. But still sky people."

Kempok tilted her head. "The story I remember is that the Dapkasamok were concerned. Something had gone wrong, and they left. Could these new sky people be the ones who drove them away?"

Foondek shrugged and snorted. "They are not sky people. You are being silly. They are probably mutations from Fengmaath. We know that there is still radiation there. It mutates living things. These are strange creatures, maybe even people, mutated, who lost their tails and their snouts."

Bongeex undulated. "Yes. That makes far more sense."

Mokfey's quills flick up and down, her nostrils flared. "Mutants from Fengmaath who steal lightning."

Foondek tilted his head. "It's probably very old. From before the Sunfire War."

Deytham snorted. "Nothing that old still works."

Kempok flicked her tail. "What matters is what can be done about it. Is there something we should be doing?"

"Why?" Mokfey asked. "The scholars in Afothameex will deal with it."

"What if they do not know?" Bongeex asked. "Someone should go tell them what happened here."

"That is a solid plan," Kempok said. "We should send someone to the observatory. Maybe have them take some bones."

"And some of what we found in the packs," Mokfey said.

"What did you find?"

"Electric equipment. Most of it smashed before I found it. A round disk. When you touch the edge here, it emits a brilliant light. Touch it again, and it goes away."

Kempok undulated. "That is certainly proof they should see.

Along with a skull, perhaps. We could send it with Depek. Have him go west first, reverse his plan."

"That black and gold visitor? He didn't survive the night. He won't be making any more journeys."

Kempok swayed. "That is sad. He was pleasant. A good visitor. Has your drummer regained his wits? Someone should send the message to Kadayax. Let his family know."

"He died here. I will send someone down to the ocean."

Kempok held motionless for a moment. Her nostrils flared slightly as she slowly undulated. "I will send someone to Afothameex to inform the scholars."

Bongeex hooted wistfully. "I will go, egg-mother. Please, let it be me."

Kempok snorted and shrugged her shoulders. "You take too many risks." She cast her eyes around the group, then thumped her tail. "If Botham is to send someone, it will be Daksey."

Daksey's quills stood up. "What? Why me? Egg-Mother, why?"

Kempok thumped her tail. "You are steady and sure. Cautious. If I send you, I will soon have two sons again. If I send Bongeex, he will join his donor-father in adventure and never return."

"What about Deytham? He is steady and sure. More than I am."

"And he has an egg in his pouch. No, it shall be you."

Deytham chut-chutted. "Sorry little brother. You and I are too much alike. She already knows Foondek is too much like Bongeex. If I hadn't been given an egg, it would certainly have been me."

Foondek snorted. "I've outgrown my risk taking. I can do it."

Kempok chut-chutted and shrugged. "We need our best hunters. Daksey will do it. You will take an extra hunt."

"I can do that. See Daksey? Botham Kempok knows how to assign tasks. I will hunt for you, while you are gone."

Daksey huffed. "I hate sand."

"You can ride the moyoxees over the sand."

"Do we have any coins to pay for it? They ask for money."

"We can send some herbs," Kempok said. "It has been done before. Leave that to me."

Espay turned to Soyok. "We should still ensure he has what he needs if he does need to walk the sand."

Soyok undulated. "I will help you pack a bag."

Kempok undulated and thumped her tail. "It's settled then. Daksey will leave in the morning."

Daksey hunched over and quietly huffed. "I hate sand."

FOONDEK AND DEYTHAM

Thursday, July 18, 3297, 2:24

S kip watched the displays in MCC, as the automated shuttle slid into the docking bay. All indicators showed green.

He sighed. "That's it, then. We can repurpose the thing for orbital operations now."

Kai nodded as she watched the shuttle be sprayed with disinfectant.

Skip waved off the monitor. He turned to look at the system diagram. Thinking about where to look next.

The image of Pam Gilliam interrupted him. "MCC, this is the shuttle bay. We...we have company, sir."

Skip's eyebrows raised. "Company?"

Pam frowned, eyes wide. "A couple natives got into the shuttle before we recalled it. They're wounded. One's gasping."

"Damn. AutoGov, match the surface atmosphere for the natives. Everyone, clear the area. We'll try to save them, but I'm not losing any more crew, understood?"

"Aye, sir. Evacuating the bay now."

"Aye. AutoGov, do you have the atmosphere set yet?"

"Atmospheric adjustment is still underway," AutoGov said. "Argon, oxygen and nitrogen levels will match in approximately 12 minutes."

"Get a drone in there and check it out."

"Acknowledged."

Skip watched as the last of the crew closed the hatch behind them.

"Can you see anything?" Pam asked.

"Give it a moment," Skip said.

Three drones circled above the shuttle while a fourth entered through the open hatch.

"There are two individuals," AutoGov said. "One appears to be deceased. The other is breathing. Unable to determine if this is a normal rate of respiration."

"Is it conscious?"

"It does not appear so. There is a large amount of blood."

"Get closer. See if you can administer first aid to the live one. And wake up Dr. Ruggiero. She'll need to be involved."

"Acknowledged."

THE LIVE SPECIMEN

Thursday, July 18, 3297, 4:48

Skip entered the conference room adjacent to MCC with Kai right behind. A well-lit room with three display walls, its wide windows of the outer wall showed the slowly rotating starfield beyond.

Maksim Borodin and Dr. Anna Ruggiero were already there. "Where are we at?" He settled into his seat.

"The live specimen has suffered multiple abrasions," Anna said, "but there appear to be no puncture wounds. The deceased specimen has a cut on the underside of the left neck ridge. It appears to be the source of the blood. Probably a major artery."

Skip sighed. "We need to set up a place to keep this thing alive."

Maksim scoffed. "Just dissect it and see what makes it tick."

"We already have a dead one for that. I want to see if we can communicate with this species."

"Remember how many of our people these things ate? Best to put it down quickly."

"We don't know if they were eaten," Anna said.

Maksim pounded the table with his fist. "Bullshit. You know damned well that was a barbeque they were building."

Skip crossed his arms. He glanced at Kai.

Anna shrugged. "It could have been a sacrificial fire."

Maksim waved his hand dismissively. "You are being an idiot."

Kai frowned. "That last image did show one of them licking his... well, lips."

"That's a human affectation," Anna said, "but I get your point. We'll be careful."

"Get security guards," Maksim said. "That new guy, the big one. Becker? Get him on it."

Skip smiled grimly. "I've made him head of security. This will be his first real job, I suppose. Need someone else big too. No idea how strong these things are, one on one."

"Maybe stunners? If it gets out of line shock it a little. Teach it to obey."

Skip frowned. "I don't want to treat it like an animal. I'll let Becker know it's an option. We'll need a space large enough for it to move around."

"I have an idea where we might put it." Kai swiped her display and shared a layout of the *Endurance*. She highlighted the small chemistry lab. "This has an adjacent area with a transparent wall. It's meant for safe observation. Also, because of the nature of the work in there, the atmosphere can be easily isolated. Makes it easy to replicate the air."

"Our readings suggest there would be a mutual compatibility there. They have more argon, but that's inert anyway. The oxygen levels are higher than ours, but not so much I think it will matter."

"Still," Skip said, "let's try to replicate it exactly, first. Just in case. Then we can run a few tests." He turned to Anna. "I want you to do a full autopsy on the dead one. The more we can learn about its physiology, the better chance we have at keeping the other one alive."

"For how long?"

"Maksim, please. This is an intelligent species. I know you are in pain at the moment. We all are. We've seen what happens to us when we are in their home. This one is in our home. We need to show it who we are."

"I've sent word to the rest of my team," Anna said. "They are preparing a dissection space now. I'll let you know what I find."

"Anything else I need to know?" Skip asked.

Maksim grumbled under his breath.

"All right then," Skip said. "Let's get the move started. Anna, you're with me. Kai, head up to MCC. It's my watch coming up, if you don't mind."

"No worries, Skip." Kai headed out first.

"Maksim, maybe you can review the drone footage. Get an idea if anything we have in the way of native plants is something they find edible."

Maksim sighed. "Yes, sir. I will see what I can find."

JUST LIKE HOME

Thursday, July 18, 3297, 7:12

Ted entered the spacious apartment and looked around. The neutral tones of the walls were dull, but welcoming. He pointed at the largest wall. "AutoGov, put a lunar landscape there. Earth as it's viewed from Moretus."

"Acknowledged."

The bottom third of the wall became a brilliant scene of lunar desolation. Earth hung above a distant peak in a sea of blackness.

"Adjust the contrast. Make it a bit more artsy. Let the stars show through."

The adjustments appeared as he listed them. The resulting scene on the display showed a partially realistic scene, similar to the one he and Debra had installed in their previous quarters on Luna.

Debra walked in carrying a small package. She glanced at the wall and sighed. "Trying to make me feel like I'm home?"

Ted smiled. "It's a starter image. Something to mark this place as ours. Much better than temporary berthing. Room to breathe."

She lifted the package. "Speaking of which, AutoGov, give us a table over here, please."

A slot in an adjacent wall opened and a vertical sheet slid out, then unfolded itself into a small table.

She set the package down and tapped the top. It unfolded into a diorama of a small restaurant. The shape made it suitable for a corner location, with eating areas on two sides with windowed views, and a kitchen section in the opposite corner. One side had a counter with a built-in grill. The other side had a long bar with a row of stools.

Ted looked it over. "Is this an exact replica?"

"It's a little bigger. Since it's going to be fully automated, we'll be able to serve more customers. But not so much bigger that it loses the flavor."

"Have you decided what to call the bartender?"

She sighed. "Uncle Etto called the new chefbot Alpha, and we shortened it to Al. I was thinking maybe Beta, but I'm not sure."

"How about Betto? Make him skinny and tan. I'll paint a thin mustache on him."

Debra giggled. "You will not." She thought for a moment. "I like it. Al and Betto."

AutoGov interrupted, "Skip Onada is calling Security Chief Becker."

"Yes, Skip," Ted said, "what can I do for you?"

"I need you up in the shuttle bay right now."

"On my way."

"Thanks." The connection dropped.

Debra frowned. "I thought you had a couple days to settle in."

"That's not how it works, honey. I'll be back when I can."

"You don't even have a uniform."

"Didn't sound like he cared," Ted said, as he walked out the door.

TED ENTERED the observation lounge where Skip and Anna were waiting. They were watching three drones lifting something from the shuttle.

"Holy crap, that's one of those creatures. How did it get inside?"

A large security guard entered the observation room. "Hey Skip. What's up? Anna." He nodded to Anna.

"Ah, Zon," Skip said. "This is Ted Becker, the guy I told you about."

"Becker, eh?" He thrust forward a beefy hand. "Name's Zontatanka B. E. Delikan. You can call me Zon for short, or Deli, if you're hungry."

Ted chuckled as he shook hands. "Most folks call me Ted." He pointed to where the drones were gently lifting the creature out of the shuttle. "We have company."

"There's another one back inside," Skip said. "It didn't survive the trip. This one is breathing. We need to get it somewhere secure."

"Secure, sure," Anna said. "But we need to get it into an atmosphere mix that it's used to. We don't know how it will respond to our air. We're going to take it down to the chemistry lab. It's right next to the lift. We can get the bots to empty it out, give us room, and it's sealed so we can run a different mix of gases in there."

Zon scratched his head. "How did they get inside the shuttle?"

"They must have tripped the lock," Skip said." Maybe climbed in while we weren't looking."

Anna opened a nearby locker and brought out two pairs of heavy duty protective gloves. "You two, take these hazmat gloves and get in there. You can help lift it out."

Ted took the gloves and handed a pair to Zon. They fit snugly.

"What about gravity?" Zon asked.

"That's a good point. The chemistry lab is down on the lower level, about ninety percent gee. AutoGov, what's the gravity down on the planet?"

"One point two five seven," AutoGov said.

"We'll need to run out an extension to get that," Anna said. "Better tell Ops what's happening."

Skip waved a finger at his display. "AutoGov, start prepping the chemistry lab. Remove anything that is easily removable, and set the gas mix to resemble the planet's surface. Try to match the region this thing came from. And send a running status to Ops."

"Acknowledged," AutoGov said.

Ted and Zon headed for the lift, each guiding and nudging one end of their charge. Once they were able to get the creature into the lift, the doors slid closed. Very slowly, the gravity increased as they neared the outer edge of the rotating habitat.

The creature's eyes opened wide, and it began to struggle. Ted gripped it firmly. It squirmed and twisted, as Zon adjusted his position to hold it down. "Easy there. Take it easy. It's going to be All right. Just relax." Ted hoped his voice conveyed calm. But what is calm to this creature?

It swung its head around and looked at Ted. Their eyes locked.

Ted released one hand and tried to gently stroke its skin.

The creature twisted and tried to break free, again.

"Let it go. Let's see if we can reason with it."

Zon complied. The creature slowly settled to the floor, its head swooshing back and forth, its quills flicking up and down. It reached out to the walls as it backed into a corner. Ted stepped back to try to give it room.

As the gravity increased, the creature became steadier on its feet. Ted could see blood dripping from a wound on its leg. He pointed at it. "You are hurt."

The creature followed where Ted pointed, saw the wound,

then placed one hand over it. Locking eyes with Ted again, it leaned forward, then thumped its back into the wall. Then again, and again. It took a deep breath and appeared to relax.

"Now if that ain't some next level shit," Zon said.

Ted watched the creature carefully. The lift slowed its descent and finally stopped. The doors behind Ted opened. He glanced over his shoulder, then started backing out. He waved Zon to come out as well, then did his best to motion the creature to follow. He tried waving his hands toward him, wiggling his fingers. The creature stared at him.

Zon clapped his hands, getting the creature's attention. He pointed at him, then pointed at a spot in front of him, then pointed at the neighboring chemistry lab entrance. Then he stepped back.

The creature took a step forward, then as if he were hitting marks, followed Zon's directions.

Ted nodded. "Nice work." The creature's wound had stopped bleeding.

"Thanks. I take it you don't have kids."

Ted frowned. "No, I... what does that have to do with it?"

"Trust me, it helps with crowd control."

With the creature inside, they closed the doors and secured them. The neighboring office had a shared window and door. They decided to set that up as the controlled entry point. It would allow them to watch the creature as well.

Skip arrived on the next lift down. After checking things were to his satisfaction, he headed back up to the operations center.

"How many people are on the security team?" Ted asked.

Zon laughed. "Including you? Let me think." He held up one hand and put one finger up. "There's me, of course. And now you." He raised a second finger and looked at his hand. "Yup. That confirms it. Two."

Ted sighed and shook his head. "We are going to need more than that. I want two people on watch at all times. That's at least six of us if we want any sort of normal day. Eight would be better."

"You'll need to talk to the supply manager. That's who I reported to before Skip stole me to be security. Oh, and my only qualification is that I'm a big strong guy, so with all that military background of yours, you get to be the new chief." He made an exaggerated military salute.

"Oh good. And here I thought we would have to wrestle for it."

"Oh, we can still wrestle. Just, you will still be the boss. Now, if you suddenly need to organize a stack of crates by index numbers and size with a cross reference to necessity and ease of access, I'll take charge, I promise."

Ted chuckled. "And here I thought this might be hard. That takes a huge load off right there, let me tell you."

The two shared a laugh.

That's when Ted noticed that the creature was looking at them through the window, watching their every move.

CONNECTION

Friday, July 19, 3297, 11:07

Foondek paced back and forth in his spacious cell. He slapped the walls with his tail at every turn. The pain in his side reminded him he hadn't healed as fast as he wanted. The window into the smaller room had gone dark a long time ago, but he knew the two large beings were inside, watching his every move. The door next to it had no latch. It could not be opened from inside. A splash of light caught his attention. A door in the little room opened and another of the creatures entered.

The room brightened, and Foondek could see the three of them clearly – the two large ones he had been tortured by before were still there, though this new creature was smaller. Probably a pouch-husband. He seemed agitated, holding a flat thing and pointing to it. He pointed directly at Foondek while still looking at the larger creatures.

Were these really egg-mothers? Probably. They wore cloth over themselves, making it hard to tell. He couldn't see if it had a pouch or not. Now that he could see the different sizes, it seemed a logical conclusion. The smaller pouch-husband appeared to have berated the larger egg-mothers into submission and now stood at the window, looking at the flat thing he had in his hand. That seemed strange, but everything here seemed strange. Were pouch-husbands in charge here?

A rectangular section of the window changed, and showed moving images. At first, it fascinated Foondek. Such clarity and movement. He saw a room filled with tables. Then he saw Deytham. His lifeless body splayed out on one of the tables. There were tremendous cuts in his body. Foondek felt a wave of grief and sadness. He knew his beloved pouch-husband had died. These cuts had been done by the creatures. They had mutilated his body.

Foondek turned away from the horrific images, swaying. A low moan filled his throat with grief and rumbled through the cell. He closed his eyes and let the emotion grip him.

He heard the door open. A hand touched his neck. He knew it wasn't Deytham, but for a moment, his mind raced. He clenched his eyes tightly, not wanting to know what new horror these creatures would inflict.

The hand stroked his neck, then took his head, and firmly aimed it back at the window. He clenched his eyes in refusal. The unexpected touch had alerted his hindbrain, and he could feel the pain relief as it once again flooded his system.

The creature spoke softly. He didn't understand what he said, but the gentleness confirmed his suspicion, this was indeed a pouch-husband. He took a deep breath, then opened his eyes.

The image had been frozen with one of the creatures putting a hand inside Deytham's pouch. A pang of agony swept over him, and Foondek imagined they were going to show him a crushed egg.

The hands started moving, and with unexpected tenderness, removed Deytham's egg whole. Intact, and wrapped it in a blanket.

The pouch-husband stepped back, and spread his arms wide. Was it waiting for a response?

Foondek pointed to the egg, then to his own pouch. "Give me

the egg." He pulled his pouch open and pointed from the image to his pouch again.

The little pouch-husband darted out the door and through the little room. Gone in an instant. The door remained open, although both of the egg-mothers stood guard.

What had happened? Could he really hope? If the egg was intact, could it still be alive? He could feel the quills of his neck stiffen in fear.

The pouch-husband came back, holding the blanket from the images. The way he moved, the care he took when handling the bundle was so unexpected, Foondek almost hooted. He took the egg and with great care, put it inside his pouch, then waited to see if the egg was alive. Barely a heartbeat later the little one began adjusting itself. Foondek reached and took the pouch-husband's hand, placing it on his pouch so that he could feel the movement too.

The pouch-husband emitted a high-pitched squeal, turned his head and said something to the egg-mothers. They said something back. He turned back to Foondek, withdrawing his hand slowly, then bared his teeth. It didn't look threatening. Those little teeth couldn't hurt him at all. Was this something good?

Foondek nodded with gratitude. He pointed to his face and said his name, then to the image on the window. "Deytham."

The little pouch-husband pointed to the window. "Deytham." He pointed to Foondek, and said his name, then pointed at his chest, between two round lumps. "Anna."

"Anna," Foondek said.

There were those little teeth, again. Foondek tried to imitate him.

Anna's eyes went wide, and his mouth opened. He might be astonished at such a beautiful display.

The other creatures, the larger ones, came running into the room. Anna raised his hands and waved at them, and said something. Such a strange language. They made sounds that Foondek found difficult to make.

Foondek looked back and forth at them. His quills flicked up, then down in confusion. The wave of realization washed from his head down to the tip of his tail. Normal teeth might have been threatening to them, while small teeth were not. These two had rushed in, not understanding that the two of them had reached an understanding. Only the little male understood.

Foondek felt a touch on his arm. Anna still spoke to the other two, and had reached back to touch his arm. He took his free hand and gently covered the creature's hand, then looked at the other two and tilted his head. In a moment of inspiration, Foondek lifted his hand back up, spread it wide as he had just seen done, and wiggled his fingers.

The other two looked at each other, and they both erupted in repetitive barking. They turned and left as the barking faded.

•• —————————— ••●•• —————————— ••

"Administrator Onada," AutoGov said, "you have a call from Anna Ruggiero."

"Yes, Anna," Skip said. "What can I do for you?"

"Administrator Onada, I'm calling to inform you that I am taking control of the efforts surrounding our visitor. Starting with a complete program of linguistic analysis and study, but will also include living conditions, feeding and care."

Skip paused. "Who was supposed to be in charge?"

"No one, sir. Not since the last disaster."

Skip took a deep breath and exhaled. "I would ask how you came to this conclusion, but I've had a very long few days, and you've solved a problem I hadn't started dealing with, so congratulations. You are now the Director of Exosapient Communications."

"I prefer sapient, sir. Or non-human sapience. Exo seems so

Earth centric, don't you think? And the reason is that I've inadvertently made a connection with her. She wants to communicate, and I think we've established a level of trust."

Skip sighed. "Make up a title and inform AutoGov what it is. AutoGov, give her anything she needs."

"Acknowledged," AutoGov said.

"Thank you, Skip," Anna said. "Any title?"

"Be reasonable, please. And make sure you start attending the department head meetings."

"Meetings?"

Skip grinned. "Sure. You didn't think it would be all play and no work, did you?"

"No sir. Just hadn't thought about that."

"Understood. Have fun figuring out what else you've overlooked."

"Yes sir." She waved off the connection.

Skip sighed. "She'll do fine."

INCIDENTALS

Saturday, July 20, 3297, 9:12

Radinka sat at the back room table drumming her simulated fingers on the simulated wood. Her frustration grew. Ferdinand had already given her a tour of his simulated ship. She wanted them all to be here before they discussed it. At last, the elf entered the room and slammed the door behind her.

"You're late," Radinka said.

Briana scoffed. "I was dealing with an interloper. Seems he likes the game and wants to explore. I wanted to check him out and make sure he wasn't a spy." She draped herself over her chair with one leg over the arm.

"What did you find out?"

"He's for real. Loves the detail you put into the place, Ferdy."

Ferdinand shook his head. "I went out of my way to make the gameplay simple, fairly boring, and highly lethal at even the slightest increase in level. With any luck at all, he'll be gone soon enough."

"How lethal?" Radinka asked.

"Once the second crystal is placed into the hilt of the sword, swinging it at full strength becomes dangerous to the wielder. Causes damage because of the sheer impact against the air itself. Adding the third stone makes it lethal to use at full strength. Just gets worse from there. Should be a real deterrent."

Briana glanced at her hand. "I'm sure it is. Can we get to business now?"

"Ferdinand said he already showed you the ship simulation. What are your thoughts?"

"It's fine. Seems accurate enough."

"I agree," Radinka said. "Ferdinand, your simulation of the ship was good. In fact, it pointed to some issues with the current plan, so I am now reconsidering."

Ferdinand tilted his head. "Why is that?"

"First, we would be too few to be a good crew," Radinka said. "Then there is the automation that we couldn't trust, and third, a whole year of jumping the ship, over and over again. Frankly, I would rather pose as a friendly passenger, hitch a ride home, and then see where everything lies up close."

"There's no telling what that would take. No one has said a thing about transfers home."

"Maybe poke around. See if there's an appetite for it among our former co-workers. You know, the ones that were loyal to the King before the borders shifted."

Briana yawned. "You two go ahead with that. I guess I can stay here and keep an eye on things. Maybe make a new recruit or two." She leaned forward. "Maybe I can have a whole regiment ready and waiting for the word to strike."

Radinka chuckled. "Interesting idea. Are you certain you don't want to come back with us?"

Briana shook her head. "I don't have anything to go back to. Well, prison, maybe. No thanks. Out here, they don't know who I used to be. I like that."

Radinka nodded. "Fine. I think we can work with what we have."

BONGEEX HUNTS ALONE

Masax had been in Kempok's room all morning. She was distraught. Nervous. Bongeex didn't know what to make of it.

He tapped on Kempok's massive door. "Egg-Mother, it's time for the hunt. I'm going to get Foondek and Deytham."

He heard her approach the door. It slid open. Kempok's nostrils were flared with worry.

"What happened?"

"Deytham and Foondek have not returned from Bamthapeem. It has been too long."

Bongeex undulated. "Then I shall set out to find them."

"No," Masax said. "It could be the sayox. A clan might have moved nearby."

Kempok huffed. "We would have heard them before now. When they claim territory, they make a lot of noise."

"I'll listen for the sayox," Bongeex said. "I agree with Kempok. They don't take territory so close to us anyway. I'll go swiftly."

"Yes, but you should also hunt. Bring back meat. If you find them, that is good. But if you do not, you are the remaining hunter."

Bongeex reeled at the thought. "I hope it isn't that bad. I'll go hunting around the side of the mountain. I'll set Daksey's traps along the way. I will make my way to the eastern steps. If I see no sign of them, I will only hunt. If I do, I will follow to see if I can find them."

"It's a good plan. Take Deytham's snares as well. As many as you can carry."

Bongeex undulated. He leapt down the hill and ran to Masax's house. One of the angular constructions, on one side an extra room held the family hunting equipment. He had helped his older brother several times before. He thought about Deytham. He and Foondek had taken the Eastern steps when they left Bamthapeem. They were to take the path directly home, but explore a little on each side to see if they could trace where the creatures had come from. They weren't supposed to be gone a full day. It had been two.

Bongeex loaded himself with all of the snares he could find. The stakes and baskets of the snares and traps together made an unwieldy load, but he would manage. He grabbed a small hand ax and thigh belt.

Setting off to the north, he headed for the eastern side of the mountain. The base of the steps were further than the southern steps, but not by much. There wasn't a river down that side. Water from Bamthapeem flowed south and west.

He thought of Daksey, heading west. So fortunate to be on an adventure. Seeing marvelous sights, new things, new places. What wonder.

He tripped and fell, sprawling onto the trail and slapping the dirt with his chin.

He took in a deep breath and sighed. "Keep your eyes on the trail."

He set traps every few paces until his load felt much lighter. He started spacing the snares out. Each had to have stakes driven into the ground, and were sometimes tricky to set. Daksey's traps had been much easier. He set the last snare, making sure to hide it well, then leapt back onto the trail. Glancing to each side as he went, looking for clues.

As he neared the base of the steps, a brief opening in the trees led to a small clearing. The trampled grass and footsteps left a clear trail. He found smaller, oval shaped markings. These were the creatures who were wearing coverings on their feet. There were also the feet of two adult pouch-husbands. Bongeex knew this was Deytham and his pouch-husband. He slowed his pace, and crept forward with care.

Heavy marks in the soil showed where something large had been, but then lifted. Yet no foot marks were on the sides. There were scorch marks around the edges. Had it burned into nothing? Leaving no ash? The prints of his family disappeared as if they had been blown away by a fiery wind.

He followed the little feet marks out of the clearing all the way to the base of the steps. He understood their fate, and there were no new tracks of that kind, just the wide four-toed marks of the Ombax foot.

He sat on a shaded section of the lower steps and unpacked some of his food. He listened for sounds that might give him clues.

Nothing but the peaceful chirrups of the dathay and the smooth buzzing of insects.

He heard the grunt of an omthey nearby. They were the large prey he preferred. Hard to catch, they were fast, smart, and it could be dangerous if it decided to stand and fight.

To best feed the tribe, catching a big omthey would do.

He put his meal away, and stepped quietly to the base of the steps, heading into the trees to the east. Tracking his prey by what he heard and the vague hints of warmth he could see.

Well into the afternoon he discovered the trees it had fed on. A few moments later, it came into sight. The omthey turned to face him. One glance, a loud grunt, and it ran into the woods.

Three others startled, and ran with it. They were out of reach and still running before Bongeex could react.

He looked at the sun, low on the horizon. He needed to turn back. Besides, the traps should have caught enough game to feed the tribe.

He made his way back to the west. It seemed much further than when he came this way. The sun had started to set when he found the eastern steps. The shadows of the trees darkened the path home. He hurried to the first trap.

He found the scraps of a smaller animal in the first snare. Something had already eaten it.

He took what he could, pulled up the stakes, then headed back. Most of the snares were empty as were the traps. Two traps had caught something, but it had chewed itself free, spoiling the trap. One trap held a small dathay inside, still intact. Enough to feed Kempok a snack. He killed it, and packed it with care, then bundled the trap onto his back, and slowly trudged into the village.

He brought his catch to Kempok. She told him to go fix the traps.

Once he was done, the egg-mothers gathered in a semi-circle around the open pavilion. Bongeex sat at their focus. He fidgeted from foot to foot.

"Tell us what you found, Bongeex," Kempok said.

"Near the eastern steps there is a small clearing. I found the creature's footprints, and I found the prints of two adult pouch-husbands. The prints of the creatures went right to the steps. None returned. The prints of the pouch-husbands went to the clearing. They did not return, either. In the clearing were marks, as if a heavy platform had been there. The prints I followed had been obliterated by a heavy wind. As if a small tornado had appeared, but not twisting, just blown away from the center, where I believe the platform had been. There were burn marks at the edges, and under where the platform should have been. But I found nothing. Just impressions in the dirt. I saw no platform. No ash, no debris. Just gone."

"Did you check all around? Are you certain they hadn't jumped into the brush?" Masax swayed with sadness.

"I searched all around the clearing. I found no other prints. They were blown away. If they went into the woods, I would have seen something."

Masax huffed. "Deytham would have found something."

Bongeex held his snort. "He might have. But I'm the one who was not lost."

Masax snorted. "He is not lost, and neither is Foondek. They must have been taken. There were more than three of those little beasts. They stole my family."

Kempok reached out to Masax and patted her neck. "Be calm, sister. We do not know what happened. Bongeex did well to remain true. There isn't any proof that the prints were even those of your pouch-husbands. Though it seems very likely, given what we know. The wind Bongeex spoke of may have destroyed evidence of a struggle. It may not have. It's something we do not know. What we do know is that they are not here. And with Daksey on a journey to Afothameex, our only remaining hunter is Bongeex. We'll need another hunter to help him carry the traps."

"Kaxooth is large for his age, and he is smart," Akfoy said. "Bongeex, can you work with him?"

Bongeex knew the child. "Even if he cannot hunt, he can carry traps. I will teach him when to be silent, if he is willing to learn. But when someone calls another a hunter, it's because they would trust him with their life. It's the highest honor one hunter can bestow another. Make sure he understands this."

"I will make him understand the importance of your training."

"I can hunt too," Moya'se said. "I'm bigger than Kaxooth, and I'm already able to be silent."

Kempok chut-chutted. "Indeed. I hadn't even realized you had hidden yourself so close to this meeting. While I believe hunting skills may be wasted on a future egg-mother, perhaps a third pair of hands will help."

Bongeex huffed. "Kempok, please. Anyone but her."

Kempok tilted her head. "It's already decided. You will teach your sister to set traps along with Kaxooth."

Bongeex undulated as his nostrils flared in concern. "Yes, Kempok."

Moya'se chutted.

•• ———————— ••●•• ———————— ••

THE NEXT MORNING, Bongeex and Moya'se packed up Daksey's traps and headed to Masax's house to retrieve Deytham's snares. He tried to give those to his sister, since they were lighter.

"You keep them. I'll take the traps and the bait pex."

Bongeex tilted his head and gave her the rest of the traps, while gathering the snares for his pack. He handed her the glass jar of the wriggly little pex they used as bait. "Kaxooth is late."

"Of course he's late. He's a child."

Bongeex snorted. "So are you, and you were awake before I was."

Moya'se stomped her foot and snorted back. They glared at each other for a moment.

"Sorry I'm late," Kaxooth said as he rounded the corner of the house. "Akfoy made me eat an extra helping for energy."

Bongeex turned and stomped toward the trail to the south. "I hunted east, yesterday. Today we go south."

"What should I carry?" Kaxooth asked.

Bongeex tilted his head. "Moya'se has all the traps. If she needs help, take a few."

"I'm fine," Moya'se said. "Just follow us and be quiet."

Kaxooth huffed and fell in line behind Moya'se. "How far are we going?"

"A lot further than this," Bongeex said. "Keep up."

Bongeex had set a steady pace he thought wouldn't be too difficult for the younger ones. Moya'se pulled beside him and hooted softly, then glanced over her shoulder. Bongeex followed her lead and looked. Kaxooth had fallen behind again.

"Let's stop here and place the first trap." He halted and waited with his sister for Kaxooth to join them.

Moya'se swung the bundle of traps off her back and lifted one out of the netting.

"Set it over there, a few paces away from the trail. Anchor it with two stakes. See the loops on each side?"

"I need the ax hammer."

Bongeex grabbed the forgotten tool and passed it to his sister. "Do you know how to set the trap?"

She huffed. "No."

"Kaxooth, come over here. I will show you both how to set the trap. First, drive in a stake on each side."

Moya'se did as instructed, while Kaxooth fidgeted nearby.

"Now, see how that one side is slanted? Push that up with your right hand, and push that little lever with your left."

Moya'se looked at the trap. "Where does this lever need to be when I'm done?"

"Under this loop," Bongeex said, pointing.

She set the trap and backed away.

"Now add the bait to the flat end."

She took the jar of bait pex from Kaxooth. "How many?"

"Just one. Two if it's small. It should fill that little depression on the trigger plate."

She undulated and placed the bait.

Bongeex hooted softly. "That is good, Moya'se. Kaxooth, did you see how she did it?"

"I know how to do this," he said.

"Good. Then you will set the second trap. Let's get moving."

When they came to the spot Bongeex thought would be good for the second trap, he stopped again. Moya'se at his side.

When Kaxooth caught up, Moya'se presented him with a trap and two stakes.

Bongeex handed him the little ax hammer.

Kaxooth set the trap down, but placed the first spike in the wrong position. Missing the loop.

"Pounding a stake in next to the trap doesn't hold it. You have to catch the loop." He pointed. "See there?"

"Oh. I forgot." Kaxooth pulled the stake out, and tried again. He remembered for the second stake, but then couldn't get the grip right to set the trap.

"Here," Moya'se said. "Let me show you."

"I can get it."

Moya'se tilted her head and crossed her arms. "Then go ahead."

Bongeex tried not to be impatient, but he could feel the frustration growing.

"Stop," Moya'se said. "Put your other hand inside and hold the door. It's so much easier."

Kaxooth's quills flicked up then down in confusion. He did as she told him to do, and after a few more tries, set the trap. He started to walk away.

"Did you forget something?" Bongeex asked.

"The trap is set," Kaxooth said. "The stakes are in the ground. Let's go to the next spot."

"You need to give the animal a reason to enter your trap. Do you know what that means?"

Kaxooth's quills twitched again.

Moya'se snorted. "Bait the trap, fish brain."

Bongeex huffed quietly. This was going to be a long day.

. . .

"Botham Kempok," Bongeex said. "Great Egg-Mother, and tribe leader. We bring meat for the family. We bring honor for you."

Kempok warbled gently. "You have done well. Come in, put the meat away and go clean yourselves. Then help your pouch-fathers in the kitchen. We'll be having guests tonight."

Moya'se pushed past Bongeex and headed down to the cold room.

"Who is coming?" Bongeex asked.

"Komay and Masax. They are both worried about Foondek, while Masax is also worried about Deytham. I must put all that aside, and work to calm their grief, without giving in to my own."

Bongeex undulated.

Kempok glanced at the passage leading downstairs. "How did Moya'se do on the hunt?"

"She asked more questions than Daksey ever did but listened when she needed to and learned quickly. Eager to help. When Kaxooth caught his own toe, she cleaned and bandaged the cut." He chut-chutted. "And her scolding of the child was a true thing of beauty, Kempok. She is certainly your daughter."

Kempok chut-chutted. "Good. Akfoy has already been by. Kaxooth won't be going out again until his wound heals. Can you and Moya'se keep hunting together?"

"Without him, we'll do much better, I think."

JAKE'S MEMORIAL

Saturday, July 20, 3297, 10:14

Ted and Debra were out on a run to help gain new strength in their legs. The great curve of the ring looked much the same as it had on Gerstenfeld Halo, the last place they had called home. The park wasn't nearly as wide, only about ten meters for about half the run, but the large loop allowed for expansion.

The path they were on split as they entered the park. An open space, two stories tall with trees and abundant greenery. The path ran down each side, so they veered left. They came upon a small clear area with fountains and benches. The sounds of children playing nearby drifted on the gentle breeze. Debra waved Ted over. "I want a break."

"No problem," said Ted. He walked over to one of the fountains and splashed some water on his face. After wiping his eyes dry, he was startled to see a familiar face. The statue he stood in front of looked strikingly like Saiki Trotter, a little girl on Gabrielle's Drum who had died in an attack. Ted had a flash of the combat. For a moment, he remembered losing one of his team, and seeing a father cradling his dead daughter. His throat tightened, and his chest constricted. His hand went to the tattoo over his heart, where the names of the two who had fallen were written. He looked around for any related information, and found a stone monument off to one side. It was indeed a dedication to Saiki Trotter.

"What's that?" Debra asked.

"Come look."

Debra jumped to her feet and bounced over. She read the words. Her hand reached out to Ted's chest. "It's her, isn't it? There must be someone here who knew her."

"I think you're right. They named his place after Endurance Halo. It had nothing to do with the meat factory."

A high-pitched shriek pierced the air followed by the giggles and approaching *thump thump thump* of a running child. A young boy about five years old burst through the bushes into the little clearing holding a pink ribbon. He spotted them and stopped. He looked up at Ted, and let his mouth drop open.

A little girl, nearly a head taller burst through after him and grabbed his shoulders, for a moment they tussled over the ribbon, then the boy let go and pointed at Ted. "Look at that big man. Who is that?"

The little girl looked at Ted and then at Debra. "I don't know you." She took a step back, pulling the boy's shoulder.

He yanked free and ran up to Ted. It made him feel a little nervous. Such a tiny kid. Debra's chuckle didn't help.

"How did you get so big?" asked the boy.

The little girl fidgeted. "Roo, get away from there. I don't know who that is."

"It's okay," Debra said. "We came on the *Pang Yu*. Just got here yesterday."

Ted spotted a woman approaching from where the children had come from, an Asian woman with dark hair pulled back in a severe ponytail, two slender curls framed her face. A sling cradled an infant to her chest.

"Children, be polite," she said. "Don't bother people you haven't met yet."

Debra stepped forward and extended her hand. "Debra and Ted Becker. We came on the *Pang Yu*."

"Malee Onada. *Pang Yu* was my husband's old ship. Glad to see it again. You here as colonists?"

Ted shuffled his feet. The little boy stood quietly, staring up at him.

"That's the plan," Debra said. "We were sent to report back. More of a diplomatic kind of thing. We're supposed to make sure you have everything you need. But that's the end of our mission. We'll send the report, and stay right here. It's nothing but bureaucratic nonsense, anyway."

Malee laughed. "That sounds familiar. I gathered from the news feed that the Federation is gone? Something new, but sounding pretty old?"

"We've united everyone in a sort of open framework. More cooperative, more democratic. A council of three, the Triumvirate, running roughshod over hundreds of delegates. A smaller set of directors acting as a higher body, but no one is sacrosanct, and murder is against the law again. Everywhere."

"That's an improvement."

Roo tugged at Ted's pants leg. "What's your name?"

Ted smiled at the boy. "I'm Ted."

"Can you pick me up? I want to see what it looks like up there."

Malee tried to shoo him away. "Aroon, please."

Ted chuckled. "If your mother says it's okay."

"Help yourself. But if he kicks you it's not my fault."

Debra laughed. "Ted's pretty sturdy."

Malee gave Ted an appraising look. "Yeah. Don't see many folks your size around here. You look taller than my dad, and he's the tallest person on *Endurance*."

Ted lifted the boy.

"My grandpa is super tall too. He puts us on his shoulders."

Ted chuckled and slid the boy onto his shoulders. "I think I met him. He's the administrator, right?"

Malee grinned and nodded.

"I'm the new Security Chief."

Malee tapped the little girl on the shoulder. "Honey, why don't you introduce yourself to Ted and Debra?"

The little girl blushed, raised her head and proudly declared, "I'm Dara Onada. Someday, I'm going to run this place, just like my grandpa."

Ted smiled. "That's a great goal. I wish you luck."

"This is my brother, Aroon. And that's Ella. She's just a baby."

Ted laughed.

"I'm five," declared Aroon.

Malee ignored him. "You're helping keep tabs on our alien visitor?"

"Yep," Ted said. "Me and Zon. A few others soon, I hope."

"I know. I've already gotten the request."

Ted paused. "Ah, so you would be the Logistics Officer, then."

"Supply Manager. I'm giving you three more people now, and some others when we wake them up next week. A lot of our crew is still in cold sleep."

Ted glanced at the statue. "That reminds me, we were looking at this statue. Do you know anything about it?"

Malee followed his glance. "That's my husband's cousin, Saiki. She died years ago. We built this park as a memorial to the Halo, and he added this."

"I see. You folks were from the Halo?"

"A lot of us here, including my family, were refugees on the *Pang Yu*. That's why my father named the ship *Endurance*. Even that's a memorial to what we lost, and a hope for what we can build in the future."

Ted gazed at the statue for a moment then turned back. "Things... got worse after you left. The Halo was the first in that war, but not the last, and not the biggest casualty."

Debra put her hand on Ted's arm. "A rough time. Even after the war ended, a lot of anger lingered on all sides."

Malee took a deep breath and sighed. "Well let's hope it never reaches us. Say, why don't the two of you come to dinner? You can meet the family."

"That would be good," Ted said. "I would like to talk to your husband." He glanced at the statue again.

ENJOYING THE VIEW

Saturday, July 20, 3297, 19:16

Brenna sat on one leg as she leaned toward the wall display. Great swaths of blue, interrupted by browns and greens on the planet below slowly slid by.

"That view is amazing."

"One of the reasons I like this place," Robert said. "Natasha keeps the displays on the view of whichever satellite is at the right time of day for us. Comparatively speaking."

Brenna took a moment to watch the serene landscapes pass by. Vast oceans, slightly greener than those on Earth, broken by unfamiliar land masses. They were largely desert with splashes of bright green, dotted by a variety of cloud formations. A large red 3 hovered over a mountain on the rim wall of a great crater. The center was one of the greener areas of the continent.

"What's the three?" she asked.

Robert sighed. "The third attempt site. Last attempt, for now."

"I heard a little about that. Bad sites?"

Robert shook his head. "Best sites on the planet. This little continent has the densest population of anywhere else. A couple of the larger land masses don't have any sign of intelligent life at all. Plenty of vegetation and abundant animal life. Nothing we can think of as people. At least, not so far as we've seen."

"This is the heart of their civilization. You looked for sites here, then. What did you find?"

"The first site seemed like the best possible place to go. Hydrocarbon emissions, electromagnetic emissions, a walled city surrounding a large oasis in the middle of the desert. They even have a few vehicles. Internal combustion types. Lots of interesting buildings."

"Other cities don't stack up?" she asked.

"No other city has a trace of electromagnetic anything. As a matter of fact, what we could find came from somewhere below ground level. Streetlights appear to be chemical, with an entire section of the town using gas lights."

"Experimental electricity?"

"And they have a working cannon," he said, "with excellent marksmanship."

"How excellent?"

"They used three cannons on the first shot. All four of our people died instantly. The next volley took out the shuttle. Hardly a hesitation. These boys know how to aim, and can fire again quickly."

"So," Brenna said, "a walled city in the desert. And they don't like guests?"

"That's the conclusion we came to. A few weeks later, we decided to go ahead at our second site. Southeast of the first spot, beyond the edge of the desert. Small farming community. Looks like an agricultural hub. We think it's a central market for dozens of smaller villages. It's the largest town on that side of the desert, and no walls."

"Maybe more peaceful?"

Robert shrugged. "After reviewing the footage, our mistake really became clear. We landed on the far side of a small grove of trees and were walking toward the town, early in the morning. An unexpected cloud bank rolled in at exactly the wrong time. They turned on their head lamps. The noises those creatures made had to be screams of terror, and judging by their size, we are nearly certain they were juveniles."

"A bunch of strange creatures with glowing eyes were coming out of the fog."

Robert sighed. "Of all the ways someone might expect to die out here among the stars, cannon fire and pitchforks weren't high on our list of possibilities."

"And the shuttle?"

"We recovered it. No issues. They are going over it now to see if they can find any extra micro-samples."

"Wait," Brenna said, "didn't you guys do that before landing?"

"Of course we did. We arrived in orbit before the end of February. Spent four months with thousands of drones scouring the planet. We've a good idea of their basic microbiome, atmosphere and wildlife. We've got some great shots of what they look like too. Found plenty of ruin sites. Yeah, we did all of that. The upshot is that there are very few things that could cross over from their species to ours. And for those that can, we can defend against. Goes the other way too. Nothing is compatible at the protein level. They do have some virus-like structures, but we haven't been able to get them to cross with our viruses, yet. If it can happen, it doesn't appear as if it would be frequent."

"Didn't mean to make you get defensive."

"Did I sound defensive? Sorry. Didn't mean to be." He smiled at her. "Tell me about you. What happened to you? Where did you go? I lost track of you after Proximus, and *Endurance* came up so soon after, I didn't have time to figure it out."

"I was supposed to spend a lot of time in recovery. But as soon as they could scoot me into a wheelchair they took me out and put me to work. I did see the farewell ceremony. You were on stage. A day later I was outbound on a jumpship to a secret research lab near Jupiter."

Robert frowned. "Look, I don't mean anything by it, but you were pretty junior. Why were they rushing you into research?"

Brenna smirked. "That trick I pulled to get all those ships to proximus without completely frying myself impressed the right folks. They wanted my input on replicating it."

"Is that what we have here?"

Brenna laughed. "No. We came up with something even better. Everyone on the team I joined was brilliant. We figured out a way to use a series of small emitters. But that took several years. Then there were the trials on the *Pang Yu*. Betsy was in command by then. We proved that it worked, and as they were ramping up production, we took off to come out here. By now there are hundreds of new ships heading out to the stars."

Robert seemed lost in thought. He took a deep breath. "Keep talking. I think this is the longest you've spoken to me without one of us going unconscious."

Brenna rolled her eyes. "You know I came so close to actually bringing a tranquilizer patch. So close." She stopped. "Wait, does this mean you actually prefer one of us to be unconscious?"

Robert shook his head, his smile, warm and inviting. "Absolutely not."

MAKSIM'S DARKNESS

Saturday, July 20, 3297, 15:38

Maksim reclined on a lounge chair near the artificial stream that ran through the park. Artificial sunlight warmed the area. "I feel her loss every moment of every day, Doc. It's like a pit in my chest that is trying to eat my soul. It consumes me. I hear laughter, and I hate it. I smell food, and I want to walk away. I don't want to talk to you, I don't want to be here. But I have been ordered to do so."

Dr. Puttkammer nodded thoughtfully. "Don't stop there. I'm listening." She adjusted her chair to give her a better view of the park.

Maksim crossed his arms. "Now you are making fun of me."

"When did you first meet Yelena?"

"On Pluto? Oh, we were young, fourteen and sixteen. We met at a community pool in the full gravity ring. Both of us loved to swim."

"What do you remember about the first time you saw her?"

"A red bikini. Skinny body. Brown, curly hair. The way she laughed. No, wait. Not the first time. She was close to the edge, dipping in her toe. I swam toward her. I only wanted a better look, but it frightened her. She thought I would splash her. I reassured her I wasn't going to. When she came in, we floated together. Talked. Smiled. Yes, a lot of smiling. We were so young."

"And the laughing?"

"After that first time, we met often at the pool. We played with friends, we laughed a lot. Such a sweet time for us. Soon came the kissing and hugging. After that, she and I were a couple. We both assumed it would last forever. The fights we had were about whose turn it was to choose where to eat. What shows to watch, what music to listen to."

"She shared your tastes?"

"We had overlap, but she liked the swing dance a little more than I did, and I liked the jump and bounce music. But you know those beats aren't that different."

"After dancing, what else did you enjoy?"

"Everything. Sex, eventually. Like two eager rabbits." Maksim's smile faded. "Then her father found out. He tried to separate us, so we ran away."

"On Pluto? Where could you go?"

"How much do you know about the bridge station?"

"Let's say I don't know anything at all. What would you tell me?"

"I would start with how Pluto and Charon are more of a double body than anything else. The barycenter between them is in space, between them. Imagine a string, stretched between them. The central ring station, Xiphion Wreath, is right at the balance point. It's where all of the system controls are for maintaining position. Then there are the two smaller stations. Melinoe is the one several thousand clicks toward Charon, while Alecto is the station a couple kilometers down on the Pluto side. Both are still well away from the worlds. The ends of each side of the bridge, at their closest approach, are still at least a kilometer off the ground. They act as stationary skyhooks. Yelena and I are from Alecto. Different sections, but the same ring."

"What happened when you ran away?"

"We decided to run up the bridge. To Melinoe. We figured it would be almost like home, but we could be free. Find work, get a place to live. We thought it would be easy. We almost made it to Xiphion. Got flagged on the transport. Unaccompanied minors. When our parents came to get us, our hearts were broken. We thought we would never see each other again."

"How long were you apart?"

"Less than two weeks. They blocked direct communication, but we had mutual friends by then. We hid our relationship from our parents until she turned seventeen. With me being nineteen, my folks didn't care at all. Her father was a bit angry, but conceded that he had no say in the matter. Her mother called it romantic."

"Where did that lead?"

"We made the climb to Pluto and back. Then spent the next few years working right there in Alecto. One day we saw the list of specialties needed for the mission on the *Endurance*. We both had required skills, and couples were preferred. Everyone out that far from Earth has the genes for cold sleep. Mandatory for the early settlers. Plus, we were with Outer Worlds Limited, and they wanted to send a contingent. We volunteered, and before you know it, we were accepted." He sighed. "On the condition we spent most of the voyage in cold sleep, of course. Six years and change later, we get a wake up, spend another few months setting up the bio labs. When we arrived here, we started collecting samples as fast as we could. It... it went so fast."

She waited for him to recover.

"Now, I have this grief that is so intense, I think it will swallow me whole. And that creature. Every time I see it, I swear I see blood on its lips. Sometimes I think I'm going to have to kill it, just to stop the nightmares."

GETTING THE PROPER FOOD

Sunday, July 21, 3297, 13:20

Foondek still occasionally paced in his cell. He had stopped slamming the walls and strode more gently, aware always of the life within his pouch.

Anna returned with his little display. This time he showed Foondek plants. Some of them were familiar. Others he didn't know.

He pointed to the screen, then to Foondek. His hand motion made it clear. He wanted to know what could be eaten. Foondek watched the images as they scrolled by. He pointed to a few items, but it wouldn't be enough. He needed meat too.

He used one hand to make a crawling motion, then grabbed it with his other hand, making it look like a struggle, then put it in his mouth. Would Anna understand?

Anna moved his fingers over the images and some of the smaller animals they hunted started showing. Daksey undulated, and chose several he knew he could cook with the plants he had already selected – if he had a flame.

The images shifted back to plants. When he saw the longwood trees, he pointed to them. Then he indicated that he wanted it about the size of his finger.

Anna nodded his head. Why did he thank him? Foondek spread his arms, showing he wanted long pieces.

He thanked him again. Such a strange creature.

After Anna left, Foondek explored the device, swiping back and forth, poking here and there. He hit something and an image of an empty box appeared, a phantom image of an ombax at one side. Hands appeared and stretched the image, then pushed it back together. As they did, the transparent ombax grew and shrunk. This was a room, and the little ombax showed him how big.

A side menu slid out and showed a line of smaller images.

He selected a basket, and it stuck to his finger. Poking it in the room dropped it into place. He hooted softly to himself.

Anna returned with a length of wood, a type he didn't recognize – flexible and sturdy like longwood, but oddly colored.

Anna pointed to the wood and said "Bamboo."

Foondek undulated and hooted softly. "Bamboo." He stretched his hands and made motions toward his chest. "Bamboo, bamboo."

Anna showed his teeth again. It must be a sign of agreement. Something like undulating his neck. He tried showing his teeth.

Anna cringed and stepped back. The two larger creatures said something and stepped forward. These two were different creatures than before. The skin color wasn't the same. Foondek closed his mouth, tilted his head and snorted.

Anna said more words to them. They backed off. Maybe this species' female wasn't as smart as the male. Wouldn't that be something? Ombax males and females were each as smart as the other when it came to learning new things. But females live much longer, so the older ones always knew much more. Maybe the males of this species live longer too. He chut-chutted.

Anna made a similar noise, but higher pitched, and breathier, but it seemed to Foondek, in that moment, he was hearing laughter.

He held his hand out, pushing the palm toward the other two, then showed Anna his teeth again.

Anna said something to the others. One of them shook his head. The other shrugged. Foondek realized they weren't saying pay attention. The movements had different meanings for them.

The other two left the room. Anna brought up the display again, and started to demonstrate a new image. That empty box again. She showed him different materials, how to select them, how to move them about, and how to change the shape of the room it displayed. He started with a room laid out like the one they were in, then pushed walls, added a water feature, and selected new colors for the walls. Then he hit one corner twice, and the entire image went back to what it had started as.

Foondek hesitated. Captured lightning. He knew that. These creatures used it like water or air. He glanced around. The lights, the images that moved. Certainly, much more that he couldn't see.

Anna reached out and caressed his neck and said some words he didn't understand, but with clear meaning. Anna thought he was frightened. Maybe he was.

After a short while, Anna left. The door to the smaller space closed behind him.

Foondek reached a finger out and tapped the display. He played with it, tried different things, then tapped twice on the corner, setting everything back the way it had been. He found all the controls he thought he needed, then started creating a space that might be suitable for his hatchling. He wondered if they were going to build it for him, or if they were simply attempting to entertain him. Nonetheless, he became determined to show them what he wanted.

He almost struck the screen when it spoke. "Foondek."

A figure of one of the creatures appeared on the screen. One he hadn't seen before. It waved a hand. "Hello, Foondek." Then it pointed at its chest. "AutoGov."

He hesitated. "Oddokof."

The display showed him various images of water. So, he said, "Water."

"Water," Oddokof said.

Foondek pointed to his mouth. "I want water."

"I Foondek water."

Foondek shrugged. "Foondek wants water. I am Foondek. I want water."

"Foondek wants water."

The display view shifted to a bowl. Water poured in until nearly full. A small opening appeared on one wall. Flashing lights made sure Foondek wouldn't miss it. A bowl of water sat there. He drank deeply.

He went back and forth with the device, teaching it how to speak Omseep. Soon, it showed him an image of one of their kind, then several, then as if it were pulling away, showing more and more of them.

It said "*Human*." The image showed Foondek, then did the same thing, pulling out until there were a very large number of images. It didn't want the name of his village. What was "Ooman?" All of them, or only the ones in this place? He thought about it. If they came from another world, they would want to learn about his world. They must want to know about all people. He said the word for *people*.

"Ombaks," Oddokof said.

Foondek shrugged. "No. Ombax, not ombaks."

"Ombax."

Foondek undulated. *A good place to start.*

DEBRA SHEFFIELD

Monday, July 22, 3297, 17:42

Ted let go of Debra's hand and waved at the door. It slid open.

Malee held her palms together and bowed in a traditional greeting. "Good to see you. Ted, Debra, this is my brother Lenny, my husband Jake. The one over there with the blank look is my brother Nando. He's in VR again. Roo, go jump on Uncle Nando, please."

The little boy squealed and began his assault on the unsuspecting uncle. His sister piled on top.

The spacious apartment was decorated with plants, all set high out of the reach of small children, and pictures of ancient Earth. Landscapes, a few oriental temples, and a wall with the faces of the entire family.

Debra grinned. "Good to see you again, Malee."

Ted smiled and turned to Jake. "Hello." He had wanted to say something about Saiki, but his throat closed. He lost the words.

Jake reached out his hand. "Malee told me she met you in the garden near the statues."

Ted looked at Jake, and carefully opened his shirt.

Jake raised his hand. "Whoa, dude. Really, I don't swing that way." Then Jake saw the tattoo, saw Saiki's name. "Oh wow. Oh wow. You're the guy my mom told me about."

"You're mom?"

"Yeah, Gina Tory. She said you guys pulled their bacon out of the oven in time for dinner."

"Gina. I remember her. Okay, so she's your mother. Saiki was your cousin, right?"

"Uncle Art's little girl. A real sweetheart. It tore me up when I heard about what happened. I got the chance to help design the landscaping in the park, so Malee and I decided to make a little tribute to her. Some place for other children to come and feel safe." He tilted his head. "The other names?"

Ted took a deep breath and nodded. "People I lost. Including Otter. She died during the battle that took your cousin."

"Otter?"

"Sergeant Ingrid Ottendorf. We called her Otter."

Jake smiled thoughtfully. "That's the kind of name you give to someone you love."

Ted refastened his shirt. His throat closed up.

Jake motioned toward the dining table. "Come on, Let's sit at the table. Something to drink?"

Nando raised his hand. Roo grabbed it and tried to pull it back down. "I'm dry as sand. I could use some water."

Malee scowled. "Get yourself out from under that pile of children and go get it yourself."

More shouts of glee as the kids struggled to keep their uncle in place.

"Not sure I'm going to make it." He let himself fall back to the chair, both children in tow. "Nope. I can't. Sorry."

Malee had laid out a meal of various traditions, from Thai noodle dishes to German bratwurst and sauerkraut. Ted helped himself to some rad na and corn on the cob, with a side of mashed potatoes. The kids freed Nando and came bounding in.

"What do you think of Zon?" Malee asked.

"Seems like a nice guy," Ted said.

"He is. Smart too. My best cargo supervisor. I hope you are putting him to good use. He hasn't had enough to do since we revived him."

"How many more people are there in cold sleep?" Debra asked.

"Over a hundred," Jake said. "Half the crew. We've been expanding the farm and stocking up so we don't have shortages when they start to eat."

Malee put her hand on Lenny's shoulder. "Lenny, stop staring at our guest. It's rude."

Lenny dropped his gaze to his hands. "Sorry. I didn't mean to stare."

Ted chuckled. "What's the matter, kid? She too cute to believe?"

Debra scoffed and elbowed her husband.

"What? You are!"

"No," Lenny said, "I'm sorry. It's just that I feel like I met you somewhere. Like I know you and I can't remember. I didn't keep any data from home that wasn't about the Halo."

Debra swiped her display and poked her history a few times, then nodded. "We've met. At the farewell ceremony. You were, what, twelve? I had fox ears."

"Fox ears?" His eyes went wide as he grinned. "I remember you now. Oh wow. You're Debra Sheffield. Dawn's sister."

Debra sighed. "I used to be both. Now, I am neither. She's gone, and I married this guy. Took his name."

Ted shook his head. "She took the name to try to hide from the public. Didn't work very well."

"With luck they'll have a hard time finding us here." She leaned into Ted.

"Why was the public so interested in you?" Nando asked. "Because of what happened to your sister?"

Debra took a deep breath. "Because of what I did in response.

Keep digging into the news packets from the transition. Just before the Triumvirate came together."

Ted put his arm around Debra. "Half the people back home want to hug her and tell her she did the right thing."

Debra chuckled and patted his hand. "The other half tend to come at me with knives or high explosives."

"We laid low for a while, had a few... adventures?" Ted shot a puzzled look at Debra.

Debra smirked. "Is that what we're calling it? Let's just say it got too interesting, and moments of peace were constantly being interrupted with one crisis after another. Way too much of it seemed focused on me."

"When we heard they were sending *Pang Yu* out here, we jumped at the chance to be on it."

"The leadership were quite happy to send us on our way."

Lenny grinned. "You're staying? Permanent residents?"

"I'm the new head of security," Ted said.

"I'm opening a restaurant," Debra said. "Permanent is the plan."

"At least for a while," Ted said. "We won't be returning on the *Pang Yu*. Can't promise we won't hop the next ship home, but we'll be staying for a while."

SHE CHANGED HER NAME

Tuesday, July 23, 3297, 7:59

Ferdinand walked into the room and slammed the door behind him with a well-practiced flourish of his robe.

Radinka paced back and forth, ignoring him. "Are you certain?"

"It checks out," Briana said.

"What checks out?" Ferdinand scowled. "Why did you call us in again so soon?"

"Sit down and shut up." She turned back to Briana. "How did you verify it?"

"The marriage contract is on file with their transfer papers. The two were married several years ago, and she changed her name from her birth name to the name of her husband."

"Look, I know we are avoiding names because we don't know who is listening, but could someone please give me a little context."

Radinka scowled. "You read the reports. You know that our King took matters into his own hands and killed the Evil Queen."

Ferdinand scowled. "I thought we were calling her the Evil Duchess."

"Shut the fuck up and follow along."

Ferdinand shrunk into his chair.

"He killed the Evil Bitch and started his quest for consolidation, attempting to bring stability and peace to the whole realm. But then, and this is the important part, the Queen's evil little sister, the Princess of Pain, killed the King, ending his plans, stealing our dreams, and handing the whole thing over to the enemy camp."

"Okay. I get that. Are you saying–"

"Yes. She's here. Right here, within our reach."

"How? Why?"

"That doesn't matter," Briana said. "All that matters is she's here. We have an opportunity for justice. We should take it."

Radinka leaned back, tapping her finger on the table. "We've other things to consider. Our goal of being on *Pang Yu* when it leaves is also important."

"I would give my life to avenge the fallen leader."

Ferdinand frowned. "When did you become such a devout follower?"

Radinka shook her head. "She's had more conditioning than either of us. I've probably had the least, and I have another mission that I'm trying to protect."

Ferdinand crossed his arms. "That's a lot of *I* and very little *we*."

Briana glared at him. "Then I will take the lead in exacting revenge. We can keep the two missions far enough apart that if I get caught, you two won't be implicated."

Radinka nodded. "Then that is your mission. Ferdinand, you will support her as best you can without leaving traces, and you will help me with the same strictures. A 100 percent success means revenge has been taken and we are not compromised. However, I want to make it perfectly clear. Having my mission completed takes priority. If at any point your mission endangers mine, you will cease. Understood?"

Briana's grin revealed a new set of sharp teeth as she dialed up the fangs. "Got it."

Ferdinand looked back and forth between the two women. "I'll do my best."

CONSTANT COMPANION

Tuesday, July 23, 3297, 12:21

Skip let Betsy enter the restaurant first. It felt warm, built like an ancient tavern with arches of brick with light cream-colored stucco. A fireplace simulator punctuated one end, and a serving counter highlighted the other. The rough-hewn timbers overhead were a work of art. In the center of it all, the familiar elegant figure of the person who built the place walking toward them.

Skip smiled. "Captain Besty Alverez, meet Natasha Telpek. She's been the light of my life for almost a decade now."

Natasha chuckled. "I keep him warm a few nights a week. He saves my life every few years. It's a good trade." She waved them inside. "Come in, let's grab a seat."

Besty laughed. "I didn't intend to set off any alarms. He told you our history?"

Natasha smiled and winked. "Like a little schoolboy with a dirty secret. No worries. Take him for a test flight, if you like. See if his engines have held up."

Betsy grinned as she took her seat opposite Skip. "I hadn't

intended on it, but if I get the urge, it's good to know you approve."

"Approve, nothing." She took a seat between them. "It's a friendly exchange. He's free to do as he likes."

Betsy shook her head. "Besides, he broke my heart pretty good back then." She froze, then glanced at Skip. "Sorry. I went too far."

Skip felt the hole in his chest throb. A constant companion since Aom had died. "It's fine. You're right. I broke it off with you because of her." His voice caught in his throat for a moment.

Natasha reached out and covered his hand with hers. "When you have such a large heart, the pain can be just as immense."

Betsy nodded. "I read about it in my mission briefing. I hadn't realized until then what had happened. Look, I didn't mean anything by it, Skip."

Skip smiled. "I liked you a great deal, Betsy. I think we could have built something if we had been given the chance. Our schedules kept splitting us up, and then..." He shrugged. "There she was. I can't even describe how it happened, because she became a part of me so quickly. We worked together like two halves of a whole. The hardest part about marrying her was letting my father know I intended to take her name. Her family tradition."

Betsy smiled. "Onada sounds better than Johnson anyway."

"Then she became pregnant, and just as quickly we had three kids." Skip took a deep breath and let it out. "Then the accident. I left Mercorps to be a full time father." He sighed. "Then they blew that place up."

"I remember that," Betsy said. "Tong Sianothai and his crew broke the *Pang Yu* out of drydock. I had been shutting my old ship down for recycling when the call came to repower and intercept them."

"Too late?" Natasha asked.

"Not entirely. But I made sure it was. Got the order, dumped the core, then acknowledged the order and told them they were too late."

"Why?"

"Because once you dump the core," Betsy said, "the fuel caps are ejected straight into the reprocessor. Within seconds it's all being shredded. You can't undo that. Have to install a whole new core, and the Rapparee was there to be shredded anyway."

"I meant why not obey the order?"

"I knew what had happened, and I knew why. Sometimes, disobedience, even a little, can save lives."

"Did you know I was on the Halo?" Skip asked.

Betsy shook her head. "Nope. Just that they had a crewmember. Jake Tory, their weapons officer."

Skip laughed. "Jake Onada, now. He married my little girl."

"Oh did he? Lucky boy."

"How did you end up in command of the *Pang Yu*?" Natasha asked.

"The last I knew," Skip said, "you had one of those new destroyers Mercorps were so proud of."

"*Conqueror*." Betsy sighed. "When the war started heating up, they ordered me to attack a string of civilian stations. I ended up in the brig right next to Tong Sianothai, Allied's missing admiral. We were lucky enough to be shoved into life pods when they destroyed the station. Allied picked up life pods instead of using them for target practice." She shook her head. "Tong vouched for me and gave me a command. I never looked back. I even managed to retake my old ship without damaging her too much. After the war, I helped build out the new Navy."

Skip chuckled. "Sounds like a desk job."

"Exactly. They were ready to test the new engine, so I jumped at the chance. By then the previous captain of the *Pang Yu* was ready to rotate, and I stepped in. That's when I met Brenna. Spent the first part of '96 testing her baby. The new engine design is fascinating, and working with Brenna Dotseth is a real pleasure. We were golden by the summer. That made us top of the list to make the first run out here. Left in October. The *Santana* should be the next one out here. Give them a few months. The intention is to make it fairly regular, while still sending us on excursions. We have a target that will delay our return trip by a few months."

"I've heard stories about Brenna," Natasha said.

Skip smiled. "She was a real hot runner when I met her. Got to know her a little bit on the refugee trip."

"I've heard more from Jake. They served together years ago."

Betsy grinned. "She's the one who came up with the dispersed bubble design. Let's use the new engine with almost none of the radiation exposure inside the ship. Makes a hell of a splash outside, but that radiates into space."

"What would you two like to eat?" Natasha asked.

"I hope you'll join us."

"Of course. I've already told the cook what I want. Take a look at the menu."

Skip raised a hand. "I'll have whatever you feel like giving me."

Natasha laughed. "Borsht it is, my little *kotik*."

Betsy made her selection and sent it to the kitchen as well.

A thin dark man in blue bibbed coveralls carrying an open crate of lettuce entered the restaurant. He spotted Natasha and headed over to the table.

"Ah, my lettuce. Excuse me while I go put this away, thank you Doctor."

"Captain Alvarez," Skip said, "this is Dr. Gabriel Mukumba. He's the head of our Agricultural Department."

"Good to meet you," Betsy said. "My friends call me Betsy."

Gabriel passed the crate to Natasha. "Nice to meet you, Captain. My friends call me Dr. Mukumba."

"Gabriel has a dry sense of humor," Natasha said. "Don't let it bother you." She headed to the kitchen.

Gabriel nodded. "Awkward social interactions such as this are why I prefer plants. If you'll excuse me, I need to grab my meal and get back to work. Unexpected mouths to feed mean that I need to increase production ahead of schedule." He scowled politely and walked to the counter.

"Dry, maybe," Betsy said. She lowered her voice. "But humor? Not really."

Skip let out a long sigh. "He's also started a petition to begin the transition to a civilian government."

"And you think it's too soon?"

"A little," Skip said. "More than half the crew are still under, including the administrative staff who were supposed to handle it. He wants to do it early, citing clear leadership failures."

"Some people don't understand the risks. I've reviewed your files, Skip. I would have done everything the same as you. Every site you selected made sense."

Skip shook his head. "The losses have been hard on the crew. I can feel the grief in the air. Thank you for lending us your doctor, by the way."

"Dr. Puttkammer is a trained psychologist." She raised her hand to ward off Skip's reply. "No need to thank me."

"The autodoc does everything needed to keep bodies working properly, but our medic isn't trained as a psychologist. She's a microbiologist. Trained to figure out alien bugs."

"Would you like her to do a full review? We have time."

"That might be a good idea. She's already started on those most personally affected."

Skip glanced at Maksim, alone at a table in the corner.

A serving bot rolled out with their dinners and set three places. The aromas were intoxicating.

Natasha rejoined them as the bot headed away. "What did I miss?"

Skip told her about Betsy's offer.

"You worry so much. Such a big heart. Everyone will be fine. You will see. The doctor will confirm it, don't you think, Betsy?"

Betsy smiled. "Dr. Puttkammer is an excellent doctor. If she does find anything to worry about, she'll jump on it and make sure it's good and healed. She's great like that."

Skip watched Maksim as he walked out the door.

"Tell me, how close were you when you jumped into the system?"

"We managed to image three potential worlds a few jumps out," Skip said. "By zig-zagging a bit on the way in, we had a pretty good idea of the orbits and only one sat in the habitable zone. We came right in, settled into a nice orbit within a week."

"Lucky you," Betsy said. "We missed you because you're on the wrong side of the star."

Skip shrugged. "Luck was with us for nearly the entire trip. We only had one real incident. Cost me my first officer."

"Anders? What happened to him?"

"Terry made the mistake of sleeping with the wrong woman."

Betsy tilted her head. "Do I even want to ask?"

"We lost him. Too much brain damage. She's still in an induced coma. They are rebuilding her whole spine. The culprit took his own life. Spaced himself."

"Saved you the trouble."

"Jake has been doing a fine job in his place," Skip said, "but it's left a big hole in the crew. Two of them were command officers, and she was one of the best xenobiologists we had. Now, we've lost three more."

"If you want, I can ask Jason to give him some pointers."

Skip raised his hand. "No need. Like I said, Jake really stepped up."

"When's your next mission to the surface?"

"After this last disaster, I won't be sending anyone else down. From now on, it's an observation mission."

"Observation?"

Skip nodded. "Once we figured out there wasn't anyone with technology around, we sent down drones. We're still making them as fast as we can. They're taking biological readings, atmospheric and all that. We've learned that their biology is different enough that most of their bugs won't infect us and vice versa, but given the tendency of viruses to mutate, and their virus-like organisms that do the same, it's probably only a matter of time before something crosses back and forth."

"Will that be dangerous?"

"Not for us. Our medtech can handle it. I worry about their population a bit."

"Skip, they ate our people."

"I know. But this is new for all of us. We don't want to condemn them because mistakes were made."

"Do you think our people might have been sick?"

Skip shook his head. "I'm more worried about our internal biome. I saw some of that last group eating brains and internal organs. All of the ones who ate the meat came down with some horrific diarrhea the next day."

Betsy smirked. "Onada's Revenge?"

"Please don't put my name on it. I'm about to go down in history as the one who blew humankind's first contact."

"What I don't understand is why they are so primitive. You said both moons have bases, and there's a partially built ring structure in orbit. We know they were in space four thousand years ago. What happened?"

"We have some clues," Skip said. "There is a residual trace of radioactive isotopes in the deeper soil samples. Dating right about that time. Some areas, like the southern end of the continent most of them live in, have contaminated soil. Given the current state of the world, it looks like they fought a nuclear war."

"Worse than what we did to the Earth?"

"Nuclear weapon wise, yes. Much worse. No sign of killbots. But if they had only gotten as far as moonshots, maybe their tech never advanced to that. Still, the landmass we chose has the largest population, and it isn't much. A dozen city-sized settlements. Only one of them gives off any electromagnetic readings."

"That's the desert city, right?" Betsy asked.

"Yes, in the northern part of the desert. There are two more in the south, but they are smaller, less advanced. Not even gas lights."

"Gas lights?"

Skip nodded. "Many of the cities have natural gas lighting. But that's not the big shocker. We found this while following one of our subjects of interest." He swiped his display and pointed to a large, fat train-like wheeled vehicle. "Look at the readings when the bandits steal those tanks."

"Oh, good lord, it's radioactive. What the hell is that?"

"Quesada says it's probably a small molten salt reactor used to boil water, make steam, to drive the engine."

"A nuclear steam engine?" Betsy shook her head. "That sounds ridiculous."

"Maybe to us. But keep in mind, most of the early reactors we made were primarily used to make superheated steam to drive turbines that generated electricity."

"I wonder how they made the seals. The monitor and control system? That would take electricity, otherwise it doesn't make sense. This can't be safe."

"Probably not by our standards," Skip said. "The question is, why? If they know how to use nuclear power, why aren't they making electricity?"

"You said they were in that one city."

Skip nodded. "We found electromagnetic activity, but no outward signs like lights. As if they're hiding it."

"Like it's something they aren't supposed to be doing."

"What are you thinking?"

Betsy tilted her head. "What if for some reason, they've all decided that electricity is bad. Then your nuclear-powered train makes sense. You can heat the water, but you have to use the physical energy directly. You can't store it as electricity. And no batteries, either. Still, there has to be electricity in there somewhere. I don't think you could build such a thing without it. Even something as simple as arc welding would make a tremendous difference. Can you get me images of the welds?"

Skip sat back and sighed. "You are now all caught up. Welcome to Wold 2384."

Betsy chuckled.

"What?"

"Steampunk dinosaurs."

Skip raised his hand. "No, don't even go there. We are *not* calling them that."

THE RUINS OF THAMTHAD

Mas'eeng Bayfod, Third Three, Early High

A long deserted ruin, the city of hills, Thamthad, its true name lost to the ages, was all that remained. A gray board, lined with streaks of debris, cracked and etched with time, had words printed on it. Daksey could make out most of it as a command to stay on the road. He glanced at it as he passed.

Angular, rectangular hills surrounded by jagged plains of rock and scrub filled his view. What may have once been wide avenues between towering buildings were now an excursion between overgrown hills dotted sparsely with trees. The occasional blockage, under thousands of years of erosion and growth were manageable hills to be climbed.

But Daksey remembered his history. He remembered that every step he took, he walked among countless of the old ones who died among these hills.

He startled an edfoth and her hatchlings. She made rude noises and nipped at Daksey's tail, as he moved away from her. He chut-chutted to himself. The little edfoth had moved well away from him, so he ignored her and continued on his way.

It reminded him of his own empty stomachs. Climbing to the top of one of the smaller mounds, he sat down and opened his bag. His pouch-fathers had made sure to pack him everything they thought he might need, food included.

As he nibbled on some dried meat and fruit, he looked out over the site. Most of the mounds were laid out on a grid, but to his left, it seemed to follow a less rigid pattern. Then he spotted something curious next to a tree. Covered in fuzzy green, it looked like it might be a carved slab of some sort. He decided to go see.

The height of the tree surprised him. It was much larger than it had appeared, as the base sat in a deep depression. Leaves were broader than he had ever seen. It had grown partially around a stone slab. He brushed his hand over it. The plant growth fell away easily, so he brushed more of the surface clear. The dark gray raised surface looked very much like someone's head in profile. It had a prominent snout and narrow nostrils. He wondered if this was a monument to someone that had once been important. Or perhaps a grave marker.

He looked around and saw several more of them, arranged in a semi-circle. He glanced at the sun. This was interesting, and maybe he would come to visit this place again, but he had something to do. He turned and started back to the main path.

The ground beneath his feet shifted and fell away. He dropped with it, hitting tree roots and tumbling onto the surface below. His fall ended in an abrupt, painful *thud*. Dust and debris, thrown up all around, rained down on him.

GENDER CONFUSION

Friday, July 26, 3297, 16:29

Foondek's cell had become far more livable. He had selected several bits of wooden furniture and cooking utensils. An area had been turned into a fire pit with a pot that swung over the heat. Running water along one side ran in a trough that Foondek hoped to decorate as a small stream. The walls all showed greenery, as if he stood in the forest.

He sat near one wall, trying to learn from the machine. With a huff of frustration, he declared, "I am male. Female penetrates donor-male, takes tiny one who is made inside male. Tiny one makes seed for female. Female makes egg, adds seed, gives egg to pouch-husband. New Ombax emerges from egg in pouch."

"Human male makes seed," AutoGov said. "Penetrates female to leave seed. Seed fertilizes tiny egg inside female. New human emerges from female."

Foondek's quilled flicked up and down in confusion. That sounded strange. But this was the third time they had done this. "Foondek is male."

"Acknowledged."

Foondek had figured that word out quickly. It was repeated often. "Anna is male."

"Negative. Anna Ruggiero is female."

"Female?"

"Affirmative."

He pointed to the single guard who remained his watchful companion. "Female."

"Negative. Ted Becker is male."

Foondek sighed. That wasn't what he had expected at all. "Human male is larger than human female?"

"Affirmative."

"Does human male live longer than human female?"

"Negative."

"No? The larger one dies faster? How fast?"

"The average life expectancy for a human male, with no anti-aging treatment, is one hundred seven years. The average for females is one hundred nine years."

"How long is a year?"

The AutoGov showed Foondek the math. After converting it he came to a realization. "That is almost the same. Not at all like us. An Ombax male lives less than a third of the life of a female."

ONE PROBLEM AT A TIME

Mas'eeng Bayfod, Third Three, Late High

Daksey's back hurt. He could feel the flood of pain relief course through his body. He was lucky. His hindbrain had felt that landing. He sat up and allowed his eyes to adjust to the darkness. Large beams of sunlight lit the mound of debris he had rolled down from. Above him the sun and sky showed through a large rectangular hole. The center had collapsed, then the corners had also given way. The edges were much further above him than he could reach, and were overhung. He had fallen into a structure that had been largely empty.

He couldn't jump out, and he didn't see any way to climb out.

He let out a rumbling growl. This is exactly the sort of thing Kempok had been afraid would happen to Bongeex. How had he been so distracted? He should never have left the path.

The sunlight created streams of light in the settling dust.

This is exactly where Bongeex would have found himself. He huffed. Except of course he would find a way out. Like knitting a rope ladder and tossing it up.

He glanced up. Oh. There's that tree, and the roots run along one edge of the collapse. That might be where Bongeex would put his rope ladder. He huffed again.

"I don't know how to knit a stupid rope ladder, and I certainly don't have any rope."

The dust had cleared enough that Daksey could see the edges of the hole more clearly. Vines lay scattered about the rubble. Long and thin, but if he weaved them into a rope, not a full ladder, but enough to climb, then maybe.

He looked more closely at those tree roots. How would he anchor the rope?

One problem at a time. He started pulling vines and stripping off the leaves. He set down his pack, cleared an area to work in, and laid the strands out. He was going to have to weave them together at odd places in order to get a decent length. Luckily, there looked to be enough vine. Soon he had a decent climbing rope.

He sat back and rummaged through the pack for something to eat. He stopped and looked at the pack. Made of a stiff cloth, very strong and durable. He pulled at the straps. Carefully, he tugged at one as hard as he could. It held. Looking at the tree root, he spotted two tendrils that separated, then came back together.

He chut-chutted. Bongeex wouldn't have thought of that.

He tied one end of the rope to both straps of his backpack. Hefting it in his hands and taking careful aim, he threw the back-pack into the air.

It fell short and crashed to the ground. He grabbed it again, and threw it harder, getting a touch angry.

It missed his mark and bounced back over his head.

He took a deep breath, calming his frustration.

"This is where Bongeex would have come to his end. He would be so angry now, he would never hit his target."

He took careful aim, and with everything he could muster, sent the pack sailing over the first limb. It swung around and dangled. With a few careful tugs, Daksey slid the pack to where it became securely wedged. Then started his climb.

Once his hands were on the tree roots, he knew he had made it. He pulled his pack free and climbed to the top.

The tree shuddered and began to fall into the hole.

Daksey leapt clear and out onto the grass. A loud *thud* and the sound of breaking wood echoed from below.

He carefully rolled the rope into a loop and put it into his pack. His heart raced as he carefully made his way back to the way he had come.

"Stick to the path, Daksey. Stick to the path." He headed out at a brisk pace. He wanted to be clear of these awful ruins.

Later that day, as the sun touched the distant hills, Daksey came to a small village. A handcrafted sign declared it Tho'peymey. A small crossroads town, with a partially completed bridge over the small river. It looked like he could use it, but there were no rails, and it didn't seem to be the sturdiest thing.

As he neared the center of town, he saw a stone bridge being built on the far side of the wooden one. As he studied it, an egg-mother, a bit smaller than Kempok, called out to him.

"Getting late. Are you looking for someplace warm? Have you eaten?"

Daksey undulated. "I am, and I have not. I ate back at the ruins of Thamthad, so I'm a little hungry."

"Thamthad? You came from further east?"

Daksey undulated again. "Botham, in the forest of Koy'am. I'm on my way west."

She looked him over and undulated slightly. "We've plenty to share, and you can sleep by the fire tonight."

Daksey nodded in gratitude. "You are very welcoming, egg-mother. I appreciate it."

He followed her inside and met the rest of the family. There were two pouch-brothers younger than him. They asked him question after question – where he came from, did he have brothers, where was he going, and on and on. Daksey decided not to bring out the skull. The children might never sleep if he did.

Then they started in on the previous year's big flood. Daksey knew it had been a wet season but had never connected it to the personal stories these people had to tell. The children talked nonstop about the big flood last year, and how they used to be on one side of the river, but it moved over, and now they were on the other side.

The next morning, the egg-mother of the house handed him a cloth filled with freshly roasted meat. The cloth had a slick side, so the juices of the meat stayed within, and would keep the meat good for days.

Daksey nodded again, as he left.

LENNY'S INTENTIONS

"Please make your morning selections," AutoGov said.

Skip stretched and yawned. He laid in his bed for a moment. "Chamomile tea. Scrambled eggs, toast, and one of Mukumba's big veggie sausages. Spicy."

"Acknowledged," AutoGov said.

Skip rolled out of bed and headed for the fresher.

By the time he had finished, his breakfast sat waiting on the counter, hot and ready. A second plate surprised him. Usually, Lenny didn't get up this early. Skip took both plates to the table, then did the same for the cups. He could smell the fresh mint aroma from his son's cup.

Lenny came out just as Skip sat down. He nodded to his father. "Morning."

"Good morning. Glad to see you up so early."

Lenny grumbled something as he put the cup of warm mint tea to his lips. He set the cup down and stared at his plate.

Skip ate quietly, watching his son. He started to get the feeling there was a reason he was up early. "Okay. Out with it. What is on your mind?"

Lenny took a deep breath and exhaled slowly. "I want to ride the *Pang Yu* back home."

Skip stopped mid-forkful. "What? Why?"

"I want to be someplace with more people my age," Lenny said. "I'm twenty-one now, and I've never had a real girlfriend. And no, a simulation isn't the same. Don't try to sell me on that crap. Even Nando's girlfriend is a real human being somewhere on *Endurance*. Look, I'll come back in a few years. A decade or so, okay? I want to see what we left behind."

"You are an adult. I couldn't stop you if I wanted. And for the record, I think you might be right." Skip put his fork back onto his plate. "When we left, you were just a kid. It didn't seem like such a stretch. I guess I never did the math on the whole girl-friend, peer group thing."

Lenny shrugged. "I have plenty of friends. It's not that. Just that they're all at least a decade older than I am. Great for school and advanced training, but pretty bad when it came to any sort of sex life." He crossed his arms. "Even that might have worked out, if I hadn't had the added bonus of being the son of the damned Administrator. You know I heard that a couple of times."

Skip raised his eyebrows. "Well, that's a new one. You want to do the whole year in cold sleep?"

"I've given that some thought too. I think it would be more fun if I joined up and became part of the crew. At least for the trip back to Earth."

"Wow. What brought that on?"

Lenny's face flushed. "You."

"I don't follow."

"I watched you for seven years as captain of *Endurance*. You loved it. You were the one everyone looked to, and you knew what you were doing. It made me think joining a ship crew might be a good way to learn leadership skills."

Skip chuckled. "Or give you ulcers."

Lenny smirked. "I think that's from this whole election thing. Once they elect you governor, you'll be back to normal."

Skip took a deep breath. "Don't jump to conclusions. We haven't settled all the candidates yet. There are at least two others who have expressed interest."

"Whatever. Big boring election and you'll win."

"Is that your problem? You bored here?"

"A bit. I mean, I don't know." He shrugged.

Skip waved at the screen showing a panoramic view of the world below. "Meeting a new species of intelligence for the first time. I know how boring that must be."

Lenny groaned. "Yes, but they look like big lizards and lay eggs. My dreams of crossbreeding with buxom green alien women are officially dead."

Skip laughed. "Yeah, we still aren't totally certain about their genders either."

"What do you mean?"

"They figured out that the one we have says he's a male, but he gives live birth to a little tentacled creature. It has brains and a heart. Circulatory system, and it can crawl around."

"That's nuts."

Skip laughed. "Yeah, more than you think. Over ninety-five percent of its body mass is testicle. The rest is barely enough for it to climb its way up inside the penetrating appendage to the guts of the egg-layer and attach itself, becoming a sperm-producing parasite."

Lenny shook his head. "That's... inside the... penetrating appendage? So, they do have penetrative sex?"

Skip smirked. "The female penetrates the male, and from what Foondek describes, pulls the little bugger out. Then it crawls up the tube. Apparently, that part is very pleasurable for the female."

Lenny frowned. "I wonder what would happen if a male human and one of their males coupled."

Skip shook his head. "The female's appendage is pretty large. If there is any sensation for either side, it wouldn't be much. Besides, consider how our people look to them."

Lenny shrugged. "You know it will happen, someday. Just seems like something a human being would try. Same for the female to female match. Someone's going to give it a go."

Skip frowned. "I'll be sure to discourage it while I'm in command."

"Afraid of hybrids?"

Skip frowned and shook his head. "Not at all. That appendage is designed to grab and pull. Might not have a happy ending there either, if you get my drift."

Lenny chuckled. "Thanks Dad."

"For what?"

"For not freaking out."

WHO OWNS THESE ROCKS?

Sunday, July 28, 3297, 14:43

The engineering control center was in the same section as MCC, but along the opposite side. Well-lit with a number of displays, it also housed a large power bank and other electronic equipment. A familiar high-pitched hum filled the room.

Brenna felt at home here as she enjoyed Robert's company.

He pointed at the display. "It's coming back around soon. Giant crater you can just make out. A big hill, small mountain on the ring near the large, forested region in the basin. Near the summit we spotted some amazing stonework. Large statues and monuments. Temples, a wide plaza, and an active community. Then we spotted this." He waved his hand and selected a new image. "That's why we chose it for the third attempt."

"Wait." She waved her finger back and forth between them. "I've seen that before."

"If you assume this chipped away part was another couple of tentacles, that's the same shape as the helmet of the ancient environmental suit they found on Proximus." He swiped and showed the helmet next to the stone figure.

Brenna fell silent.

"Sorry. Bad memories?"

She shook her head. "No. I'm alive, thank you again. But it means those aliens were here too. That's pretty solid evidence."

"Exactly. Another is that it has these really long staircases. Ancient things, but they look maintained. The one on the east side made it so anyone climbing would have been visible for hours before reaching the top."

"Hours?"

"Yeah. It gave the aliens a good long look at the team, slowly climbing up. When they got to the top, they sat down and waited. At first, everything seemed to go well." He took a deep breath. "Then one of them started attacking, and a bunch of others followed."

Brenna frowned. "That seems like it should have worked."

Robert took another deep, slow breath.

Brenna reached out her hand and covered his. "You lost friends."

"We are a tight community. Skip makes us all feel like family. Everyone has lost someone."

"Makes me wish we could automate it all."

Robert shrugged. "Maybe someday."

The shadows of the clouds had grown long. Pink edges lined part of the terminator.

"Looks like storm clouds over there," he said.

Brenna caught herself watching the light play over Robert's face. He looked good. Better than last time? She frowned. After what, seven or eight years?

Robert smiled at her. "What?"

Brenna felt the warm flush explode onto her face. "Sorry. I was just... you look good. Better than the last time I saw you. It got me thinking."

Robert smirked. "Most of us started treatment when we left. The general idea is that we're going to be out here for a very long time. Slowing down old age, living longer, that will help. And there aren't any social costs here. Everyone understands, at the very least. Besides, we aren't starved for resources."

"Even back home things are better, now. Plenty for almost everyone. Still, not too many people are jumping on that rocket."

"You haven't?" Robert asked.

"Nope. I'm getting old."

Robert laughed. "You look amazing. Especially your hair."

She rolled her eyes. "Last time you saw me, it had started falling out. With my skin flaking off, I must have been a horrid sight. I don't think that's a fair comparison."

"True. But I did know you before that." He nodded at her hair. "It was a lot more unruly back then."

"So was I."

Robert chuckled.

"Now about the materials I'll need. I've noted where the current supplies are inadequate. I didn't see anything in the way of mining schedules, except for the water acquisition project. I want to get that set up, then lay out the plans for the extra processing and manufacturing facilities that will be needed."

"Isn't the factory we brought up to the task?"

"It's fine to start with. We need to build a couple more factories first, then increase mining to scale before we dive solidly into production. The engines themselves are only slightly more complex than the ones you have, but the distribution network is massive in comparison. It's going to take resources."

"We were prepared for any eventuality, but I think everyone assumed we would find a technological civilization here. At least, someone to ask permission from. The other possibility was that we would find nothing, then there's no problem. But what we have is a species that apparently established bases on their moons over four thousand years ago, but are now incapable of spaceflight. Do we need to ask permission? Who owns these rocks?" He shook his head. "That's where we sit. Debating. Now, to be fair, we haven't needed anything but water, and retrieving one small iceteroid didn't seem harmful. Tearing into their system in a meaningful way?" He shrugged.

"From what I've seen of their population numbers, there's plenty to go around for centuries."

Robert leaned forward. "That doesn't mean we can just take it. Besides, most folks I know are in this for the long haul. We may never try to move *Endurance* again."

Brenna leaned back. "Are you saying I came all the way out here for nothing?"

Robert blushed. "Not at all. Assuming we do claim some of those resources, we'll be building new ships in no time. This place is only the first step."

MAKSIM AND DEBRA

Monday, July 29, 3297, 10:16

Maksim was on his knees, leaning between two shrubs, planting a seedling, when he was interrupted.

"Maksim Borodin?" she asked.

He pushed dirt around the seedling. "Shestakova."

"Oh. Is there more than one Maksim?"

"No, no." His fingers pressed the dirt into place. "I decided to change my name. To honor someone I lost."

"One of the landing party?"

Maksim sat back and looked into her eyes. He saw a flash of recognition.

Her shoulders dropped. "I understand."

"Few people do, it seems."

"I'm Debra Becker." She swiped through her display, then tossed an image of Buck to him. "This was Buck."

He glanced at it. "I see why they called him Buck."

"I had similar mods back then. We were quite the pair." She paused. "He's the one I lost. It... it was the most painful experience of my life, up to that point. Even losing my parents, while painful, wasn't a match for what we went through. I felt him die, and I knew I couldn't do anything. I think that feeling of helplessness will haunt me forever."

"I don't know how to do it. How did you escape the pain? I want to know how you get through the day without something, anything, triggering the pain and the tears. Yesterday, as I tended the east garden, I noticed the buds of a new flower. Without hesitation the thought came to me, she will never see this bud, never smell the bloom, and it broke me. The pain came at me like something heavy had stepped on my chest, and I just wept. How do you stop this?"

Debra reached out and gently stroked his shoulder. "You don't. You can't. The pain you feel is real. Not something you can turn off. It's there because you loved her. Everything good reminds you of her, and it will keep hitting you, over and over again. I didn't get through it because I found a key. I got through it because I wasn't given a choice. Every day for what seemed like an eternity I stumbled over something that made me think of him. It tore me up. All I know is that after a while, I got used to it. There's a hole inside me that can never be repaired. You learn where it is. Learn how to walk close to it, without falling inside. Eventually, you can sit at the edge, and remember all the good parts that went missing. It still makes you sad, but you get to the point where you think you've cried all you can. Life goes on, and it keeps dragging you with it. At some point, laughing stopped making me feel guilty. Smiling didn't hurt as much.

"I can't tell you how you are going to get through this. I can only tell you that you will. No, it won't be better than before. That hole in your heart will always be there. It won't stop you from having some happiness later. It takes more time than you're going to want to give it. And even then, years later, something unexpected will remind you of her, and it's going to hurt, and tears will come to your eyes. Or like now, with you. I'm sitting here talking to you about your loss, and so much of my internal dialogue is about my own loss, and it brings up what I felt. I can feel some of what you are feeling in the echoes of my own pain. I don't want to say it's a good thing, because that's a horrible thought, but it means I understand where you're coming from, and what you're going through. So, you never, ever have to apologize to me for your pain, or your tears."

Maksim took a deep shuddering breath. He felt tears run down his cheeks into his beard. A thought came to him, and he started to chuckle, tears flowing. "I just realized how much she would have liked you. I felt the pain, and then it all seemed so stupid." He took a deep, steady breath. "Thank you, *prelesten zhena*. It is good to know there are people like you still in this world."

He watched as her eyes briefly darted to her display. He could tell when she read the translation by her smile.

"Now, you didn't track me down just for that conversation. What can I do for you?"

She chuckled. "Yeah. Got more than I bargained for with you. I'm establishing a restaurant. I have plenty for the menu from the farm, but I was thinking long term. Maybe we should put some thought into feeding guests from the planet below."

Maksim's face grew dark. "Maybe we could discuss it some other time. The thought of more of those creatures up here, I can't right now."

"I'm sorry. Look, forget about it for now. It was only a thought I had."

"I will keep it in the back of my mind. I'm helping the creature eat as it is. Maybe I can take notes. See what it likes best."

"Thank you." She turned to leave, then hesitated. "If you ever want to talk..."

Maksim didn't answer. He couldn't. He only watched as she walked away.

LET'S EXPLORE THE RING

Monday, July 29, 3297, 12:13

At Natasha's, enjoying a midday meal with Robert, Brenna caught a glimpse of the orbital ring structure. She tapped the display and expanded the image. "Tell me about this thing."

Robert smiled. "The ring is a touch over a thousand meters wide, and over fifteen hundred in diameter. It's rotating in two axes. A slight amount of motion along the circumference, as one would expect for artificial gravity, but mainly perpendicular. We've spotted an impact site that would explain the latter movement." He waved at the display and zoomed in to show the described location. "The whole thing is flipping instead of spinning. Simulations suggest it will continue to wobble like that indefinitely. The effect is that in some places along the inner hull you'll have about a sixth of a gee. Walking along the curve would be like going uphill. The hull is thick enough to have four or five decks for humans, although if this thing was built by the Proximus aliens, it could be twice that, as they were more horizontal."

"If? You haven't gone to take a look, yet?"

"Nope. We were more focused on the inhabitants of the

planet. We sent missions to the moon bases, though. The ring is on the list of things to look at, but it hasn't been a priority."

"Why is that?" Brenna asked.

"It's not completed. It's got all the markings of a construction project that wasn't finished. That means it's probably a higher risk target."

"What about drones? You sent drones?"

"Not yet. It's on the docket, but we're focused on either the planet below or resource gathering. We're still pumping out drones as fast as we can, but it's a big planet. It will probably be pushed back further when we add in everything we'll need for your little project."

Brenna shrugged. "Sorry. Still, maybe we can take a shuttle over and have a look around. A handful of crawler bots with human overseers would give us a better understanding, wouldn't it?"

Robert's eyebrows knit together as he tried to come up with something cute to say. "I suppose you would want to come along, right?"

Brenna grinned. "Two engineers exploring an ancient engineering project. It's almost romantic."

"They'll want archeologists along for the ride. We wouldn't be alone."

Brenna shrugged. "Who said anything about being alone? They'll want to stream the entire trip, I'm sure. Not a moment of privacy." She leaned forward. "But think of the adventure we could have."

Robert smiled. "Fine. I'll create a proposal and send it to Skip. Maybe we can make it our first official date."

Brenna's mouth dropped open. "What? This isn't an official date? I've been robbed!"

LOCATION SCOUTING

Tuesday, July 30, 3297, 13:11

Ted followed Debra as she wandered through the ship. They came to the park with young trees, flowers, and children playing. She pointed at the far side. "There's a storage area over there that might do. See that passageway going back to the elevators? That would be perfect."

"Wouldn't you want the front to be facing the park?"

She shook her head. "People coming from other levels will be able to pop right in, and that leaves the whole side here for views of the park. More people sit on this side, remember."

"Got it. Now we need to clear it."

"AutoGov, put in a request for this space, please. Send the detailed plans to whoever makes that decision."

"Please classify the intended usage," AutoGov said.

Debra furled her eyebrows. "Entertainment, food consumption, socialization. A gathering place for people to enjoy."

"Acknowledged. Usage plan accepted. Storage area clearance has been scheduled."

"That was quick. Who approved it?"

"The usage of space aboard *Endurance* is coordinated by the

Automated Governor. Excess storage in zone seven lower level easily accommodates the containers within this space. Suggested usage coupled with existing location guidelines meet acceptable criteria."

"Apply the template to this space," Debra said. "Let's have a look at anything that doesn't fit."

The displayed overlay let them expand the seating area in one location and adjust the kitchen to fit. Ted thought it was a nice design. Debra looked it over one last time.

She held her breath for a moment, then exhaled. "It looks good. Implement this, please."

"Acknowledged," AutoGov said.

"How long until it opens?" Ted asked.

"The initial iteration will be available for review in approximately seventy-eight hours."

He turned to Debra. "What are we going to do for seventy-eight hours?"

Debra looked around at the greenery. "I want to see the world. AutoGov, where can we get a good view of the world we are in orbit over? Real view, not screens."

"The lounge in zone six lower level," AutoGov said. "The port side of the station is currently facing the planet."

●● —————————— ●●◉●● —————————— ●●

THE VIEW out the portal was spectacular. The night side of the planet below, dark patches of ocean with splashes of slightly less dark land masses, the further moon, a slim crescent, rising off to one side.

"I was hoping to see more green," Debra said.

Ted chuckled. "Just wait. In a little while we'll be on the daylight side. There's plenty of green and blue."

"It's so different from Earth. Do you think humanity will come and try to take this place from them?"

"I hope not." He stretched. "I didn't realize they wouldn't have the big farm set up by now."

"There's plenty of time for that." She smiled up at him. "They probably didn't expect company this quickly. Remember, they've only been here six months. We can help oversee the farm expansion and make sure we have the crops we need for Keegan's. Until then, there's already a little bake shop here. We can arrange for bread. Maybe even mix for waffles and pancakes."

"Yeah, but no bacon, yet. That meat factory is tiny."

"It met their needs on the way out here. Remember, they are just now waking up the rest of the crew."

"AutoGov," Ted said, "how long until the meat factory can make extra bacon?"

"The expansion for specialty meats has been scheduled," AutoGov said, "however the exact timing is dependent upon resource mining operations. Prospecting drones are making their initial surveys now."

"Ugh," Debra said. "It's like we have to set everything up from scratch here."

"It's exactly like it, darling wife. Everything here is starting from scratch."

Debra looked into Ted's eyes. "They don't even have the aquarium set up."

"AutoGov," Ted said, "aquarium timeline?"

"The designated iceteroid has been identified," AutoGov said. "The retrieval drone is on the way. Expected arrival in eleven months. This time frame is well; before the estimated time of completion for the watertight enclosure in the second habitat."

"Second habitat?" Debra asked. "When is that going to be completed?"

"The completion date is projected to be one year, three months and five days from project start, which has yet to be scheduled."

Ted frowned. "No bacon and no prawn. I mean, without those, how can you cook anything and call it Keegan's?"

Debra smirked. "You didn't spend enough time there. Keegan's menu was vastly larger than the common things people loved. First of all, you never had breakfast. Pancakes, waffles, French toast, kasha, sweet rolls... bread is going to be a big deal. Eggs too."

"Natasha serves eggs, all styles."

"They would have had the egg maker set up before they left home. Kind of basic." She swung around and touched Ted's chest with her fingertips. "We'll have to adapt to whatever is available, and work from there."

"We can talk to Natasha," Ted said. "We should try to make sure that people can get what they want, but have the two places be distinct. Make it so people pick one place or the other, and it's a hard choice, because both are good."

"Maybe she can help with bread too."

SECRETS WITH MOYA'SE

Mas'eeng Bayfod, Third Eight, Early High

Bongeex snorted in anger. He crossed his arms and huffed at his sister. "I showed you how to do that a full count ago. Such a simple thing. Now look. The entire clutch is wasted."

Moya'se shrunk in embarrassment. She locked eyes with him and huffed back. "You mentioned it one time, and then we never used it again until now. Just a little reminder would have been enough. You wanted this to happen. You wanted me to fail." She flicked her tail then thumped it hard on the ground and winced.

Bongeex tilted his head. "That was a solid thump. Did it hurt much?"

Moya'se filled her lungs expanding her chest and held it. When she finally let it go she did so slowly, with self-control. "Bite my tail."

Bongeex chutted.

Moya'se tried to snort at him, but made a snort-chut instead. They chut-chutted together at the odd noise.

"Clean up the mess," he said. "You will remember next time.

You are right. I could have reminded you. Truth is, I forgot you needed reminding."

"You mean I am so good a hunter that you no longer feel the need to teach me?"

Bongeex chutted again. "No. It means I'm not a very good teacher. But it's commendable how much you have learned despite that." He turned and stepped out of her way.

Moya'se glanced at her brother's foot. The quills on her neck sprang forward, as she sucked in air.

Bongeex didn't have time to react. His foot exploded with pain. He tried to shake the pain away, then saw what he had stepped into. Pook'yef, a carnivorous plant. Nice to have around to keep pests under control, a real pain to step on. His foot firmly in its spiky grasp.

He pried himself loose and tried to tenderly step on it. No good. The spikes had pierced his skin. He waited for a moment. Nothing happened. He glanced around.

"What are you looking for?"

"Nothing. Don't worry about it." He stood with his wounded foot slightly raised. "Finish what you were doing."

He watched as she cleaned the mess and carefully put the remaining supplies into her pack. She glanced at his foot, then looked again. "You are still bleeding."

Bongeex huffed. "I know."

"Why are you still bleeding?"

Bongeex shrunk. "It's nothing."

Her nostrils flared.

"I said it's nothing. Don't worry about it."

She glared at the wounds. "The blood is still seeping from the little holes."

Bongeex took a deep breath. He caught himself about to sway. He huffed. "Go find a stick. I need my hindbrain tapped."

Her eyes went wide. She dove into the underbrush and returned with a branch as long as his tail and as wide as his forearm. He raised both hands. "Sister, please. I need a tapping, not a bludgeoning."

Her nostrils flared again, as she returned to the underbrush. The stick she returned with was a good size for a light tapping.

"Do you know how to do it?"

"I've seen Kempok do it for Daksey." She rounded his side and held the stick above the lower part of his back.

"A little further down. Good. Right there. Not too hard."

The stick hit his back with more force than he would have liked. After the third tap he raised his hand. "Enough. I can feel it working now."

"You have a slow hindbrain, just like Daksey."

"Not as bad as his. It only happens to me once in a while. His needs tapping all the time." He locked eyes with his sister. "Please don't tell anyone."

"What? Why?"

"It's embarrassing."

She chutted. "It's because you teased him and don't want him to find out."

Bongeex snorted.

Moya'se crossed her arms. "Why should I keep such a thing secret? It would take effort not to mention it. That sort of thing gets talked about all the time."

"Effort?" He huffed. "It takes effort to not say a thing?"

"It takes effort to remember that what I know is not to be shared." She paused. Her head tilted slightly. "Perhaps if I had a fond memory to secure it in my mind." Her head tilted further. "A sweet memory."

He huffed again and chutted. "You just want my koox."

She hooted wistfully. "Yes, I think that would do it very nicely, dear brother. I would be sure to remember to never mention it to anyone."

Bongeex snorted.

"I would remember not to tell my friends. Daksey would

never hear it from me. I wouldn't even mention it to our pouch-fathers or Kempok, who might already know."

He raised his hand. "Enough. It's in my pack. The pocket under the strap. Help yourself."

She pounced on his pack and eagerly retrieved her prize.

"Not a word."

"A word about what? This koox is making me forget everything." She pinched off a large chunk and put it into her mouth. Her eyes closed and she hooted softly.

Bongeex tilted his head and huffed.

Moya'se pinched off another chunk and held it out to her brother.

He chutted and accepted the peace offering.

THE ALMOST ANTS

Thursday, August 1, 3297, 9:35

"The local garden wing is sealed to prevent cross contamination," Maksim said, "and it's a damn good thing too."

"Why is that?" Kamalov asked.

"We managed to bring up a smattering of their version of ants. Nasty little critters. They swarm and bite at the slightest provocation."

"Have you shown them to Foondek?"

Maksim could feel the heat on his face. "No, I have not bothered with that creature. I am a scientist, and I'm researching the plants and insects and how they work together. I have no interest in one of those blood sucking menaces."

"Easy, now. We're talking about the first sentient species mankind has ever encountered. We should at least keep an open mind."

"Neo Chimps could do everything those things can do, and dolphin poetry and dance were some of the highest forms of art there was for a time. These things are monsters. Not worthy of the sentient label."

"We altered chimps to make them smarter," Kamalov said, "and the interface needed to communicate with dolphins is something we invented. Not them. The people of this world built ships that took them at least as far as their moons. That larger base could have been permanently inhabited. Humans are the only living species we know of that did the same. Besides, you know why they cancelled the chimp program. Aggressive little beasts. How many people died?"

Maksim lowered his voice. "Not as many as these have killed."

"That's a load of *layno*, Maksim. Thirty people died in the Denver uprising alone. We've lost eleven. Yes, it's terrible, but we can get through this, and it doesn't mean these creatures aren't sentient."

"They may have walked on their moons four thousand years ago, but that doesn't mean what we see down there today are intelligent. They may not even be the same things that built those bases."

Kamalov frowned. "It seems like a stretch that an advanced civilization would be replaced so quickly by a new one. Humans replaced competing species far before recorded history."

"That doesn't mean that's the way it happened here."

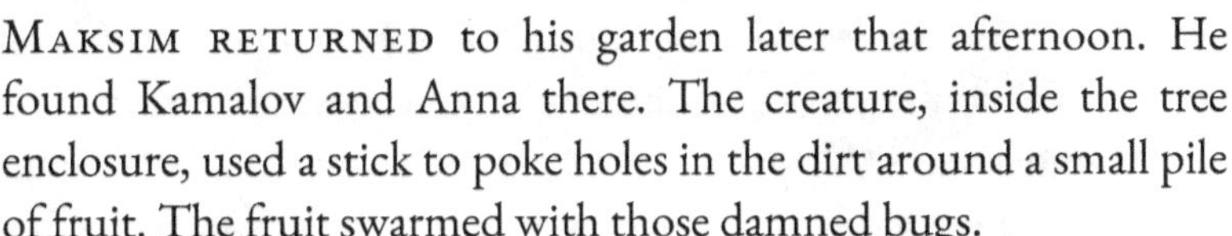

MAKSIM RETURNED to his garden later that afternoon. He found Kamalov and Anna there. The creature, inside the tree enclosure, used a stick to poke holes in the dirt around a small pile of fruit. The fruit swarmed with those damned bugs.

"What the hell is that thing doing?" Maksim asked.

"I showed him those little ant things you were having trouble with," Kamalov said. "He pointed to the other room at the trees. So, I let him in."

"We've managed to keep those things away from the trees. It took a hell of a lot of work, and now it's just serving the fruit right to them. We'll be overrun in a day."

"It's not even a dozen fruit. Give it a chance."

"Bullshit," Maksim said. "Get that goddamn thing out of my garden. Now."

Anna put her hand on his shoulder. "Calm down, Maksim. Foondek is only trying to help."

"I don't want that thing's help. I want it gone. Now."

Anna waved to the beast.

Its eyes gazed at Maksim. He could feel the hatred burning through his skull. "Now."

Anna guided the beast to the lift, and they were soon gone.

How dare she invade his space with that thing. Maksim wanted to punch the bulkhead, wanted to scream. "It isn't fair."

"Maksim, you need to calm down," Kamalov said.

"Why? Why should I calm down? What right does that thing have to be alive when Yelena is dead? How much of her did it eat? How much of my Yelena went into that thing's belly?"

"Maksim, you know the footage is clear on that. He was part of that second group. The ones from the forest to the south. The green and black group."

"I don't want to hear it, Kamalov. I don't want that thing back in here."

"I'll see what I can do, but Onada gave her the run of the station. Not sure how you will be able to stop him, if he wants to come back."

"Him. He. Listen to you. You think of it as a person. It's an animal. We don't even know the gender for certain. Just stop."

"I understand. A pouch and an egg," Kamalov said. "It thinks of itself as the male of the species, but you're right, we are making assumptions about their biology. Just like you are making assumptions about their malicious intent."

Maksim's head pounded. He gritted his teeth. "They ate Yelena. How can that do anything but make my blood boil? Every time I think of it, my vision clouds, my head tries to explode." He slammed a fist into the other palm. "I want to go down there and butcher the whole lot of them, and then this thing is prancing around here, all happy and fat like it belongs. You keep it away from me." Maksim pointed at Kamalov. "I am warning you. Do not bring it back."

Kamalov furrowed his eyebrows and raised his hands. "All right, Maksim. I'll speak with Anna, make sure she understands. Just don't go do something you'll regret."

Maksim shook his head vigorously. It didn't help. He took a deep breath and let it out. "I'll be fine. It's... more intense than I ever expected."

"I understand. You know you can always talk to me. I'm here for you."

"Thank you. I know. This is something I have to deal with on my own. The pain is inside me. Burning me hollow. I have to wait until the fire dies down. Right?"

SOURDOUGH BREAD

Thursday, August 1, 3297, 16:55

"Brick?" Ted looked at the brickwork on the arches and the cream stucco. "This can't be real."

"What does it matter if it's not? Real is overrated. I've always liked the look of brick. We don't get enough of it on orbital habitats."

"You must be Natasha." Debra held out her hand.

Natasha gripped her hand. "Welcome. You hungry?"

Ted grinned. "Yes."

Debra elbowed him in the ribs. "No. We wanted to talk shop."

Natasha smiled. "Maybe we can feed him, and you and I can talk."

Debra laughed. "Fine. Just something light on the carbs. He needs to get back into shape."

Natasha called over her shoulder, "Hey Nancy, top shelf to the left. Bring the big platter."

The waitress smiled and waved, then went for the food.

"One of our most popular features are the sandwiches. For

those, we need bread. More than one kind if possible, but it could be anything."

"I do a lot of those too." She motioned for Ted to take a seat. "I could make extra bread and share it with you. But you know, now that I'm thinking about it, I recently decided I don't have time for an experimental yeast project I had started. What would you think of managing that and making sourdough?"

"Sourdough?"

"Sure. You could use it in a lot of ways too. Everything from pancakes to dinner rolls, and bread of course. And it would give your place a distinct taste."

"You wouldn't want any?" Debra took the seat next to Ted.

"Sure. But when I do, I'll drop by and eat at your place. I simply don't have the time. They keep bringing more of the crew out of cold sleep, and your ship arrived on top of that. I can't wait for you to open and take some of the traffic."

"That sounds great. We've a whole section of sourdough recipes we can try."

"Which library do you use?" Natasha sat on the other side of the table.

"My Uncle Keegan's. He built up his own list."

"Really? Are you willing to share?"

"Of course!" Debra grinned. 'There are thousands of dishes in there. We're still limited in a few ways, though."

"I know. We still have a long way to go before we can start making real ketchup. The artificial stuff is all right, but I want to play with the spices, get a new blend."

"Me too. And my big dream is a prawn tank."

"Prawns?"

Debra nodded. "One of the most popular dishes were his prawn rings. Had them several times a week. They were like a fall-back for anytime I wanted something good and couldn't decide on anything else."

"What about you, Ted? What kind of food do you like?"

"I'm an ex-Marine," Ted said. "Anything that isn't condensed or dehydrated into a sealed package is fine with me."

"Oh, that reminds me. I've got a box of number five cheese noodles and gravy. Interested?"

Ted laughed. "Oh hell no. Thanks for the offer, but not on your life ... Unless you have ketchup."

The ladies laughed.

"We're still a long way off from being able to make it locally," Natasha said.

"I'm from Luna," Debra said. "We've got thousands of varieties. That's what I miss. The artificial stuff has maybe four marked popular and that's it. As if someone wasn't paying attention and thought it wouldn't matter."

"You must have had it real nice there," Natasha said. "The Halo had to import it. Two brands, depending on what shipment was most recent. And if you take the labels off there's no difference between them. Standard mix from identical machines. But we had baked goods and greens like you wouldn't believe. That's what we exported, you know. Salad. We shipped out salad fixings and imported ketchup. A few other things too."

"You're both privileged," Ted said. "In Mercorps, we got whatever they procured for us, and since it came with the same labels, we never noticed any differences."

"Probably all from the same machines that made ours."

"No doubt."

"I guess that leaves me being the privileged one," Debra said.

"Works to our advantage. You have a lot more flavors to miss here. Like I said, we are a long way out from having everything we need to make it from scratch."

Debra smiled. "Good thing we brought supplies. Before we left we made sure to look over what you brought with you. Noticed some places we could help."

Natasha frowned. "Did you bring cinnamon?"

"Yup. And three different strains of tree."

"Tell me you have Cassia. I would love to make cinnamon rolls."

Debra swiped her display and brought up the list. "Yup. Pure Chinese Cassia, Indonesian Burmanni, and a strain of Verum from Ceylon."

"Wait, there's more than one kind of cinnamon?" Ted asked.

"Dear lord, where did you get this guy?"

Debra laughed. "I found him on a battlefield."

Ted chuckled. "Yeah. A battlefield we left behind. Time for me to learn about things like cinnamon, I suppose."

"And making bread," Natasha said. "Don't leave that to a machine."

Debra frowned. "What? We brought bots to do all that."

Natasha shook her head. "Learn to do it for yourself first. That way, when the bot makes a mistake, you'll know what it did wrong, because you'll have done it yourself. Tell you what. Come work in my kitchen tomorrow. I'll show you all there is to know, and we can make enough for us both."

"That sounds like a deal." She smiled at Ted. "Now we both have jobs."

Ted entered the apartment to find Debra already home.

"So how did your first day go?"

Debra groaned. Her face still had traces of flour dusting one cheek, and that might be a small dab of dough in her hair. Ted reached for it.

She swatted his hand away. "What are you doing?"

"You have dough in your hair."

She reached up and found it. "Oh. Crap. I need a shower."

Ted smiled. "Go. Do it."

"No, tell me how your day went, first."

Ted shrugged. "Today they came and told us Foondek is actually a he. Or at least, that's the way he sees it. So now we get to swap pronouns."

"That can't be all that hard," Debra said.

"No. But the thing is, Foondek said it surprised him too. He thought I was female and Anna was male."

She laughed. "With curves like that?"

Ted shrugged. "Apparently Foondek judges by size. In his species, males are smaller than the females."

Debra smirked, stepped into Ted's chest and smiled up at him. "Oops. Excuse me, miss."

Ted wrapped his hands around her and smiled. "I like it this way."

THE SKULL AT BEETHAX

Mas'eeng Bayfod, Last Two, Late

Daksey's feet hurt. He had been walking every day from dawn to dusk since crawling out of the ruins. He had left Bamthapeem with a pack on his back, and his thigh pouch strapped in place. A small bag packed by family members hid in his pouch.

The road ran straight through occasional stands of trees. Some places opened to broad meadows. Small game, abundant in either habitat, scurried away from him as he strode by.

As he topped a tree-tufted hill, he spotted workers on the road in the distance. The river road had once been a smooth, solid surface. Over the centuries, repairs had been made whenever a large crack or hole appeared. Those areas were less smooth, more abrasive to his feet. Now it was more repair than original.

As he approached them, he noticed the cart with a pile of salt bags, and other materials. He walked closer to the edge to give them room.

"Hello traveler," said one of the workers, a tan pouch-brother with dark green stripes. "Mind your step. We just fed that side. It's not as firm as you would expect."

Daksey stopped and looked. He could see a section with small bubbles emerging.

"It will grow solid in a few days. In a week, it will be good as new."

Daksey undulated. "Thank you for your warning."

The worker undulated back. "Have a fortunate journey."

Daksey continued on.

The road ran straighter than the river, and so he found himself walking up and down hills, while the river meandered great distances away, only to come back and flow beside him.

As he topped the next rise, he saw a strip of forest below, and hills of meadows beyond that. Further away, he could make out the yellow sands of the desert. Somewhere among those meadows and stands of trees sat Beethax, the old town. He would stop there to rest.

Before the sun had set, he topped another hill and spotted the little town, down in the shallow valley, where the river he followed met a much larger river flowing north. The central buildings were round huts made of stone and straw, with a few built of brick. There were older, fallen buildings on either side of the river. To the north, a large stand of trees stood adjacent to the town. Planted fields stretched to the east and across the small river to the south. A patchwork of trees and meadow decorated the far side of the larger river. The road went through the middle of town, and crossed a wide bridge. From there, he could follow the line of the road toward the desert. He cringed. Sand. Hot, slippery sand. He hated it.

As he neared the center of town, he saw a large hastily constructed platform. He stopped. Set on top of that platform were four more of those odd creatures. Dead fong'sak surrounded the bodies. Several more circled above. The smell of decomposition assaulted his nose. He noticed a few furtive glances his way, as he stood staring at the display.

"Odd things are happening, stranger. Have you ever seen anything like it?" The local pouch-husband was elderly, but had a look in his eye like he had sized Daksey up, and had decided he posed no threat. His faded green stripes blended with his light green skin, looking more like long smudges.

Daksey undulated. "Three of them climbed the steps to Bamthapeem not long ago. They were eaten."

The old one swayed. "Did any of them live?"

"Only one died. Our egg-mother knew what medicine to use."

"From Bamthapeem?"

Daksey shrugged. "No, I am Botham."

"Botham. I don't know that one."

"We are one of the forest tribes in Koy'am."

"Ah. From the other side of the mountains. I understand. Where are you going?"

"I have one of the skulls from Bamthapeem. I'm taking it to the Observatory to let the scholars see it."

The old one undulated slightly. "That is an excellent idea. You should take something from here too. It might be important."

"Could you remove the meat first? The stench is horrible."

The old one chut-chutted. "I'm sure we can get one of the younger brothers to take the task."

"Is there anything left of their packs?"

"Yes. And something on their heads gave a bright light. We think they used lightning."

Daksey undulated. "A disk about this big. I have one."

"There is also a device that is small and flat. If you touch one corner, it lights up and shows symbols. We believe it's some sort of translation tool. But again, it uses lightning."

"It seems to be their way, whatever they are."

"What do you believe they are?"

"The agreement of the two tribes is that they are mutants from Fengmaath."

The old one undulated slightly. "You did not answer my question. Be direct."

Daksey looked at the old father. "Have you been looking in the night sky?"

The old one shrugged. "What have you seen?"

"There is a fast star at night. It passes overhead often and at regular times."

The old one undulated more vigorously. "I see. Something to awaken the legends, then."

"Something important." Daksey shifted his pack to one side and set it on the ground. "I will need someplace to sleep tonight. Is there a room I might borrow in town?"

"I have a daughter who has recently chosen her name. Will you be polite?"

Daksey chut-chutted. "I'm still too young. One more molt."

"That is a shame. But the room is yours. She won't mind. Perhaps, after your adulthood arrives, you will return and be polite to my daughter."

"It would be my honor. I must admit, I'm not on okdeyok. I do not have the desire to travel. I want a stable home. I will be a pouch-husband."

"I'm the same. I hope your journey is pleasant and swift then."

He pointed to the bodies. "Could I bring the device to the observatory?"

The old one undulated his approval. "I am Bangsekmo Ekaath Axsong."

"Botham Kempok Daksey. Bangsekmo? I thought this place was Beethax."

Axsong chut-chutted. "Beethax is the name of the town. It's shared by three clans. When you get to places larger than this, you will find many more tribes all living together."

Daksey nodded in gratitude. "I've never been this far from home. This is new for me."

"Have you ever seen the Deym'okfad?"

"There is a small desert to the east of our forest. I've been there. Hot. Sand. It was unpleasant."

"The Deym'okfad is far worse. You will be taking the moyox-ees, correct?"

"My egg-mother told me I would need to trade something valuable. She gave me axmodok leaves."

Axsong chut-chutted. "That should be fine. Those folk will appreciate the intoxication. Just be sure to split the payment. Half when you board, and half when you arrive at the other side."

"You don't trust them?"

"I trust them quite a bit, but if you give them too much, they may steer you in circles."

Daksey chut-chutted and undulated.

THE NEXT DAY, Axsong presented Daksey with a newly cleaned skull, the little flat device, and two of the little glow disks. He took care to wrap them together and placed the bundles into his pack. In the late afternoon, the townsfolk prepared a feast near the river. Freshly chopped angthey were added to a large cauldron. The rich aroma of the stew made Daksey's first stomach rumble. Axsong's daughter, Bangsekmo Moysespay, churned the pot. They had shared warmth over the night. She hadn't seemed disappointed at his immaturity. Still, he felt he owed her a debt.

"May I offer my help with the cauldron?"

Moysespay shrugged her shoulders. "No need, Daksey." She pointed her nose in the direction of a small platform. "Go over there. The elders will want to speak with you."

Daksey nodded. "You are very kind."

Moysespay chutted.

Daksey didn't think it funny. He turned and headed to the elder's platform. Near the center of the open plaza where the dead bodies had been, an open wooden structure, decorated with colorful strips of cloth, provided partial shade for the elders who gathered beneath. A number of people were there already. There were introductions all around, but their names didn't stay long in his mind. He remembered the clan names and colors, Baxmang, the tan and green people, Mokafed, red with golden stripes, and of course, Bangsekmo, the grass green people with dark green stripes. Several egg-mothers of each clan were there to greet him, as well as a handful of pouch-husbands. One of them, Baxmang Kakong Doybes, stepped forward to tell the story.

"The young ones had been sent out for morning duties. They were to gather okas and herbs in the forest. A cold wind blew in from the north, and a bank of fog rolled in soon after." Doybes flicked his tail. "The fog wasn't unusual, but the howling of the children was. We thought a predator might have come upon them, so we grabbed whatever tools we could, and ran toward them. These things were in the fog. Bright light coming from their heads, piercing the fog like some evil from ancient myth. We acted quickly and shoved every point we had into them. They died easily when we spiked their heads or their chest. We kept at it until the last of them stopped moving. The lights were another matter. They flashed through the fog, even as the creatures died."

Axsong stepped forward. "Once we cleaned up, we took one of the bodies to Mokafed Beythofop."

A large dark red egg-mother stood and stepped into the center. Her golden stripes started thin near her neck and became very wide closer to her tail. "They brought the dead carcass to me. I cut away the cloth and examined it. The features of this creature are not Ombax. Their legs are straight, and thin. Round heads, with long fur at the top, and a light, mostly useless fur on both the front and back, down the legs." Beythofop snorted. "External genitalia hung between the legs. I believe if I were to guess at the gender, I would get it wrong. There were two round things in a sack." Beythofop's bead-decorated quills rattled as they flicked up, then down. "I don't know. No evidence at all of anything I've seen before. Yet they captured lightning. They could undoubtedly speak. The cloth they wore had been sewn with such care, you could barely see the seams."

Beythofop sat back on her tail, bracing her hands on her thighs.

"I opened it up and looked around inside," she continued. "It had two lungs and a heart. Only one stomach, but it had intestines. All the things we would think it should have. Just not in the right places. No sign of a hindbrain, though, and the rest of the organs were very peculiar. Once I opened the skull, I found a brain. Lots of wrinkles, like you would expect, but it seemed to have two halves. Two sides. It makes me wonder if the hindbrain of this species is conjoined with the forebrain."

Nervous chuts came from the crowd.

Beythofop took a deep breath and exhaled. "I decided to slice the brain into sections to see what the internal structure looked like. That's when I found these." She opened her hand to show the others.

Daksey leaned forward. There were three silver balls, in her hand no bigger than a pebble. Each had several thin threads connected.

"These things are metal, unless I'm being fooled. They are not organic. The thinnest, metal threads I have ever seen ran into the brain tissue."

"What do you think it means?" asked a younger pouch-husband of her clan.

"Remember your biology, Kex. A brain uses naturally occurring lightning for command and control. Metal such as this might allow the lighting to flow."

Kex flicked his quills up and back in confusion. "Were these things controlling them, or allowing them to control something else?"

"Remote talking?" asked another elder.

"Either is possible," Beythofop said. "I don't have the knowledge to say more."

"The scholars at the observatory should know of this," Daksey said.

"We should make images," Axsong said.

"Good idea." Beythofop turned to face him. "Daksey, can you stay another day or two? I will create images you can carry with you to Afothameex. We'll also send a message with you to Dathopsak Safoy in Soypasod. She will give you the permission you need to see the scholars. It will save you time."

Daksey undulated. "I did not realize I needed permission to see the scholars."

"Your people don't have as much contact with the city as we do. Even ours is infrequent and often brief. But we do know something of the curious path one must traverse in order to speak with those in the observatory. Safoy will shorten that path."

"I will gratefully accept your help and the images. I will wait for them to be created." He turned to Axsong. "If I'm still a welcomed guest."

Much of the crowd chut-chutted, as did Axsong. "Your egg-mother has taught you to be such a kind and honest Ombax. You are welcome here, Daksey."

"Why is he so concerned?" Kex asked. "There are many egg-mothers here who would welcome him."

"He hasn't had his adult molt, yet. He can provide warmth but nothing more. Somehow, he seems to think the more is required."

Several others chut-chutted.

Daksey wanted to find a very small hole and crawl inside.

LENNY PLUS TWO

Monday, August 5, 3297, 12:03

Skip entered his apartment to find Lenny and the two women he had been hanging out with in the midst of a conversation at the kitchen table.

"I love you both," said Lenny, "and I couldn't stand to hurt either one of you. So instead of choosing, maybe I need to go back to my original plan and go back to Earth."

Valerie shook her head and crossed her arms. "If you really want to go back to Earth, that's fine. She and I will be great out here on the frontier. But you should have said something a long time ago about your little dilemma, kiddo."

"Yeah," Amida said. "The idea that you need to choose one of us or the other is the dumbest thing I've ever heard."

"What?" Lenny's eyebrows were a mess of confusion. "But, I thought–"

"You thought wrong," Valerie said. "We love each other. Sharing you wouldn't be a big deal. You're great. A really nice guy. Even so, neither of us wants to over commit. We've already agreed we would share you for as long as it worked."

Lenny sat back down. "Share?"

Skip started giggling.

"Dad, stop."

"Sorry," Skip said. "I'll let you three work it out."

"Sorry," Amida said. "We don't mean to be crude or anything."

"Honey, I was in the Mercorps Navy for over a decade. You can't offend me. Just be careful with my little boy. I think you two are confusing the hell out of him."

"Dad," Lenny said, "please stop."

Valerie put her hand on Lenny's shoulder. "It's okay, Lenny. Look, let's be a thruple for a while. See if you like it that way, and then think about going back to Earth. You can go if you want to."

"We won't stop you," Amida said, "but we sure won't complain if you stay."

Skip shrugged. "Gee, Lenny. I would give you some fatherly advice about this whole situation, but I think you can't really make a bad choice here. Just be honest with yourself, and with these young ladies."

Lenny shook his head. "This... is not how I expected this conversation to go."

Skip chuckled and headed for the door. "Let me know if you need anything. I'm heading over to Nat's. I won't be back until sometime late tomorrow."

Both women giggled.

"Dad. Just. Go. Okay, yeah." Lenny had started to have ideas. Good boy.

Skip smiled as the door closed behind him. He stood for a moment. "Dammit, I forgot lunch." He shook his head and headed for Natasha's.

THE ANCIENT RING

Monday, August 5, 3297, 10:22

The approach to the ring appeared painfully slow. Brenna perched quietly near the viewport, waiting for every glint. The massive ring spun slowly, but not the way you would do it to make gravity. It flipped over, edge over edge, so slowly it produced less than one sixth of a gee at the outermost parts.

The quiet hum of electronics, the smooth flow of air. The shuttle was well equipped for their mission. It reminded Brenna of her early days on the *Pang Yu*, before they added the habitat ring.

Kamalov tapped on the viewport. "That thing's over fifteen hundred meters in diameter."

"We've built bigger," Brenna said.

"That one is four thousand years old," Kimi said.

Brenna frowned.

"And not made by human beings," Lexi said.

"I get it. But who made it? The folks down below or the ones they met four thousand years ago?"

Kamalov smiled. "That is the question I am going to try to answer."

"Not if I figure it out first," Kimi said.

Kamalov chuckled. "Sorry, Dr. Sasaki, but I have a great feeling it will be me. Neither you nor Dr. Nadine have been awake as long as I. My head start in this area will work to my advantage."

"Leave me out of it," Lexi said. "Kimi, don't let him rattle you. Just a bunch of macho bravado."

Kamalov smiled. "Indeed. The best kind."

Brenna rolled her eyes and twisted around to look out the viewport again.

Tony Visconti's voice filled the air. "Everyone secure yourselves. We are five minutes from contact."

The shuttle thumped into the ring and rocked as the landing struts bounced on one side.

"No worries, folks," Robert said. "We are down, but there isn't a lot of pull here, so we should look for a way to latch on to things where we can. Sub-Commander Dotseth and I will each lead one team."

Brenna chuckled. "Master Lieutenant Quesada, you sound so sexy when you get all military."

Kimi and Lexi laughed as they pulled on their helmets. Their voices transferred to coms.

"We're used to it. The military folks run the show, so we just roll with it."

"I think he's trying to show off."

The skin of Robert's cheeks began turning a bright shade of red. "Sometimes the civilian compliment likes to be too unprofessional. But if you prefer, we can use first names." He fastened his helmet.

Kamalov's laugh blasted through the coms. "Go ahead. Try it." He opened the inner hatch of the airlock and entered.

Lexi laughed. "Even his mother calls him Kamalov, and she's the one who named him."

"It's true," said Kamalov. "Old family names can be a burden."

"Besides, you military types are going to become civilians soon anyway, right?"

"I know," said Robert. "But on missions like this, don't we need some sort of decorum?" The last one to enter the airlock, he closed and secured the inner hatch, then hit the control to begin pumping out the air.

Brenna swiped her personal display and read Kamalov's name. *Gadzhimurat*. She chuckled. "First thing I thought of was Gadzooks."

Robert frowned.

Kamalov's eyebrows rose. "Dear lady, that's the best first try I have ever heard. Good for you."

"Decorum, I said. Decorum."

Brenna smiled and saluted. "Yes sir."

The light indicated the last of the air had been removed from the airlock. Robert hit the release and the outer hatch swung aside.

They stepped out onto a broad expanse of metal. The surface, pockmarked with divots. Some small, some that looked a bit worrisome. They had touched down in an area where the metal sheeting was more complete. Looking along the ring they could see many areas that were far less complete. Struts loomed overhead, connecting the edges of the ring to spots along the opposite side of the ring, like the spokes bicycle wheel without a central axle.

"Up close it really does look like a construction project they never finished," Lexi said.

"Any sign of tools, or automated builders?" Brenna asked.

"Not yet," Robert said. "You take Kamalov and Kimi. Head that way. I'll take Tony and Lexi this way."

"Aye." Brenna moved off and took great care where she stepped. Kamalov followed closely. The plating looked solid, but she worried about gaps. The light kept shifting in odd ways as the ring slowly flipped. One of the drones floated past to her left. It scanned the surface as it headed for an open area.

"How many drones did you release?" Kamalov asked.

"Six," Robert said. "One for each team headed across the span, and two in each direction up the sides. They'll get up to the poles and cross over to the other side. We can leave them behind to explore."

"It looks like nothing but infrastructure," Kimi said. "What you would build first, before you added anything interesting."

"Like a plaque with your name on it?" Brenna asked.

Robert chuckled. "Or a map to your home star system."

"Oh, wouldn't that be nice," Lexi said.

"Drone four found something that looks like a lower deck," Brenna said. "I've authorized it to take a look."

"Drone four," Kamalov said. "You military types never have any fun. We should have given them real names before we left."

"You could have made the suggestion," Robert said. "I wouldn't have objected."

Brenna smiled to herself. "Let's call the one with my team, Sparky."

"Not a great name for electronic technology."

"Na. It's perfect. Trust me."

Robert chuckled. "Fine, but the one with my team is Clyde."

"You need to let us name the others," Lexi said.

"Fine. Brenna and I have officially renamed drone five and six. Each of you pick a bot. Name it."

"Let's call drone one, Odin," Kamalov said.

"After the god?" Brenna asked.

"What? No. It's Russian for the number one."

"I claim drone two," Lexi said. "I want to call it Bobby."

"I've always hated that name," Robert said. "Pick another."

"Why? I'm not calling you Bobby, it's the drone."

"Pick another."

"Fine," Lexi said. "How about Bee."

"Good enough. Kimi, you're next."

"I'll take number three, I guess," Kimi said. "Call it Lee, after my mother."

"Aw," Brenna said. "That's sweet."

"That leaves four," Robert said. "Tony?"

"That's the one exploring down below, right?" Tony asked.

"Yup."

"How about Bilbo?"

"Why that?" Lexi asked.

"Because the little guy's on a quest. Might find a dragon." Tony chuckled.

"All right, what am I missing?" Kimi asked. "I've no idea what he's talking about."

"It's part of early industrial European mythology," Kamalov said. "I studied it as part of my history certifications."

"Speaking of which, anyone got a signal from Bilbo?" Robert asked. "He's dropped off my display."

Brenna checked and didn't see the drone's signal. No one else answered.

"I'm going to reposition, which one is that, now, Lee? I'll put Lee on a course that should get it closer to where Bilbo descended."

"Maybe we should all take a look," Kimi said. "I'll bet the insides are a lot more interesting than what we have out here?"

"What do you mean?" Kamalov asked. "Thousands of years of spatial degradation for us to study. Not interesting?"

"All right Kamalov, you can stay out here. Kimi and I will head downstairs. See if there's anything interesting."

"You are attempting to give her an advantage," he said. "It won't work."

"Nope. Just this place looks a bit tight, and you are bigger than either of us."

"Probably just wiring conduits," Kimi said. "Can't be all that great."

"Fine, I'll stay," Kamalov said. "Just make sure you take lots of pictures. I'll want to know what I missed."

"Tell you what," Brenna said, "if it's anything exciting we'll switch places."

"Deal."

* * *

BRENNA FLOATED into the wide gap. Her suit light cast a harsh light, creating crisp, black shadows. She pulled up her display and selected Sparky's illumination settings. The entire area flooded with light as Sparky crawled along the edge of the opening.

Brenna smiled to herself as she saw the contours of a passageway large enough to stand in. "Good news, everyone. Room enough to stand."

"This looks like it's a hallway," Kimi said. "Tall too."

"A-ha. Made for something taller than the Proximus aliens. So this was for the ones down below."

"Ombax," Kimi said. "We are calling them the Ombax, now."

"Yes, the Ombax."

"Let's not jump to conclusions, people," Brenna said. "We know the species of this world are taller, and they were in space back then. This could be designed for both species."

"Or a third species we haven't even found yet," Kimi said.

"Or it could be an empty wiring conduit," Kamalov said. "Focus, people. Brenna, do we bring everyone down?"

"This passageway goes both ways. It might be worth it to explore both ends. Robert, what do you want to do?"

"We're heading back toward you. Nothing interesting up here."

"Right."

"Brenna," Kamalov said, "heads up. I'm sending Clyde down to you now."

"Aye." She watched as the drone entered her view and proceeded down near her position.

Robert was the last one down. He shined his light along the passage in each direction. "All right, Lexi and Kamalov, take Clyde and head that way. Brenna and I will take Sparky and go this way. Tony, you and Kimi follow us. There is a junction this way that leads to the left. If it's another passage, you two can follow it. Keep an active signal lock so we don't fall out of comms range. If you lose the signal, turn around. We'll do the same until we are back in contact. If all else fails, meet back here at the opening."

"Sounds like a plan," Kamalov said. "Come on Clyde. Lead the way."

Brenna walked a step beyond and to the right of Robert. The light gravity made their movements a little too bouncy. She almost hit her head more than once.

"Damn," Robert said. "This isn't a passage. Just an alcove. Let's all keep moving forward."

"Got it," Tony said.

The walls were smooth. The ceilings didn't look as if they ever provided light. No fittings, either.

"There's another break in the tunnel up ahead," Robert said. "Maybe just another alcove."

Robert stopped quickly. Brenna bumped into him.

"Hey," Kimi said, "that's not nothing."

"Looks like it might be a hatch of some sort," Tony said.

"Do you think it's an airlock?"

"Would it be part of the original design? Would that mean this passage was supposed to be exposed?"

"Hush you two," Robert said. "Brenna, see if you can figure out the mechanism. I'll hold the light. Kimi, take Sparky and check up ahead a few meters. See if there are any more details. Tony, check out this weld. It looks different from what we've seen before."

"That looks like something done by hand," Brenna said. "See

the wobbles? Machine welds are always super straight. Just like what we saw before."

"So why all of a sudden do we have a hand-welded hatch inside a passageway?"

"Guys," Tony said, "this thing opens up, and there is a lever and a wheel inside. My bet is this is the locking mechanism. A wheel to turn gears and retract or engage the locks. Maybe this is a latch lever."

"It would make sense," Robert said.

"So, there is the question we need to answer," Brenna said. "Do we open it up?"

"My biggest concern is that there might be someone inside. What if we kill them accidentally?"

"After four thousand years?" Kimi scoffed. "Highly unlikely."

"Extremely remote possibility," Tony said.

"I would say impossible, but I've read too many science fiction novels. This is where we release the monster, and it kills all but one of us."

Brenna giggled. "Well then, the three of you should step back. It's always the guys who die first."

"Yes," Kimi said, "the survivor is invariably a very cute young woman. Sorry, Brenna."

"The hell you say? No, it's the cute junior girl that buys it first. The sexy, slightly older, far more experienced female is the survivor."

"Are you two done? Tony already pulled the lever. The door cracked open. No escaping gasses."

"Robert, you really are no fun." Brenna stuck her tongue out at him, but he didn't see it.

"It's an airlock. Look up here. A mechanical interlock. Can't open the next hatch without this one being closed."

"It's big enough for all four of us," Kimi said.

"I noticed," Robert said. "Com check. Kamalov, Lexi, can you hear me?"

The reply came back with a little breakage. Like digital chunks that weren't coming together quite in the right order. "We hear you. Choppy."

"We found an airlock. Heading inside. Might lose comms."

"Airlock," Kamalov said. "Good find. We will turn around. Nothing in here but emptiness, and we are nearly weightless. Found Bilbo."

"Understood."

"Okay," Brenna said, "everyone inside. Let's go see what they left us."

When the inner hatch opened, Robert and Brenna put their lights on a diffuse setting, brightening the entire space.

"Are those trees?" Kimi asked.

"I don't think so," Brenna said. "The trunks are too precise. It looks less natural."

"Look over at this one. There is a residue."

"Organic?" Robert asked.

"I'll take a sample."

"This could have been a hydroponics farm," Brenna said.

"Sure," Robert said. "It has that look to it. These trees might be supporting structures for some sort of vine, perhaps."

"It's what I would do for tomatoes. These things look heavy enough for that, but are too light for much else."

"Pipes," Tony said. "Here, connected to this basin under the trees."

"Wait," Kimi said, "there might be traces of organics in the pipes."

"That's going to have to wait," Robert said. "We've already broken the spirit of our orders by coming inside. Breaking open a pipe is going way too far. Put it on your wish list for the next mission. We'll bring the proper equipment."

Brenna noticed a mound of something near one wall. She bent closer to look. "Hey Robert, you're going to want to see this. I think we have bodies."

"Bodies? After four thousand years?"

"Yeah, they look pretty crumbly, but that looks like the right shape. See there? Curled around, but that's a tail."

"Oh my god," Kimi said. "Did they leave someone behind?"

"I wonder how long they survived?" Tony asked.

"This level of decay can only happen in an atmosphere," Brenna said. "Maybe they ran out of food or water."

"Get lots of pictures," Robert said. "No samples this time. Leave that to the scientists. They can send drones for that."

"This is amazing," Brenna said.

Kimi laughed. "I can't wait to get some of those samples."

"All right people," Robert said. "I'm going to call this a huge success, but it's time to get back out into the open and start heading back to the shuttle."

Robert's voice sounded off. Brenna switched over to the private channel. "You sound a bit spooked, Robert. What did you see?"

"I got a good look at its arms. It looked like the adult might have been clutching a juvenile. Makes me feel like a grave robber." He switched back to the main channel. "Brenna, let's you and I take a good look at the seals."

"Do you want to see if there is any way we can make this thing airtight?"

"I'm more curious to see if we can find out if they failed. We don't have enough to fill the compartment in any meaningful way."

"If this is metal," Brenna said, "I wonder how it lasted four thousand years without corroding or fusing together."

"It might be some sort of ceramic," Tony said. "We'll have to bring in better equipment to take a good look at it."

"I don't see any sort of residue," Robert said. "No sign of a gasket. It looks to me like the seal is simply smooth surfaces pressed together."

Brenna felt a vibration under her fingers. "I think the other team is inside the airlock."

They waited a moment, The internal door unlatched and swung open.

"Robert." Kamalov's voice sounded gruffer than before. "We have a flare alert. Coronal mass ejection inbound. Headed in our general direction. They said it would probably graze us."

"That's not good," Tony said.

"They advised us to take cover, shelter in place for a while."

"We should tell the other bots to come this way," Robert said. "Send a couple to fetch tanks so we can either swap out or replenish our supplies."

"Got it," Kamalov said. "I'll go back out. Clyde is right outside, and we left Bilbo near the opening. They can both go back, too."

"Maybe you should move the shuttle instead," Brenna said. "Save us time if we need it later."

"Good idea," Robert said. "Tony, you go with Kamalov. Bring the shuttle close. See if you can orient one of the hatches to make entry easy."

"Got it, boss."

"And check on the other bots. See how far they've gotten." He waved his hand. "Scratch that. Just call them back."

"We should see about ensuring communications to the outside from this area," Brenna said. "Set up a relay through the bots."

"Got it," Kamalov said. "I'll also retrieve continuous radiation readings from the shuttle. We can compare them to here. Set an alert if it gets too high."

"What happens if it's too high?" Kimi asked.

"Then we'll have to try to get back to the opening," Robert said.

"That will take time," Kamalov said.

"I know. Not my first option. I'm thinking this place will provide better shielding. I hope I'm not wrong."

FOONDEK IN THE SHIP'S GARDEN

Monday, August 5, 3297, 9:19

Foondek stepped out into the open. His eyes followed the curve of the station down the passageway in both directions. The room he had been in felt more like home with all the greenery he had asked for. This was entirely new.

Anna waved her hand. "Well? What do you think?"

Foondek spoke and the words were translated by Oddokof. "It is spinning?"

"Yes," she said.

"Like a bucket on a rope. You can spin it around your head. This is how we can walk."

"That's right." Anna nodded. That meant agreement, or affirmative.

"The air smells sweet."

"That might be the flowers."

"Flowers." Foondek flicked his tail.

"This way. See, there's a flower garden."

"For eating?"

"Some," Anna said. "Mostly to look nice."

Foondek pointed at a row of red tulips. "Even red leaves?"

"Yes. Is there something about red leaves?"

"Yes. For us, red is a warning. Red leaves of the *daydoykey* turn black near *ongdoyam*. It makes you sick if you are not careful. We do not eat them, so they can warn us."

"Ongdoyam?" Anna asked.

"Yes. Like from the sun, but you cannot see. Left from when our world fought itself, and lost."

"Radiation, I'll bet. Interesting, the leaves turn black?"

Foondek undulated in agreement. "They are meant to be a warning. To keep young ones from straying near. We are taught to stay away."

"Meant to be a warning? Meant by whom?"

Foondek looked confused.

"Did someone make the plants turn black to warn you?"

"Oh. Yes. I see. The old ones. After the great war. They created plants for warnings."

"Your people could change plants easily. Do you know they once traveled to your moons?"

"Of course. We know our history. Before the Sunfire war, they went to them both. It's where they met *Dapkasamok*."

"Dapkasamok?"

"The Sky People. We called them the finger faced. Dapkas amok."

"Ah, it's a compound word."

"How long ago did your people meet Dapkasamok?" Foondek asked.

"We never met them. We found traces of them a few years ago. We know they existed long ago. It's how we knew to come here. Something they left behind had a clue. But we don't know what happened to them or where they went, and we don't know where they came from either."

"We know where. It's in a book."

Anna stopped walking. "In a book?"

Foondek undulated. "I saw it when I was young. We have a copy in my village. The Book of Worlds. Written long ago."

Anna walked quietly for a time.

Foondek realized he must have said something important.

CLOSE QUARTERS

Monday, August 5, 3297, 20:48

With air running low and an ebb in the storm, Robert decided the team should make a dash for the shuttle. They sent the bots out first, then followed. The shuttle waited for them above their heads when they came to the gap in the ceiling they had dropped into. In the light gravity they hopped out and headed to the shuttle.

The bots lined up and entered through a service hatch while the people entered through the cargo hold. The door lowered and cycled closed. As the hold repressurized they all ran checks to be sure of no lasting damage. Once given the all clear, helmets came off, and they began disassembling their protective gear.

Brenna had stayed next to Robert, and at one point her bare shoulder touched his. She felt him pause, then he pressed, ever so gently, expanding the contact. Her nostrils flared when she caught wind of his ripeness. She smiled and glanced at the others. The two of them were the only ones standing so close.

Why did her heart race? She giggled and took a little bounce forward, separating them.

They each took turns in one of the zero gravity washrooms.

So many hours inside an environment suit tended to accumulate body odors. Why did he smell so good?

"*ENDURANCE*," Robert said, "have you gotten a reading on how much longer this storm will last?"

"Affirmative," Kai said. "Our current estimate is that the arm that grazed you will have passed within the next few minutes. The worst of the radiation is already past. How is your oxygen supply holding up?"

"We're good. The bots just came back from their second run. Hardy little things. We've enough for several more hours, and the ship is recycling what we sent back."

"Affirmative. We'll send you the all clear shortly."

"Aye," Robert said. "Thank you."

Lexi interrupted. "Can we get the cutting tools and open up this interior hatch?"

"Absolutely not. We found the hatch, that's better than expected, but we've already gone much further than we were supposed to."

Kamalov held up his hand. "But we've established that this station would have been built to support the Ombax."

"Yes," Kimi said. "You and I both came to that conclusion together."

"Only because you weaseled your way onto my team."

"My team, Kamalov," Brenna said. "The two of you were on my team. So perhaps I should get the credit instead, eh?"

Both Kamalov and Kimi started yelling indignantly. Brenna smiled to herself. "Then maybe the two of you can share the credit, and stop arguing about it."

Kamalov grunted. "Da. Fine."

"We should be sure to use his first name on the plaque," Kimi said.

"Now that was uncalled for. My name has a rich, if nearly unpronounceable heritage."

Kimi giggled.

Robert pinged Brenna on a private channel as he drifted toward the opposite end of the enclosed space.

"What can I do for you?" She slowly bounced in his general direction.

"Thanks for cooling that spat. Sometimes these civilians can get out of hand over stupid things like that."

"Yeah, I get it. No worries. In a hundred years, no one will care."

Robert held out both arms. "I'm already working on the proposal to come back and work on opening that inner hatch. I'm curious about what's on the other side. You game for a second trip?"

"Would that be another date?"

"This one has gone better than the first two. Neither of us went unconscious. No near death experiences. I would call that a win."

Brenna laughed. "I would run my fingers through my hair, but it's a bit hard in this suit. Sure. I'm in. But I'll need a bit of downtime between them to get all of the work set up for the factory build."

"Still in a hurry?"

"A bit. *Pang Yu* isn't going to stay here forever, you know."

"I know," Robert said, "and I've been thinking about that. Look, what if I said I didn't want you to leave. That I wanted you to stay here."

"Stay here. As an engineer?"

"Partly, yes. Having you here would mean the project would be well supervised from start to finish."

"Partly?" Brenna waited in silence for a moment. "Come on, Robert. You said *partly*. What's the other part on your mind?"

"The other part is that I've really enjoyed your company. I thought... that it would be very nice if we had some time, this time around, to actually get to know each other."

Brenna sighed, then chuckled.

"Was that so funny?"

"No. I just remembered how much I hated you the moment I set eyes on you."

"I remember," Robert said. "It was a difficult time."

"And then I–"

"Yeah. You did what you had to do. I respect that."

Brenna floated near him so she could see inside his helmet. "And then you saved my life. Holy crap, Robert. Did you save my life because you wanted to get into my pants?"

Robert laughed. "Of course not. I saved your life because at the time, I was the only one who could. I would never have been able to live with myself otherwise. Your pants had nothing to do with it."

"You never wanted to get into my pants?" She slid one leg around his, pulling herself closer.

"That would not be a correct statement. Look, we have history. A stranger one than most. All I'm asking is for some time to... explore what might be."

Brenna smiled. "Robert. Do you remember the second time I kissed you?"

"You were drugged and half dead. I didn't think it counted."

"I was very much aware of what I was doing, and never second guessed myself about it. Not once. I may have been a bit sedated, but still fully aware."

He cocked his head to one side. "The second kiss counts?"

"But I still think the first one shouldn't. I was distracting you so I could slap the tranq patch on your neck."

Robert laughed. "Doesn't matter. Doesn't matter at all."

. . .

BRENNA WAVED her display off and sighed. The shuttle, on course for *Endurance*, same as before. Everything looked good. No problems to fix. No warnings to investigate. She flipped to a display of various ship systems. At every possible trouble point she found an alert flag. One obscure reading that had once caused her trouble still sat two points lower than standard. She chuckled. Robert was on the ball as always. When she had first met him, she had chaffed under his strict, by the books manner. Now, after years of experience, she was more cautious. Same as him. She unlatched her seat and swung it around to face the open area of the cabin.

"So," Lexi said. "Everything good?"

"Do you hear me yelling orders?"

"Um, no?"

"No," Brenna said. "So, everything is exactly perfect. Anything less and I would be giving orders to make it right."

Robert chuckled and shook his head.

"What?"

Robert tilted his head. "Sounds like you have a lot more experience under your belt than the first time we met."

Brenna's cheeks grew warm. She scowled. "That was a very long time ago, old man."

"Old man? Who – what?"

Brenna's scowl broke into a giggle. "Okay, so I learned a few lessons the hard way. I'm still alive, and I still have seven original fingers."

Robert laughed.

"Anyone for poker?" Kamalov asked.

Kimi spun to face him. "Wait, you have cards?"

Lexi waved her off. "We can do it all virtual, silly."

"I suppose," Kimi said. "What do you have in mind?"

"Anything but Rainbow," Robert said. "I am so tired of playing that game."

Kimi frowned. "Seriously?"

"Yeah. My shift would play it almost non-stop while we were in jump. Let's play six card draw or Sliders."

"Sliders?"

"I know that one," Lexi said. "Six card hand. You slide what you don't want to the left after the deal. Then you start the betting. Once that's done, everyone gets a new card and then discards get slid again."

"Any wild cards?" Brenna asked.

"Nope," Robert said. "They stay out of the deck for this game."

"Too bad," Kimi said. "I like to use them to change the direction of play."

Brenna laughed. "We could always add them in. Local rule. Call it Sliders with Rainbow Wilds."

Robert rolled his eyes.

"I like that idea," Kamalov said. "Let's play. Brenna, you deal first."

•• ———————— ••●•• ———————— ••

"I'T's almost too easy. AutoGov will take us in. And since it controls the docking bay scheduling, there's nothing left for us to do."

"All hands man the maneuvering watch," AutoGov said.

Everyone took their assigned places. Brenna strapped into the co-pilot seat next to Robert. She glanced at him and smiled.

"We'll have to send the bots off with the samples as soon as we dock."

"I've already given them their instructions," Brenna said.

"Efficient. Thank you. Then all we have to deal with will be the mission debrief."

"De brief? How brief will de brief be?"

Robert smirked. "Skip loves long meetings. At least three, maybe four hours."

Kamalov's chuckle told her Robert exaggerated. She smiled. "Good. I love a nice extended meeting before I run back to my place for a good long nap."

•• ——————— ••●•• ——————— ••

"THERE IS a large section that has completed infrastructure." Robert tilted the schematic display of the ring, highlighting the areas he mentioned. "The room we were able to access, at one point, had been pressurized. Seems likely to have been growing plants. Probably for food."

"The hatch in there is secured from the other side," Maksim said. "We'll have to bring a cutter."

"A bunch of light drones would help, too," Kimi said.

"The samples from the bodies we found," Lexi said, "have been sent to the biology lab. It looked like an adult and a child. No way to tell, at this point, how it happened. They were barely recognizable."

Skip frowned. "You would think being frozen in a vacuum would have been a better preservative."

"We don't think the place was open to space. More likely the atmosphere leaked out over time. Plenty for heavy decomposition."

"That seems odd. I suppose we'll have to wait until we explore further to see if we find anything."

Robert nodded. "And that about wraps it up, sir."

Skip's eyebrows furled. "That's it?"

Robert shrugged. "I sent you a list of the samples we took,

and where we routed them. We should know for certain about those things we couldn't identify on site."

"Anyone else have something to contribute?" Skip waited for a moment.

Brenna fidgeted. "I think we're all a bit worn out, sir. Zero gee sleep isn't the best."

Skip nodded. "Fine. Let me know when you want to schedule the follow-up. Go get some rest."

"Aye, sir."

One by one they filed out of the room. Brenna followed Robert. When they had moved out of earshot of the others Robert stopped and faced her. "How tired are you?"

Brenna felt her cheeks flush. "Zero gee sleep may not be the best, Robert. But I still got plenty of it. You?"

Robert tilted his head. A smile lifted one side of his mouth. "Same. Want to come back to my place?"

Brenna smirked and batted her eyes with a little smile. "But I don't have a tranq patch."

They were still laughing as they entered his apartment.

THE FARM

Tuesday, August 6, 3297, 9:11

The large section on the lower deck below the park had been set aside for the hydroponics farm. Rows of stacked planters sandwiched between light panels, tubing neatly fastened and routed to each. Robotic arms tending the plans moved swiftly, yet handled the plants with a delicate touch. A wide, deep basin under it all where much of the ship's farm water was held.

Amidst the greenery, Debra spotted a small, dark skinned man in a white coat, taking cuttings from one of the plants. The nearby robotic arm sat silently.

"Dr. Mukumba?" she asked.

"That's me." He stood. A flash of recognition crossed his face.

Ted adjusted his stance and glanced at the man's hands.

"What can I do for you, Mrs. Becker?"

"Debra. Just call me Debra. I'm here to see about the produce situation. I'm setting up a new restaurant."

Gabriel scowled. "I've heard. It will still be twelve days before the first of the baby leaf lettuce is harvestable. It's usually harvested at about three to four weeks from seeding. Until then you'll have to share with Natasha. Two weeks after that, we will have the new full head lettuce ready as well as the new long beans. A fresh line of cherry tomatoes is also coming along shortly."

"What kinds of soil do you have?"

"We have three types," Gabriel said. "Bratsk, Congolese, and Rio Novo Terra Preta."

Debra smiled. "Now you have four. We've brought a box of Lunar Special Blend with us. We want to contribute it to your farm."

"Thank you very much. What are you hoping to have grown in it?"

"Standard salad makings. Nothing too crazy. The idea is that we'll be a new distribution point for the community. We wanted to be sure we made a meaningful contribution up front. We won't be picky about the produce, but Loonie dirt turned out really well, and is more radiation resistant than most Earth blends."

"Radiation resistant dirt?" Gabriel tilted his head.

"Microbiome. Oh, wait, you were kidding."

Gabriel smiled knowingly. "Just wanted to see what you knew. This will be a big help. We brought up samples of the native soil. It's a different chemistry behind their biology."

"And yet the natives look a lot like dinosaurs," Debra said.

He shrugged. "Evolution weeds out the stuff that doesn't work, and the things that do keep going. Besides, appearances don't tell the whole story. Dinosaurs often had feathers. From what we've seen, these folks have colored skin."

"What colors?"

"Usually a solid color with brown, black or gray stripes. We've spotted what might even be dark green stripes, but haven't confirmed that, yet. Oh, and spots. Such variety. The one we have on board is dark green with black stripes. We've also seen skin that's gray, brown, red or black. Our latest survey showed that most smaller towns had a single type. Larger towns might have two or three, with maybe a dozen different types in their larger cities."

They stepped through an access hatch into a large open area that gently curved upwards in the distance. The scents of various flowers were heavy in the air. In the distance, several drones floated above the fields, their ducted fans gently blowing tiny bubbles downward.

"What are those for?"

"Those are the pollinator drones."

"Pollinators? Wow. I knew you guys were using artificial pollinators, but somehow I always thought of tiny bee-bots."

Gabriel laughed. "That would be terribly inefficient. I would rather we had brought bees. I miss the honey."

"Don't they manufacture honey?"

"Of course they do, but nothing matches the taste and texture of the real thing. No, they decided to limit our potential impact on the new world. No insects at all, and a careful microbiological study and precautions before contact." He sighed. "Tea isn't quite the same without honey." He paused for a moment. His eyebrows furled together. "Say, I haven't asked you about the petition. I've sponsored a petition to create a civilian government. Nothing terribly out of the ordinary, since we were going to do it anyway. I felt we should get on with it. The sooner the better. Would you be interested in adding your approvals? I'm sure your name would carry quite a bit of weight."

"Maybe," Debra said. "Let us look it over, first."

Gabriel swiped a finger and jabbed the air, sending the command through his personal display.

Ted nudged his wife.

She frowned at him. "Thank you for your time, Doctor."

"You are quite welcome. Please, come again soon. I would love to hear more of your story."

Debra nodded with a smile, then headed toward the lift. Once the doors closed she turned on Ted. "What's up?"

"He knew you. Seemed overly friendly. Like he was trying too hard. Made me uneasy."

Debra thought for a moment. She began waving her hand

through the air, her eyes scanning a display only she could see. "He's former FoodCo. That doesn't mean anything. They were still independent when this ship left home."

"I know. Didn't say I had a reason, just this twitch in my gut that said to keep an eye on him, that's all."

Debra sighed. "I hope that, just this once, you're wrong. But I suppose I'll be sure to have plenty of security around me when he delivers."

"You have no idea how much I hate that feeling."

SAY WHAT?

Tuesday, August 6, 3297, 16:22

"Whatever you do, don't give the dragon flowers," Briana said. "You can stab it, poke it, throw fireballs at it, and it'll fight back and keep the game moving forward."

"What happens if someone gives it flowers?" Radinka asked.

"The dragon cries. Sits down, curls up around the flowers, and that's it."

"Dead?"

"Nope," Briana said. "Just napping for the rest of the day. But you'll get no points, and when it's in that state, you can't do damage, so no victory. Makes the game impossible to advance to the next stage until dawn."

"What possible use is that in a game like this?"

Briana blushed. "It makes that entire meadow a safe area. Nice tall grass, soft loamy ground. Use your imagination. Not every time here has to be about fighting dragons."

"Oh good grief. In virtual? Why don't you just go shag the guy in person?"

Briana crossed her arms. "Operational security. I actually do take this seriously, you know. A little fun on the side isn't going to make me jeopardize the mission. Besides, that's how I hooked him."

Radinka shook her head. "Have it your way."

Ferdinand entered the room and let the door close behind him. "There's been a development."

"What do you have?" Radinka asked.

He sat with a big flourish of his cape and grinned. "She is opening a new place to eat. According to my contact, she'll be taking regular deliveries from the farm."

"What does that mean?" Briana asked.

"It means, little elf girl, that we might have a way to get close to her. Something involving those deliveries."

Radinka scoffed. "Just be sure you don't hurt any of the farm personnel."

Ferdinand frowned. "If you say so. Although a few extra casualties might be good for the overall objective."

"Perhaps. Let's take it one step at a time, shall we? Farm deliveries won't be the only point of access. Find as many alternatives as you can. But that's a good start."

Briana's elven ears twitched in anticipation. "Now that we have a better location than residential, it gives us a more open target. I'll start looking into her routine. See if I can find the best cycle."

"I'll start looking for ways to help her," Ferdinand said. "I'll let you know as soon as I find something."

Radinka stood. "Good meeting. Very productive. See you in three days."

THE SAND

Mas'eeng Bayfod, Last Four, Highest

Daksey had left Beethax only yesterday and already the ground showed more brown, vegetation became sparse, and the few trees he could see were sickly, or dead. As the sun rose in the sky, few clouds offered him their shade.

He arrived at the long brick building where a dozen others had gathered. A stand of trees next to it, with shaded benches for people to wait. A tall wooden water tower dominated the skyline. The egg-mother inside collected the axmodok leaves he offered, demanding them all in advance. Daksey tried to protest, but she was very large. The most attractive female he had ever seen. He scolded himself for giving in so easily.

Benches under a small grove of trees provided a place to rest while he waited for the moyoxees, the vehicle that would take him across the desert. He closed his eyes and tried to nap in the shade.

A steam whistle screamed into the air. Daksey jumped to his feet, his eyes wide, heart pounding. He must have drifted off. The large, wheeled machine rolled to a stop near the station. Six cars were pulled behind it. Each had spoked metal tires that stood taller than Daksey and almost as wide where they met the ground.

The engine in front belched white steam and glowed with heat. The legendary moyoxees. Bongeex had been so excited when they had first learned of them. He would be jumping as fast as his heart beat if he were here.

Daksey felt a pang of loneliness in his chest. He missed his pouch-brother, and all of the family. He looked at the moyoxees. Workers were filling the tanks with fresh water. He looked back at the road he had walked to get here. What would happen if he turned around and went home?

He took a deep breath and exhaled. Duty demanded he complete the mission. He dug into his pack and ate a few bites of the dried meat he had with him. The people at Beethax had warned him that the ride would be almost three days, and you had to bring your own food. They had given him dried fish and a few strips of meat he hadn't recognized. It tasted good.

When he climbed aboard the car he had been assigned to, the first thing he noticed were the flower boxes along each window. He recognized those little red plants. They were daydoykey, the ones whose leaves turned black near radiation. The red they showed now was meant to give comfort. Daksey realized they were there because of the way they flashed the water into steam. He and Bongeex had studied how the machines worked when they were able to choose an optional course of study. Daksey chutted to himself. Bongeex had been persistent, learning far more than the rest of the class.

Bongeex would have eagerly gone to explore the engine, to learn the inner workings. Daksey had no desire to see those leaves turn black. He settled onto a bench near a window. His pack fit snugly underneath. A blast of cool air surprised him. It came from a vent above his head. Maybe the desert crossing wasn't going to be so bad.

When at long last the moyoxees began moving, another loud call from the steam whistle pierced the air. The bench Daksey had perched on slid from under him, and he sprawled onto the floor.

Several onlookers chut-chutted. Daksey hauled himself back

to the bench, and held on more tightly. The initial lurch never repeated, however. The train followed a rocky trail in a wide circle until it looped back on itself and headed the way it had come. It slowly gathered speed, and soon the landscape passed by his window much faster than he could run.

The landscape became more barren, rockier, then they topped a ridge and swept down into the desert basin. Strange at first, Daksey soon grew tired of watching the sand and rocks sweep past. He dug out a little more meat from his pack, then settled down in an attempt to sleep.

The motion of the train and the blast of cool air thundering down on him kept him from becoming comfortable enough for sleep.

Later, as night fell outside, he noticed the jars mounted at regular intervals along the cabin. They were filled with a glowing liquid. As the last light of the sun faded, the liquid glowed brighter. Dimmer than the sunlight had been, but enough to see by. One of the lamps seemed much dimmer than the others. Daksey wondered what was in them.

A train worker passing through the car stopped at the dim light and tapped it. He went back the way he came, and returned a little while later. He carefully opened the dim jar and produced a bottle of white liquid from his pouch. A few drops from the bottle was all he added, then closed the two containers. He went to the next car on his rounds. By the time he returned, the dim jar had become brighter. After he left, Daksey watched as the jar that had once faded so badly, became the brightest jar in the cabin.

It soon became another reason Daksey couldn't sleep. He turned his head in another direction and closed his eyes again.

The train lurched in the wrong direction, waking Daksey on his way to the floor. This time, he wasn't alone. Most of the other passengers had also been tossed off their benches. The train lurched and creaked to a stop. Daksey climbed back onto the bench, and heard low growls outside. They didn't seem to be animals. He could only make out shadows, but he caught a glimpse of several two-wheeled vehicles, and three that were larger, three wheeled vehicles.

Several Ombax dismounted and began waving weapons in the air. Daksey had never seen weapons like that in real life, but he knew what they were. A small explosive propelled chunks of metal out one end at high velocity. Lethal. He tried to remember the name for it. Engpoy. That sounded right. The newcomers each carried an engpoy. Some were long, a few were shorter versions.

A loud noise issued from the front of the train, and a gurgle rippled through the air. The train crew climbed down and gathered near the newcomers. Glowing jars were brought out. Daksey opened his window to listen.

"Here," said the one with a large floppy hat. "Put this bundle on the fire early in the morning. It will give off a plume of black smoke. The people at the station will see it, and they will send help. In the meantime, dig down into the sand. Everyone. Dig yourselves a hole and cover with one of the tarps they have in the engine. You won't want to be exposed to the sun all day, tomorrow."

"They have cold air on the train," said one of the passengers. "Why can't we stay inside?"

"Because we are taking what makes the steam, and the steam makes cold air for you. The compressed air you have won't last all night and all day tomorrow. You should plan ahead. When the clouds come, keep the windows open until the sand starts to blow, then close them and climb back aboard. It will be safer during the storm, and with luck, you won't get overly hot once the clouds block the sun. Just remember to get out and make yourselves shade when it's over."

Two people wearing thick cloth over their bodies, eyes covered by glass discs strapped to their faces each carried one end of a long pole. In the center hung a cylinder. Daksey could see by the heat glow that they would be hot enough to burn someone's skin. Out of the corner of his eye, he saw one of the leaves start to blacken.

He slid away from the window and crossed over to the other side. He stood on the bench. There were two other pairs of covered people, pouch-husbands or scouts, perhaps, each carrying a steaming cylinder.

He watched as they took one each to the three-wheeled vehicles, and carefully wrapped them in metallic looking blankets. He glanced at the leaves. Only a few, scattered here and there, had darkened.

"Maysam, Osmay, come with me," said the one with the floppy hat. "We'll check the passengers for coins. Our little bonus."

Daksey felt relieved. He had no coins. They would leave him alone.

They approached the end cabin first. Daksey's cabin was next. "Take out your coins and hand them over. Be quick about it."

One of them stood over Daksey. "Where are your coins, child? Give us all your fong."

Daksey's quills rose. "I have none."

The bandit chut-chutted. "Hey, Thoy'eeng, this one says he has none."

Thoy'eeng snorted. "He must be lying. Take him outside. Grab his pack. I see it there under his bench." He adjusted his floppy hat, so it rode higher on his head.

They pulled and prodded Daksey out of the coach onto the sand. His feet slid in the wrong direction. He hated that feeling. All those tiny grains of rock wouldn't let him grab hold of anything.

"Maysam, search him while your brother holds his arms."

Maysam snorted. "Why does Osmay get the easy part?" He looked Daksey in the eyes. "Where are your coins? In your pack, or did you stash them in your pouch?"

"I don't have any coins. My people don't use them."

Osmay pulled back on Daksey's arms. The brief pain made him yelp. "Don't give my brother a story, little one, or your egg-mother won't be getting you back."

"I am Botham, from Koy'am. We hunt for food and build with trees. We sing to ourselves and don't need your stupid coins."

The leader of the train workers called over. "That one tells the truth. He paid for his ride with herbs. Good for cooking."

"Herbs? For a train ride?"

"The station keeper called it a fair trade. They were what she liked. We don't argue with that one."

Daksey would have laughed if a bandit wasn't holding his arms. Axmodok leaves didn't taste good at all, but were a beloved intoxicant of everyone who chewed them.

Thoy'eeng called over. "Leave the child alone, then. We've no use for him."

Osmay dropped Daksey's arms. "We've no use for you, child."

Daksey snorted softly. He had heard it the first time.

"Oh look," Maysam said. "He has a father's bag."

Osmay tilted his head. "Poor lost child with a father's bag? What could it contain? Maybe some snack meat? Or koox, I want koox." He grabbed the smaller bag from Daksey and opened it. He chut-chutted. "Nose filters. Fathers packed him nose filters. And look, clean foot bags. Not a speck of sand on them."

"Nose filters and clean foot bags," Maysam said. "Father must love his little child."

Thoy'eeng approached. "What are you two doing? I told you to leave him alone."

Osmay pointed to the bag. "Thoy'eeng, look. Little lost one has a father's bag with nose filters and clean foot bags."

"Imagine that. Someone thinking to be prepared for the desert. Why does it surprise you, Osmay?"

Osmay stamped a foot. "Nose filters? It's a silly thing. A weakness."

"It is a trait of the forest dwellers and the villagers that they do not breathe sand as well as our people. All you are seeing is someone who is well prepared for a difficult journey. Child, did you prepare this bag? Did you plan ahead?"

Daksey huffed in frustration. "My pouch-fathers prepared the bag for me. They gave me each item, and explained why it was needed. The foot bags and nose filters, and there is also a jar of balm, to keep my face from cracking. And yes, on the bottom, tightly wrapped, are dried snack meat strips."

Osmay and Maysam were chut-chutting in laughter.

Thoy'eeng gave a short, stiff undulation. "Give him back his bag. Obviously neither of you were loved by your pouch-fathers, or you would see what I see."

"What? A weak young child carrying a neat little bag his pouch-fathers packed?"

"A young one embarking on a dangerous journey, with a family who allowed it, and cared enough to help him prepare. I also see a young one who, even in the face of derision, spoke true words. He didn't attempt to claim the foresight to pack a desert bag himself."

Osmay tilted his head. "Whatever." He tossed the bag at Daksey's feet, snorted, and stomped away.

"One thing I wonder," Thoy'eeng said, "why have you come all this way? Why dare the desert crossing? Are you going okdeyok so young?"

Daksey kicked at the pack and swung it around. He opened it, and removed the carefully wrapped skulls. He unfolded the cloth on the ground, and let the bandits see them.

Thoy'eeng stooped low and sniffed at them. Looking closely, but not touching them.

"What animal is that?" Maysam asked.

Thoy'eeng lifted his head and matched his eyes to Daksey. "You're going to Afothameex to see the scholars at the observatory."

Daksey undulated in agreement.

Thoy'eeng flicked his tail and turned to Maysam. "Pack him up. He's coming with us." He swung back to Daksey. "You are taking a longer path. Better put your footbags on."

Daksey was about to respond, but Thoy'eeng turned and

stomped away. He called back over his shoulder. "And the nose filters. Don't forget those."

Daksey gathered the skulls into a bundle and repacked them. A smaller package bumped his hand. He opened it and chutted.

"What's so funny?" Maysam asked.

He held out the smaller package with one edge opened to reveal the soft cake inside. "The koox was in the pack."

Maysam chut-chutted. "Keep it hidden from Osmay. He would take it from you."

Daksey followed Maysam to the two-wheeled vehicles. He saw one of them placing an open bag of chalk onto the back side of the vehicle. He looked around, and saw that several of them had similar bags of chalk, and all the vehicles were being lightly sprinkled with chalk dust.

Daksey climbed aboard the same vehicle as Maysam. A division in the long seat allowed Maysam to slide his tail under the back part. Daksey had to keep his tail lifted above the wheel.

Osmay settled in on his own vehicle, glanced at Daksey and snorted. He slammed the rear seat with his tail.

A foot lever at one side allowed the driver to start the engine. Daksey cringed at the sudden explosion of sound. It sounded much louder when you were sitting on top of it. He had never heard such a thing. Like a growling thunder, it shook his teeth. Maysam reached over and passed Daksey something he didn't understand, until he saw Osmay setting one on his head. It had two large pads, one for each ear. Once Daksey had it in place, the noise became bearable, but still shook his chest.

The vehicles rode south for most of the night. They came to a ridge and climbed to the top where the rough stone surface opened to a wide plateau.

Three large, flat vehicles awaited them. The metal frames were covered in sturdy cloth with flexible transparent panels sewn into the front and sides. Flexible skirts were fitted around the bottom edges. A large fan mounted at the rear with fins gave them control of the wind direction.

Once they came to a stop, Thoy'eeng barked commands. "Pull up here, stay to the right. Maysam, take all the longwood and light three fires off to the left. Leave them far enough apart to look like three cook fires. The rest of you, brush off each three-wheeler and load them onto your bepthod. Then load the two-wheelers behind. Remove all chalk and all sand. When we start moving, be sure you leave no trace to show our true course. You," he pointed at Daksey, "climb into the front bepthod, over there. Wait for us."

When the fires were lit, the vehicles cleaned and loaded, they boarded the three large bepthods and started west. Moving slowly, in parallel to each other, they left the fires behind. The engine noise of the bepthod was far quieter. A smooth, low buzz from outside the cabin. No one needed the ear protection anymore.

Daksey thought about the longwood. He remembered the longwood forest at the edge of the desert to the south. They had now turned northwest, along the curved, rocky ridge. If they followed the curve, which seemed likely, they would eventually be headed north. A diversion. A trick to confuse any pursuers. Daksey had thought these were the bandits known to live near that longwood forest. Now, he wasn't so sure.

NATASHA

Wednesday, August 7, 3297, 20:32

"I tell you the look on his face, priceless." Skip grinned. A pop and crackle from the faux fireplace caught his attention. Natasha's diner was quiet at the moment.

"Both of them?" Natasha scowled. "I'm not sure I trust it." She took a sip from her mug.

"They were up front about it." He shrugged. "He's older than they expected, and their goal is children. Long term relationship is an option, but simple parenthood will do. They have their own relationship, and that seems stable."

"So do they really lean both ways, or are they more into each other?"

"That I couldn't tell you." Skip chuckled. "Still, if it kept him here a few years longer, I would be happy." He raised his mug as if to toast his good fortune. After deeply inhaling the steam and appreciating the aroma, he took a careful sip.

"He's still intent on going back?"

"I think he wants to look for more survivors. All he ever knew was the Halo. He lost a lot of friends that day, and there are others who may have survived, but ended up scattered. Say, this is differ-ent. What did you do to it?"

"Added a little cinnamon." She sighed. "*Pang Yu* wasn't big enough for everyone. We all lost a lot of people. I'm grateful you gave me a heads up."

Skip gazed into his mug. "I should have done more. I wish–"

"No more of that, old man. The universe has spoken. It is done. Your part is to build a better future. Here. Now."

"With you?"

"I'm here," Natasha said. "Now."

Skip raised his mug to his lips and smiled at her through the steam. "You certainly are."

CHALLENGES AHEAD

Monday, August 12, 3297, 6:57

Brenna drifted awake and became aware of the warm body in bed next to her. She took a deep, slow breath and let it out. Her entire body relaxed. At peace. She thought of the challenge ahead of Robert and his team. Establishing a mining, processing and factory system even before the first emitters could be built. Then the installation, balance calculations. The *Pang Yu* would be another year of routine watches, minor repairs, drills, training, and in the end, where would she be? Home? Back to Europa? Everyone was gone. The people she knew had long since rotated out. But here...

Robert snored. Light at first, the rattle grew louder until he snorted, then rolled over, still asleep. She smiled. He had an automatic reset.

After an eternity, an alarm shattered the peace. Not the bad kind. The kind people used when they didn't want to have the alarm in their heads.

Robert took a deep breath. His hand sought her out. They lay quietly for a time, smiling at each other.

Finally, he spoke. "AutoGov, coffee. What kind do you like?"

"Extra dark smooth roast, sweetened, medium light, with a dash of cinnamon."

"AutoGov, make that for her, my usual for me."

"Acknowledged. You have forty-five minutes before your watch."

THE CREPE INCIDENT

"Crap."

Ted frowned. "Debra, are you getting hostile in the kitchen again?"

"Oh, shut up," she said. "I learned something new."

"Making crepes?"

"Yes. I learned that if you start with beating the eggs, then add your melted butter, you cook the damned eggs."

Ted tried very hard not to laugh. "Scrambled eggs, then?"

"No. I think I'm going to press ahead. I mean, how bad can it be, anyway? A few chunks of cooked egg in the mix might make it a little lumpy, but if it still rolls like it's supposed to, it should be fine."

"Maybe you should ask Natasha about it."

"No. And I don't want to waste the eggs either. We've a limited supply."

"When are they setting up the second egg machine?"

"Should be done this week."

"After breakfast, want to go for a run?"

"Not yet. I'm still a little unstable in this gravity. I wish they would have settled on a half gee. Full spin makes my back hurt."

"Maybe you need more support. Get some new muscle laid in."

"I'm doing the bendy stretches. It'll grow. Just not ready to walk all the way around the station, again."

"Okay. No worries."

"Oh hey, these look great. No lumps after all. Come get yours while they're hot."

Ted sat at the table. He looked at the rolled crepes on the serving plate. "What did you put in them?"

"These two have scrambled eggs and cheddar cheese, that one has cream cheese and a raspberry, those two have a pumpkin and cinnamon mix. Be careful with the cream cheese. It's a little runny. I don't think they have the mix right, or at least it's not what I'm used to."

"Only one raspberry?"

Debra shrugged. "Some of them accidentally jumped into my mouth while I made the crepes. Fatal, I'm afraid."

"You have bread and crepes, which I suppose means you also have waffles and pancakes, right?"

"Yup. And dinner rolls. I think we can skip the pasta for a bit, as long as I can get some greens for a salad. Oh, and I'll need a salad dressing."

"What does Natasha use?"

"Oil and vinegar. But Uncle Keegan used to make a really good thousand island dressing." She tilted her head. "AutoGov, does Al have Keegan's recipe for thousand island dressing?"

"Affirmative," AutoGov said.

"Are all of the ingredients available on *Endurance*?"

"Negative."

Debra frowned. "No? What's missing?"

Ted watched as she scanned an invisible list.

Her face darkened. "No mustard seed? No black pepper?"

"There's black pepper in Thousand Island dressing?" Ted asked.

"It's in the ketchup that goes into the dressing."

"Oh. Wait, no ketchup?"

She swiped her hand and made a selection. "Real, not the artificial crap. We have apples, but they haven't started making apple cider vinegar yet. It's scheduled for next year."

"Next year?"

"Yeah. Have to wait for the harvest, then the fermentation takes time. The schedule has it available in early February."

"So, we have until then to find substitutes for everything else that's missing. Then you can make your own version of thousand island dressing."

Debra sighed. "I'm still going to need something tasty to put on the salads."

"Sounds like you have almost everything you need for the mayo. Maybe add some spices to that. See what we can come up with."

"That might do, for now."

"At least they have an egg machine. These egg filled crepes are delicious."

Debra rolled her eyes and shook her head. "Oh, thank you so much."

"What?"

"It hardly took anything to fry up some batter and roll it around scrambled eggs. There are so many things Keegan used to make that we won't have the ingredients for on opening day."

Ted shrugged. "So what? You'll have something, and Natasha is making sure it's different from what she serves, while still being great food."

"I know. She's been a real angel. We should do something nice for her."

"What do you have in mind?"

"I should make her a dress."

Ted felt his heart drop. "Debra."

"What?"

"This whole thing with the restaurant themed for your uncle's place, that's one thing. But now you want to start making dresses? What happens if I die? Will you start commanding an elite strike team?"

Derba crossed her arms. "Been there, done that. No, I wasn't thinking I would make it by my own hands, but I could design one. I used to do that on my own."

Ted smiled. "Sorry. I didn't mean–"

"Mean what? That all this is because the two most important members of my family–" She caught her breath.

Ted stood and stepped over to her side of the table. He put his arm around her and kissed her forehead. "Sorry."

She put her hand over his and looked up at him. "It still hurts."

"Only because you loved them."

She looked into his eyes for a moment. "Are we going to stay here?"

Ted rubbed her shoulder, moved his free hand to the other shoulder and began to kneed. "Wasn't that the plan?"

"I don't know. I keep thinking that we're only here to set up the restaurant, then we go somewhere else. But this feels more permanent."

"When we first talked about it, I thought it was permanent. What brought this on?"

She took a deep breath and sighed. "No one has been rude to me. No one has pointed at me and gawked. Everyone is open and accepting here. I feel like we could stay."

"Sure. We could stay."

"Maybe start a family."

Ted froze. "A... family?"

"Look, I know you have reservations, but I'm serious. You would be an amazing father. I want to take our safeties off."

Ted continued to rub her shoulders while his mind soared through space.

"Look, just think about it, okay."

"I'll think about it. Just–"

"AutoGov turn off my pregnancy blocker."

"Acknowledged. Pregnancy block removed. Regular ovulation cycle will be fully functional within fourteen days."

"You don't have to do it right now, Ted. I wanted you to know how certain I was. I'll wait for you to decide."

Ted felt his mouth dry out. He became acutely aware of his own pregnancy prevention. He focused on breathing steadily and rubbing his wife's shoulders.

A CHOICE

Tuesday, August 13, 3297, 8:17

Despite being offered a nice apartment on *Endurance*, Betsy had elected to stay in her own stateroom aboard *Pang Yu*. With the bed folded away, it was also her shipboard office, although it was still cramped for two people.

Brenna sat facing her commanding officer over the display little table that served as a workstation. "Captain, you know I've given this a lot of thought. We talked about it before we even left."

"Here it comes," Betsy said.

"I officially want to stay here. Transfer to *Endurance*. Wayne is qualified to take over for me, and with Dugan cross training they can stay in four sections at least half the time. You have plenty of crew, so if you don't mind, if it's okay with you, I would like to request a transfer."

"This thing with you and Quesada is going well, I take it."

Brenna blushed and nodded.

"Are you sure he's the one? The man of your dreams?"

"I don't know. I'm not sure. But if I don't stay and give it a shot, how will I ever know? Every time we met in the past, we were never together. Now..." She shrugged. "...it's like we connected, and it might be good, but we haven't done the full battery of tests. No real metrics. And if I leave and go back to Earth, who knows if we'll ever have a chance to try again."

Betsy smiled. "Good answer. I'll tell Jason, get it moving on our end."

Brenna smiled. "Thanks, Captain. Thank you very much."

THE PRISONER

Mas'eeng Masassof, First One, Rising

Daksey had no idea how long he had been in this poorly lit, damp cell. Food came periodically, but he didn't know how often, as he tended to sleep when he wasn't eating. Water ran in a trough through his cell. It appeared to be clean when it came in. It was all he had to drink, and the only way to deal with his waste. He worried there might be someone downstream of him, who wouldn't appreciate that part.

He tried to count. One meal a day? Two? How many days? Six days? A full count? He began to think he might be forgetting meals.

He longed for his brother. For his pouch-fathers, Soyok, and Espay. Kempok had chosen him, and he had failed. He had been given this great honor and had disgraced himself. She had sent him because she had been certain he would return, and yet he was going to spend the rest of his life as a prisoner of bandits. Or worse, a slave. Forced to labor against his will. His shoulder itched. He didn't want to think about it. He wanted to go home.

The familiar rattle of the lock at the end of the passage. The familiar footsteps. He waited for the sliding of the bowl filled with chunks of old meat. It didn't come.

"How are you doing in there, child?" Thoy'eeng, the one who had put him here. Still wearing that large floppy hat.

"I want to go home," Daksey said. "Please, let me go home."

"I thought you were going to Afothameex. Taking two skulls and some other interesting things to the scholars."

"I no longer have any of that. You took everything from me, even my freedom. Just let me go home so I can tell my egg-mother how badly I've failed."

Thoy'eeng thumped his tail. "Enough of that. You've been here two days. How can you be half mad after two days?"

"Two days? I counted the meals. So much time."

"The meals?"

"One meal a day," Daksey said. "I've been here a long time."

"Four meals a day, and you've been here two."

"Four meals?"

Thoy'eeng gave a short, stiff undulation. "We fed you on our schedule. No idea what your custom is."

Daksey stood. His quills flicked up and down in confusion.

"Never mind that now. You are wanted upstairs. It's time to talk to the egg-mother of Seeng'dod." He turned the latch, sliding the gate open. "Follow me."

After climbing a long and winding staircase, Daksey followed Thoy'eeng to a large room with an open balcony at one end and large drapes at the other. A wide table in the center held the contents of his pack. The two strange skulls, unwrapped, and the assorted items he was to bring to Afothameex. The images he had been given in Beethax were set out in a row at one end of the table.

With a grand flourish the majestic drapes were flung back and the largest, most beautiful egg-mother he had ever seen strode boldly into the room, leading a handful of others. She was partially covered in ornate cloth, patterns of several complimentary colors. Her quills were carefully painted, with tiny silver tips.

A delicate scrollwork decorated her tan skin while glistening sparkles gave extra life to her thin brown stripes.

Thoy'eeng removed his large hat and held it before him.

Daksey hooted wistfully.

Thoy'eeng chut-chutted and thumped his hand on top of Daksey's head. "Keep calm, child."

Daksey huffed and shrugged away from the hand.

"This is the forest child?" she asked. "What is your name?"

"Botham Kempok Daksey."

"Botham Kempok. I've heard of your egg-mother. You may call me Samam, for I am samam of this city."

Daksey undulated. He had no idea what the title meant. "Yes, Samam."

Samam chut-chutted and exchanged glances with Thoy'eeng. "I wanted to speak with you about the items you were carrying. Where did you get all this?"

Daksey stepped forward. He pointed to the skull with blackened patches. "This is the first skull given to me in Bamthapeem. Three of them climbed to the top in full daylight. The whole tribe saw them. They sat at the top of the steps as if to talk, but then showed their stolen lightning. It startled the tribe. The three were killed, and eaten."

Samam gave the same short, stiff undulation Thoy'eeng used. "How many of the tribe died?"

Daksey shrugged. "Just one died. A scout from Kadayax. My egg-mother led many of us to the mountain top with medicine. Once she knew what had made them sick, she selected an herb that helped. We gave it to them, and helped them drink a lot of clean water."

Samam snorted and huffed. She turned to one of the others. "Bring the physician. We will have words once I'm done here." She turned back to Daksey. "What medicine did you use?"

"We gave them o'saf leaves. It settles the stomach, and helps to flush out the bowels."

Samam snorted again. Her eyes narrowed. "Once the medicine was given, how did you come to be given these skulls?"

Daksey swayed. "I'm a young hunter. An older hunter offered to hunt in my place, in addition to his own duties. My egg-mother chose me because I don't take as many risks as my pouch-brother. She gave me the first skull. She thought I would be more reliable." He snorted. "She made a mistake."

Samam looked at him, her eyes drilling into his. "And the second skull?"

"I followed the road to the desert. The last town before the edge is Beethax. I came into town, and there were four more bodies on display in the center of town."

"How many people died there?"

Daksey shrugged again. "None. They did not eat them. There were many dead fong'sak near the bodies. They may have seen they were poison before it was too late. Or it might not be their tradition. I didn't think to ask."

Samam let out a low moan. "We lost five of our best egg-mothers, and over a full count of our brothers."

"I'm sorry to hear that, Samam."

"Tell me, what happened in Beethax?"

"The event in Beethax took place much earlier than at Bamthapeem. A full-count, at least. The creatures came in the morning through the fog. They used lights from their heads. Those discs over there. A group of frightened children screamed, and the adults came running with pointed farm implements. They say the creatures die easily when you stick them in the head or chest."

Samam chut-chutted softly. "They don't do so well against cannon fire either."

Daksey's quills flicked up and down. "What?"

"They were here. Three months ago. They came from the sky, landed beyond our gate. We didn't know what they were, but our guard opened fire before anyone could find out. We are very cautious with visitors. We examined the wreckage and found four strange bodies. Their skulls look like this."

"Then they have come to us at least three times."

Samam undulated briefly. "And have been defeated three times."

Daksey flicked his tail. "Or failed to communicate three times."

Samam snorted loudly. "Communicate? If that's what they wanted they should have walked up to the gate."

"They tried that at Beethax and Bamthapeem. It didn't work there, any better than landing outside your gate did here."

Samam glowered at him and thumped her tail. "Are you arguing with me?"

Daksey shrunk back and sat on his tail. "I'm telling you what I saw. Giving you my thoughts. Nothing more, Samam."

She spun quickly and walked toward the drapes. "Follow."

Daksey scurried after her. Thoy'eeng fell in beside him. In a very low voice he said, "Take care not to anger her, child."

Daksey undulated.

The large egg-mother led them down a grand stairwell and into a wide hall with display cases on each side. She stopped and pointed to one side.

There were three skeletons in various states of dismemberment set in blocks of a clear material Daksey had not seen before. He reached out and tapped one of the displays. Smooth to the touch but not cool. It didn't feel quite like glass.

"These are the creatures with their bones laid out, nearly as we found them. I would give you a skull, but it takes a lot of effort to release it once it's set in foydeng." She turned to him and pointed to the other side of the hall. There was a largely intact creature, also preserved. The chest had been opened to reveal organs, intestines and bones. Parts of the cloth these things wore had also been left on the body.

Daksey stepped forward and examined the display. "This is amazing work."

Samam undulated briefly. "We studied this one while the others were butchered and distributed." She turned and watched Daksey take in the sight.

Thoy'eeng cleared his throat. "Samam, what are you going to do with the child?"

She turned to him. "I've not yet decided. Our specimens here are already preserved, and he has samples of the devices they carried. If you had left him where you found him, he would be on his way to the scholars by now. As it is, he has seen enough to cause us a great deal of trouble."

Daksey's quills rose. "I have?"

Samam snorted. "Do not pretend to be foolish. You know what they stole and how you came to be here. How could you explain it to Afothameex?"

Daksey undulated slowly and deeply. "How could I explain that the bandits came here, to your city, and perhaps neglected to tell you the source of their wares?"

Samam chut-chutted. "Thoy'eeng, you dare to sell me what you've stolen? I shall banish you from this city. How long will your next raid take?"

"At least a full-count, Samam. We leave in three days for the west."

"You are banished for a full-count. If you are caught again, the consequences will be more severe. This banishment shall begin in three days. You can give our friend here a ride to a western outpost."

Daksey chut-chutted. "I heard with my own ears that the bandit leader has been banished."

Samam undulated and gazed at Thoy'eeng. "He may be from the forest, but he thinks quickly." She turned to Daksey. "Your egg-mother was right to choose you. I will have images of all this created. You will take them to Afothameex. You might also mention how well we've treated you here."

Daksey chut-chutted. "After I spend three more days in a cell?

Please forgive me, Samam. I am not that good at telling falsehoods."

Samam eyed Daksey, her spines flicked up and down. "You were well fed and kept from the heat."

"Confined in a tiny room, with no sunlight. I'm unused to such a thing."

Saman chut-chutted. "Perhaps we should let you see more of the city. Thoy'eeng, arrange a better room and give him sixty-four fong. Show him the city."

Thoy'eeng snorted softly, then gave a brief, short undulation. "Yes, Samam."

He led Daksey out of the room to a long, wide corridor. "You need to stop undulating like that. It's embarrassing."

"What? I don't know what you mean."

"You undulate like a child. Do it quickly, less deeply. I'm sure you've seen how I do it."

"I have," Daksey said. "It seems impolite. I thought you were being rude."

Thoy'eeng chut-chutted. "And the way you do it looks silly to people from Seeng'dod. Pay attention. You aren't among the trees anymore."

Daksey gave a brief, stiff undulation.

"Better. Watch others. See how they do it. And keep watching for differences. Everywhere you go, people are a little different. They move differently, speak differently, and sometimes think differently. Now, have you ever actually used fong before? Ever bought something?"

Daksey undulated. "Not fong, coins from Kadayax. I don't remember what they were called. My pouch-father took us there once when we were young."

"That is a good start. Now, as a measure of value, one fong is worth... Oh I don't know. A bite of meat. A piece of fruit. Five fong is a small meal."

SECRET OF THE KO'DEX

Mas'eeng Masassof, First One, Early High

The trees were much closer together this far south of Botham. Bongeex led Moya'se along a game trail he remembered from last season. He had been hunting with Deytham, learning how to track animals through the dense undergrowth.

Moya'se froze and gave the hand signal for quiet.

Bongeex stopped and remained silent. A broken twig to the left, a rustle further ahead, still on the left. A deep inhale allowed him to taste the air. He dropped his tense shoulders and snorted. "Ko'dex hunters. I can smell you. Did you forget to use scented oils this morning? You won't catch anything with that cloud rolling in front of you."

"Oh. I can hear it now," came the reply. "The little cry of that tiny Botham who pretends to hunt with his brothers. Speak louder, little one. I don't see where you are. This bush is nearly as high as my pouch."

Moya'se turned to stare at her brother. "Tiny?"

Bongeex chutted.

Three hunters made their way out of the forest to the trail.

They were dark green, with black stripes far thinner than those of the Botham. The leader, slightly taller than Bongeex, stepped to face him. He snorted in Bongeex's face.

Bongeex made as if to retch. "Oh, my stomach. You've turned it with that stench!"

Moya'se chut-chutted.

The leader turned, tilted his head, then hooted. "A sister! He hunts with a sister!"

Bongeex pointed at the leader. "Moya'se, this is Ko'dex Foyam Pongsok. And yes, she is my sister. Kempok Moya'se."

Pongsok glared at Bongeex. "But why? Why would Kempok do this?"

"Some of our hunters have gone missing. There are strange things happening. But we must still hunt."

"But... a sister?" Pongsok glanced at Moya'se, who stood with her neck straight. A powerful and defiant stance.

That made Bongeex proud of her, especially since it caused so much consternation in the members of the other tribe. "She is better than nothing, and even better than brothers her age. But what about you? Why do Ko'dex hunt so far west of your home?"

"We are going to the ruins–"

Pongsok raised his hand. "Quiet Sopoth."

Bongeex snorted. "I see. That big secret of yours."

"What secret?" Moya'se asked.

The quills on Pongsok's neck stood up. "Please. Do not share this with her. She is a sister. This is a brother thing."

Bongeex chutted. "Moya'se, let this go down the river for a while. It will keep the weather clear."

Moya'se knew what he meant. Leave it be, so the three hunters would not become confrontational. The weather would stay clear.

"We are also heading in the direction of the ruins. I'm going to show her the way to the fruit trees. She and I are setting traps along the path. You are welcome to walk with us, or perhaps you would want to run ahead. Take care of your business, before we join you later, between late high and highest."

Pongsok undulated. "We run fast for fun. Your tiny legs would never keep up. We'll meet you later, near the tree in the wall. You know the one?"

"Yes," Bongeex said. "Where the wall has been ripped apart over hundreds of years by a slow-growing tree. The branches provide a shaded rest area and fruit."

"Don't count on any fruit. Enjoy your trap setting." He tilted his head at Moya'se and started off to the south. The other two fell in behind him.

Moya'se snorted. "They are so impolite. He tilted at me. Such an insult."

"Moya'se, it's the way of the hunter to speak rudely to other hunters. His tilt of the head, the tiniest insult there is, which, come to think of it, is pretty insulting. If he had made derogatory comments about your quills, or your tail, then he would be declaring his respect for you."

"That is the dumbest thing I've ever heard."

Bongeex chutted. "I didn't say it was smart. Just that it was."

They took their time setting traps along the path. Bongeex watched Moya'se as she started catching glimpses of the old buildings in the forest. She never lost her footing as Bongeex once had. He snorted softly.

When they arrived at the tree in the wall they found the three hunters resting in the shade. Several of the fruit bearing trees were nearly empty, but still quite a bit left on several others.

"Moya'se, look. The hunters have been kind to you, they left you fruit."

Pongsok snorted. "We filled our bellies. There was simply too much."

Moya'se hooted softly as she tasted the first of her handful of fruit.

Bongeex chutted. "Looks like she likes it."

"Everyone does," Pongsok said.

"What is this place?" Moya'se asked.

"An old temple," Bongeex said. "Something from thousands of years ago."

"The story in our tribe," Pongsok said, "is that it was built after the Sunfire War. An outpost for research, before they forbid it. Destroyed in an attack, then many generations later, abandoned by the settlers who had claimed it."

"Who were they?" Moya'se flicked her tail. "Where did they go?"

Pongsok chut-chutted. "They were us. They were you. All the green families of the forest here came from this place. Only the Kayax came from somewhere else."

"And Bamthapeem," said the smallest of their group. "The gray and black ones."

Pongsok snorted. "The mountain people don't count, Thefdoy. I'm talking about our valley, the Koy'am."

Bongeex swung his bag around and opened it. "I have some things to share. And you?"

Pongsok's nose moved forward. "Koox? I smell koox."

"Traded for what?"

"Ah." He pointed to Thefdoy. "His pouch-father made us some dathay cakes. And Sopoth and I both have koyo crunches." He tilted his head toward Moya'se. "Does she carry anything?"

Moya'se snorted. "I have dried angthey chews." She held up a handful of the aromatic delight.

The three Ko'dex hunters started hopping from foot to foot.

They all contributed and shared, then sat for a while recounting hunting adventures. Bongeex kept an eye on his sister. She didn't have any stories to tell, but she listened intently. The other hunters seemed to enjoy her attention.

Bongeex told them of his climb to Bamthapeem, and what they found, then of the disappearance of Foondek and Deytham. From a great distance to the south, Bongeex heard a screech that made him stop talking.

The other hunters all looked south at the same time.

Moya'se listened, her quills flicked up and down. "What is that?"

Pongsok chutted quietly. "You are teaching her to hunt, and you haven't taught her the call of the sayox?"

"How close do you think that was?" Bongeex asked.

"Not so close; we are in their territory. Not far enough, though. I think it's a new clan."

"What does that mean?" Moya'se asked.

"Sayox live in small clans," Thefdoy said. "They claim territory with their noises and hunt quietly. Do you know about their colors?"

"Sayox can change how they look," Bongeex said. "Even their glow at night can change. They can cool themselves to blend in with a bush. Very sneaky."

"Why do you call them clans? Animals live in herds," Moya'se said.

Pongsak chutted. "Sayox are smart. Clans. Sometimes, they might even trade."

"If they aren't hungry," Thefdoy said.

Bongeex chutted. "Hard to trade with someone who might eat you."

When the time came to return to the trail, the Ko'dex hunters gave insults to Bongeex, and either ignored or tilted their head at Moya'se. Bongeex huffed. Respect must be earned.

They retraced their steps and picked up several of the smaller game animals. Before long they had a nice haul.

As the two neared a twist in the trail, Bongeex heard the angry growls of a fay'spay. Nasty things. Sharp toothed pack hunters. If one made such noise, several others were silent and close. He waved his hand to tell his sister to crouch and be quiet. She followed his lead as he carefully made his way through the trees to get a better look.

They came to a stand of low trees and undergrowth. Beyond the trees he spotted more of the pack. He suppressed a chut or two when he realized the Ko'dex hunters were hiding in the trees above the pack, and they were being hunted. At least two fay'spay under each tree containing a hunter, with two more wandering the perimeter.

Bongeex gave Moya'se the hand that said to stay back. She responded with an urgent denial. She pointed, then gave the sign that said she intended to attack from her direction, then sprint to another tree and climb. Bongeex understood. When they turned their attention to her, he would have a clear shot at the fay'spay at the other end. He could pick it off. He looked at Pongsok, and gave him the hand signals, telling him what they were doing. He signed back.

Bongeex turned to his sister, and gave her the go hand, then crouched, ready to spring the trap.

Moya'se charged in, remaining remarkably silent. She struck the closest fay'spay with her fist.

Then Bongeex noticed that her fist carried a trap stake. The fay'spay yelped and twisted, running off in fright, leaving a trail of blood. The rest of the pack turned. As one they jumped in the direction of his sister.

Bongeex waited until the last fay'spay was about to pass by, then leapt and stomped its neck. He both heard and felt the snap. A quick look confirmed Moya'se had made the tree, then he saw Pongsok jump into the fray. In short order the survivors had run off after the wounded one. Moya'se hopped down and stood tall among the hunters.

Pongsok snorted at her. "You ran with such a thundering noise you scared the fay'spay into standing still."

Sopoth chutted. "You climbed that tree so slowly they had to stop and wait for you to get out of their way, so they wouldn't have to taste your sour flesh."

Thefdoy huffed. "You ruined my entire plan with your stupid dance."

Bongeex waited. He understood what had happened. But did his sister?

She turned to Bongeex and snorted. "I hadn't been so close

before, but the stench is amazing. No wonder they were after them. They smell like a family of wild omthey."

All of them started chut-chutting.

Pongsok flicked his tail at Moya'se as he turned to leave. "We'll see you again soon, hunters of Botham." He kicked the fay'spay he had killed and continued on without looking back.

Bongeex felt his chest swell with pride. His sister had proven herself to be a hunter.

She looked at him, her quills flicking up and down. "So how do we gut these things?"

THE CITY IN THE SAND

Mas'eeng Masassof, First One, Highest

The smell hit him first. Food, people, animals, and more food. There were spices he couldn't identify and flowers he had never seen. One large bloom smelled of death. The owner offered the ugly brown pods for two coins each and did a brisk business.

The streets ran between walls of stone buildings with shops jutting out at the base. The height of the walls blocked much of the oppressive sunlight, leaving the streets almost cool.

He spotted a familiar fruit arranged at the front of a shop. Something that grew on vines he climbed as an ankle-biter. The pouch-husband in the stall attempted to sell it to a pouch-brother about his age. Dark red with black stripes. He claimed it would cure all ailments, an exotic treat. Daksey chut-chutted.

"Why do you laugh?" asked the merchant. "This fruit comes from a land far away and offers healing to all those who consume it."

"That fruit grows from vines that grow on my house," Daksey said. "It's sweetest when it's purple, but bitter when it turns brown, like what you have."

The shopkeeper's quills rose. He turned to the red and black customer. "Ignore the child. These are the best tasting fruit there is."

"I saw the same fruit down the street," Daksey said. "Nice and purple. They are very good."

"Do they have the same health benefits?" asked the other customer.

Daksey tilted his head. "They are just fruit. If you want medicines, the o'saf leaves, or the koyo nuts are best. At least, from my part of the forest."

"You are from the forest? Where?"

"Koy'am."

The shopkeeper snorted. "You are hurting my business, child. Move along."

"Yes, let us both move along," said the customer, "and you can show me the sweet purple fruit."

"I am Botham Kempok Daksey."

"Call me Amthek."

"Amthek? How did you earn that name?"

"By being unusually clumsy and energetic as a child. With a slow hindbrain, I always had to ask others for help. I had my adult molt last season, so I know how you feel about being called a child. I saw your reaction when he said it."

"I've been getting it a lot recently. I will molt this season. I shouldn't let it bother me." Daksey pointed out where the purple fruit was being sold.

"I see it. Stay here. I'll be right back." Amthek walked in the direction of the stall, appearing to ignore it. As he walked by, the shopkeeper was talking to a customer. Amthek quickly turned his head to the left and leaned forward, as if something caught his interest. When the shopkeeper turned, Amthek grabbed a handful of fruit, and slid them into his pouch. The keeper didn't notice. Amthek continued to walk, then crossed slowly to the other side of the street. Making his way back to Daksey with a calm step. He took out one of the fruits and tossed it to Daksey.

The keeper of the stall saw Daksey holding the fruit, and sounded the alarm, pointing at him. Arms from all directions grabbed him, both arms and his tail.

Daksey's eyes darted left and right. He could feel his heart racing as the large egg-mother approached.

"That fruit is stolen. I'll have you thrown into a cage for this."

There came a scuffle behind Daksey. He glanced over his shoulder. Thoy'eeng had a firm grip on Amthek's arm and was leading him through the crowd.

Daksey let out a quiet hoot.

"I've caught your thief," Thoy'eeng said. "This one you are yelling at did nothing wrong."

"I saw him catch the fruit," said the shopkeeper.

"You saw him catch the blame. This one still has three more."

"I see. Then we shall put that one in a cage. But this one still has one of my fruits."

"I can pay," Daksey said. "I'll pay for all four of them."

"Oh? All four? What about the trouble you've caused?"

"I'm sorry for your trouble. Being yelled at wasn't fun either. I'll pay for five."

She chut-chutted. "Six, and this one goes into the cage."

"Seven, and Amthek stays free."

She snorted. "Done. Pay me."

Daksey sorted through his coins and selected seven small, flattened ovals, dropping them into the outstretched hand of the large shopkeeper.

She clenched her fist and spun around, heading back to her stall.

"That should keep her happy," Thoy'eeng said, "but why did you pay for this one's freedom? He's the cause of your trouble, after all."

"I didn't mean anything by it," Amthek said. "I'm just hungry."

"Then go home. Your pouch-father should still feed you."

Amthek swayed with sadness. "My family is gone. I'm alone."

"How did you come to be alone? All of your family is gone?"

Amthek undulated. "My egg-mother died in the storm with one of my pouch-fathers. The other died of thirst in the desert, before we made it here."

"The storm?"

"I'm from Keyoompax, a fishing village on the north coast on Moyafaf Bay. A great cyclone hit with both storm walls, then many smaller cyclones followed. Our entire village was destroyed. Many were killed. Those that remained knew of this place, knew they would take in refugees. So, we came. Those that survived were let in, but we have to find our own way now."

"So, you steal food?"

"Sometimes. Most of the time I run messages. Clean stables."

"We should get moving," Daksey said. "That shopkeeper keeps glancing our way. She might start trouble again."

Thoy'eeng led them down another path, taking a left, then walking quickly down a side passage. Daksey's nose flared when he smelled the delicious aroma of meat, roasting on an open grill. They rounded the corner to an open plaza with many large tables. He could see by the different colors that people from a variety of tribes sat at the tables. Most kept to their own kind, but some tables were mixed. Thoy'eeng directed them to a table near the back wall where a mixed group feasted.

"Amthek, sit there. Daksey, you too." Thoy'eeng turned toward the open serving window. "Ankadax, I brought you three more mouths to feed. Are you interested?"

"Can they pay?"

"Two of us can."

"And the third?"

Thoy'eeng locked eyes with Amthek. "Willing to clean tables for a meal."

Ankadax strode forward. Her large frame dominated the serving window. "Clean tables? I have plenty doing that. We had a load of refugees from the north."

"That is amazing. This one is also a refugee from the north."

"I'll pay," Daksey said. "How much for his meal?"

Ankadax eyed Amthek. "One dey. Be sure he behaves."

Thoy'eeng chut-chutted.

"Thank you," Amthek said. "You are being very generous."

Daksey's quills flicked up and down. "Eight? Is that eight fongs?"

"No. An eighth of one fong. A dey."

Daksey relaxed. "I see."

"Not used to money?"

Daksey shrugged. "No. We don't use it in our part of the world. Things are more simple."

"That's fine. Just think of it like this, one fong is made up of eight dey. You can cut a dey in half, and you get an apod. One sixteenth of a fong."

"Are there other sizes? Like a fourth?"

Thoy'eeng shrugged. "Not here. In Afothameex they do, but they also have sak, fey, and doy. That's four, eight, and sixteen fong. Not fractions. Bigger money. But be careful. Sometimes they'll call them something like bayfong, and you'll think they mean bay, but they mean four whole fong. If you agree to the price, you could be paying a lot more than you expected."

"That doesn't sound honest."

"That is exactly what I am telling you." Thoy'eeng thumped his tail. "Not everyone is honest."

"I understand that, but how can they have a business and not be honest? Why would they treat a customer like that?"

"Mainly because you wouldn't be a regular customer. Just some forest dweller passing through who doesn't know a bay from a bayfong."

Amthek chut-chutted.

"You bought your friend food, and he laughs at you. Is that how to show gratitude?"

Amthek shrunk.

Daksey chutted. "He's poking fun at us. Be who you are."

Amthek's quills flicked up and down. "Be who I am?"

"Something we say in Botham. You be who you are, and I will be who I am. If it's good, we'll be friends. If it's not, it doesn't matter. We still won't be enemies."

Amthek chutted. "It's a saying of trust. I understand. In my home, we would say, swim with your own tail. It means you make your own way, I'll make my own way. Something like that."

One of the members of Amthek's tribe brought a large serving platter with three bowls on it. Daksey inhaled the savory aroma. "This smells good."

TED AND JAKE

Wednesday, August 14, 3297, 10:10

"I'm not sure what to do," Ted said.

"Why?" Jake asked. "You aren't getting any younger." He tapped a control and brought up a view of the planet onto the main display of MCC. "This seems like the perfect place to start a family."

"I know, but I have no idea how to raise a child."

"No one does, Ted. It's something you learn on the job."

"How did you decide?" Ted asked.

"Me? What makes you think I'm in charge?"

"Didn't you have to turn off your safeties?"

"Malee turned hers off before we even got married," Jake said. "She's always been a lot more certain than me. We talked about it on our wedding night but decided to wait until we were under-way. Then, after a couple jumps in, she brought it up." Jake shrugged. "Best idea ever."

"Oh? How so?"

"The kids. It's like you get to create your own little group of people who love you. They make you laugh and dance and experience a whole new way of life. I love Malee. With all my heart. Our children are an extension of that."

Ted sighed.

"Look, don't take my word for it. Go ask Skip. He'll tell you the same thing."

"I guess I keep hearing the same answers at this point."

"So why are you holding back?"

Ted shook his head. "I don't know. I mean, I've been on plenty of missions, seen lots of action, and it never made me as nervous as I get when I think about trying to raise little humans to be good people."

"What, like you might screw it up?"

"Maybe."

"Seriously, man. It's not an issue. Just the fact that you are worried about it tells me you will be a great father."

TED AND SKIP

Friday, August 16, 3297, 14:12

"I didn't have a great relationship with Nando," Skip said. "Mercorps had me gone a lot. I think he resented it. Malee was all smiles and laughter whenever I came home. And Lenny was so young, he would just crawl all over me. But then their mother died, and it all fell to me. I didn't hesitate. I resigned my commission and went back to the Halo. Became a full-time father. It was hard, at first. But it's been so worthwhile. Even Nando and I have a better relationship now. Malee grew to be strong and independent, and Lenny has the makings of a fine leader. He knows he wants more, and he's brave enough to get it."

"Yeah," Ted said. "But what about this place? How long are you folks going to stay here?"

"Our orders were to establish contact here. We failed, but our backup mission is to establish an observation post if there were intelligent life, and there is. So, *Endurance* is here for the long haul." He waved at the MCC display and brought up a view of the long-abandoned ring structure. "There is so much to learn here."

"Even if you never make friends with the natives?"

Skip shrugged. "It beats going home to be ridiculed for our failure."

"You shouldn't be so hard on yourself, Skip. No one could have predicted what happened."

"You know how people can get. It's all politics and posturing back there. I like it here. I want my grandkids to grow up out here, too. A new branch of humanity."

"A new branch?" Ted asked.

"That might be a bit rich. With those new engines, we'll probably be a big tourist attraction for the rich folks."

Ted laughed. "Yeah, not as many of those left these days."

Skip looked startled. "What?"

"It happened shortly after you guys left. They call it the purge. Most of the corporate owners were killed or at least separated from their ownership when the federation collapsed. Later, the new powers that took over transitioned to the Lunar economic model. That got a bit messy, but eventually the wealth inequality will evaporate, and everyone will get the same share."

"That sounds like a lot of utopian bullshit."

Ted shrugged. "And that's part of why Debra and I left."

"Didn't believe the government line?"

"Not that. We left because the ones who opposed the transition kept targeting Debra. Made the whole thing her fault."

Skip shook his head. "That won't happen here. I won't stand for it."

Ted nodded. "I know. So does she, which is why I think she wants to start a family."

"Ah. That's why you asked. I get it. It's a personal choice, son. But I've seen the two of you together. I think you'll make excellent parents. That is, when you decide to give it a chance."

JUST BRING IT

Mas'eeng Masassof, First Three, Late High

Daksey and Amthek worked at Thoy'eeng's fuel distillery, cleaning tools for him in the vehicle storage building. The job had been given to Amthek, as Daksey was a guest, but he enjoyed the company. The smell of the algae vats reminded him of the swamps back home. The open space was large enough for the four bepthods, but one had been pulled out to the courtyard to give them room to work. On one side the building was attached to an adjacent hall where their living quarters were.

The large door from the hall swung open, filled with an agitated Thoy'eeng. "Daksey. Time to go. Samam has sent word. She will see you now."

"I'm coming." Daksey glanced at his friend. "Can Amthek come?"

"Amthek? Why? He has work to do. That load of fertilizer needs to go out to the farmer. Don't worry, Samam won't send you out of the city without allowing you time to gather your things. Come now. She can be impatient."

Daksey followed Thoy'eeng through the passages then out

onto the narrow street. Soon they entered a door that would have been easy to miss. A back entrance, of sorts. They passed through the cooking areas and into an alcove where water fell like a waterfall, and drained away.

"You smell like fuel. Clean yourself here. Use the scented oil, it will help."

Daksey quickly cleaned himself and slapped some of the oil onto his skin. He wondered if he had smelled bad the last time he had met with Samam. He remembered the time he spent in that tiny room. *I must have become very self-conscious. If she had asked that I be bathed, my aroma must have been powerful.*

"That's enough, child. You'll scrape yourself into adulthood. Here, take this cloth and dry off."

Daksey did as told, then followed Thoy'eeng through the compound to where Samam awaited. She sat in a mound of folded and stuffed cloth. Ample padding for her majestic form. Once again, Daksey was amazed at her beauty.

"He's wet. Did you bathe the poor child just to see me?"

"I thought it best, Samam. I meant nothing by it."

"Perhaps you were a little jealous, Thoy'eeng. He smelled so wonderful. Not like you, with all that petroleum and grease. You smell like your engines."

Thoy'eeng undulated, dropping his head low. "As you say, Samam."

She huffed. "Daksey, step forward." She held out a flat package. "Here are the images. Please take them with you when you leave for Afothameex. They will add to your presentation."

Daksey took the package and undulated as briefly as he could. "Thank you, Samam. I will do as you say. But I'm at a loss. I do not know how to get to Afothameex from here." He glanced at Thoy'eeng. "My previous journey was interrupted."

"I understand. As you will recall, I'm about to banish Thoy'eeng from my city. I have decided that he will be allowed to compensate me by taking you to Afothameex. If he does that, I shall allow him to return."

Daksey tilted his head. "That seems like such a sacrifice. I'm glad he will be able to return home."

"You no longer think ill of him? The bandit who interrupted your journey?"

"I've come to appreciate him for who he is."

Samam chut-chutted. "Then you may understand why I am entrusting your safety to him."

"I do. Thank you." He had a thought. "Samam, as much as I appreciate Thoy'eeng's help, there is another I would like to bring to Afothameex."

Samam waved her hand and rumbled. "Do as you wish, child. Thoy'eeng. How soon will you leave?"

"The trip to Epkodek takes almost a day by bepthod. If we start at dawn, we should reach it in time for the evening meal. We'll stay at the boyok, then proceed up the canyon. It's much slower going along the river, but we should make good time. We'll take to the water above the falls where there aren't any obstructions."

Samam undulated. "Then perhaps you will join me for a late meal tonight."

Thoy'eeng undulated. "I will be sure to have everything prepared today. I will return to you at sundown." He touched Daksey's shoulder, then turned to leave.

Daksey followed. Once they were back in the food making area, Daksey asked, "A meal with her? You must be closer to her than I had thought."

"Sometimes things are best left unsaid. We have work to do before sundown. Then I want you to be sure to see the city tonight. Go find some music and food. You can sleep in the desert tomorrow."

●● ——————— ●●◉●● ——————— ●●

AMTHEK HAD TAKEN Daksey to a tavern near the center of the city. It was well lit, and a band played near one end. The music was lively, but the drummers weren't as good as Deytham and Foondek. He remembered how his older brother had always been tapping things with his sticks. When Kempok gave him his first drum set, he and Bongeex had to run outside, or be treated to another performance. Sitting and watching at that age felt like torture. Even so, he would give anything to watch his brother play again. Foondek too. Together, they were a far better team than these were.

Amthek brought over two tall bowls filled with odd colored juice. "Here is something we had plenty of in the north."

Daksey nodded in gratitude. He took a taste. The burning sensation down his throat felt unusual, but he liked it. A flavor he had never tasted before. Like a mixture of fruit and nuts, with a hint of fish.

"Do you like it?"

Daksey undulated. "What is it?"

"Meng. The one who made it is from my village. Something he is able to do here to make money. It has become very popular."

"I can see why." Daksey hooted softly and took a deeper drink.

"Easy. Meng is intoxicating."

"I recognize the burning sensation. We have a root in our forest that does much the same. You eat two or three of them, and the afternoon is all beauty and shooting stars."

Amthek chut-chutted. "It might be the same root. I wouldn't know. But I like the way you describe it. For me, I think of it as being rolled over and over by a wave that does not drown you. Like you are underwater, but can always breathe."

Daksey chut-chutted and looked into his tall bowl. "I thought I smelled fish in here. Maybe that's why."

One of the workers passed by the table and dropped a basket filled with dried fish onto it.

Amthek nodded his gratitude.

Daksey leaned forward and peered into the basket. "Those look nice. Can I have one?"

Amthek chut-chutted. "They are for us to share. From the one I told you about. He's helped me in the past. Seems happy to see me. There are a lot of familiar faces here, and a lot of faces not from the north. I think he will do well." He reached in and took one of the dried fish, offering it to Daksey. "Have a taste."

Daksey took the fish and bit into it. It tasted of the sea, of fish, and of a spicy mixture that made his tongue tingle. It felt strange, but good. "I like it. What is that spice?"

"Feemos. It's something from the west, I think. This place has people from all directions. They mix their food together, and come up with something new. We had dried fish all my life, but I never loved it like I do this. Maybe we were meant to be here. Maybe..." His voice trailed off. "Maybe it's just the meng."

Daksey undulated. "Nothing is ever worth losing those you love. That doesn't mean you can never find happiness again."

Amthek looked away and took a deep breath. "I miss my pouch-brothers. My egg-mother, my pouch-fathers. I miss my friends."

Daksey reached out and put his hand on Amthek's shoulder. "Never forget the friends you've lost. And always remember that you will find new friends in the future. Even now, you have found me."

Amthek put his hand on Daksey's and nodded. "Thank you. I was going to leave you to rot in a cage, and yet here you are, being nothing but kind and generous to me." He turned and locked eyes with Daksey. "I won't make that mistake again. I see who you are, Daksey. You are a true friend to me. I will try very hard to be a true friend to you."

Daksey could feel the room turn ever so slightly. He felt the warmth in his chest. He wasn't sure if it was the deepening friendship he found with Amthek, or the strange juice he had been drinking. Either way, he enjoyed it.

The music caught Daksey's attention as they started to play a familiar tune. Daksey couldn't remember what they called it, but he remembered Deytham breaking a drumstick while playing it. He moved to the music and soon found himself dancing with Amthek in a crowd. The heat and the bodies and the intoxicating drink mixed together in a swirl.

Daksey awoke with a start. His mouth tasted rotten. His arm, numb. Something lay on top of it. He turned to find Amthek sprawled at his side, sleeping on his arm. The pounding at the door brought him awake. "I'm awake."

"Get up and get ready," Thoy'eeng said. "It's time to leave."

"Coming."

"Is Amthek in there with you? He isn't in his room."

"Yes, he is. I think he's still alive." He gave Amthek a shove.

"Ack," Amthek said.

"The two of you shouldn't be slow this morning. Grab what you packed yesterday. You can go back to sleep on the way."

Daksey pulled his arm out from under Amthek.

"Oh. I slept on it? Wait. This isn't my room."

Daksey chut-chutted. "I don't remember how we got here, either."

Amthek sat up and shook his head. "Yuck. My mouth tastes like week old fish left too damp."

Daksey stretched, then reached for his bag. "Let's go get your bag. Thoy'eeng sounds as if he wants to be gone."

"He always sounds that way. But I get your meaning." He stood and cried out in pain.

"What happened?"

"Nothing. Just a stiff tail muscle. I must have slept strangely." He stretched his tail.

They went to Amthek's room and gathered his bag, then headed to the workshop. Thoy'eeng waited there with Osmay and Maysam.

Osmay snorted. "Why are we bringing the northerner?"

"He is traveling with Daksey. Unless one of you would like to climb the stairs to Fengpax."

"No. That is fine. We can tolerate him. Maysam and I will enjoy the city's attractions."

"You and Maysam will wait under the waterfall with the bepthod. They don't allow vehicles like this in their precious city. Too much dust on their streets. I'm concerned that someone might claim it as abandoned and take it."

Osmay snorted again. "This trip keeps improving every time we talk about it."

"Then talk less, dear brother. And stop expecting great rewards at every turn."

"If it's time in the city you want, I will be sure to give you time, but I will do it by being there to watch the bepthod myself, after I've sent these two on their way."

Packing went quickly and soon they were off. The clean swept street they used allowed them to glide by without much of a storm. After a few turns they passed through the city walls at a large gate and headed out onto the open. Thoy'eeng drove slowly past the fields, keeping the dust low, then let the engine roar into life once they hit the open plains. Daksey had intended to stay awake and enjoy the ride, but soon Amthek shook him awake. The sun was setting and there were low level shrubs and greenery everywhere.

"We are nearing Epkodek."

"I slept the whole day?"

Amthek chut-chutted. "You did."

"I'm sorry. I didn't mean to."

"Don't apologize to him," Thoy'eeng said. "I just woke him up. First thing he did was wake you. You both slept all day."

Daksey and Amthek chut-chutted together.

"Now pay attention to this area," Thoy'eeng said, "Keep an eye out for bandits. They don't usually bother me here, but I would rather be safe than be caught by surprise."

"Are we going to Soypasod from here?"

"Soypasod? No. Too far south. We'll head up to Afothameex, next."

Daksey sat back. "I was supposed to visit someone in Soypasod. Someone who would make my journey to the observatory shorter."

"We took you much further to the north. It's quicker to go through the canyon."

Epkodek, an open village, had no walls, and no paved streets. Thoy'eeng brought the vehicle to a stop near a large wooden structure at the edge of town.

"This is where we'll spend the night. Don't go wandering into town. They don't like strangers." He turned to Maysam and Osmay who were wrapping their heads in colorful cloth. "Don't be too late. The canyon isn't far and it's a dangerous road."

Maysam undulated and turned to leave.

Amthek snorted. "Why do they get to go?"

Osmay chut-chutted. He flung the loose end of the head cloth over his shoulder. "Because we are not strangers."

THE MEMORIAL GARDEN

Saturday, August 17, 3297, 18:32

Skip had been very clear. Everyone should come by the park at some time during the two-hour window. With ample food being served, and being held during a watch turnover, in theory, everyone could come and pay their respects. So here he stood, drink in one hand, tiny plate of nibbles in the other, wishing he had a third hand.

Maksim didn't realize at first. The sudden realization that the statue of Yelena Shestakova stood in front of him caught him off guard. He had thought she was on the other side of the garden. He had meant to steer clear. His heart sank into a void of despair, exactly what he didn't want to experience. He stepped forward, then stood there, unable to move forward.

So beautiful. At this distance, almost exactly the right height. He closed his eyes and took a deep breath. When he opened them he got another surprise. Just off to the left, Foondek stood looking at him. The creature looked at the statue, then back at Maksim, and walked toward him. Maksim froze.

When Foondek came near, it reached out a hand and took his, pulling gently. Maksim followed, not sure what was about to happen. They rounded a tall shrub, revealing a statue of a creature like Foondek.

Foondek pointed at it. "Deytham."

Maksim was bewildered.

Foondek spoke in his language while AutoGov provided the audio translation in real-time. "You look at that one, I can feel your sadness. I feel it when I look at this one. This is Deytham."

"I am sorry for your loss."

"I am sorry for your loss. She was at Bamthapeem, yes?"

Maksim nodded.

"Bamthapeem is a very old culture. They have traditions most others would never approve of. I am Botham. We are a different people with different traditions."

"Are you saying your people would not have killed them?"

"I'm not sure why they were killed. I will say when I know. We would not have done what followed. I think it must be very diffi-cult for you. I think you see me as one of them."

"I,...maybe. I don't know."

"You all look alike to me as well," Foondek said. "Except when I see you, I always see your anger. I wanted to say, now I see your pain. I understand where it comes from."

Maksim could feel his eyes welling up with tears. He didn't know what to say.

Foondek turned and started walking away. He stopped and looked back at Maksim over his shoulder. "I don't know if you would be friends. Small hope for me. I love to work in a garden. It smells of home." He turned and ambled down the path.

Maksim felt a tumble of emotions. Grief, confusion, and perhaps compassion. He shook his head. "What a weird day this is, Yelena."

UPLIFT

Monday, August 19, 3297, 8:30

Maxsim met Foondek in the big agricultural lab. This time, he decided to try talking.

"Hello Foondek."

Foondek locked eyes with him, then hooted softly. "Maksim Shestakova, do you wish me to leave?"

Maksim shook his head. "No. Stay. I think, perhaps, I should talk to you. I think it's what Yelena would have wanted."

Foondek undulated. "You have done well here. Many plants are growing nicely. It smells like home. Do you intend to bring animals here as well?"

"Perhaps. We don't really have the space for it, yet. Maybe when we build the second ring."

"Second ring?"

"Yes," Maksim said. "Joined in a framework to this ring, but counter rotating." He spun his fingers in the air to demonstrate.

"For stability?"

Maksim smiled. "Yes, that's right. And to support the full crew as it expands. From there, we can extend both drums lengthwise, and make them into two cylinders. That is, if we decide to stay."

"If you decide to stay?"

Maksim shrugged. "Our contact attempts were more costly than we had anticipated. A lot of people want to give up and go home once the new engines are in place."

"And what do you want, Maksim Shestakova?"

Maksim felt that emptiness in his heart again. "I want us to complete the mission Yelena died for. To make contact with your people."

"Perhaps I can help. If I could find what went wrong, I could help you avoid the same mistake."

"I think I can do that. But, if you don't mind. There are parts I would rather not see again."

"See? You have images?"

"Moving images. I'll arrange for you to watch everything."

"You have so many useful things here. We are taught that it is wrong to capture the lightning. Electricity is forbidden."

"Forbidden?"

Foondek undulated. "The egg-mothers know more, and there are old books containing the stories. I only remember it is forbidden."

"But you are okay using it here?"

"I do not have a choice. And even if I did, I think it might be more important to learn about you. To know who you are."

Maksim sighed. "Good luck with that. We're still trying to find out for ourselves."

Foondek chut-chutted. "A very good answer, Maksim Shestakova."

"Just Maksim. You don't need to say Shestakova every time."

"Does this mean we are friends now, Maksim?"

Maksim stared into Foondek's eyes. Tears came to his eyes. "Perhaps in time, Foondek. For now, we are not enemies. That I know for certain."

FOONDEK HAD MASTERED the controls of the video feed quickly. It zoomed and panned. He watched the humans near the second town they had attempted contact with. A stand of trees, then some fields, before a vast forest.

"I believe the people of Beethax have a beast problem in their forest. See here? This is a place where sayox nest. It's large, like you might expect for a family, or small clan."

"Clan implies intelligence. You mean a small herd, perhaps?"

"No, they are not quite animals. They have clans and use tools. This structure has two levels."

"Not quite animals?"

Foondek undulated. "Long ago, lesser animals were altered, made more intelligent. Something common in those days. Sayox are like that. I think the villagers might fear them, and so they would respond to the alarm of their children. With weapons. Such as you saw."

"And if you have weapons in hand..."

Foondek turned to Maksim. "Did your people do this on your world?"

"There were two attempts back on Earth to improve the intelligence of animals. The first were the chimpanzees." He brought up images of a troop of chimps. "An entire tribe bred with what we thought to be better intelligence."

"I'm not sure I understand. You make it sound as if you were wrong. Did you make a mistake?"

"Yes. What we ended up with were a bunch of cunning xenophobic murderers. They broke free of their compound, stalked and killed dozens of people before they were finally wiped out."

"Wiped out?" Foondek's quills flicked back and forth. "They were destroyed? Couldn't you have rounded them up?"

"They had broken into an armory. You would be surprised

how easy it is to learn to use a gun. They had been watching the guards target practice for months before they made their break."

"And the second?"

"Dolphins," Maksim said. "An aquatic animal. No hands. They thought it would be harmless enough."

"What happened there? The same?"

"No, quite different. They studied. Learned our legal system. Eventually they sued for the right to be recognized under law as citizens, with the rights and privileges that humans had."

"How is that bad?" Foondek flicked his tail.

"After winning, they turned around and sued several of the largest corporations for polluting the oceans. Won that too."

"I see. Again, I am not seeing something bad."

"Not saying it was," Maksim said, "but the corporation that had bred them had made sure the genes that made them more intelligent were not dominant."

"What does that mean?"

"Within two generations they were back to what they had been before. Their citizenship claim was challenged and revoked, and the corporations quietly resumed dumping their crap into the oceans."

"Do you consider us to be an inferior animal species?" Foondek locked eyes with Maksim. "Are you going to attempt to improve us?"

"First of all, no, we do not consider you to be inferior or an animal species. You are intelligent beings, and you had a techno-logical civilization that was thousands of years advanced of ours."

"And you see us now, as not advanced?"

He hesitated. "We want to understand. Your people built bases on both of your moons, and that incomplete ring structure rivals anything we've built, even today. What happened?"

"We study our ancient history. I don't remember anything about the ring, but it is said for a time, we lived on both moons. Then Dapkasamok came, and we celebrated with joy. We knew that among the stars, we were not alone. Then they left. As suddenly as they had arrived, they went away."

"Do you know why?"

"There are things written in the books," Foondek said. "I apologize for not being a better student. I only know that *Axdayek* soon followed."

AutoGov interrupted him, and they exchanged a few words.

"Sunfire War," Foondek said through the translator. "Is that better? The world burned. Cities melted into the sand. Poison spread upon the ground that will last a very long time. The place we live, *Thoxmoyang*, the least damaged. People from all around the world gathered, and began again. Scholars adapted us to better survive the poisons. Like your own efforts to improve those animals. Our ancestors created us from themselves. Then, sometime later, came the chosen ones. Our religion that included a deep hatred of captured lightning. We study it. We know it happened and why. We still have a deep hatred, even a fear, of electricity."

"Does it make you uncomfortable, now?"

"I was uncomfortable in the shuttle. I feel as if I died, and now I'm someone new. It doesn't bother me the way it did. I don't know if that is a good thing."

"I think it is. You've been very helpful to us. We understand your people now, in a way we couldn't have without you."

"Yes. You've learned much. What will you do with that knowledge?"

He furled his eyebrows. "Do with it? I'm not sure. We came to meet you. To find others like ourselves. This isn't what we hoped for, but I feel as if our people can be friends. Maybe we can work together to find out what happened four thousand years ago. Where did the Dapkasomak go? Why did they never return?"

"When I learned those stories, part of my mind thought it wasn't real. Some invented fantasy to teach us life lessons. Now that I know it happened, it scares me a little."

"Scares you?"

Foondek undulated, then carefully nodded his head. "Four thousand years ago, they walked among the stars. They knew your people and ours. Yet they went away and never returned. My fear is that the reason may threaten us all, if we go looking for it. Like the *sesom* slumbering in the shallow water, if you poke it with a stick, only the stick will survive."

UP THE CANYON

Mas'eeng Masassof, First Five, Early High

The canyon looked more dangerous than Daksey had imagined. The road they had been following narrowed, pushing the edge of their vehicle too close to the edge for Daksey's comfort. He understood that for the bepthod to work, the air cushion must be preserved.

Amthek gasped. He grabbed Daksey's shoulder and pointed down into the canyon. What had once been a massive dam that held back an immense amount of water had long ago split apart. The gap in the center, a jagged tear. At the bottom, a much wider arch had formed as the water had worn away the edges of the dam over millennia. Still, the narrowing of the river and the scattered debris made the waters there formidable. Along the shore on the other side of the river were rectangular heaps that resembled large, buried buildings. As they passed beyond the broken dam, Daksey couldn't help but be overwhelmed at the size.

"Here we go," Thoy'eeng said, "Everyone hang on."

The bepthod lurched over the edge and down the steep embankment. Daksey felt his heart bump up and down between his stomachs. He gripped his seat tightly. The front of the bepthod thundered into the water and bounced upward. Water splashed over the top as the bepthod took off over the surface. Thoy'eeng turned south, to move them upriver.

The ride smoothed out over the water. They passed the occasional cluster of houses and a few people fishing with nets along the way. Thoy'eeng made sure to slow down whenever they spotted someone in the water, which always brought a snort of derision from Osmay.

THE END of their journey came when they reached a wide lake. At the western side water cascaded down a wide series of waterfalls from the sheer side of a mountain. The water seemed to emerge from the cliff itself. A carved structure above the water hinted at another source for the flow. Billows of steam rose from above.

"The Steamworks." Thoy'eeng pointed to a large round building built into the cliff face. "It supplies the steam for the city, as well as hydraulic power. Keeping those pressure lines going to turn machinery and keep the city functioning. Head for the left side of the falls, then angle in behind. You'll see. Plenty of room back there."

As they rounded the base of the falls a building could be seen with several other ships moored to a dock.

"Someone has claimed our mooring," Osmay said.

"What does that mean?" Amthek asked.

"I don't know yet," Thoy'eeng said, "Let me do the talking."

An older pouch-husband walked out onto the nearest dock and greeted them. "Thoy'eeng, is that you?"

"Ah. Kepthey. What have you done to our private little beach?"

"I built a business. City people love to come see the lake. This spot behind the waterfall is beautiful, you know."

"I need to leave my bepthod somewhere safe."

Kepthey snorted. "It's been a while since I let anyone stay for free, old friend."

"Has it been that long? And you've been charging a fee all this time?"

"Indeed."

"Is your charity so out of practice? Maybe you need to try again. Just to be sure you are still able."

Kepthey huffed. "That is not what I was aiming for."

"I understood that from the start. I don't mean to make you uncomfortable. If you are incapable of remaining friends, I'll find another place where we are welcome."

"That's not what I meant at all. I am quite capable of still being your friend."

"Excellent. Where should we park?"

Kepthey's quills flicked up and down. "Just pull it in behind the building."

"I see. And what would that service cost me?"

"Cost? Ah yes. Well, I could use some of that delightful beverage I know you are carrying. Would one cask be too much to ask for?"

Thoy'eeng huffed. "Fine. But I don't know how long we'll be. Could be a day, could be a few full counts."

"No worries. Take the time you need. For two casks, I'll keep it safe as long as you need."

Thoy'eeng huffed again with a hint of a rumble from his throat.

HIGH PROTEIN

Tuesday, August 27, 3297, 13:00

Maksim entered the conference room next to MCC and bobbed his head in silent greeting. He took a seat next to Anna. From here he had a clear view of the slowly rotating stars outside.

"Start recording," Jake said. "In attendance today, in addition to myself, we have Gadzhimurat Kamalov, our lead Archeologist. Maksim Borodin–"

"Shestakova," Maksim said.

"Sorry, yes, Maksim Shestakova, our Agriculturalist. Anna Ruggiero, our Lead Biologist and chief liaison to Foondek, and Cheri Allen, our Lead Linguist. Maksim, how are things going in the native garden?"

Maksim cleared his throat. "We've had an interesting development, and come to a rather interesting conclusion. Initially we were doing our best to keep some ant-like creatures from devouring one of the fruit trees we've been growing. The pests kept appearing from nowhere. We call them 'almost ants.' The tree bears two slightly different kinds of fruit." He displayed a small fruit. "These little bumpy ones, the large and very fleshy fruit. We had gotten so far as to realize the almost ants were emerging from the bumpy ones. Every time we opened one up, we found it infected. We thought they were a pest, so we clipped them, and tossed them into a different terrarium so that we might study them."

"Any luck?" Cheri asked.

"Not then. The almost ants wandered around, biting anything in their path, then died very quickly. The fruit would stay for a few days, then drop. No seeds. No new plants. I had no clue."

"What happened?"

"Foondek happened," Maksim said. "By making a little pile of the larger fruit, and putting the almost ants on top of it, then poking little holes all around the pile, Foondek demonstrated what we had entirely missed. The almost ants and the fruit tree are the same biological entity."

"Say what?" Jake's eyebrows rose high.

"The almost ants devoured the plump fruit, then ran to the nearest unoccupied holes and buried themselves. As far as we can tell, the transformation begins at once. Within a week we had twenty new plants a yard tall. We've confirmed that the almost ants are seeds with legs. It's a plant with an insect stage."

"Legs, brains, and they eat?"

"Eat, yes, but they consume only one meal, and use it to transform themselves into a seedling. So, no digestive system. Not a lot of brains, either. Which is why they will bite anything they come into contact with."

"So Foondek has been helpful?" Jake asked.

"Yes. As a matter of fact, he has taken to working in the garden. We are learning quite a bit. It also helps the food situation, as both fruits are edible for him. One for carbs, the other for protein."

"Wait, he eats the almost ants?" Cheri asked.

Maksim shrugged. "With apparent glee. When I questioned

him, he lifted one up and said, 'high protein.' Seemed rather proud of it."

Jake turned his attention to the linguist. "Cheri, what sort of progress are you making?"

"I think I've finally worked out how their numbers work," she said.

"Why was it so difficult? You have examples from the bases and a living specimen. Last I heard, the translator could handle most of their spoken language."

"Yes, but in order to translate numbers, you have to know all the ins and outs. The examples we found on those bases were very old. The way they were written made us think they were using octal. See here, this second set is similar to the first seven, but with this curved line here. It's the same for almost all the rest up to fifteen. But then we started finding these. This second set acts in a math-like way, but it's odd."

"How so?" Jake asked.

"They never double up. Take this one, it means sixteen. But you don't see two of them, instead you see this. That's thirty-two. And here's sixty-four."

"Good grief," Anna said. "How did they ever do math?"

"That was a point of contention. Eventually, with Foondek's help, we realized that there are two ways of doing numbers. The traditional way, and what Foondek calls simple numbers. Simple only uses the first set of eight characters. Zero to seven. Part of their dates are written in traditional numbers, specifically, the year. Traditional is full on hexadecimal."

Jake leaned back. "We have dates?"

"Yes and no. We have the dates of things like when they met those other aliens, that's on the base. But Foondek doesn't have a clue what year it is now. She says that's a thing scholars know."

"Still. Doesn't seem all that complicated."

"Two things. One, they don't write the numbers quite like they used to. There has been some drift over the millennia. Second, our friend Foondek has horrible handwriting."

"You guys keep referring to Foondek as male," Jake said. "When did that change?"

"I meant to tell you," Anna said, "we learned more about their genders. We kept thinking of Foondek as female because of the pouch and what we think of as the uterus we discovered in the other. Then we found the egg. We assumed that the uterus would somehow produce an egg. Closed case."

"What did you learn?" Jake asked.

"Foondek has told us that he and the other one are not egg layers. They do not produce the eggs. There is a physically larger gender that does that. So that one is definitely our female. What we didn't get was the sperm producer. See, that's not this guy either."

"They have three genders?" Cheri asked.

"That's what I thought at first, and I'm going to have to say the jury is out on that one."

"What do you mean?" Jake asked.

"Foondek," Anna said, "is also kind of a female."

Jake's eyebrows shot up again. "He lays eggs?"

"Nope. Live birth."

"Wait–"

Anna shook her head. "No, no, not a live born Ombax. Not exactly. Here, look at this."

"What the crap is that?" Cheri asked.

"That is what Foondek grows internally in that uterus-like structure, and then basically gives birth to. In a way."

"Not following you," Jake said. "In a way?"

"The egg layer has a sexual appendage that enters him and... sucks it out."

"Enters?"

"That's correct," Anna said. "Near as I can get from him, the egglayers have an appendage that enters him through his cloaca and removes this little guy. That thing is pretty much a little tentacled testicle. I dissected a dead one. Less brain than a snail. Apparently the egglayer stores it internally. Foondek is a little confused on that part. Says it's an egglayer thing and I should ask one of them about it. He seemed a bit embarrassed, actually."

"How did you manage to get one?" Cheri asked.

"We found one inside Deytham," Anna said. "We thought it might be a pregnancy."

Cheri shook her head. "Now that's some strange biology."

"Yeah, but there's a twist that I also managed to get from him. See, an egglayer stores a number of these internally. They become a permanent part of her. But, if she's not interested enough for a permanent relationship, she can direct the little fellow down another route to one of her stomachs. Foondek says he would never know. What comes out of him is taken by the egg layer, embedded inside her body where they become parasites. Foondek says the older the female, the more she can hold. She uses them to occasionally fertilize an egg, which she then gives to one of her pouch-husbands."

"She can hold many?" Jake asked. "Does that mean the male genetics might come from outside the group?"

"Foondek says that's the way it's supposed to be. Some males wander and are 'polite' to a female in exchange for food and lodging. The marriage group is more about producing and tending to the offspring."

"And one female has multiple husbands," Cheri said.

Anna nodded. "Foondek says that by his tribe's tradition, one female usually has two or three husbands. But he says it's different in bigger cities."

"How so?"

"He didn't say. I think it makes him uncomfortable. Maybe a social taboo."

Cheri smirked. "I'm wondering if it's more, or less."

"You would prefer they were monogamous?" Jake asked.

"At least it would be familiar."

"Monogamy," Anna said, "is based on the premise that a dedicated male mate will be the one producing the offspring. These people don't even think that way. They mix the genes up willy-nilly. You get a better variety, I'll bet. The rest is just family grouping for the sake of having a family. A work group to raise children, if you will."

"If they mix their genes," Jake said, "why have we observed the same coloration grouped by location?"

"Ah, there's the rub. Those traits all come from the mother. Skin color, stripes, even the quills. The males appear to donate more to the internal characteristics."

"So these aren't fifty-fifty splits like ours?" Jake asked.

"Still working that out. We don't know how their eggs work and who knows what goes on inside the female. There's one clue that we got from Foondek. The female can control the internal body temperature of her egg sack, and that's how the gender gets set. She holds the egg through the temperature-sensitive period."

"So she chooses to lay a female or a male?" Cheri asked.

Anna nodded. "Foondek said that his village has sixteen breeding age females. He has a little sister, and there is a very old female in his village she will replace. When the young one comes of age, the older female will expel all of her testicle parasites and stop producing fertilized eggs."

"Population control," Jake said.

"That's why they haven't overrun their landmass," Anna said.

"They've eliminated the pressure to grow and expand," Cheri said.

"The egglayers are in total control of reproduction, then?" Jake asked.

"It would seem so," Anna said. "They decide when they will fertilize an egg, and then they present the egg to one of Foondek's gender for nurturing, hatching and raising. It's a long-term commitment."

"That can't have evolved naturally, can it?" Jake asked.

"Hard to say," Anna said. "I don't see why it couldn't. A female could produce a large number of new females from her repository of parasites and replenish a whole village in a generation with the help of very few males. Moreover, they would all look like her, and have an immediate affinity, regardless as to the origin of the male genetic material."

"I would love to know what else happens inside an egglayer," Cheri said.

"Perhaps we can task a few drones to the study," Maksim said.

"AutoGov," Jake said, "new task for the drones. Mid-priority, as the opportunity presents itself, study the larger gender of the species, the egg layers, for indications of their internal mechanism."

"Acknowledged," AutoGov said.

"Are we going to settle on calling Foondek a male?" Jake asked.

"Worried about the pronouns?" Anna asked.

"I don't want to cause offense. Doesn't it affect the translation?"

"Actually," Anna said, "the translations for both sides were technically reversed. I've already adjusted AutoGov's translation matrix to account for it."

"Good. Anything else? Maksim?"

Maksim shook his head. "All I haven't mentioned is that I am growing extra plants, and feeding Foondek."

"Are you okay with that?" Anna asked. "I still remember your first reaction to him."

Maksim shrugged. "I'm better now. And Foondek... is a good person."

"Wonderful. If that's all, then thank you everyone. I'll give you back your time." Jake stood and strode out the door.

Maksim took a deep breath. *Time to get back to work.*

DEFROSTED DISTRACTION

Wednesday, August 28, 3297, 8:00

Radinka appeared at her seat in the private back room of the fictional tavern. She nodded at Briana and turned her attention to Ferdinand. His large, pointed hat perched atop his head. "Good work on the security filters. Talking like idiots was annoying."

"We should still take care not to alert the system. But yes. I do good work."

"Where do we stand on gaining access?"

Ferdinand shook his head. "Making some progress. The *Endurance* has disconnected and physically removed its external secured network antenna normally used for updates, however I found a copy of the encryption algorithm."

"Can we insert a packet internally?"

"No. The trace program would filter us out quickly. Might even raise alarms."

"How did they get the update from *Pang Yu*?" Briana asked.

"Direct authorized link. Hard wire. And there is something that might work. *Pang Yu*'s antenna is still in place, but I can't tell if it's turned off or unplugged. If we can get aboard, we might be able to bypass the monitor and reactivate it without being noticed. We could broadcast an update, a minor upgrade, if you will. It would be processed aboard the ship, but since they are still connected, *Endurance* would get it too, from a legal source."

Radinka sat back. "So, the question is–"

A loud scream from the tavern interrupted them.

Radinka scowled at the wizard. "Your program is getting distracting."

Ferdinand waved his hands and consulted a glowing scroll. "The characters are reacting to a new player. He's tearing the place apart. Wait... damn. He's one of us. As a troll."

"Why didn't he follow protocol?" Radinka swiped her display and opened a scene of the tavern. A large brutish creature tossed patrons about like rag dolls. "Clear the room. Lock the doors."

Ferdinand adjusted controls and the simulated victims evaporated, leaving the troll standing along amid the carnage of broken furniture.

Radinka leaned forward and spoke into her display. "Why are you bothering with this stupid game? We have business to discuss."

The troll grinned and chuckled deeply. "I like my cover not to be blown. But if you insist, where is the damned door?"

"Walk to the left of the stack of firewood, then look behind it." She turned to Ferdinand. "When he enters the room, reset the Tavern back to the defaults."

Ferdinand shook his head. "Idiot."

The troll squeezed his bulk through the door and sat on the floor next to the table. His wide face punctuated by a broad flat nose that sat a little too high. Pale blue eyes peering out from under a heavy brow. The creature's gray-green skin looked stiff and thick, like mossy stone, barely flexible. The ill-fitting loin cloth kept threatening to come loose.

Briana wrinkled her nose. "Why did you pick such a repulsive avatar?"

"And who are you?" Ferdinand asked.

Radinka held up a hand. "Character name only. Then give us a general idea of your role."

"Ha," said the troll. "Hammerfist. I break things. What are you supposed to be?"

Radinka smirked. "Pirate Captain, and you have joined my crew."

"Did I, now? I seem to recall seeing that my friend didn't make the journey."

"I'm a last minute replacement. From the top. Which, in here, we refer to as the King."

The brute nodded slowly. "And they murdered the King. That much I saw. So, who do we kill in revenge, and how can I do damage?"

Radinka sighed. "We have a few ideas. Just to be clear, no unauthorized actions. Do you understand?"

Hammerfist's lips pulled back into a grotesque grin. "Sure boss. No problem."

SHOULD HAVE GONE TO SOYPASOD

Mas'eeng Masassof, Second Four, Early

Thoy'eeng paced from one corner of the rented room to the opposite, then back again. With their bedding all packed away, there was space for them to sit and talk. Thoy'eeng strode back and forth in the gap. "It's been a full count, and they still haven't said when you will be able to state your case."

Daksey sighed. "I think this is what they warned me about in Beethax."

"Warned?"

"Yes. I have a letter to someone in Soypasod. I was to show her the skulls and the images and give her the letter. They said she would help me."

Thoy'eeng huffed. "It shouldn't be this difficult. They've refused to even talk to you."

"We should go home," Osmay said. "Leave him here to wait as long as it takes."

"Have patience, brother," Maysam said.

"You have patience. I'm tired of patience. I'm running out of money. What happens when we all run out of money?"

Thoy'eeng glared at Osmay, then glanced at Daksey. "I promised Samam that I would be sure he reached the observatory. I shall keep my word. I made no such promise on your behalf. Leave if you wish. Walk back to Seeng'dod. The choice is yours."

Osmay cringed.

"I'll go again and see if I can talk to the gatekeepers. Maysam, come with me. The rest of you stay here and wait."

Daksey huffed. "Shouldn't I come?"

"If they agree to speak with you, I'll send Maysam to get you. Otherwise, find something more constructive to do."

After Thoy'eeng and Maysam had left, Amthek turned to Daksey. "What do you think he meant by more constructive?"

Osmay chut-chutted. "He means that this has taken much longer than he planned for, we are running out of money. We should find work."

"Work?" Amthek's nostrils flared. "I only know fishing."

"You are half decent at stealing," Daksey said.

Amthek tilted his head. "I would be better with a decent partner."

Osmay shrugged. "We should not risk their prison."

"Let's go for a walk through the city," Daksey said. "See what we can find."

"You two go. I'm going to rest."

Amthek chut-chutted. "You and Maysam stay out too late. How much does that cost?"

Osmay grabbed a large pillow and threw it at Amthek. "Go, before I throw a table."

Amthek and Daksey ran into the street, chut-chutting. Osmay slammed the large door behind them.

"Come on," Amthek said. "The center of the city is this way. I have an idea."

Daksey followed Amthek through the wide streets. The houses were spread out with ample green surrounding them. Trees and shrubbery, neatly tended, decorated many of them. He noticed that while many were made of brick, the occasional wooden home made an appearance. Those reminded him of home.

When they came to the central square, Amthek stopped and started searching for something.

"What are you looking for?"

"In Seeng'dod I once found a place near the middle of the lower enclosure where people would post notices of work they needed done." He pointed. "There. Come with me."

They approached a statue with a metal worker, a wood-worker, a weaver, and... Daksey wasn't sure what that last one depicted. It had some sort of container hooked into curled tubes.

"Here, see? On the wall at the base."

Beneath the statues were hundreds of bits of ofmay with notes written on them. Some were very hard to read, while others looked as if they had been typeset and printed with a machine.

"Look, here is one we can do." Amthek pointed to a note that asked for someone to clean a house.

Daksey snorted. "Cleaning someone else's mess? I had to do that with my brother and little sister."

Amthek chut-chutted. "We can do it in half a day. Let's try it and see. If you don't like it, we can try something else."

Daksey undulated hesitantly. "So, what do we do?"

Amthek grabbed the note and turned it over. "See, there is a street and a description of the house on the back. Boothos Path, blue brick house with a white door."

"How do we find Boothos Path?"

Amthek sat back. "Oh. Right. Seeng'dod was all grids and walls. Easy to find. This is very different."

Daksey took a deep breath and closed his eyes. When he opened them, he started looking around. Off to his left he spotted a store with a pile of old books in the window.

"Follow me." He led the way to the shop and peered inside. "Hello?"

"Right here," said the old pouch-husband. "No need to shout."

"I'm sorry. I didn't think I was being loud."

"Hush now, calm down, child."

Daksey tried very hard to keep his voice low. "Is this better?"

"Now that is much better. What kind of story would you like to read?"

"We don't need a story, we are new to the city, and we don't know the streets. We need to know how to get from one place to another."

"You need a map."

Daksey undulated. "Yes. A map."

"I have one right over here. Six fong and a quarter, each."

Daksey choked. "Six fong?"

The old pouch-husband chut-chutted. "Let me guess, you were sent into town with no money."

Amthek held out the job note. "We need to find this place. Boothos path."

The old shopkeeper looked at the note, then back at the young ones. "I see. So, you don't have six fong."

"That's why we are going to go clean someone's house."

"I will strike you a bargain. I'll let you borrow a map. You use it to find your way today. Then you bring it back."

"And in return?"

"In return, when you can afford it, you buy a copy for yourselves."

Daksey nodded in gratitude. "Thank you... What do we call you?"

"People call me De'pey." He shrugged and waved at the books. "No idea why."

"I am Daksey, this is Amthek."

"Amthek? And I thought being called after books was bad. Who gave you that name?"

Amthek chut-chutted. "Everyone. I earned it."

"As did I. I look forward to seeing you again. Tonight then?"

Daksey paused. "We don't know how long it will take. If not tonight, then tomorrow morning."

De'pey undulated. "Good enough. I wish you luck."

They used the map to find the proper path, and soon found the blue house, but the door, while it might have once been white, stood in dire need of new paint. The wood beneath had long since greyed, and the few flecks of paint left were their only clue.

Daksey stepped forward and pounded on the door. The two waited. Nothing happened. Daksey pounded again.

A voice from inside said something that couldn't be made out. They waited.

The door finally opened and an old, tan pouch-husband with white stripes looked up at them. "What do you want?"

Amthek held out the note. "We would like this job, please."

The little pouch-husband chut-chutted. "Fine. On the other side of the street. The one that is stone and wood with the cracked door. It's empty of furniture, but needs to be cleaned. Do you have your own tools?"

Daksey shrugged. "We've never done this before."

The tiny one undulated then turned and went inside. "Follow me."

He led them through a spacious living area. In one corner, Daksey saw what he thought to be a tremendous mound of blankets. Then he noticed it stir.

"Who is it, Odfay?" asked the pile of blankets.

"Two younglings come to clean your sister's house."

The top of the blanket pile erupted, and the aged face of a large tan and black egg-mother appeared. Her eyes were discolored. She blinked hard several times, then extended her hand to the floor, searching.

Daksey spotted the glasses she reached for. They were nowhere near her hand. He stepped forward, picked them up, and put them into her hand.

She set her glasses on her snout, the brace wrapping behind her head and peered at Daksey. "Green with black stripes?" Then she looked at Amthek. "Red with black stripes? Not from around here. Have you come to steal from my sister's house?"

"No Egg-Mother. We are here to earn money."

The tiny pouch-husband emerged from the other room with a handful of cleaning tools and a large bucket. "There is nothing left to steal anyway. Please rest. They are here to help." He motioned them to step back outside while the old egg-mother settled back into her pile. "You watch them, Odfay. Be sure they don't take anything."

"Yes, Thopaak. I will be sure of it."

They followed to the other side of the street and watched as Odfay fumbled at the door, then carefully pushed it open. The crack made it stick to the sides of the frame.

"This was her sister's?" Daksey asked.

"Yes. She passed away last year. We haven't been able to sell the place. I thought a cleaning might help."

Amthek stepped into the center of the room. The old floorboards creaked, and the sound of splintering came loud and clear.

"These floors are too old."

"Yes, I know. But we can't afford to have them replaced. We are hoping to sell the place and let the next owner fix the floors."

Daksey looked around at the place. A layer of dust covered every surface, but didn't seem to be all that dirty. "It doesn't look hard. Just dust."

Odfay chut-chutted. "You aren't from here, so you don't understand. That isn't dust. It's the scattering from the trees outside. They are very tiny little bubbles, and when you wipe them, it becomes very sticky. You'll need solvent, and you'll need to scrub. Once you start, it gets worse."

Daksey's quills flicked up and down. "Why not swoosh it back outside?"

"Swoosh it?"

Daksey took the wide broom and made a sweeping motion slightly above the floor. The tree pollen swirled and floated to a location a bit further away.

Odfay undulated. "That takes a delicate hand. If you can do it, your job will be much easier."

Amthek tilted his head. "So, you want the floors and flat surfaces cleaned of this. Is that all?"

"Yes, that should do. Perhaps clean out the basin in the kitchen."

"We'll use that for the scrubbers anyway," Daksey said. "We'll be sure it's clean when we're done."

"Not to be impolite," Amthek said, "but how much will we be earning for this job?"

"Not impolite at all," Odfay said. "It's smart to ask before you start work. I had that note posted for at least two full counts. You are the first to come, so I'll give you sixty-four."

Amthek tilted his head.

"Each. Sixty-four each. And I'll give you a meal."

Daksey undulated. "We accept."

Amthek undulated as well. "We thank you for the offer of the meal. We'll be sure to earn it."

Odfay hooted softly. "Well spoken. I will go tend to my wife. She's still sad from the loss of her sister. They were very close."

After Odfay had left, Daksey and Amthek got to work. Daksey carefully swooshed the pollen out the door as best he could, then he and Amthek buckled down on those spots that needed more than a swoosh.

As they cleaned their tools, Odfay returned with a tray filled with food. "Oh my. You have done a very nice job. Even these old floors almost look good."

"They are clean but still very old," Amthek said.

"You did well," Odfay said. "Here is your meal, as promised. And here is your money." He counted out eight large coins for Amthek, and seven for Daksey, then added four smaller ones.

Daksey knew the totals were the same, but also knew what it might mean. He nodded in gratitude.

Amthek bundled up the food and the two were shortly back in their room. Osmay and Maysam were both there.

"Where have you runts been?" demanded Osmay. "Why were you gone so long?"

Amthek set the food onto the central table and opened it. "We were earning food. With anger like that, you must be very hungry."

Osmay growled. "I'm angry because we are still here." He turned to glare at Daksey. "And now, because of you, Thoy'eeng is in prison. They took all his money, everything he had on him."

"Prison? Why? How?"

Maysam sighed. "Thoy'eeng lost his temper and yelled at the egg-mother priestess. Who knew they made a law against that? He's been put into prison until he has a tribunal. After that, he could be in there for a very long time."

"And it's all your fault."

"Osmay, please," Maysam said. "You were there when we found him. Thoy'eeng is the one who took him. This is all his own doing."

"What are we going to do? How are we going to eat?"

Amthek kicked the table leg. "Daksey and I brought food. Enough for us all tonight."

Maysam glanced at Amthek. "See? If they can bring food, we can bring rent. We'll be fine. And when Thoy'eeng gets out, and he will get out, we will go home."

Daksey shrunk. He decided not to remind them why they were here.

MAKSIM AND FOONDEK

Thursday, August 29, 3297, 15:11

"I am wondering," Maksim said, "what are your beliefs about the purpose of life?"

Foondek flicked his tail. "Purpose? You mean, why are we here?"

Maksim nodded.

"My people exist because those who came before us could not have survived. After the great Sunfire War, the land and air were poisoned. They made us better able to resist the radiation. Better able to repair genetic damage. We are taught that our purpose is to survive long enough that we'll one day be able to repopulate the entire world, once the radiation has faded."

"And until then?"

"Until then, we persist. We survive and enjoy what life brings us. We remember, and teach our past to the children who will build the future. We keep the books, copy them from generation to generation in the So'ke'fes." He tilted his head and spoke again. This time it translated to "Great Library."

"Ah," Maksim said.

"And what about you?"

"Some of us believe in a creator, others do not." He shook his head. "I believed my purpose was to make Yelena happy. To make a family, and to live a very long time. Now, I have no idea."

"I see. Without her, you feel you have no purpose in life. Nothing to offer."

"Well, that's a little blunt, but yes. I think that's right."

"I have no doubt it's how you feel," Foondek said, "but it is incorrect."

"How so?"

"You have given me your friendship. I place great value on that, Maksim. You have taught me much about your culture. How your people interact with each other. Most significantly, you have shown me the depth of your love for one another. Your ability to share your feelings with me has shown that your people feel the loss of your life-mates as deeply as we do. This is a significant thing our species have in common. It is your unique, priceless and horrifically painful gift."

Maksim sat quietly for a moment.

"Do you need to shed tears again?"

"I am strongly considering it."

Foondek looked down as a small head poked through the opening of his pouch. "I think someone wants to see you, Maksim."

Maksim smiled as a tear rolled down his cheek.

ODD JOBS

Mas'eeng Masassof, Second Five, Early

Daksey and Amthek went back to the job wall and searched for something else they could do. They spent the next few days running errands, cleaning rooms, none of which were as easy as the first, and tending to the occasional livestock.

One day, as Daksey looked over the notes, something caught his eye. He pointed to a note. "Look at that."

"Someone selling furniture," Amthek said. "Chairs, table. Bed. So?"

He shifted down several paces. "Now look here."

"Wanted, used furniture in good condition. I need a bed and chairs."

Daksey flicked his tail. "What if we put these two together?"

"How so?"

"First, let's go look at the furniture. Then we will know."

They went to the address, stopping by the bookstore first to consult the map, then were off.

The furniture was to come out of an older home. It all seemed to be in good order. Daksey had Amthek wait with it while he ran to the buyer. She only wanted the bed and chairs, but she offered more than the set, so Daksey agreed.

He ran back to Amthek. They pooled their money to buy the furniture, then went to rent a cart. The haul netted them a tidy profit, and at the end of the day they returned to the bookstore.

"We have this table left over. Would you like to trade it for the map?'

De'pey chut-chutted. "That is a very good deal for me. Come, let me get the map for you."

"You had a good idea," Amthek said. "This is the most money we made in one day."

Daksey flicked his tail. "I saw something else. I've been thinking about it all day. But I don't know if we can do it alone. We might need the other two to help."

They bought enough food for the four of them and returned to their room. Osmay kept to himself. Maysam seemed distracted.

"Is there a problem?" Daksey asked.

Maysam huffed. "We haven't been able to find enough for rent. We are going to lose this room."

"How much longer do we have?"

"Another half count."

"Four days is not long," Daksey said. "What will we do?"

"When we lose the room, I'm going home. Osmay agrees. It's too difficult here. We don't know anyone. We've no way to begin."

Daksey cringed. Just when things were looking better. Now this?

That night he and Amthek lay quietly in the large bed they shared. Daksey couldn't sleep. His mind raced. What next?

The next morning, as Amthek looked at the jobs, Daksey tried to remember something. It felt important. Then he saw it. That's what he remembered. "Amthek, look at this one."

"Tree cutting? That is a hard job. Fourteen trees. How much does it pay?"

"No, look at what kind of trees they are."

"Koyosek?"

Daksey flicked his tail. "We use those at home for floors."

"Floors? So what?"

"Remember that first house we cleaned? It needed new floors. They were having a hard time selling it with the old ones."

Amthek undulated. "And that cracked front door."

"We should go talk to Odfay again. I have an idea."

"NICE TO SEE YOU," Odfay said, "but I'm sorry, we cannot afford another cleaning so soon."

Daksey hopped from one foot to another. "I have an idea. About your sister's house."

"Yes?"

"How much are you trying to sell it for?"

"We are asking thirty-two kesfong. That would be enough for us to live on for a very long time."

"Someone is asking for trees to be cut down. Koyosek trees."

"Yes, that makes for very nice floors, but we simply cannot afford it."

"What if we refloored the house on our own. Did all the work for you. Could you ask for more money?"

Odfay huffed. "We certainly could. Our neighbor got over eighty kesfong last summer for their house."

"Then you could afford to pay us, and you would have your money."

"What if it doesn't sell?"

Daksey tilted his head. "Our other problem is that we need a place to stay. Four of us."

"Ah. I see. So, you stay there, do all the work, and if we sell the house, we all make out good. But if the house doesn't sell, you have a place to stay. For how long?" He shuddered. "No, never mind. You can stay until the summer comes around again, or we sell the house. How's that?"

Daksey undulated. "That is quite long enough. We have a deal. Thank you."

The two of them raced through town, coming at last to the place with the trees. The owner wanted to expand her house. The trees were in the way.

"The last one who came here asked an okfong a tree and intended to leave the stumps."

"We'll do it for half that. One doyfong, and we'll carve the stumps even with the ground."

"I want the roots removed."

"I'm sorry, Egg-Mother. We do not have the tools for that. Koyosek roots are very hard to dig out. Doyfong a tree."

She huffed, then flicked her tail. "Flat to the ground, then. You have a deal."

"We'll return in the morning. We have to gather our tools, and arrange to move the trees."

"Good enough."

They left. Once they were near the bottom of the hill Amthek stopped. "Daksey, I don't know how much help I will be. I cannot lay flooring. I have no skill."

Daksey chut-chutted. "If you argue for your limitations, you get to keep them. Convince yourself of your inabilities, and you guarantee that they will hold you back."

Amthek huffed. "If you say so. What next?"

"The lumber mill. They will be able to move trees and cut them."

"And that will make them into flooring?"

Daksey paused. "Almost. We may have to pay more."

"You seem to know what you are doing. If I think you are going to make a mistake, I will ask."

Daksey tilted his head. "I don't know everything."

They arrived at the mill. A stout, older pouch-husband

greeted them. The sawyer's toolbelt declared his trade. "What can I do for you?"

"We have fourteen koyosek trees to cut tomorrow. We wanted to talk to you about them."

The sawyer undulated. "They make good flooring. You want to sell them?"

"We need flooring for a house," Daksey said. "Two rooms."

The sawyer shook his head back and forth as he spoke. "You will need to slice and boil it first, then wait for it to dry and cut in the grooves. It will take a full count at least. But with that many trees, you will end up with a lot more than two room's worth."

"Do you have enough existing flooring for our project?"

"What are you suggesting?"

Daksey flicked his tail. "We trade you the trees in exchange for enough flooring to complete our two rooms."

The sawyer tilted his head. "That seems like a roundabout way to get it done."

"We also need hauling," Amthek said.

"From where to where?"

Daksey put his hand on Amthek's shoulder. "From where the trees stand after we cut them to here, and for the flooring delivered to the home."

The sawyer huffed. "I see. Not as much profit for me as I would hope."

"I understand. It would be of great help to us if you could see your way to agreeing."

"I get plenty of trees. This sounds like more work."

"Just hauling," Daksey said. "We do the cutting."

"I don't cut my own trees, and the cutters haul them to me."

"And then you pay them."

"Of course."

"With these, you don't have to pay. Just haul."

"And the cost of the flooring," the sawyer said.

Daksey undulated. "And the cost of having your employees cut new flooring from your fourteen trees. Yes."

The sawyer sighed deeply and thought it over. "I'll need to see the trees first."

Daksey hooted. "Very good. When can you come?"

"Right now. It's time for a meal anyway. Otha, watch the shop. I'll be back later."

"WHERE HAVE YOU TWO BEEN?" Osmay asked.

"We found a place for us to live," Amthek said. "A house."

"How can we afford it?"

"We'll need to do some work on the place," Daksey said, "but it's nice, and we can live there until the owner sells it, or until summer. Whichever comes first."

Osmay huffed. "So, we find a way to delay the sale? How is that a good thing?"

"No, because when it sells, we share in the profit because of the work we'll be doing."

"What kind of work?" Maysam asked.

"It needs new floors. A simple job. Daksey made all the arrangements. The new flooring will be there in a few days. Tomorrow, we'll need to cut down trees to pay for the flooring."

"Oh, look at you," Osmay said. "You think you are so smart, don't you?"

Daksey tilted his head. "We are also being paid to cut down the trees and take them away."

Maysam chut-chutted. "Look at the little dealmaker go. Sounds like a good enough plan. Anything you need help with?"

Daksey hunched. "We need to cut down fourteen trees tomorrow. The sawyer will come to get them tomorrow evening. Then we take delivery of the flooring the next morning."

"When can we move into the place?"

"Anytime we want. It's ours until it's all done with."

"That sounds ridiculous," Osmay said. "It sounds like a great deal of work only to have the house sold from under us. They'll cheat you on the price, and you'll get nothing."

"Come on, Osmay. Don't be like that. Not everyone is only out for themselves."

"You'll see. You are wrong. I won't have any part of it."

Maysam huffed. "Osmay–"

"No. I'm leaving. I'll find my own way back to Seeng'dod." He turned and stomped out the door.

Daksey's nostrils flared. "With three of us, it will take too long. We need that wood tomorrow."

FOONDEK AND THE DRONES

"I miss my family," Foondek said. "I miss Masax, and I miss the people of my village. I wish I could see them again."

Anna frowned. "I understand, and we appreciate you staying to teach us. There might be something I can do for you. Do you remember how we made images of Bamthapeem during our last attempt at contact?"

Foondek undulated, then nodded. "Yes. Flying machines."

"We call them drones, and there are still two of them near Bamthapeem. I might be able to convince the research team to move them down to your village."

"You could tell them how much different the Botham are, and that a contrasting study would be to their benefit."

Anna chuckled. "Maybe I'll let you tell them. You seem to understand exactly what might motivate them."

Foondek's quills flicked up and down. "I merely try to think as they do. The reasoning seems obvious, then."

"If only everyone tried that. All right then, let's do it."

Foondek watched the images on large flat screens. Two for each drone, one front, and one rear as they flew furtively near his village. None of the humans were using screens. They saw these images in their heads. Captured lightning. Foondek shuddered and took a deep breath.

"There, to the left on one," said Sid, one of the operations technicians. "Anyone you know?"

Foondek looked. He had been learning their numbers. Two of the screens had the number they called "one" in a lower corner. This display's colors were strange, flat and cold. He turned his head from side to side. "It's difficult to tell. Your images have such strange colors. The people don't look any different than the trees."

"I forgot, sorry. AutoGov, adjust the pickups and displays to show a spectrum similar to Foondek's eyesight."

"Acknowledged."

The images shifted, and suddenly the people stood out brightly against the background. "Ah, that is Soyok. One of Kempok's pouch-husbands."

"How different is their eyesight?" Sid asked.

"They see nearly the same width of a spectrum," Anna said, "slightly shifted more into near infrared. To them, warm things start to glow at much lower temps, and their night vision is far better than ours."

"But he doesn't see violet," Maksim said. "Some of my prettiest flowers look gray to him."

Foondek chutted. "They still smell nice. Ah, there is Bongeex, and his sister Moya'se."

"Who are they?"

"Deytham's family. His younger brother and sister. They are heading to the gear hut. Bongeex is going hunting. Is he taking Moya'se?"

"Is that unusual?" Sid asked.

"Females don't often hunt, and even so, she is still young." Foondek swayed. "Deytham and I were to be hunting with Bongeex until Daksey returned from the city."

"Why don't any of the other males join the hunt?" Maksim asked.

"Most are too old, or simply don't have the skills. If you don't know what to do, or you are clumsy, what you are hunting might decide you are their prey instead. Some of the creatures we hunt like how we taste."

"Can you tell if the sister is scared?" Anna asked.

"Scared?" Foondek watched how Moya'se moved, watched her drape the traps over her arm and adjust them. "She knows how to handle the traps. She seems confident. Perhaps content." Foondek chutted. "She probably demanded to go, if I know her. She's a lot like her mother."

"Her mother?"

"Kempok. A force of nature, that one. She is the leader of the Botham, has been since before I was born."

They spent the next few hours watching Bongeex and Moya'se hunt. The drones angled through the trees, keeping far enough that they wouldn't be heard, darting behind a tree before being seen.

Foondek spotted the sinkhole first. He pointed to the screen. "That is new. It wasn't there when we last hunted this area."

On the display, Bongeex stalked his prey, as he slid slowly closer to a small bush at the edge of the pit.

"Bongeex needs to stop," Foondek said. "He needs to look to his left. Look left. No. You idiot."

Bongeex brushed against the small bush, and it gave way, along with some of the ground he had been standing on. He tumbled into the deep pit, out of view.

Foondek's nostrils flared. "I can't see him. Go higher. Look inside that hole."

The view shifted as the drone rose higher.

"It's too dark," Maksim said. "I can't see him."

"He is right there." Sid pointed. "Sprawled out. He isn't moving. It's a long way down."

"The sister is coming," Anna said. "Over there."

Foondek flicked his tail. "Moya'se. Yes, she can help her brother."

"She doesn't see the pit either."

"She will. She has to."

They watched as she nearly missed it, then saw where the earth had been disturbed. She crept to the edge and peered inside.

Sid pointed. "Hey, look. That animal they were hunting is coming back. See it? It's over there behind her in the tall grass. It's crouching."

"We call it fay'spay," Foondek said. "It's hunting her, and she doesn't see it. Please, help her."

"She'll see the drone."

"Or she'll be dead. Are your secrets more important than her life?"

"Damn," Sid said. "AutoGov, intercept that creature. Distract it, get it to follow you."

Foondek watched as the images raced past. A flash of teeth and eyes, then the creature backed away.

The other drone watched a wider view. Foondek's heart sank as he watched Moya'se. Frightened by what she had seen, stepped too close to the edge and tumbled after her brother.

The fay'spay started to circle around the drone. It batted at it with a foreclaw.

Maksim shook his head. "This thing isn't going to take long to figure out the drone is too light to do any real damage."

"Check the hole," Anna said. "Is she all right?"

Foondek pointed. "There, she's moving. Sitting up and holding one arm. She's fine. We have to keep the fay'spay out of that hole."

"Send the other drone to get help," Maksim said.

The others exchanged glances.

"Yeah, I know." Sid sighed. "Someone figure out how to tell Skip how badly we messed up his orders. AutoGov, take drone two back to the village. Let's get them some help."

Foondek watched as the village came into sight on one of the screens. He pointed to one of the homes. Two Ombax were outside in a small garden. Foondek pointed. "There are Espay and Soyok. Settle down at eye height in front of them. Don't get too close."

The image shifted. Soyok saw it first and looked startled, holding still, but when Espay's eyes landed on the drone, his entire body shifted, and he lunged at the machine. The drone skipped out of reach, but Espay chased after it. Soyok ran to the tool hut and soon followed with a bow.

Espay's lunges were unsettlingly erratic, as if he were in a blind fury.

"I've never seen him this angry," Foondek said. "He's always such a kind and gentle being. I don't understand."

"That's the look they had at Bamthapeem when they suddenly decided to attack," Maksim said quietly. "Like they all went crazy at once."

The drone stayed ahead of Espay as it led the two pouch-husbands down the path.

The other image tumbled furiously. The animal had landed a blow. The images became unstable, but the drone still stayed in the air.

"What happened to drone one?" Sid asked.

"The predatory animal approached the pit with the two hunters," AutoGov said. "A distraction maneuver was required to keep the creature at a safe distance. The animal is slightly more dexterous than anticipated. Flight characteristics have been adjusted accordingly, however the drone has been damaged."

One of the two screens flickered, then went blank. The other tilted wildly. The ground rushed closer. Then teeth and blackness.

"That drone's gone. How far is the other one?"

"The angry guy is keeping up," Anna said, "but we are leaving the other one behind."

"That's good enough," Sid said. "Get him over to the pit, then dive bomb the fay'spay. Chase it off, or at least make sure it isn't hidden."

A few moments later, the drone veered into the woods. Espay's angry teeth in one screen, dense woods in the other, until it swung around the pit. The fay'spay peered over the edge at the two down below. The drone swooped into the creature's face and sped into the trees. It climbed high, and found a perch where it could fall silent and observe.

Espay tackled the creature and pummeled its head. With a scrape of claws and a shriek, it clawed its way free and ran off into the woods. Espay's chest was lined with blood, most of it his own. He sat at the edge of the pit looking around for the drone. "Where are you? Come out."

Moya'se called to him from below. "Espay, we are down here."

He leaned over and saw the two at the bottom.

Soyok caught up. "Pouch-husband, you are hurt." He used a cloth to wipe away the blood from Espay's chest. The wounds were already closing. He would be fine.

"Moya'se. Where is Bongeex?"

"Down here with me. He is breathing, but not awake. And he is bleeding. A bone is sticking out of his arm. It isn't healing."

"You go back and get a rope. I'll climb down and tend to Bongeex."

"I will, but first, are you all right? I've never seen you like that."

Espay shrunk. His quills flicked up, then back. "I've never felt that way before. So angry I couldn't think. We can talk about it later. Go get the rope."

Soyok swung back toward the path.

Espay found handholds and carefully made his way down the

side of the pit. When he came close enough, he let himself drop to the floor.

The image shifted as the drone rose up and took a position far above the pit, angling one camera down.

"Are you injured, daughter?"

Moya'se tilted her head. "I landed on my feet. The pain was a shock, but brief. I'm healing now."

Espay turned his attention to Bongeex's broken arm. "I will need to set this. You should watch, so you know how it's done." As she looked on, He pulled the arm and let the bone slip back under the skin.

Bongeex moaned and flinched but remained unconscious.

Espay felt the bone and pulled again. "You have to be sure the ends of the bones are where they began, so it will heal straight. We'll need a stick as long as this part of the arm, and something to secure it to his arm.

Moya'se's nostrils flared. "It should have stopped bleeding by now." She picked up a sturdy branch, long and straight enough to do the job and began pulling off the smaller branches.

Espay huffed. "He may have damaged his hindbrain."

She handed the split to him and started gathering vines.

He set the stick at his side and made another examination of the arm. Once satisfied, he put the stick against the arm and pulled a ball of string from his bag. He carefully tied it in place. He slid his hand over the unconscious body, seeking out that area where the hindbrain sat. "I don't feel any broken bones. Is there another stick over there?'

Moya'se saw the string and dropped the vines. She undulated and grabbed a smaller branch. "Will this one do?"

Espay took the stick, tore off the smaller branches, and started tapping Bongeex's back.

"Just like Daksey."

Espay undulated. "And like Soyok. His hindbrain is slow too, sometimes. It's more common than you think."

Bongeex inhaled sharply, then let out a shuddering sigh." Don't move, yet. Give yourself time."

Bongeex opened his eyes and blinked. "That. Hurt."

Moya'se chutted. She looked up into the trees, searching.

Foondek sat back as the drone hid behind a tree, spoiling his view. "He will be fine. You saved their lives."

"Yeah," Sid said. "We did. Now, who is going to explain this to Skip?"

WOOD WORK

Mas'eeng Masassof, Second Seven, Rising

Sawing proved harder than it looked. The three of them worked in shifts. Two on the saw, the third resting. It wore them out, but the last tree came down while the sawyer hauled away the first load. By the time they arrived at the old house, they were exhausted.

The next morning, true to his word, the sawyer delivered several large pallets of beautiful flooring. He took his time wandering around the house. "The workmanship on this one is very nice. But the front door is pitiful. Those edgings are rotting from the inside too. Did you see that?"

Daksey looked where he pointed. "We only agreed to do the floor. How much to replace the door and edgings?"

He shook his head. "Several hundred for new edgings. You'll need to replace them both. And the door? You can rarely find a matched set."

"Why is that?"

"Hand made. Machines don't do that kind of work very well. Those were made by skilled craftsmen."

"Like yourself?"

"Eh? Oh. I haven't done that sort of work in a long time."

"If they are worth hundreds, why not?"

He locked eyes with Daksey. "Not that many new houses get built. Can't make a living at it." He sighed wistfully. "Still." He glanced at the roof and turned to leave. He stopped and took a longer look at the roof. "If you need anything else, be sure to come by the mill."

FOONDEK EXPLAINS

Saturday, September 7, 3297, 12:41

Skip's gaze drifted among the stars as he sat in the large chair in MCC. Kai left him to his thoughts when it was a quiet watch. Something he much appreciated. An alert popped up.

"Administrator Onada," AutoGov said, "you have a call from Sidney Nameth."

Skip sighed and tapped the glowing icon. "Yes?"

"Skip, the native wishes to speak with you," Sid said.

"Aye," Skip said. "Where is he?"

"Cargo bay three."

"Any idea what this is about?"

Sid hesitated. "About an incident we had a little while ago. You need to know. He's asked to explain it to you himself, sir. In person."

"Fine," Skip said. "Kai, you have the watch until I get back."

When Skip stepped into the large open bay, he marveled at the transformation. The floor that had been covered in piping and drainage systems now lay hidden under a thick layer of soil.

Foondek and a handful of humans were on the far side, putting plants into the ground.

"Foondek, you wished to speak with me?"

Foondek undulated, then gave a curt nod. He started speaking and AutoGov piped the translated words into Skip's ears. "Hello, Skip Onada. Gratitude for coming to speak with me. I wish to explain the drone mission, and what we did."

"Drone mission?"

Skip heard his own voice speaking alien words, then Foondek responded.

"Yes. When I asked to join the observation team to help them understand my people, I had not expected the situation to develop as it did."

"What happened?"

"My pouch-husband and I were supposed to be hunting. Instead, Deytham's younger brother, Bongeex, and their little sister, Moya'se, were hunting. We followed them with both drones. The team wanted to study hunting techniques. I wanted to see my people. Bongeex fell into a pit and became incapacitated. The animal Bongeex had been hunting attacked Moya'se. I asked the team to help. In contradiction to your orders, we saved both of their lives, lost one drone, and alerted my people to your presence."

Skip sighed deeply. "Saved two lives. Lost one drone. And we are no longer operating in secret."

Foondek undulated then nodded. "I wanted to act only to save my family from injury."

Skip nodded back. "The secret was a preference. We'll have to deal with it. We can print a new drone on demand. No loss there. I'm glad we could help."

"The others thought you may be angry. The exposure of the drones might cause problems."

"Yes, it certainly might. However, having the drones help save two of your people might be a good thing. Either way, the fact that we rendered aid is fine with me. "

Foondek hooted softly. "That is very generous of you. After all that has happened."

"After all that has happened, I think it's best we keep looking for ways to be seen in a good light. We still want to make contact, some day."

"Will you try again, soon?"

"No. I've canceled all further manned missions to the surface. I won't risk any more of my crew."

"There is something else you should know," Foondek said. "Something I had never seen before. When Espay, the pouch-father of Bongeex and Moya'se, saw the drone we had sent to alert them, he flew into a rage. It's the way you described your other encounters. I do not understand it, and I thought you should know that."

"Something more for the researchers to investigate. Thank you, Foondek. I appreciate everything you are doing, and I'm glad we could help your friends."

Foondek hooted softly as Skip turned to leave.

"Skip," Foondek said, "you said no more of your people will journey to the surface. What of my return?"

"I'll make that one exception. You can arrange to go back any time you wish. But the crew will drop you off and return. Nothing more."

Foondek undulated. "You have spoken. I understand. Thank you."

Anna joined Skip as he headed back to the command center.

"He seems to have become very familiar with our technology," Skip said.

"I'll say. He's smart. Picks things up quickly, understands well. According to AutoGov, he's been taking courses on physics and quantum mechanics. He's earned a high rating."

"Not the primitive bumpkin we might have expected."

She shook her head. "More like a species that walked on their moons four thousand years ago, then stopped but didn't forget."

"That part about the uncontrollable anger. Have they looked

into that? I mean, a couple of flashing lights shouldn't trigger someone to freak out and go insane, should it?"

"No. But it could explain why we've done so poorly when we tried to contact them. Maybe an overt display of technology triggers something. I'll have the bio team go back over Deytham's body. See if they can find anything physical. They're still trying to work out everything that little hindbrain does."

"I thought that handled locomotion," Skip said, "similar to dinosaurs on Earth."

"That was the first hypothesis, and it might have once served that purpose, but it's not hooked up that way. It's surrounded by a cluster of glands, some of which we still haven't figured out. From what we've gathered from Foondek, it provides pain relief and accelerates healing."

"Like a medtech controller?"

Anna nodded. "And a couple of those glands look like little chemical factories that create specialized virus-like structures capable of helping with repairs."

Skip shook his head. "That sounds way too good to be natural."

She shrugged. "Nothing says it has to be natural. But in function, yes. It's exactly like our controllers with their own biologic version of nanomedics."

Skip thought for a moment. "Maybe the anger issue is in the programming then."

THE SAWYER AND THE ROOFER

Mas'eeng Masassof, Third Four, Early High

A single day was all it took to rip out the old floors and clean up the mess. Two more days to put the new floor in and secure it. Next came the sealant. They had to sleep outside that night. The fumes were horrid.

The sawyer showed up again with a cart. "I have your door, and two edgings for either side. I found those in my scrap pile, and remembered how badly yours were getting."

"Thank you. Very kind of you."

"I had another reason to come by. My friend makes roof tiles. He has a little problem, and I think you two can help each other. I might be wrong, but I think those tiles are the right color."

"Yes, but many of them are broken, and the roof leaks."

"That is what I thought. Good. Maybe you can both benefit. He'll be along shortly."

The roofer came up the hill and passed by the sawyer on his way down. As he approached the house he cast long looks at the roof. "Those are the color I need."

"We still need them for our roof," Daksey said.

"I could replace your roof with something else, if you will let me take those tiles."

"Why?"

"Ah," the roofer said. "An error. We made enough for a customer, but they were the wrong color. Now she's demanding the correct color, and we have to make more. With those, we would have more than half the order done already."

"What color are the bad ones?"

"Dark brown. A shade darker than your trim."

"You would give us those in exchange for the ones we have?" Daksey asked.

"Yes. An even trade?"

"And you would remove the old roof?"

The roofer undulated.

"And you would install the new roof? Make sure it doesn't leak?"

The roofer hesitated. "I would have to pay my workers."

"And how much would that be? That might be more than we can afford right now. We are attempting to sell the house to earn money."

"I know. You could add it to the price of the house. Two days labor for six workers. I can bring it down to twelve hundred. I get my share before anyone else."

"You would get your share after the old egg-mother we are trying to help but before us."

"That will do. How soon can we get in to do the work?"

"You are in a hurry? Start as soon as you like. As long as we have a roof when it rains, we'll be good."

The roof workers came in the afternoon, and that night the house was covered in tarps. The next day the new tiles arrived along with workers. By the end of the following day, the roof had new tiles, the floors were new, the door and edgings had been replaced. And just like that, they were done.

Odfay and Thopaak were delighted and brought people to see the house. Daksey and Amthek returned to the job wall every morning to find work. When he had time, Daksey stopped in at the bookstore and bought another book to read.

THREE DAYS LATER, a bid was made on the house.

"They offered one hundred and thirty one kesfong," Odfay said. "We only needed thirty-two. That will give you ninety-nine kesfong."

Daksey shrugged. "We asked for a split down the middle before. We should do it that way. Take sixty-five."

Odfay chut-chutted. "I told you he would say that. We said no. We agreed to thirty-two. That is where we will stay."

"Please. I don't feel right taking so much. It was your sister's home."

"Fine. We'll take forty-eight kesfong. No more."

Daksey undulated. "Agreed. Thank you for your generosity."

"Thank you for your hard work."

COMPLAINTS

Monday, September 23, 3297 8:01

Radinka materialized in the hidden room of the tavern directly behind her chair. Ferdinand and Brianna were already there. She sat with a flourish and sighed. "I do appreciate your promptness. What do you have to report?"

Ferdinand tapped the table. "I've been working on a new section of this simulation. It will give us better insight as to the vulnerabilities of the enemy ship. I may have something, but I would rather not say until I'm certain."

"I would rather have all the information I can. What are you working on?"

"It has to do with the delivery system. The one on the station. I think I might be able to delay the delivery."

"How long," asked Brianna. "Long enough to alter the contents?"

"Is that useful?" Radinka asked.

Ferdinand smiled. "I hope so."

Brianna grinned and nodded. "Maybe even to the point Hammerfist likes it."

"Speaking of which, where is the oaf?" Radinka swiped her

display and brought up the character list. "There he is. Fighting that damned dragon."

Ferdinand laughed.

She poked the chat button. "Hammerfist, you are late for the meeting."

"Do you have anything for me to do?" came the gruff response.

"Not yet. But soon."

"Then fuck off. Call me when you are ready for something to be broken." He dropped the connection.

Radinka scowled.

"We don't need him," Brianna said. "Even for this, he's not a good fit."

Ferdinand frowned. "Do you want to use... measures?"

Radinka shook her head. "Not yet. He's not a good fit, but he's still an asset."

SECRETS OF THE DARK FOREST

Mas'eeng Foythey, Second Seven, Early High

Moya'se set the last of her snares while Bongeex sniffed the forest air. The fresh wind brought nothing in the way of possible game. Sunlight glittered from the dense canopy overhead.

"Can we get some fruit from the ruins today?" Moya'se asked.

"That was part of the plan."

"What plan? Hunting plan?"

Bongeex shrugged. "Kempok's plan. She wanted me to show you something."

Moya'se hooted softly. "I hope it tastes good."

"If you are hungry, eat some of those koyo nuts we picked up. We have plenty."

"I'm saving those for the ankle biters."

They came to a section of the wall surrounding the old ruin. A large collapsed section allowed them to enter the grounds.

Moya'se stepped to the right.

Bongeex turned left and headed in the opposite direction. A series of low walls and embankments hid an opening between several dense bushes. He could never forget his first time here.

Deytham had shown him the secret inside. Now, it was his turn to be the teacher. "It's in here. Follow me. Keep your head down, and be careful until your eyes adjust. It's very dark."

"Dark?"

Bongeex stepped down into the first chamber. Light from the opening kept the place from being too dark. To the right a hallway curved down and to the left.

Moya'se followed quietly.

He stopped and stepped to the side when they came to the next chamber. So dark he could only tell by the sound.

Moya'se gasped.

He reached out and touched her arm. "You are safe. Wait and see."

Slowly the contours of the room became evident. Small glimpses of the heat glow of several small dathay scurrying about gave them scant illumination. A single slightly larger glow revealed what might be a mother.

"It smells like moss in here," Moya'se said. "Moss and stale water."

"There is a small pond on the far side. Don't drink that water."

"Why are we here?"

"I will show you soon. Can you see the floor?"

"A little. It's cold. Dark. I just see where my feet stop."

Bongeex slipped his hand into the crevice he had been quietly looking for. He gripped the handle and while his sister looked at her feet, he pulled.

The far wall lit with patches of light in shapes easily seen. Triangles, squares, circles. They flashed, changed color, and moved about.

Moya'se watched them, holding steady in place. After a few moments, she huffed. "What is this place?"

Bongeex released the lever and the lights went dark. "Turn back and head outside. I'll explain in the light."

She moved quickly. By the time Bongeex made it to the first

chamber, she had already climbed outside. He climbed out into the light and froze with the sharp end of a spear at the back of his neck.

The green bushes turned brilliant red, as three more sayox revealed themselves. Each held deadly spears.

THE TAVERN ON THE HILL

Mas'eeng Foythey, Second Seven, Late

The proceeds from the house sale were enough to invest in a small tavern that Maysam had found. A cozy place built into the side of a hill near the edge of town, it included a small stage in the main hall and several rooms for sleeping above. After cleaning and purchasing supplies, they opened to a steady stream of customers. They even hired a band to play three nights every half count. The other five nights were quiet.

One night, he and Amthek were reading near the window. Daksey heard Amthek trying to sound out a word.

"Did you find a word you don't know?"

Amthek cringed. "There are plenty of words I don't know. But most of the books De'pey gives me I can read easily enough. This one is harder. But it's about the sea, so I want to read it."

"What is the word?"

Amthek spelled it out.

"Ah, that's an old one. You would know it as Athmo'tham, the Dead Forest, but since your book must be so old, it uses the long form instead."

"Oh. Now I see. Long form. I remember something in school about how our language has shifted from the time of the Sunfire War. Before that, there were many languages all over the world."

Daksey nodded. "I remember that too. It must be in all our teaching books."

"Thank you."

"No problem. It's just a word."

"No, I mean, thank you for being so kind. And smart. Yes, that too."

Daksey sighed. "I'm only being myself, Amthek. I think everyone should go through life being who they really are."

"What if they aren't kind? What if they are cruel, mean?"

"Someone who is cruel to another is usually someone who has been hurt. They aren't being themselves, they are being a pained version of themselves, and they take out their pain by trying to give it to someone else. When a person is who they really are, we learn very quickly that others are just being who they are, and nearly everyone is good. Trying to do the right thing, even if it doesn't seem that way."

"Nearly everyone."

"There are always exceptions to every rule, but even the people keeping me from seeing the scholars believe they are doing the right thing."

"There must be a way to convince them to change their minds."

"I think that's what that egg-mother in Soypasod was supposed to help with."

"Soypasod?"

"Yes. In Beethax, they gave me a letter of introduction and was told to show her the skulls. They said she would help me at the temple. The old one who gave it to me seemed certain he did me a great favor."

"And you ended up in Seeng'dod instead."

Daksey flicked his tail. "Doesn't matter. We will get through this."

"Why don't you go to Soypasod now?"

"Because I'm afraid that they will call for me, and if I'm missing, they'll decide I wasn't telling the truth."

Amthek glanced at the window. "I see."

Daksey sighed. "It will work out. It has to."

Amthek put his book away and laid his head down to sleep. After a while, Daksey covered the glowlight and did the same.

THE NEXT MORNING, Amthek had already awoken and gone. Daksey stretched and headed to the basin to wash. When he returned, he found Maysam eating in the front room near the stage.

"Daksey, I've been thinking. I believe we should hire the gray one, who both plucks the strings, and sings the words. That way, we could have music on more nights."

Daksey tilted his head. "If you think so. Where's Amthek?"

"No idea. Didn't see him this morning."

Daksey snorted. "I wonder where he went." He thought for a moment about the previous night, and their conversation. "Oh no." He got up and ran to his bag.

"What's wrong?"

"One of the skulls is missing. And a kesfong."

"He stole our money and ran. Typical."

Daksey shook his head. "My letter is gone as well. And there are a lot more of those coins in there. I think he only took one."

"A lot more?"

Daksey snorted. "I've been taking a little each day and setting it aside. When I have a thousand and twenty-four, I go trade it for a kesfong and set the coin aside. That is why when we need repairs, we always have enough money. I don't think Amthek found where I hid the smaller coins, so a kesfong is the smallest he could take. And again, he only took one. I think Amthek is going to Soypasod."

Osmay chut-chutted. "Eager to impress you, I'll bet."

"Impress me? What do you mean?"

"I should think it obvious. He's taken with you. He's going to do his best to live up to your standards."

"But I would never ask him to do such a thing."

"Of course not. That's why he waited until you were sleeping. He knew you wouldn't let him go."

"If he gets hurt, if something happens to him…"

"I understand your concern. But remember, he's been on his own for many seasons. He'll be fine. Besides, he's long past the city gates by now. With the money he took, he may have bought a cart too. Or a wheeled rider."

Daksey moaned. "He's been looking at those things for weeks."

CLAN OF THE SAYOX

Mas'eeng Foythey, Second Seven, High

His head ached. His wrists were bound together. Bongeex kept his eyes closed and inhaled, searching for a scent.

Something sharp prodded his leg. He recoiled.

Loud *clicks* and what sounded like burps and sniffles ensued.

Bongeex opened his eyes. He had been laid on his side, bound foot and wrists. He tried to find Moya'se but couldn't see anything beyond the several full counts of little sayox. "Where is my sister?"

The sayox danced back. Their colors shifted from orange to red and back.

He struggled to roll onto his knees but failed. He huffed. "Where is my sister?"

One of the little sayox hopped forward. Its head feathers flicked up and down. A flashier display that his own quills. He wondered if it meant the same thing. Was it confused?

"Sister. Where is my sister?"

The sayox clicked and burbled then said, "sisker."

"Sister. Where is she?"

"Sister," it repeated then burbled and clicked. Others joined in, burbling, clicking and dancing.

He looked at the rough rope around his wrists. A well-formed knot kept the bindings tight. He brought it to his teeth and tried to untie it.

Four of the sayox leapt forward with spears.

The first, the one who had spoken, waved them off.

Bongeex got a good look at their arms. There were feathers trailing off them. As if they might be more related to birds.

"Sister," it repeated with burbles and clicks.

"Where is she?"

"She. She ster."

"No. She is my sister. Where is my sister? Where is she?" He huffed. "This is silly. You have no idea what I'm saying."

A larger sayox who had stayed back moved forward. The others made way. When it came close to the one who spoke, it waved it off. "Speak big talk. Sister. Other big. We have. We take."

Bongeex froze. "Sister. My sister. Family. Give back."

The thing chut-chutted like an ombax. "Eat food. Feed we now."

Bongeex felt the rage inside. "You are not going to eat my sister." He clenched his fists and twisted with all his might. The rope snapped free. He reached for the closest spear and pulled it from the hands of the smaller sayox then pointed it at the larger one. "My sister. Give back."

A dozen more spear carriers jumped forward. One spear thrust into his leg from behind.

He howled, turned on the owner of the offending spear and shoved the back end of the one he held into the sayox's abdomen. It flew back.

The large sayox clicked and burbled with intensity. The spear holders fell back. Then it stepped forward and centered itself on the spear Bongeex held. With a puffed out chest, it grabbed the spear and pulled it until the tip touched, then let go.

Bongeex looked into the eyes of the creature, trying to figure out what it had just done. "Sister. Give back. Please." He swayed with that last word. Trying to give more meaning. Then he sat back on his haunches and drove the spear through the rope that bound his feet. It came loose.

"Bad knot," said the larger sayox.

"Good knot. Bad rope."

The thing chutted again, then warbled and burbled to the crowd. Suddenly the entire clan was chut-chutting.

Bongeex stood and planted the blunt end of the spear into the ground. He stood tall. "My sister. No eat my sister."

The clan grew still. Many brought out their spears.

The largest of the sayox opened its arms wide. "Feed we. Sister feed we. Good in mouth." It patted its belly. "Good here."

Bongeex's quills flicked up and down.

HAMMERFIST

As with most meetings, the unruly troll hadn't bothered to show up.

Radinka concluded her plan. "If there's no more, I would say we've been productive. Gather your materials and construct the devices. Ferdinand, I want you to do at least two test runs. Be sure you are not tracked, and the delay is unnoticed."

The door burst open, and the virtual barmaid's limp body flew across the table and slid to the floor on the other side with a thud. Hammerfist's bulk barreled into the room. "I'm tired of waiting. When do I get to break something out in the real? This fake wreckage is tasteless garbage."

Radinka glanced at the others. "You two are dismissed. I'll handle this."

Ferdinand evaporated in a puff of smoke that billowed through the sparkles left behind by the elf.

Hammerfist grunted. "Showy. A waste of time."

"Sit down. We need to talk."

He stomped to the table, pulled it away from Radinka, then

sat on it and grinned. "There. Speak up, boss lady. You have my attention."

"There are four of us. I've checked the reserves. We've as many as five more in cold sleep, but they won't show up for months at best."

"And?"

"And it means we are vulnerable. If you act prematurely, you risk exposing our entire effort."

"And what the fuck is that effort supposed to be? Xavier hired me because he knew I loved to fuck shit up. I have no idea what your plan is, but I haven't gotten to do a damned thing out there."

"I understand. Your skills are rather limited. I apologize for the delay. However, our original plans have to be carefully moderated to include the fact that we are left only with revenge and back-up plans."

"And where exactly does that leave me?"

Radinka crossed her arms. "Fighting dragons until we identify a more useful target."

Hammerfist stood and lifted the table over his head, then slammed it to the floor. It didn't bend. "Who wrote this shitty game? That should have been a satisfying crunch."

Radinka nodded. "I promise you. I will find you a target. But for now, I need you to have patience."

"I have none left. I'll do as you ask for as long as I can, but you need to give me something." He vanished silently.

Radinka shook her head. "Message to Ferdinand. I want to trace his every move."

WRATH OF KEMPOK

Mas'eeng Foythey, Third One, Early High

Bongeex adjusted his heavy pack once more. Moya'se led the way through the river crossing. On the other side, one of the ankle-biters spotted them and alerted the others.

"No secret arrival for us," Moya'se said.

"It's the koyo nuts. They expect a treat, so keep watch."

Several of the youth flocked toward them. Many adults as well. Trailing behind, but thundering forward, Kempok stormed at them.

"She looks..."

"Angry," Bongeex said. "Kempok is angry."

Moya'se tossed koyo nuts to the ankle-biters as the adults gathered around.

"Bongeex." Kempok's voice drowned out the rest of the world. "Explain yourself." Her throat rumbled in anger.

Bongeex shrunk. "Botham Kempok, Great Egg-Mother, and–"

"Stop. Enough. Where have you been?"

"I took Moya'se to the ruins. All went well inside." He locked eyes with Kempok. "As well as expected. After, when we left the ruin, we were ambushed by a clan of sayox."

"You fought them?"

"They had spears. The tip they pushed into me put me to sleep. When I awoke, I could not see Moya'se and the sayox had me tied."

"Moya'se, are you injured?"

"No, Kempok. The ropes hurt, but when I awoke, I tried to communicate with them."

"Bongeex, did you communicate as well?"

"Not as well as my sister, Kempok. I broke their tiny ropes, and they fought me."

"Did you kill any?"

He shrugged. "One of them got itself under my foot. A very young one, instead of stomping on it, I pushed it out of the way. Their leader saw what I did, and stopped the fighting."

"Just like that? Stopped fighting?"

"They made clear to me that they return acts of kindness with the same. They hadn't expected it from me, but did so. I kept asking about Moya'se, but they don't speak well. At first I thought they either wanted to eat her, or already had."

Moya'se chutted. "They were hungry. I fed them."

"You already had game?" Kempok asked.

"No, I had koyo nuts and koox."

"Egg-Mother," Bongeex said, "there should be great books written about your koox. The sayox loved it. They treated her like an honored guest."

Kempok's eyes went wide. She threw her head back and chut-chutted again and again.

NO SIGN OF AMTHEK

Mas'eeng Bayok, First Two, Setting

A delivery arrived at the tavern. Daksey took it, thanking the Ombax who brought it. He opened it and read the contents.

"What did you get?" asked Maysam.

Daksey huffed. "A response to my last letter of inquiry. I'm on the waiting list for a preliminary interview to assess my criteria to be placed on the advancement interview waiting list. It's very congratulatory."

Maysam snorted.

The music had picked up the pace. Tonight's crowd, larger than before, showed how well they were doing. Daksey sighed. Not all bad.

"Excuse me." A mid-sized female, tan with wide black stripes, stood in the open doorway. "Who do I speak to about the drums?"

Maysam undulated. "We own this tavern. Do you wish to ask the musicians a question?"

"No. I wondered if you could get them to quiet down. I can hear the drumming in my room, and I'm trying to rest."

Maysam slid around the counter. "My apologies. We have a large crowd tonight. The band is getting excited. They are very good."

"Yes, quite good. And I do enjoy the music, but I'm tired and want to sleep."

Maysam flicked his tail. "I will make you a deal. Share a drink with me. It's called Meng. When we are done, I'll ask the band to lower their efforts for you."

Daksey chutted softly.

Maysam nudged him. "Maysam. I am Tho'ombax Foypang Maysam."

"I am Mo'beex Foysom," she said. "The drink sounds nice."

Maysam led her into the open area. They sat at a table far from the band.

Daksey turned back to the entrance. Still no sign of Amthek.

WHAT ARE THE RULES?

Friday, September 6, 3297, 21:34

Foondek sat at the table on a seat Debra had custom made for him so he could visit her new restaurant. Ted sat opposite and Maksim sat on the far side. She handed Foondek a bundle of greens she had picked and took the open seat. "These are growing nicely. You said they were good for the little one?"

Foondek flicked his tail. "While Deypax is still in the pouch, I have to eat extra and provide him with nutrition."

"Do you chew it up and put it into his mouth?"

Foondek's throat rumbled. "No, of course not. I am not a bird. Deypax has something inside my pouch that provides for him."

"Oh. Like milk?"

"What is milk?"

AutoGov projected a quick explanation of milk to him. He chut-chutted. "Not as liquid. Thicker. But yes. Like that."

"Wait," Ted said. "Does that mean he is a mammal? Are we back to him being a her?"

Foondek huffed. "You are too concerned with your labels.

I'm a pouch-husband. Now, a pouch-father. I was once a pouch-brother as well. I have a pouch. There is nothing confusing to me. The pouch is for the child to grow and feed until it can go free."

Ted raised his hand. "I didn't mean to get you upset. Sorry."

Maksim shook his head. "Foondek, that's the first time I think I saw you angry."

Foondek's quills flicked up and down. "Angry? Not at all. It's just that your definitions are not ours. I'm trying to make it simple. Ombax are two. I have a pouch. My egg-mother made the egg. My pouch-father took the egg and grew it into me. This is not confusing to me."

Debra patted Ted's arm. "I don't think we need to worry about it. Besides, don't you have an appointment with Zon, soon?"

"Sorry. Yes." Ted turned to Maksim. "If you two want to stop by, Zon and I are sparring downstairs. Right next to Foondek's quarters in Cargo 3."

Maksim waved as Ted and Debra left. "Tell me more about egg-mothers. How does it work?"

Foondek shook his head back and forth. "When the egg-mother decides to create a child, she holds an egg for incubation. While it's there, she... tastes it? To see if it's a good egg. Sometimes, it is not. Those go to the lower stomach. When the egg is good, and the incubation is at the proper stage, she will present it to a pouch-husband. Almost always one of hers."

"And the egg-mother has two husbands?" Maksim asked.

"At least. Two, three, four. It depends on how many she wants."

"How do you know if the child is yours?"

"If the egg-mother gives you the egg," Foondek said, "the child is yours."

"But how do you know it isn't fertilized by another?"

"What does that matter? The egg becomes the pouch-husband's when it's given to him. The donor of the seed only matters to the egg-mother when she chooses to hold an egg. She chooses the seed she likes at that time."

Maksim's eyes went wide. "Wait, so when she wants to make a child, she chooses the sex partner then?"

"No. Of course not. The sex part is done when the donor is available and ready to be polite. The choosing of the seed happens much later. Days, weeks, years."

"Now I am very confused."

Foondek huffed quietly. "This happens a lot when I talk about reproduction with your people. However, having studied your reproductive system, I can see the cause of the confusion. Your sex act is directly responsible for the seed fertilizing the egg. For us, there is a storage mechanism that allows them to be separate and controlled by the egg-mother."

"So, she has sex once, and can then have as many children as she wants from the same father?"

"She has sex with as many as she likes and then uses the seed she likes at the moment to create a child. A full-grown female can hold fifteen or sixteen seedlings."

Maksim tilted his head. "Wait, seedlings?"

"Yes. Our sex act is where the egg-mother penetrates the donor and takes a seedling. It will then crawl up her *untranslatable* and find a spot inside. There is an *untranslatable* with hexagonal pockets. Once it attaches, it lives there, producing seed when she demands it."

"She can only ever have reproductive sex with sixteen males?"

Foondek's nostrils flared. "Not exactly. The egg-mother can taste the seedling, and if she decides she doesn't like it, she pushes it into her lower stomach."

"Doesn't the donor get offended?"

"It's not something that is shared, so he would never know. Besides, most donors move on after that. Only the pouch-husbands might get a hint of the status of their seedlings, but it's considered impolite to speak of such things."

Maksim sat back and crossed his arms. "Which gives the egg-mother total control over reproduction."

Foondek hooted softly. "Exactly. Isn't it wonderful?"

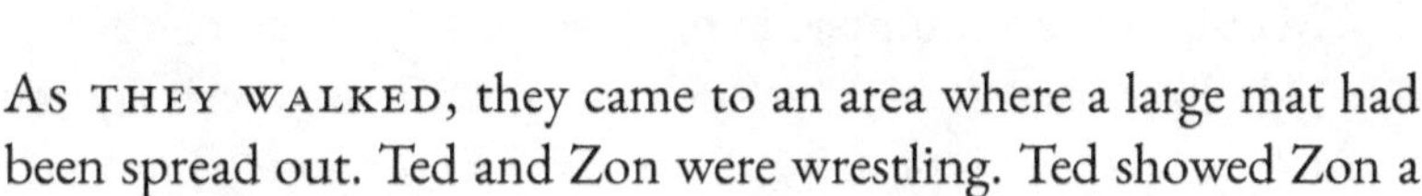

As they walked, they came to an area where a large mat had been spread out. Ted and Zon were wrestling. Ted showed Zon a move to disarm an opponent with a gun while Debra stood to one side holding towels.

"Fighting," Foondek said.

Maksim looked at Foondek. "They aren't really fighting. Just practicing. Remember, Ted said he and Zon had an appointment. This is it."

Foondek chut-chutted. "I see no displays of anger. Now I understand. Just now, when Ted had Zon on the ground, Zon tapped Ted on the leg. Two times. Ted released him. We do something like this. But with three taps. The result is the same. Peaceful disentanglement."

"Peaceful disentanglement," Debra said. "That's a nice way to put it."

"Indeed," Maksim said.

"Do you think they would let me play?" Foondek asked.

"Maybe. Hey Ted, Zon. You guys want to let Foondek play with you? He thinks it looks like fun."

Ted and Zon looked at each other.

"That might be a good idea," Ted said. "I think it would help us learn more about each other."

Foondek flicked his tail. "The disarming move you showed Zon. The item you took, a weapon, correct? Perhaps a projectile thrower? Or did it represent something more dangerous?"

Ted grinned. "Projectiles. We've found them to be cheap and

easy to make, while also being very effective in close range. Helps defend against animals."

"Sometimes they are made by my people as well. Not always because of animals."

"Come on in and let's see what you can do."

Foondek took a step forward, then placed a hand on his bulging pouch. He turned to Maksim. "Would you hold Deypax?"

Maksim's heart thumped in his chest. "Are you sure?"

"He likes you. It will be safer for him. In case we play too hard." He opened his pouch and gently lifted the young Ombax.

"My how he's grown."

Foondek gently placed his ward into Maksim's arms. "They grow quickly in the pouch. It's all eating and resting in there. It will slow when he begins to scamper about."

"Will he slow down his eating?"

Foondek chutted. "No. And it will be difficult to walk without stepping on his tail."

Maksim smiled down at his charge. Two large eyes looked up at him. The green scaly skin turned into a small black ring around the eye, only to return to green before revealing the dark amber eye punctuated with the little black dot of his pupil. Deypax blinked and curled into his embrace, all settled in for a nap.

Foondek had already entered the ring by the time Maksim looked back up.

"He seems excited," Debra said.

"Who Foondek?"

"Of course. The little one looks like he went right to sleep. But I swear I saw Foondek smile."

Maksim smirked. "Showing teeth is a sign of aggression for them."

· · ·

TED GRINNED LOPSIDEDLY. "That makes the third time he has beaten you, Zon."

Zon scoffed. "He's more slippery than he looks, and that tail can land a nasty thump."

Foondek's nostrils flared. "Did I cause you an excess of pain? Is there any injury?"

Zon shook his head. "Maybe a bruised ego. You are very good, Foondek."

"I feel lighter in this place. I'm able to use that to my advantage. This last time you came close. If I hadn't been able to knock you off balance with my tail, you would have prevailed again."

Ted laughed. "That's being generous."

"Do your people play at fighting for fun?" Debra asked.

Foondek flicked his tail. "For fun and for tradition. We have a game we call *endurance*. The same as you call this city in the stars."

Ted grinned. "A game with fighting?"

"Teams who run toward a goal, individual combat, mild bondage, and trust are all parts of the game."

Zon chuckled. "Mild bondage?"

Debra stood on her toes. "Ooh. Now that sounds fun."

Ted's face flushed red.

Foondek undulated. "When a combat round is resolved, the winner will bind the loser, give them water, and leave them for later retrieval."

"What if they untie themselves?" Zon asked.

"That is where the trust comes in. A candidate who loses but then breaks the trust is deemed to be a great failure. One can lose an individual combat but still find a mate. But one who fails the test of trust will find no female interested in him. He will return from whence he came, and word will spread. This sort would eventually have to leave his home and wander the world, searching for redemption."

"That's harsh," Zon said.

Ted put his hand on Debra's shoulder.

"I know how that feels," Debra said. "Does it happen often?"

Foondek chutted. "Only in the stories we are told as ankle-biters. I've never heard of it happening in recent memory. However, that would only be in our region of the world. There are many areas I know little about. It could be a bigger problem than I know."

"You say the games affect your chances of finding a mate," Ted said. "Is that how you do it all of the time?"

"All the time?" Foondek shrugged. "No. Most of the time a female will find pouch-husbands attractive and suitable within the village. The games are held between villages. It helps us find mates in other places. Keeps the population mixed. Makes us healthier. We do it at least once or twice a year. I remember once we had three. Anyone who participates could find an egg-mother. The winner becomes an honorary member of the tribe, if he wasn't already. Then there is a celebration with music and food."

"Is your tribe on good terms with all of your neighbors?"

Foondek looked him in the eyes. "Some, more than others. All the tribes of the Koy'am are related and good friends. The people up in Bamthapeem are not close relations. We see them less, but there are no conflicts between us."

"According to our data, all the tribes down in the crater have similar markings. Some variation of green and black. The mountain folk are gray with black stripes."

Foondek shrugged. "The Moyak have gold stripes. But the green is the same as the Botham and the Ko'dex. The Kayax are black, with green stripes. They are less related, but we still consider them family. We are the four tribes of the Koy'am. The forest in the crater. Bamthapeem is high on the edge."

"So those little villages outside the rim wall, not related?"

Foondek shrugged. "Not as much. All Ombax are related in one way or another, but the connection may be many generations removed."

"Does each tribe have its own variation of colors?"

"Most do. There are some places where two or three villages might have families of the same colors. In the cities there is more variety. You might find samples from many of the surrounding villages there. If you go far enough to the west, you will find some with spots instead of stripes. Is it the same with your people? Your skin is much darker than his skin. Are your mothers from different tribes?"

Ted laughed. "Our colors come from both parents. Male and female. We have much larger communities, and there is a lot more mixing but still a wide variety. I may be darker than him, but I have ancestors who were much darker and much lighter."

"Foondek," Debra said, "tell me more about that game. What are the rules?"

THE SCHOLARS

Mas'eeng Masassof, Third Eight, Late

The last full count had passed quietly. Maysam and Foysom saw more and more of each other, until finally Maysam moved into her home. She began helping to manage the place, organizing and cleaning. At first, Daksey worried she would try to take over, but she accepted the fact that she wasn't an owner and played the role of support very well.

One evening after closing the door swung open. A very old and large black and silver egg-mother strode into the room.

"Geen and black. Are you Daksey?"

Daksey undulated. "I am. Do I know you?"

A familiar red and black face poked out from under her arm.

"Amthek!" Daksey hopped from foot to foot.

Amthek pushed past the elder egg-mother and leapt onto Daksey. "I did it. I knew I could. I did it."

"Did what?" Daksey paused. "Are you...?"

"I am Dathopsak Safoy of Soypasod. Your friend came to get me. He said you were having difficulty reaching the observatory."

Daksey chut-chutted. "Come and have a seat. I'll tell you

everything. Amthek, run up to my room, the first room on the left. Fetch my pack. It's in the far corner."

Amthek started up the stairs then stopped. "First room? Where's Maysam?"

"Married. Lives next door. I moved into the small room so we could rent out the other."

Amthek huffed. "Of all things." He scampered off.

•• ——————————— ••●•• ——————————— ••

THE NEXT MORNING, Daksey and Amthek followed Safoy to the temple. She strode in without so much as a glance at the adornments. Almost as if she owned the place. "Bayam? Where are you?"

Moments later Bayam appeared. The head priest who had dismissed Daksey before. "I hadn't expected you would ever return here."

"I hadn't expected it either," she said, "but I'm quite concerned over the reports I've been hearing."

"What reports?" He blinked, glanced at Daksey, but didn't seem to recognize him.

"There are reports of unusual creatures about. How is the investigation going?"

"Investigation?" He glared at Daksey. "I recognize you now. Yes, a report of a mutant or two. Silly speculation."

"Silly? One or two? Didn't you even bother to listen to this one's story? Examine his evidence?"

Bayam shrugged. "A malformed skull, I'm sure. It's–"

"Similarly strange skulls from three different events scattered over half the continent. A group of four at Seeng'dod, another four at Beethax, and three more up in a little mountain village called Bamthapeem. All adorned with similar cloth, all showing some form of electrical devices, and all three came in flying ships."

"Flying ships?"

"The one at Seeng'dod was destroyed. They have the parts. Why haven't you examined them?"

"I had no idea. These can't be mutant creatures. It sounds too preposterous."

"Exactly." She thumped her tail. "Which is why that new little moon may hold the key."

"New little moon? It's surely a captured asteroid."

"Have you looked at it with a telescope?"

"No, but the scholars must know about it."

"Perhaps. And they should know about all of this as well. We should give them the images and the physical evidence this one has brought to you, and we should do it right now."

"Yes, Egg-Mother. Right away." He led the group through the hall to a large circular staircase.

"Send them up in the elevator."

Bayam shrunk. "Yes, Egg-Mother."

Amthek nudged Daksey. "She's really his egg-mother. He's not simply being courteous, he's Dathopsak Safoy Bayam."

Normally Daksey might feel sorry for the pouch-husband, but in this case, he deserved the embarrassment. "It explains why the people in Beethax told me to meet her."

Amthek chut-chutted.

The elevator was a wide cage of wrought metal with ornate copper coils. Once the three of them entered, Bayam closed the gate from the outside and pointed to a lever. "Pull that backwards. Then leave it alone. It will reset at the top by itself. Open the gate when the car has come to a complete halt."

Daksey undulated deeply. "Thank you for your help."

Bayam started. His eyes went wide. He undulated, then turned and followed his egg-mother, who had already leapt to the stairs.

She stopped him. "Before you come up, go ask your wife if she would kindly free the one called Thoy'eeng and forgive him. He is this one's protector and so a friend of mine."

Bayam shrunk. "Yes, Egg-Mother." He turned and scampered off.

"I will meet the rest of you up there. Pull that lever now."

"Are you sure you don't want to ride with us?" Daksey asked.

"No." She huffed. "Never again. But you will be fine. I'm sure they've fixed it by now."

Amthek pulled the lever before Daksey could stop him. The cage lurched upwards and began a steady ascent.

The light faded into darkness several times, then returned with a pane of glass, or a small balcony, before the darkness returned. Eventually the light grew strong and stayed. The cage shuddered to a stop.

Daksey opened the gate and stepped out into the small stone walled room. Open arches leading outside were framed with vines. Flowerpots lined the walls. Vegetation partially obscured words that had been chiseled into the stone. Daksey recognized the first part as being the words of warning. *It is wrong to catch the lightning.* He knew all three of them, but this stone had a fourth at the bottom. Something he had never heard of before. *Sky People ride the lightning.*

"Welcome. We haven't had visitors up here for quite some time." A large, gray egg-mother filled an archway. Her black spots glistened in the sunlight. "I am Bengdoy. Welcome to my domain. What brings you here?"

Amthek leapt forward. "Daksey has things to show you. Important things."

Daksey huffed. "Amthek, please."

"What things? Why are they important?"

Daksey shifted his pack and dug out the skull. He carefully unwrapped it.

Bengdoy leaned forward. "Interesting. Very interesting." She backed out of the room and headed toward another building. "Follow me. Bring everything."

They entered a room filled with strange equipment. A table piled high with clutter occupied the center. Bengdoy began shifting things from the table onto shelves along the walls. "As I make space, feel free to fill it up with what you have brought. I'll try to be quick."

"I can help clear the table," Amthek said.

"No, no. That won't help. I need to know where everything is, and if I don't put it there myself, I'll lose track."

Daksey put the first few items onto the table.

Once the tabletop had been transformed into a display of the contents of Daksey's pack, Bengdoy began examining each item. When her hand hovered over one of the small disks, Daksey stopped her. "If you touch it in a certain way, it glows. It's not a natural light."

Bengdoy's hand withdrew. "You have seen it?"

"I have," Daksey said.

She sat back and put her hands onto her hips. "Tell me your story. Start where you think it starts. Don't leave anything out. The rest of you, if you get bored, please leave quietly. Akbay, fetch water and something to eat for everyone, please."

The pouch-husband flicked his tail and headed to the kitchen.

Daksey started with the sighting of the strange new moonlet, and spoke for a long time. The food and water came, and Amthek eventually fell asleep.

Safoy arrived and sat quietly.

"Safoy, would you like me to start over?" Daksey asked.

"No, no," Safoy said. "Please keep going as you were. She's the scholar here. She's the one who needs to know."

Bengdoy flicked her tail and urged Daksey to continue. She asked questions only when she wanted clarification, or more details. When Daksey finally described the delay in getting the information to the scholars, her throat rumbled in anger. "Those stupid priests. How in the world can they wield so much power? Oh, sorry, Safoy. He is your son. I mean no offense."

"No offense can be taken at the truth, Bengdoy. If my work at Soypasad wasn't so important, I would have been here. I came when the little red and black arrived to fetch me."

Bengdoy gazed at the sleeping Amthek. "Someday, Daksey, you will have to tell me that part of the story as well."

Akbay entered pushing a large cart laden with food. "I thought you might want another meal."

Amthek sat up. "Food?"

While they ate, Bengdoy examined the treasures Daksey had brought while he retold the first part of his story to Safoy.

Amthek had his fill and wandered out to stretch in the sun.

"So now tell me about him," Safoy said. "How did the two of you meet?"

"We met at the market in Seeng'dod and became friends. His family is gone. A storm on the north coast where he lived. Many of the survivors came south to find a new home."

Bengdoy huffed. "The winter storms were bad this year. Keyoompax is the name of the town, I'll bet. He's lucky to have survived."

"Even luckier to have found such a good friend," Safoy said.

Daksey shrunk. "I inspired him to risk his life, and then didn't drop everything and go after him. What kind of friend is that?"

Bengdoy and Safoy both chut-chutted.

"Inspirational," Bengdoy said.

"And trusting," Safoy said.

Bayam arrived as Akbay finished clearing the dishes. Amthek followed him in and set about helping with the cleanup.

Bayam huffed. "Have you determined anything of import?"

Bengdoy snorted. "People from another world are trying to contact us, and they are failing badly."

"Impossible. You must have it wrong." He pointed to the skull. "That is a mutation. Nothing more. Something from one of the other continents."

Safoy huffed. "Bayam, please allow the scholar to be the final arbiter of the facts here. Your dogma is getting in the way of the truth again."

"Esteemed Egg-Mother, I respect your opinion and will do my best to take it into consideration always, however you no longer rule here. The truth cannot conflict with what has been written, because what has been written is the truth."

"Bayam we've had this discussion before, and you know how I feel about it. However, you are correct. You are now in charge."

"I propose we take the airship to Seeng'dod," Bengdoy said. "They have more evidence which should help us determine if these skulls are simply a mutilation, or something that breeds true."

Safoy flicked her tail. "Agreed. Seeng'dod and back again."

"I would prefer to go to Bamthapeem as well."

"That is a long way to go. Surely you will find enough evidence at Seeng'dod. Wouldn't that be repetitious? Unless you can think of something new that could be of scientific value, the airship should not go further than the desert."

Daksey glanced at Bengdoy.

She huffed in clear frustration.

"What about Thamthad?"

"Thamthad? Isn't that one of the eastern ruins?"

Daksey continued, "I strayed from the marked path, and the ground collapsed. I ended up beneath the surface. There are tunnels, passageways that have not been explored."

"You never mentioned that."

"It has nothing to do with the skulls. I didn't think it would help."

"Thamthad, you say," Bayam said.

Safoy crossed her arms and tilted her head and huffed.

"Fine. Take an expeditionary team to Thamthad as well. Make sure they are well provisioned. That is a long way from the city. Then return."

Bengdoy flicked her tail. "Thank you, Bayam. We'll do as you say."

Safoy undulated. "A reasonable call. Bengdoy, can you work with this?"

Bengdoy chutted. "You know me, Safoy."

"Good. Now, let's go down and speak with your wife, Bayam. I would enjoy the opportunity to catch up before I return to Soypasod."

THE AIRSHIP

Mas'eeng Masassof, Last One, Early High

Every day, Bengdoy asked more questions about his journey. He was careful when he explained about his change of plans. The rest of the time she ordered and organized as workers moved supplies toward the far side of the enclosure.

"Where are they taking everything?" he asked.

"To the crater. This ledge we built on sites between the cliff on one side, and a deep crater. Come, let me show you."

Daksey followed her. They came to a railing, and Bengdoy made room for him. He peered carefully over the edge into the deep crater below. All he could see was the oblong shape of the giant gas bag. Somewhere below that, Daksey assumed, hung the gondola.

Once they had climbed down, Daksey realized there was no gondola. At one end of the oblong shaped material, a wide doorway made of koyosek slats. The light wood made sense. But that must mean the people rode inside the bag itself. The bottom structure turned out to be something else entirely. Beyond the bag Daksey could see a large lake in the crater below. Nearly solid green, with what looked like collection stations placed in positions in the water.

"The plants use sunlight to consume the water," Bengdoy said. "They extract oxygen, and release the hydrogen. We simply capture it, and use it for our lifting gas. As you can see, our supply is limited. That's why we only have one airship at a time." She waved at the airship. "This one is the Exkeesak."

"So if this doorway takes us inside, what is in the bottom part? That's where my brother and I always thought people rode."

Bengdoy chut-chutted. "The bottom houses the compression tanks and the landing gear. There are also hook mounts for the occasional cargo netting. We don't usually need it, since so much can fit inside the main hold. But it's nice to know we can use it in a pinch. We call this a cargo hatch, but it's just a big door. There is another way in from the bottom, but it's much smaller. We use it for maintenance, primarily."

Two pouch-husbands took one side each of the hatch and lifted. The horizontal slats were arranged so that when it neared the top, it followed a curved track and rolled itself into a bundle at the top.

A large open area inside had been filled with regularly spaced pallets of cargo crates. Some seemed much larger than others, and it looked lopsided.

Daksey had a thought. He undulated to himself. "You space these out by weight, not size."

Bengdoy flicked her tail. "Yes, of course. We want the Exkeesak to be balanced. It makes it easier to handle in flight."

"Close that hatch," came a deep, booming voice from within. "I'm not done with the ventilation checks."

"That would be my daughter, Kayfox."

The pouch-husbands were scrambling to close the hatch.

Kayfox emerged from the darkness into the well-lit cargo bay. She stood a little taller than Daksey, with the same coloration as her mother, except her spots seemed bolder. Sharper edges, and smaller ones that ran up her neck that were very delicate and interesting.

"You can stop staring now."

Daksey blinked, then bowed deeply. "My apologies. Your spots are very interesting. I've never seen people with spots before."

Kayfox's quills flicked up and back. "They are only rare in the far east."

Daksey flicked his tail. "I am Botham Kempok Daksey. I come from the East. From the forest of Koy'am."

Kayfox huffed, then inhaled sharply. "My test." She spun and hurried back into the darkness.

Daksey glanced at Bengdoy. She was watching him, but he couldn't figure out what was on her mind.

She undulated gently. "Let's proceed to the control room. The Exkeesak is a complicated machine. We'll need to show you what not to touch."

EXKEESAK

Mas'eeng Masassof, Last One, Late

When Daksey and Amthek returned to the tavern, Thoy'eeng greeted them at the door. Osmay sat at a nearby table. His head hung low.

"Good to see you again, Thoy'eeng," Daksey said. "I'm sorry for my part in your imprisonment."

"Say nothing more of it. The fault is mine. I let my temper get the better of me. But then I had company, as Osmay came to join me."

Osmay grunted and buried his head in his arms.

Thoy'eeng chutted. "I was about to settle into a room upstairs."

Daksey chut-chutted. "Don't bother. We need to pack and get back up the mountain. We can sleep there from now on. We'll be leaving soon for Seeng'dod."

"Back down the river?"

"No," Amthek said. "By airship." He hopped from foot to foot. "They call it the Exkeesak."

Thoy'eeng's nostrils flared. "Airship?"

Daksey turned to Maysam. "You and Foysom can have my share of the tavern. I won't be back"

"Me neither," Amthek said. "Same deal. May your life be full of good things."

Thoy'eeng swayed. "Airship?"

HYDROPONICS

Thursday, November 21, 3297, 11:11

Maksim led Foondek to the hydroponics section of the lower level. "Just like I told you. Long channels of nutrient rich water with plants packed in as tightly as they will allow. Tons of lights providing light that is identical to our home star's light."

Foondek squinted. "I cannot see a difference. Your sun is like ours?"

"To our eyes they are the same. The scientists say they are slightly different, but it's not by much, if you ask me." Maksim pointed to the far end. "See where the lights end? That's the next expansion area. Some of us are thinking we might be able to grow food from your world there. We just have to get the nutrients mixed right. Our studies show the atmosphere mix is close enough that the plants can comingle."

"What about pollen? Or pollinators?"

"One problem at a time. Yes, we may have to install partitions and filters. And we already have artificial pollinators at work. We didn't want to bring our own insects, because they tend to get everywhere, and we didn't want them getting down to your world."

"Like how ours came to be on your ship."

"Exactly. We use small drones to do the work. The AutoGov oversees it all."

The lights flickered then went out. Emergency lamps every few meters provided enough light to move in. A large person came running toward them. Maybe they needed Maksim. He turned to look at Maksim, but his friend had crouched over. Maksim leapt at the running figure, they tumbled.

An attack. Foondek's eyes went wide. Maksim smashed his hand into the other's face, while clutching his side.

Foondek smelled blood. Maksim was wounded. He scooped Deypax from his pouch and thrust him into Maksim's arms, then jumped with all his might at the attacker.

Both feet struck the large man's chest. Foondek pushed himself upwards, landed where the rolling man had been. He spun on one leg and his tail, kicking out at the other, catching the attacker under the chin. The assailant flipped backwards over the rail, into the water.

Maksim stepped to Foondek's side and peered over. The attacker was lost in the darkness. Both listened for any motion.

Maksim spoke to his communications system. "Foondek and I have been attacked, lower level, hydroponics. The attacker went into the water, but we can't see where he went. Send someone at once."

A few minutes later, Ted and his partner arrived. Zon slid into the water, and after a few minutes, found the attacker, dead, wedged between two supports.

Maksim shook his head. "What the hell was that about?"

Foondek took a deep breath and looked at his child. He looked around, content, not scared. Then Foondek put his arm on Maksim's shoulder and pointed to the pouchling. "He trusts you."

Maksim showed his teeth. "I wouldn't let any harm come to

him." He held the child out so Foondek could slip him back into the pouch.

"All you need is a pouch, and you would be a good pouch-husband."

Maksim made those barking noises again. "Perhaps in time."

Ted turned to them. "You two should head back up. Zon and I will wait for the body recovery team. We've already got the data team doing a full trace. I'll let you both know what we find."

Foondek followed Maksim up the steps. As he watched the alien creature, he thought how Maksim was no longer alien. No longer a stranger. Maksim was a friend. Foondek hooted softly to himself.

FALLOUT

Thursday, November 21, 3297, 14:24

Radinka entered the simulation in a foul mood. She stormed though the Tipsy Raven's automated patrons, shoving them aside as she stalked to the hidden door. She entered the room and found only two of her three compatriots. "Why did you make me come around the long way?"

"I turned off direct materialization as a precaution. I've also deleted the asshole's records," Ferdinand said. "Nothing in the system connects him to us."

Radinka fell into her chair. "That was the most stupid, idiotic thing I have ever heard."

"It might have worked out," Briana said. "If he had killed that thing–"

"He would still be just as dead. Or worse, captured and interrogated. Stupid filthy bastard. How the hell did he ever qualify for this team?"

"Your predecessor chose him," Ferdinand said. "That's all I know."

"Another good reason for him to have been replaced. We could have used another pair of hands. How goes the coding? Are you going to be ready to plant the program when the time comes?"

"I think so. I should be able to start testing the code in my simulated environment next week."

"Next week?" Radinka's face burned hot. "Why next week? Why not tomorrow?"

"Because I'm involved in a dozen different official projects and they are tracking all of my time while I'm working. I can only do this in my downtime. But early next week. Four days, tops. I promise. I need to be sure the simulator is properly partitioned from the main system. Can't afford any leaks. That would tip them off as surely as an unprovoked attack might."

Radinka scowled. "Elf, have you heard anything about an investigation?"

"No," Briana said. "My guy on the inside has been moody. He is angry because I won't meet him in the real."

"Is he male?"

Briana nodded.

"Are you female?"

"Yes. I'm damned pretty too. I don't want to blow my cover, remember?"

"Do it anyway," Radinka said. "Pump him for everything he knows. See if you can motivate him to learn more if you have to. We need to know what's happening."

Briana took a deep breath. "You're pinning a lot on me having the body type he's looking for."

Radinka paused. "Do you need mods?"

"What?" She blushed. "No. It's that my avatar is a lot taller than I am. I think he might like tall women."

"Wear high heels. Then spin his head so hard it falls off. We need that information, and that's the best lead we have right now."

Briana growled and crossed her arms.

MAYBE 60/40

Saturday, November 23, 3297, 10:33

Ted found Jake on watch alone in MCC. "No backup?"

"We got used to shorting the weekend watch. One can handle it most times, and with a small crew, the extra free time was appreciated. Is this about the attack?"

Ted nodded. "TuckerMale1a TuckerMale1b was brought out of cold sleep on August 26. He's listed as an agricultural specialist. Was helping Gabriel on the farm."

"Anything on his past?"

Ted shook his head. "No history files from before he was put on ice. FoodCo, though."

"Did Gabriel know him?"

"He said he had never heard of him, and pointed out that FoodCo was the largest nutrition manufacturer when we left." He shrugged. "He said he had no problems with the guy, and he seemed to know his job. No idea what brought on the attack."

Jake sighed.

"Gets better. The guy's social life was normal. Mostly. He spent time at Natasha's bar but never got drunk. Talked to few people but didn't seem rude. The only other thing was he had VR gear in his room."

"Where did he go there?"

"He spent time in several games and then a ton of adult content. Again, nothing strange."

"Next steps?"

"I want to set AutoGov up to analyze his VR time, but there isn't enough to go on to even look at anyone else."

"Okay. Keep me posted."

Ted smiled. "One more thing I wanted to run by you. I want to try again." He nodded out the wide curved window where the expanse of the planet below rotated into view. "Down there."

Jake's eyebrows shot up. "You want to do what?"

"You heard me," Ted said. "I want to take a team down and attempt first contact again."

"Dad gave specific orders against doing anything of the sort. You saw what happened. We tried three times, and lost eleven people. All three attempts failed."

"Yes, but this time we have Foondek, and we've got a plan."

"Ted, please." Jake signaled for him to lower his voice. "Have you run this by Debra? You would be risking your life."

"Okay, let me stop you right there, Mr. Onada. You are just as married as I am."

"Oh. Right. So this was her idea?"

"She's leading the team."

"He will say no," Jake said. "He's dead set against losing more people. Even if your idea works and Foondek is right, it's still a risk he has explicitly said he does not want to take."

Ted tilted his head. "But he did say we could take Foondek home, right?"

Jake's eyes narrowed. "Yes. He did say that. Has the attack soured him on us?"

"No. He was already talking about going home. In fact, we've been working on this plan for a while. So, can I assume your father didn't put any parameters around Foondek's return mission?"

Jake crossed his arms. "So now you want me to forget our previous conversation, and pretend you guys only want to be the team that returns Foondek to his home."

Ted nodded with a grin.

Jake frowned. "And since there are no specific parameters from my father, and if I said to use your best judgment as to how to accomplish that..."

Ted spread his hands in a wide shrug. "I think we've found our way in. Now, you need to act surprised when we do what we plan to do."

"Which is what, exactly?"

"Now, now, if I told you, it wouldn't be a surprise. But between me and you, it was Foondek's idea. He seems convinced it will work."

"How sure is he that no one else will die?" Jake asked.

Ted shrugged. "We think we understand the main issues involved. The response to technology, the way we look. Pretty sure. Maybe. I don't know, ninety... maybe eighty-five percent chance we all make it out alive. Hey, it's way better odds than I've had on previous missions."

"Okay. I'll set it up. But you're Chief of Security so I'm listing you as the one in charge. Anyone else you draft is on you. Got it?"

"Got it. And thanks. I'll let you know when we're ready to drop."

•• —————————— ••●•• —————————— ••

"Slight change of plans," Ted said as he entered the restaurant.

Debra smiled. "What's up?"

"I'm leading the security team to take Foondek home."

"No first contact?"

"I didn't say that," Ted said. "Just that we won't have official permission as such."

"Mission parameters?"

"I lead a team of my selection, and I accomplish the goal of returning Foondek to his people as I see fit."

Debra grinned. "We're on, but we can't say it that way."

Ted waved his hand above her head. "I hereby select you to be on the team as my second in command. Get the rest together and let's get ready."

She nodded intently as she swiped her display. "Maksim is a go. That makes three of us. We need a fourth to fill out the team."

"Make sure it's someone without family."

Debra frowned. "You still think this is too risky?"

"Everything is risky. This could turn upside down in a heartbeat. You saw what happened before."

"We have reasonable explanations for each event. Plus, we have Foondek. That has to count for something."

"Hey," Ted said, "can Foondek be on the team?"

Debra shook her head. "He has his own mission. He needs to be in position near the end zone. I don't want to interfere with that part of the plan. Besides, he's married and wants to take his kid home to meet the mother. If nothing else, that part needs to go smoothly. He's going to have to explain what happened to the other one, too."

"Right. It still needs to be someone who would trust Foondek, and be able to hold their own in a fight. It should be someone without a family, for obvious reasons."

"What about that biologist?" She swiped and poked the display. "Anna Ruggiero. She's friends with Foondek. I saw her sparring with Zon the other day. Seems competent. Let's ask her."

Ted smiled. "I like that idea. Make the call. Be sure to be discreet, and honest. Don't oversell our chances."

Debra sighed. "I know."

· · ·

ANNA'S HEAD and shoulders bobbed in Debra's display as she frowned. "Are you fucking crazy?"

Debra tried to smile. "Kind of. But we think it will work."

"Skip said we weren't going to try this again. What changed his mind?"

"Technically, his mind hasn't changed. Our official mission is to return Foondek to his family."

"So, the rest," Anna said, "that whole thing is what, off the books?"

Debra took a deep breath. "It stays within the technical bounds of our orders, but yes, it stretches the hell out of them, and if Skip gets wind of it he'll shut it down. But Foondek is sure his plan will work, and he's going to be right there next to the one who decides. The leader of the tribe. She's something close to family. I think he'll be–"

"Family, as in the mother of the one who died. You are not making your case right now, lady."

"I know. And we've given it a lot of thought. But here's the thing, I trust Foondek. I think he's right, and we just hit a streak of bad luck. Bad timing, and an underestimation of their reaction to displays of technology."

Anna nodded thoughtfully. "I've read that report. It does seem pretty convincing."

"You did? Good. What did you make of it?"

"Remember, I'm the one who did the autopsy. I saw what that hindbrain looked like, and from the way Foondek described it, it seems quite plausible. I think he is basically correct."

"From that standpoint, what do you think our chances of success are?"

Anna sat back and crossed her arms. "Objectively, fifty-fifty. Maybe sixty-forty in your favor."

"Would you like a chance at meeting more of these people?"

Anna sighed. "Look, I'll need to talk it over with Cheri first. This is a big risk."

"Oh crap. I hadn't realized. Ted told me not to ask anyone with a family, and I completely forgot to check your personal profile."

"Too late. Besides, that list is damned short, and I'm the best qualified to actually accomplish some science down there if this plan of yours works. So yes, let me talk to my wife. When do you need to know?"

"We're already packing. Maybe a day at the outside."

Anna nodded. "I will let you know in the morning. That gives me all night to bring her around."

"Look, I feel guilty for asking, now. Maybe–"

Anna raised her hand. "Nope. Like I said, too late. And I think your odds are better than sixty percent anyway. I'll let you know when I know."

"Okay. Thanks."

SHUTTLE TALK

Sunday, November 24, 3297, 8:19

Ted activated the chef and stood back.

It puttered about behind the counter and started sorting dinnerware.

"I got it started on the dishes."

"Good, honey," Debra said from the table in the front corner.

Anna sat quietly, looking out the window at the park.

"Our shuttle might need a little work," Debra said. "We are going to have to fit four humans and Foondek inside, all while making sure everyone can strap in safely – not to mention extra padding for his pouch."

Anna thought for a moment. "What about the *Pang Yu's* shuttle? Isn't that bigger?"

"Bigger wingspan, more fuel, but the cargo space is about the same. Plus, it's never actually made an atmospheric entry. I would rather take something that's been fully checked out."

Ted sat next to Debra. "Not to mention that would put Captain Alvarez in the mix, and she's bound to ask questions."

"Good point," Debra said. "Okay then, we take one of the *Endurance* shuttles. Make sure it's rigged out. Pack it with a little camping gear just in case. Food rations for a week at most. Am I missing anything?"

"Pilot?" Anna frowned.

Debra smirked. "AutoGov. Best pilot we have."

"Look," Anna said, "don't get me wrong, but I have a hard time trusting that thing."

"I grew up with automation. AutoGov was born on Luna like me. I trust it."

"I grew up in a habitat that had precious little of that. We did things for ourselves, and most of our folk didn't like heavy automation any more than they liked rich know-it-alls from super rich wonderlands. No offence."

"Hmm... super rich." Debra shrugged. "Comparatively speaking, that's true. Luna was great. And the only reason I tend to have answers is because my controllers connect me directly to the AutoGov. I can look up any fact I need. I really don't know it all, just look it up very quickly. Aren't you connected to AutoGov, now?"

Anna scoffed. "Yes. I got the upgrade before we left Earth. I don't use it much."

"Maybe if you did you might learn to like it. At any rate, AutoGov is the most qualified to pilot the shuttle. It means we don't have to find a fifth body to take."

"Fine. But put me down for a mild tranquilizer, just in case."

"To keep you from freaking out?" Ted asked.

Debra scoffed.

Anna laughed. "To let me sleep through your screams of terror before we crash. I don't want to be awake for that shit."

"I'm more worried about how Foondek will take it. His last flight was a nightmare."

Anna sobered. "Oh yeah. Not good at all. I'll have a talk with him. See if he has any concerns."

"Good idea. See you at the end of your next shift."

RETURN TO THE SAND

Mas'eeng Masassof, Last Seven, Late High

Thoy'eeng pointed to the north side of Seeng'dod. "Head to the fields near the north gate. Keep a good distance from the city."

"Any reason why the north, in particular?" Bengdoy asked.

Thoy'eeng nodded. "No one from the north has ever attacked us. We use it as a sort of signal. If it's in the north, wait and see. Any other direction and you get cannon fire first. Questions are asked later."

"When was the last time you were attacked?"

"Don't they teach you your own history? Your people attacked us less than 128 years ago."

"That was a long time ago." Bengdoy chutted. "And they aren't my people. I come from the East. I ended up in the city because of my love of books."

"In the desert, we remember such things. And now that I'm telling you about the north, if the people of Afothameex use it to their advantage the next time they attack us, we will blame you."

"I have no intention of telling them the best way of attacking you. I'm a scholar. I'm not even in charge of attacks and rarely condone them."

"No, but what you learn here... well that is not for me to say. Get us close to that farmhouse over there. Come near the ground, but don't land until I negotiate a fee."

"A fee? For landing?"

"The only place to land in this area that is inside the outer wall is a field. It will damage someone's crop."

Bengdoy huffed. "Being inside the wall is a good thing, I suppose."

Thoy'eeng flicked his tail. "It's also a sign of respect. Inside the protective wall, outside the main city wall."

When they came near the ground two young pouch-brothers could be seen jumping and running in circles. A large egg-mother emerged from the farmhouse and gazed up at them. When they came near to the ground, but stayed above the crops, she waved and walked over to them. Thoy'eeng leaned out of the open window and called down a greeting.

"Hello. We've come to see Samam, and we need a place to land the ship. It will very likely damage crops. I'm authorized to negotiate the price of that damage."

"You speak like a local, but this ship looks to be from Afothameex."

"You are correct on both counts. I am Tho'ombax Boyap Thoy'eeng. This is the Exkeesak. We carry a delegation to speak with Samam."

"The ship is large and flat, but it doesn't seem very heavy if it's lighter than the air. Will it rest on the ground, or float above it."

"We would prefer to land," Bengdoy said. "There are skids below, and a system that draws air up, holding the craft to the ground when the wind blows. The lifting gas is then compressed, which makes the ship heavier. Not its full weight, but a good deal of it will rest on the ground."

"I see," said the farmer. "Then there will be some damage. How long will you stay?"

"At least a full count," Thoy'eeng said.

"If you stay in one place that long, the entire spot will go dead. Sixty-four fong a day."

"We can move it every two days. Sixteen fong a day."

The young ones started shouting at their egg-mother. "Oh please! Yes, yes!"

She waved them off. "You will move it every day. I will mark places for you to land. Thirty-two fong a day."

"We'll move every day, and we can throw in rides for the younglings when we do. Twenty-four."

She tilted her head. "Twenty-eight, and if they break the ship, it's on you."

Thoy'eeng flicked his tail and nodded. "Twenty-eight is good. And if they come back with their tails bitten off, that is on you."

Both of the young ones stopped and cowered, grabbing their tails and looking at their egg-mother.

She chut-chutted. "We have an agreement. Just be sure you bandage them to stop the bleeding. I have nice wooden floors, and I don't want them stained."

Thoy'eeng chut-chutted with her. "Agreed. I look forward to having them aboard."

The young ones looked at each other, then back to their egg-mother, then each other.

"We won't break your ship," said the nearest one.

Thoy'eeng locked eyes with that one. "You will do as you are told, and ask before you touch anything. If you can do that, you will enjoy the rides, I promise you."

"You handled that well, Thoy'eeng," Daksey said.

"I know children. I seem to deal with them every day." He gazed at Daksey.

"You do see that my skin has started to loosen, even as we speak?" Daksey huffed. "My adult molt has started."

"Yes, and you are already starting to sound too big for your skin. Be careful not to let your transition affect your tongue. Especially with Samam."

"Thoy'eeng," Bengdoy interrupted, "I want you and Daksey to accompany me. I will speak to Samam."

Thoy'eeng undulated deeply. "I will be with you."

Daksey's quills flicked up and down as he undulated. "I don't understand why you want me there."

Bengdoy chut-chutted. "You are the link that has brought it all together. You came from the far lands, you visited this city, and you came to me in Afothameex. I believe this is for a reason, and that you should continue to learn. What I will speak of with Samam may be of great importance. Come, they are opening the gate as we speak." She swung her bulk around and headed inside, toward the rear loading gate.

Thoy'eeng and Daksey followed.

The gate opened into a great courtyard. Several fruit trees and a small garden near the wall were decorated with colors banners and strips of cloth. Along the far wall a row of stalls with merchants selling rolls of cloth sat quietly.

Thoy'eeng led them to the right for a short time, then through an inner gate, smaller than before. Inside stairs wound upward.

The hallway at the top was lined with statues of egg-mothers Daksey had never seen before. All were painted in life-like colors with bright strips of cloth, and coverings.

Two pouch-fathers in leather armor stood outside a grand door.

"You never took me this way," Daksey said.

"You said you saw Samam here," Bengdoy said.

"I took him up the back way," Thoy'eeng said. "This is the front. More official."

Daksey huffed as the doors opened.

Thoy'eeng strode into the great room. He was about to speak when Bengdoy announced herself. "Great Samam of Seeng'dod. It is good to see you again. Are you doing well?"

"Bengdoy, greatest scholar of all Thoxmoyang. I didn't believe I'd ever see you again. I'm well. My city thrives, even as we absorb refugees from the north."

"Indeed. It does thrive. So much that it also invites visitors of another sort."

Samam's quills flicked slightly. She tilted her head, then glanced at Daksey. "It's good you received my report. Have you been able to determine which landmass they may have come from?"

Bengdoy shrugged. "There are still too many unanswered questions. Such as why they chose your city over mine."

"I'm sure they came because we are isolated. Perhaps they thought we would be an easy target."

"You suspect they intended to invade? With four people? By walking in daylight?"

Samam huffed. "What are you suggesting?"

"You know what I'm suggesting, and you know it should not be spoken of with ears in every corner. Perhaps we should move somewhere more private, or at least with more trusted ears."

Samam leaned back. "All the ears that can hear us are my most trusted. I've been following your breeding suggestions for a long time. I have many who are suitable."

"Then I can say plainly that lightning generation produces invisible forces which could be detectable at great distances. It's my suspicion that this is why you were visited first."

Samam huffed. "It is against the law to do such–"

"Enough. I'm not the law, and I don't care one tail flick for those dogmatic traditions, and you know it."

Samam chut-chutted. "I apologize. I'm not in the habit of discussing any of it, and denying everything is my base reaction. Yes. Our work could well have brought them here. We felt that since no Ombax used lightning, no Ombax could detect our emissions. And indeed, it appears no Ombax did."

Bengdoy flicked her tail. "Then that confirms a suspicion I've had ever since Daksey came to me with his story."

Samam eyed Daksey. "You mean about the new little moon?"

Bengdoy undulated slowly. "We've seen it in the telescope. It's not a moon. It's a structure, built by intelligent hands. It passes close enough in the sky to easily have detected your work. The train-works at Soypasod is too deep inside the mountain to be detected."

Samam huffed. "Then they are not mutant Ombax. Not unless they have launched themselves into orbit."

"My current theory is that they are not from our Thad'pek. They are from elsewhere, as were Dapkasamok."

"Could they be the ones who drove them away?"

Bengdoy's quills flicked up and down. "I hope not. If they were powerful enough to be victorious four thousand years ago, what chance would we stand today?"

•• —————————— ••●•• —————————— ••

"YOU HAVE QUESTIONS," Bengdoy said. "I can feel it eating at you. Ask them."

Daksey undulated. "I understand most of what you said concerning the lightning. Samam must be using the pa'boos to create the power needed to generate it. But what did she mean about the breeding suggestions, and having ears that were suitable."

Bengdoy chut-chutted. "You would make a very good scholar, Daksey. Do not speak of this openly. For now, these are things we need to protect. How much do you know about the days after the Sunfire War? The time of the great burning, and the creation of the Ombax?"

"I know the war was caused by the first ones using electricity. It's the evil they blamed for the destruction."

"What if I told you that philosophy was several hundred years younger than the Ombax themselves? That when we were first created, adapted from the first ones to survive the ruined world they left us, Ombax used lightning every day. Had the skill to capture lightning, and were free to use it as we saw fit?"

Daksey's quills shot up. "But what of the texts warning against its use?"

"Written four hundred years after the war ended. There was another war, one of religion. The use of electricity became their evil. Then they did something more. You see, we still had the knowledge of the first ones. They altered our genome again. Added a little bit of automatic behavior into the hindbrain. When someone with this alteration sees captured lightning, specifically in the form of unnatural light, they fly into a rage and attack with a fury that is unstoppable."

"I've never seen such a thing."

"Of course not. But I have. Too many times. So has Samam. Females have, over time, lost that urge almost entirely. While some still have sudden bouts of hatred and anger, the rage is gone, and it's manageable. However, far too many males still retain the behavior."

"Would I fly into a rage?"

"Over the last few generations, a covert network of us have been working to breed this out of males. We've been largely successful, and many males now react more like females. However, there has been a complication. A side effect. The male hindbrain of those who can tolerate unnatural light are often slow to respond to injury, and may require the occasional tapping."

Daksey stopped walking. "Slow hindbrain?"

Bengdoy turned and chutted. "Yes, Daksey. Kempok is one of my followers."

PITSTOP

Mas'eeng Foythey, First Five, Early High

Daksey pointed to the hole amid the ruins. "There. That is where I fell."

"Good." Bengdoy turned to the pilot. "Find a stretch of road that is wide enough for us as close to that hole as possible. And be sure to put our gate end on the side toward the hole. That will make it easy for us to move cargo."

"Yes, Bengdoy. Coming around now."

Soon the airship had settled into place, west of the hole with the gate on the road at the east side.

Kayfox stood in the cargo hold giving orders as the gate lifted. "The camp will be here. Be sure to leave a path for passersby to go through. No need to block travelers."

Soon supplies, bedding, tents and climbing gear were arrayed along one side of the road or the other.

Daksey gathered his things and started heading to the camp. Bengdoy was there amid the chaos.

"Bengdoy, I want to thank you for everything. I've learned so much, seen so much. I'm looking forward to being at home with my family again, so I can share it all."

Bengdoy chut-chutted. "Perhaps I should be more open about my plans. This was never meant to be the stopping point. I intend to go to Bamthapeem. To investigate the visit there."

Daksey's quills flicked up and down. "You were told not to."

"Implied, yes. I was not told which way to travel when I returned home. Does that make me a bad Ombax?"

"I don't think so. The visits are important. I think you see that, more than Bayam."

"And since we'll be so nearby, I believe it would be appropriate to stop briefly in Botham before we head back home. No need for you to walk back."

Daksey hooted softly. "If that is your plan, then when we are at Bamthapeem, there is something I would very much like to do."

THE DRUMS OF BAMTHAPEEM

Mas'eeng Foythey, First Seven, Late

The drums of Bamthapeem thumped in the distance. Bongeex paused to listen. He grew excited as he recognized his name in the message. They were inviting him to Bamthapeem. The airship was there. The message ended with Daksey's name. He broke into a steady trot and soon arrived home.

Kempok waited for him. "Did you put your brother up to this? What is this about an airship at Bamthapeem?"

Bongeex hooted and jumped in place. "I do not know, but Daksey knows how much I love the airship. He invited me to see it."

"Or he's pulling your tail. Given how the two of you treat each other, I'm tempted to believe that."

"This is because Daksey knows me as a pouch-brother, while you only see me as your egg. Daksey is being what he has always been, a very good brother. He knows I love the airships."

"And if I do not let you go, can I expect you will sulk for a week?" Kempok asked.

"No mother. If I cannot go, I will sulk until the end of time.

In my entire life I've seen only one airship, and it did not land anywhere close. If you deny me this gift from my pouch-brother, the next opportunity may never come."

"Are you threatening me, child?"

"No mother. I'm expressing my heart to you. Decide what you will. I'll always obey."

"Bongeex, I will demand something from you, and if you comply, I'll allow it."

"Anything Mother."

"Now that your adult molt is complete, you shall enter into the marriage I select for you. You will then do all in your power to find happiness and joy in that marriage, and raise offspring to strengthen the tribe you end up in."

Bongeex stiffened. His nostrils flared, then slowly he undulated his neck in agreement. "It shall be as you say, Mother."

"Climb the hill to Bamthapeem," Kempok said. "Meet your pouch-brother, and touch the airship if it's allowed. Return with Daksey quickly. We'll raise the banners on the day you arrive. You will both join as defenders in the next contest. Then I shall find a marriage for you."

He thumped his tail. "Yes Mother. I shall leave at once."

Kempok paused to ensure her eager son still listened. "You may go now."

Bongeex backed out of the room and leapt with joy. He was soon on the path with a small bag strapped to his shoulders, heading to the base of the grand stairs that led to the hilltop.

DAKSEY AND BONGEEX

Mas'eeng Foythey, First Eight, Late High

Daksey sat at the top of the stone steps. He had been watching Bongeex climb for what seemed like forever. His brother had waved in his direction a few times, but was still a few minutes from the top.

Kayfox tapped him on the shoulder. "I need help with the engine. I need to make a few adjustments to the manifold."

"I don't know anything about engines."

"I need someone to hand me tools as I call for them. Everyone else is busy."

Daksey cast a gaze at Bongeex. "Let me greet my pouch-brother. He's almost at the top."

Kayfox looked at Bongeex and huffed. "Perhaps you are too busy. I'll do it myself."

"No, please. I think you should wait." Daksey had a sudden inspiration. He bounced from foot to foot. He shouted down to his brother. "Bongeex, come here faster."

Bongeex stopped and gazed up at him. Then he saw Kayfox and started climbing two steps at a time. A few moments later he reached the top, gasping for air. "Did you miss me so badly, brother?"

"I didn't miss you at all," Daksey said. "This is Maykath Kayfox, the engineer of the airship. She has asked me to hold her tools while she works on the engine."

Bongeex hunched, his eyes wide. "I can hold tools."

Kayfox tilted her head.

"She's asked me because I'm not busy, but when she saw you were coming, she thought I should stay and meet with you for a time."

"I can hold tools." Bongeex looked from Daksey to Kayfox. "I can count them, I can hold them. I can pass them along. I can hold tools."

Kayfox chut-chutted. "Is this why you wanted me to wait?"

Daksey flicked his tail and chut-chutted. "If you let him have a moment to touch the skin of the ship, his childhood dream will be realized."

"And you don't want to catch up with your brother, Bongeex?"

Bongeex glanced at Daksey. "You hurt?"

"No," Daksey said. "You?"

"No. We're caught up. Please. Let me hold your tools."

Kayfox chut-chutted. "Let's go then."

"First I think Bongeex, you should go visit the river."

"I'm not thirsty."

"I mean the dirty river."

Bongeex shrunk and glanced at his brother. "Yes. Good idea. Sorry. Be back soon." He ran off to empty his bowels as quickly as he could.

"I thought you were the one eager to learn how the ship works," Kayfox said. "It appears your brother is far more interested."

Daksey flicked his tail. "I had an amazing trip, and I would gladly help you, but if I went off to the airship and left my brother to sit in Bamthapeem to wait for me, I would never hear the end of it. Besides, I called for him so that he could ride the ship to Botham. He doesn't know that part, yet. It will explode his braincase."

Kayfox chut-chutted. "I'll be sure to have a mop nearby when you tell him."

Daksey undulated. "If the subject comes up, you could tell him. I think the effect would be more profound."

"The effect? On your brother?"

Daksey undulated. "If I tell him, he will also remember that I've ridden it first. I know it might disappoint him. But if you give him that dream, it comes from a place more pure."

"You don't want the credit?"

Daksey tilted his head. "He knows who called him."

Kayfox undulated slowly and chutted. Daksey's heart beat faster. Such beauty.

•• ———————— ••●•• ———————— ••

Bongeex hurried back to his brother and that lovely spotted egg-mother. She waved him to follow as soon as he got near. He looked at his brother, who waved him on and undulated.

He followed the egg-mother toward the airship. "Kayfox, how many times have you ridden the airship?"

Kayfox chut-chutted. "How many times have you eaten a meal?"

"There's no counting."

She flicked her tail "There's no counting."

"You trained at an early age?" Bongeex asked.

"My pouch-father was engineer before me. I watched from the pouch. I learned how parts fit together before I learned to read, and I learned to read so that I could consult the technical documents. I grew up on the ship, near the ship, and for a little while in a school overlooking the ship. It's my home, and my life."

Bongeex kept looking from the ship, growing closer, to the gray skin and bold black spots leading the way in front of him. "Beautiful."

"Don't step on my tail." Her deep voice sounded playful, not scolding.

Bongeex's heart raced. He took extra care not to step on her tail.

•• ——————————— ••●•• ——————————— ••

"HAND ME THE SECOND ONE," Kayfox said. "I think that's what I need."

Bongeex could see where she looked. He lifted two tools and handed her the one she requested. "Here is the one you asked for. From here, it looks like this other one is what you need." He held out the second tool.

Kayfox looked at the tool in her hand and tried it on the part. Then without looking, held her hand out for the second tool. She set it where it belonged and pushed. The part turned slightly and made a popping sound. She handed both tools out. "You have a good eye."

Bongeex nodded his gratitude. "I have a better angle to see it from."

She slid her large frame out from under the machinery and gazed up at him. She had grease spots among her own. "No one I have ever had help me has even tried to correct me. You saw the error, and selected the correct tool. You handed me what I asked for in case you were wrong, then offered me the second. You are kind, considerate, and intelligent. You are also so eager to work on this machinery I think you would jump at the chance to see it working."

Bongeex nearly took to the air as he hopped from foot to foot. "I would, I really would."

"My egg-mother wants to go down to Botham."

Bongeex undulated. "I see. I could take her down."

Kayfox chut-chutted. "She wants to fly down. In the airship."

Bongeex froze. "Fly?"

Kayfox undulated slowly. "Would you prefer to be near a window to see from far up high, or would you want to be here in the engine room?"

Bongeex chut-chutted. "I think I would tear myself in two."

"I think I'm glad I got that mop."

Bongeex froze then looked under his tail.

Kayfox shrieked and chut-chutted loudly. "I meant for the blood that would result from your halving."

Bongeex chut-chutted with her. "Maybe I'll just walk back and forth."

Daksey saw his brother emerge from the ship at long last. He and Kayfox were still talking. She turned and went back inside.

Bongeex saw his brother. "Daksey! Daksey!"

"I'm right here. No need to yell."

"Daksey! Daksey! Daksey!"

Daksey chut-chutted. "You have no idea how happy it makes me to see your glee."

Amthek chut-chutted. "Is he always like this?"

"Yes. Every moment until he sleeps. Bongeex, this is Amthek, my friend from Seeng'dod."

Amthek bowed slightly. "I am actually Keyoompax Deyomaf Amfoydek, but everyone calls me Amthek."

"Why?" Bongeex flicked his tail. "Are you exceptionally clumsy?"

"As a child. I outgrew it, but the name stuck."

"A friend of my brother is a friend of the whole tribe. You are welcome among us."

"What did you think?" Daksey asked.

"Beautiful." He hooted softly. "Absolutely beautiful."

"Are you talking about the ship or the engineer?"

"Yes, Daksey." He hooted loudly. "Most certainly, yes."

Daksey chut-chutted. "She has nice spots, but they are often covered in grease."

"All the better."

THE ASCENT

Mas'eeng Foythey, Second Two, Rising

Bongeex spotted his brother near one of the widows. He ran over to join him. "Are we in the air, yet?"

Daksey chutted. "Not yet. You will know it from the way the deck shifts under your feet."

Bongeex huffed. "You sound as if it's boring you."

"Of course not. I've only felt it a few times. But even so, I find that looking out when we are far above the land is far more thrilling than when we are leaving the ground. But I remember my first time. I know you will–"

The deck tilted slightly. The lower side quickly caught up. Bongeex looked outside and watched as the mountaintops sank below the airship. He hopped from foot to foot. "We're flying." He chutted and looked at his brother.

Daksey hooted softly. "Seeing you like this makes it all the much better."

"I'm going back to the engine room. See you later."

Daksey chut-chutted.

Bongeex headed back to the engine room at the center of the ship. Kayfox watched some gauges, one hand on a handle, the other on a railing. A small puff of steam behind her, partially obscured the light. Bongeex felt his heart leap.

"Did you enjoy the view?"

He chutted. "Now you are making fun of me. The view is magnificent."

•• ———————— ••●•• ———————— ••

DAKSEY STAYED NEAR THE WINDOW, watching the mountains slide by as they moved away, then started their descent. It seems as if no time had passed before the call went out to lower the mooring line.

"Akbay is on the roof now. He has secured us to the trunk. Reel it in, bring us into docking position."

The end of the airship with the large cargo door settled toward the rooftop platform of the tallest house in Botham. Daksey hooted softly. He and Bongeex would step off the airship onto their own home.

He looked around. His brother had missed the whole thing.

KEMPOK GREETS AMTHEK

Daksey nudged Amthek. "Do not worry. She can be a little stern, but she is a good egg-mother. She will welcome you."

Amthek's nostrils flared. "It's so different here. Even the trees seem greener."

Bongeex chut-chutted.

The three of them climbed down into Daksey's family home and reached the top floor entry. The wide doors flew open, and Kempok filled the frame. She locked eyes with Daksey, then turned her attention to Amthek.

"Egg-Mother," Daksey said, "I would like to present my friend, Amthek."

Before he finished pronouncing his full name, Kempok barreled out the door, put a hand on each of Amthek's shoulders and planted her snout tight against his. "Amthek of Keyoompax. I have word of you from Soypasod, Seeng'dod, and Afothameex. Letters written about my son that also mention you. After full consideration of their content, I declare you family. A member of the Botham tribe from this day forward. No matter where you go, or what you do, you will always have a home here." She released him and stepped back.

Bongeex nudged Daksey. "Does his jaw always hang open like that?"

Daksey chut-chutted. "I knew he would be welcomed, but—wait. What word did you receive?"

"Letters," Kempok said. "The first a brief one from the Samam of Seeng'dod, assured me you were well and apologized for your delay. Then..." she glanced at Daksey, then looked back to Amthek. "She warned me that you had taken up with a refugee who may be a bad influence. She said they called him Amthek."

Amthek shrunk.

Kempok chut-chutted. "The second came from Mo'beex Foysom of Afothameex. She told me of the work you did, and of how proud I should be. And she told me of your friend, Amthek, by your side, just as wonderful, kind, and thoughtful."

Amthek tried to make himself even smaller.

"The third came from Soypasod. Suffice it to say it was impressive as well. I realized that the Samam must be mistaken as to Amthek's character. Not a bad influence, in need of family."

Amthek shuddered and bowed deeply.

"Well at least he closed his mouth," Bongeex said.

Daksey lightly punched his pouch-brother in the shoulder.

Kempok looked at them and chutted. She glanced at the activity above. "You rode the airship?"

Bongeex undulated vigorously. "It was wonderful. I think I'm in love."

"With the airship or the engineer?" Daksey asked.

"Hush!"

"Engineer?" Kempok's quills rose.

"It's a long story," Daksey said. "May we come in? Amthek needs to be fed soon."

Amthek sputtered. "I don't!"

Kempok chut-chutted and waved them inside. "Yes you do.

But head down to the common ground. The feast is nearly ready. I will join you shortly."

She returned to the home and the others headed into the village.

"You were right about her welcoming me," Amthek said.

Daksey chut-chutted. "Even I didn't expect her to adopt you, Amthek."

"You think she meant it?"

Daksey thumped his tail. "You are part of the tribe now."

Bongeex butted shoulders with Amthek. "Yeah. Like another brother. You hunt?"

"I fish."

"Fish? I love fish. Just be sure to use the clean river to the north."

•• ——————— ••●•• ——————— ••

DAKSEY QUICKLY REALIZED they were hosting a contest feast, not one set out just for his return. There were members of two other tribes here.

The gathering quieted as Kempok entered the pavilion. "It's good to see you all. Welcome. For an additional surprise, Maykath Bengdoy and her two daughters are also here. They have brought home our Daksey, and a new member of our tribe, Keyoompax Deyomaf Amfoydek. He is called Amthek. Apparently, he was less graceful when younger."

Amthek stepped forward and dropped his head low.

The sounds of approval floated through the crowd.

"Now, everyone enjoy the first day of the feast. Tomorrow brings the contest. Then we have a day of celebration and interesting encounters."

ENDURANCE

Friday, December 13, 3297, 12:50 & Mas'eeng Bayok, Last Four, Early High

Foondek felt the floor nudge his feet as the little ship settled into the clearing. He unhooked the harness and turned to Maksim. "Time to go."

Maksim's eyes darted around. Then he said, "*Bom. Ath saydoy pofood, maypaf bayamthay*"

"*Bayaad*," Foondek said. "Hope for good luck, not question it. It's strange to hear you speak Omseep without AutoGov."

Maksim bobbed his head as close as he could get to undulating.

"Will AutoGov continue to learn while we are here?"

"Yes," Anna said. She continued in Omseep. "Our ears are his ears. Our eyes too. With luck, our language skills will grow."

Foondek chutted. "Improve. Skills improve. Ankle-biters get bigger."

Anna gave a full throated chut-chut.

"Time to head out," Ted said. "Good luck, Foondek."

Foondek stepped out into the warm sun as it peaked over the mountains. The air carried the heavy scents of the wildflowers and budding trees. He hooted softly to himself. With the rising sun to his back, he headed home.

MAKSIM WATCHED as Foondek headed up the gentle slope into the deep forest. He turned and followed the others as they made their way south to the river. In less than an hour, they arrived at the open field where the platforms marked the starting positions. Each starting platform rose half a meter above the ground. The worn stone slabs had once been full hexagons, but the centuries had chipped away at the edges. Vegetation sprouted from the cracks.

"Did anyone else notice the time before we left?" Debra asked.

"Late," Ted said. "Past midnight. Why?"

"Did you check the date? I hadn't thought about it until I saw it. Today is Friday the 13th."

Maksim sighed. "God help us, then."

Ted stepped up onto the first platform he came to and urged the others to step aboard quickly. Maksim followed his gaze and saw a group of Ombax approaching from the east. They were following the river upstream. He stepped up and the four of them stood and waited.

The four Ombax came near, one of them jumped as if to attack, but didn't step onto the platform.

AutoGov provided a running translation.

"Break no rules," said one of them.

"Their faces break the rules."

"Stand back, Sopoth. See how they stand still? They are here to compete."

"Compete?" The quills on the back of Sopoth's neck stood

stiffly. His nostrils flared. "What egg-mother would ever marry a creature such as this?"

Three of them chut-chutted. It sounded forced. Not the free laugher Foondek used.

Sopoth glanced to the west. "Here come the others."

Maksim followed his glance. Three more were coming. These had the same green coloration, but they had wider black stripes, like Foondek. One stood back. The other two joined Sopoth.

"Good so see you have returned, Daksey. Bongeex did you and your brother invite these things?"

Bongeex shrugged. "No Sopoth. I thought we were only running two teams today. This is new."

Daksey's quills stayed relaxed. He chutted. "They are even uglier with their skin on."

Maksim cringed. He felt Anna's warm hand on his shoulder.

"You have seen them before?" Sopoth asked.

Bongeex thumped his tail. "These are the creatures who were killed at Bamthapeem."

Daksey stood tall and raised his voice. "Whatever happens today, do not eat these things. You will be lifting your tail for days."

"Meem saap fos eskoy boykoy o'kayfam," Ted said. *Not kill we will happy tomorrow.*

All the Ombax froze, their eyes on Ted.

Sopoth's eyes bulged wide. Then his shoulders shook, and he chut-chutted loudly.

"They speak like children," Bongeex said.

Daksey undulated. "At least they are too big to get underfoot."

A distant low tone echoed from the forest. The Ombax split into their two teams, and each stepped onto different platforms.

Daksey looked at Ted. "Third high tone is the start. You know this?"

Ted undulated as best he could.

Bongeex chutted. "They have no necks, but I believe they know the rules."

"How would they have learned?" Sopoth asked.

The high tones started, cutting off the conversation. On the third tone, all three groups headed into the trees at a run.

•• —————————— ••●•• —————————— ••

TED'S LEG WENT FIRST, then slipped. He quickly slid over the edge of the cliff, flailing to grasp the edge. His hand caught another hand. The unexpectedly tight grip could only have come from one source. He looked up. Sure enough, his alien opponent had grabbed his hand, preventing him from falling. "Well, what do you know?"

Bongeex snorted and shook his head back and forth. His other hand pushed against the top of the cliff as he helped Ted to safety.

At the top, Bongeex carefully let go, backing away.

Ted saw how wary his savior looked. He knelt and raised his wrists.

Bongeex pointed to a small grove of trees and took a step.

Ted stood and followed at a distance then sat in the shade at the base of a tree.

Bongeex snorted and moved near him, tied his hands, then took his water bottle and opened the top.

Ted tilted his head back and drank the water.

When he had his fill, Bongeex set the empty bottle next to Ted, then looked into his eyes. He spoke while AutoGov translated. "I am Bongeex. I have *untranslatable* questions. Perhaps later. I must catch up with the others, for I am their leader." He leapt into the forest, quickly gone from sight.

AFTER THE GAME

Friday, December 13, 3297, 21:13 & Mas'eeng Bayok, Last Four, Late

Foondek could see through the trees where Kempok sat. She was at the edge of the circle in the clearing. The last runner, Daksey, entered the end area. Debra right on his tail. Daksey spun to face her. They were the same height if he didn't stretch his neck. Daksey looked a little heavier, but Foondek was well aware of how swiftly Debra could move. Daksey's stripes were dark and clear. He had recently completed his adult molt. Good for him.

As Foondek made his way down to where Kempok and Masax were seated, he kept a close eye on the fight. Daksey lunged to the left and lowered his head, then twisted and repositioned to the right. He lunged past outstretched arms and slid in the dirt. Debra, much quicker than Daksey had expected, wasn't where he thought. His quills flicked in confusion. Foondek chutted to himself as he realized that he wasn't sure who he wanted to win. Daksey, Deytham's brother, or Debra, a friend.

Foondek passed behind a stand of trees. When he looked again, Daksey had landed on the ground, Debra's arms wrapped around his neck. Foondek had to look away again, so he didn't step on anyone's tail as he made his way down the slope. When he looked again, Daksey lay on his back, Debra high above him, falling. How had that happened? She landed as he rolled and ended with her at his side, arms once again around his neck.

He decided to stop and watch. He wanted to see Masax, but this fight was really fun.

•• ——————————— ••●•• ——————————— ••

DAKSEY COULD FEEL THE CONSTRICTION. He arched his back and bucked in another attempt to dislodge it, but he could feel the lack of air starting to fuzz his brain. If this had been an Ombax, he would have given the three taps. He hesitated. They must know about that. He reached up and tapped one arm three times. The grip relaxed, and he went free.

He rolled to his feet and spun to look at his opponent. It locked eyes with Daksey. They both paused. It played by the rules, like the others. He took a deep breath, held his wrists together, and sat back on his haunches, wrapping his tail around his ankles.

The creature looped a strand of rope around his wrists and snugged it. Then reached down to Daksey's side, took out the water flask and made the traditional offering. Daksey opened his mouth.

A yell from the crowd and gasps were followed by an eruption of red and black. Amthek landed on the creature from the side. It rolled and spun Amthek underneath, one its legs landed on Amthek's arm. He let out a loud, high pitched yelp of pain.

Kempok bolted to her feet.

The creature reacted like it had received a blow, jumped off Amthek, reached out a hand to his arm, and said something soft, and strange. Then it said "*Omem, omem,*" their word of apology.

The tone was not in the least aggressive. Amthek cradled his arm, looked at the creature, then his arm.

Amthek saw Kempok, then glanced at Daksey. He took a deep breath and relaxed. He rolled into a seated position, and held out his wrists, lowering his head.

The creature looped a bit of rope around his wrists so loose it almost slipped off. It looked for a water flask, but since Amthek wasn't a contestant, he had none. It took a flask from its side and offered it to him.

Amthek looked at Daksey then at Kempok, who had sat back down but was still, leaned forward, her eyes not leaving the scene. He lifted his chin and opened his mouth.

Daksey watched as his friend drank something. It looked clear, like water. But he couldn't be sure.

Amthek shook his head and splashed the liquid over his face. "It's water. Clean, pure, and cold. Like spring water. Very good." He leaned forward and said, "More please?"

The creature made a repetitive sound, like a short barking, then poured more water into Amthek's awaiting maw. He gurgled it and splashed again, then started chut-chutting.

Others saw the humor as well, and started chut-chutting.

The creature looked around the area, then must have seen the circle. It walked over, and stood in the center. It dropped to its knees, and sat back onto its very tiny feet.

Kempok rose and walked slowly around the circle. "Amthek, shake yourself loose of your bonds and free Daksey."

"Yes, Kempok." He did as told and freed Daksey. "What should we do now?"

Kempok had made the complete circle and stood in front of the creature, towering over it. "Amthek, go free the others. Bring them all in." When she stepped behind the creature, she used her hands to signal Daksey to remain alert. He shifted his eyes to the creature and kept them there.

"But Kempok," Akfoy said, "the winner is supposed to accompany the last tied. It's tradition that they do it together."

Daksey quietly moved to be behind the creature's back at the edge of the circle and waited, observing every move.

"It's a game," Kempok said. "These creatures have shown they can honor our traditions and play by our rules. Now, we can do them the honor of bending our tradition a little, so that we can accomplish more important things."

"What is more important than tradition?"

"Saying hello. Making new friends, I hope." She lowered herself down, and soon sat directly in front of the creature. "Bengdoy, come join us."

Masax shrieked and began hooting loudly. Daksey only gave it a glance, but saw Foondek had returned. His mind raced, but he fought it, and remained alert. He watched the creature.

Kempok's voice joined the hooting, and soon much of the crowd was busy hooting and chutting, welcoming Foondek back. Daksey still watched the creature. It remained still and seemed relaxed. Perhaps it expected this commotion, but made no moves to take advantage of it.

"Join us, Foondek. We'll have to wait to ask you more questions. We must address our new guests."

Daksey could see them on the other side of the creature. Kempok in the middle with Foondek and Masax on one side, Bengdoy and Kayfox on the other. The crowd settled down to a low chorus of fading hoots.

Foondek nodded at Debra. She nodded back, but remained silent.

"Do you know him, Foondek?" Kempok asked.

Foondek flicked his tail. "Before we returned, this one and her family trained with me to be sure they knew the rules of the contest. She is a female of their people."

"Female? So small?"

"Their males are a little larger, but the difference isn't as much as it is with us. And... well, their genders are strange, Kempok."

Bengdoy leaned forward. "Strange, how?"

"The males have an appendage that penetrates the female to

plant their seed. The egg never emerges, instead she gives live birth."

Kempok's quills flicked up and down. "Live birth? Does she also have a pouch?"

Foondek shrugged. "Neither gender has a pouch." He pointed at Debra's chest. "Those bulges are milk sacs. She will cradle a newborn offspring and feed it from them."

"Can we see?"

Debra started to giggle.

"What is that?"

"She finds our conversation funny," Foondek said. "The female's milk sacs are considered to be private and kept covered. Usually only shown to a mate or close friends."

Bengdoy stared at Foondek. "You seem to know quite a bit about them."

"I lived on their ship in the sky for a time. They treated me well, and they returned me when I requested it."

Kempok snorted. "They didn't return Deytham?"

Debra's head fell. She took a deep breath and recited in her best Omseep. "Egg-Mother of Deytham. Our people beg you to forgive us for our mistake. When we called our craft back to the sky ship, we did not look to be sure it remained empty. It's flown by machine, and machines do not need to be gentle. The course was too hard. Both Foondek and Deytham were injured. Deytham could not be repaired."

Kempok took a deep breath and exhaled slowly. "Why was this mistake made?"

"Our people watched as their loved ones were killed and eaten. They were distraught."

Kempok undulated slowly, then looked at Bengdoy. "They make mistakes. They care for their own people. Amthek proved that they react to other creatures in pain with compassion. Bengdoy, I'm of the opinion that they are not here to hurt us."

Bengdoy undulated. "Just as well. Creatures with their abilities would be a formidable foe." She looked at Debra. "There are small balls of metal in your head. What are they for?"

Debra attempted to undulate. "They connect us to the machines. Give us information. This is how I can know what your words mean. Then, I tell it what I want to say to you, and it gives me the words I need. But some of your words are hard to say. Our throats do not close as loudly as yours."

Kempok's mouth dropped open. She threw her head to the sky and chut-chutted. She kept laughing for a good long time. It spread through the crowd.

Daksey held his breath, not wanting to remind the creature that he remained. Still, that was a funny thing to say.

"One thing you said puzzles me," said Bengdoy. "You said they saw the others killed. From the sky? So far above?"

Debra shrugged a solid *no* in her best imitation of Ombax body language. "Before we sent our people, we sent small machines. They fly through the air, and swim in the water. They see things, and they tell us what they see."

"We know about those." Kempok thumped the ground with her tail.

Bengdoy held herself still. "Messages through the air? You are using lightning."

A murmur rippled through the crowd.

Debra did a well-rehearsed undulation. "Yes. We use lightning in many forms, in every part of our lives. It's as natural to us as the air we breathe. Which, in space, we make using lightning."

The crowd remained silent.

Debra's shoulders slumped. "I'm hoping very much that you don't eat me now."

Kempok took a deep breath and looked at the faces in the crowd. "It's one of our most sacred laws." She raised her voice. "It is wrong to catch the Lightning."

The crowd repeated the phrase, then added, "Thunder warns the people. Electric power is lightning!"

Debra spread her arms out and touched the ground.

Daksey looked at her, looked at the crowd, then remembered what he had found. He stood, and in his loudest voice, "Sky People ride the lightning."

The crowd silent, one voice called out. "What was that?"

"Sky People ride the lightning," Daksey repeated. "It's what the next line reads. I found it carved in stone on the wall of the observatory."

Bengdoy stood. "Daksey is correct. That last line is true. Sky People ride the lightning."

"But what does it mean?" Akfoy asked.

Bengdoy sat with a thud. "It means we should stop killing our visitors just because their ways are different from ours. Dapkasamok used lightning to fly among the stars. If these creatures came from another star, they must have used it too. She said it's natural to them. As natural to them as for Dapkasamok."

"And for Ombax," Kayfox said. "We used to use it too."

"Until the Sunfire War," Kempok said.

"It caused the Sunfire War," Akfoy said. "It destroyed everything."

"It did not cause the war," Bengdoy said. "Our predecessors caused the war. The edict against using captured lightning did not come from them. It came much later, after the survivors had gathered on Thoxmoyang and after they created us. We created the edict after the last of the old ones died. Many generations after."

Debra shook her head and said something to herself.

Kempok leaned forward. "Did you speak?"

"I'm sorry, Kempok. Everything we say is being listened to by my people above. When she said what she did about the predecessors making you, many of my people became very excited and were asking too many questions at once. I had to tell them to be quiet."

Bengdoy leaned over to Kempok. "Add scientific curiosity to the list. I think I like these people."

Kempok huffed.

Amthek arrived with the rest of the contestants, including

three more of the creatures. Two were larger than the one seated. The last was nearly the same size, but thicker.

Kempok chut-chutted. "She is smaller than they are. And yet she won. Daksey, she held you tightly. Could you not break free?"

Daksey shrugged. "She had locked one arm with the other around my throat. I could feel the hold was gentle, but firm, and effective. I would have taken a nap. I tapped three times, and it released me."

"You there, stop gawking and sit. Now, do any of you wish to recount your encounter with our guests? Were they honorable, or deceitful with you? Be who you are and speak freely."

Bongeex rose and pointed to the largest of the creatures. "This one fell into a ravine that stank of dead air. I reacted as if one of our own had fallen, and grabbed an arm. I helped it climb to the top. It stood tall above me. I thought for a moment it might attack, but it knelt, and offered up wrists. I pointed to a tree further away from the ravine. It moved to where I pointed, and again, offered wrists. I tied them, and found a container at its side. It held water. I made the offering. It sat. Oh, and it crossed its legs in front of it. Very strange. I did not feel threatened after that. It acted like people. So, I treated it like people."

Pongsok stood and pointed at Anna. "This one attacked me from behind. The fight ended quickly. I also tapped three times and was released. It tied me too loosely but made the proper offering and left."

"Is attacking from behind a complaint?"

Pongsok shrugged. "Only that it moved quieter than I had hoped. It was a good move."

Foondek stood to address the crowd. He stepped down toward the circle and stood facing Maksim. "When I lived among them, I noticed that one of their males appeared agitated when I came near." He put his hand on Maksim's shoulder. "This one. His name is Maksim. It did not take long for me to understand that these people can carry hatred in their hindbrain. I soon learned that his mate had been at Bamthapeem. Killed and eaten. I understood his pain. At first, I avoided him. But he is a gardener, as am I. Our paths kept crossing, and he grew more agitated each time. Then the leaders of the ship created a garden of statues, a memorial to those who lost their lives during this first contact between us." He turned and looked into Kempok's eyes. "Deytham stands among them in that garden."

He looked around again. "I saw Maksim looking at one particular statue. A female. I took care not to draw his attention but came close enough to look at his eyes. I saw the pain in them. I could feel his loss as surely as I could feel my own."

"Does he hate us all?" Akfoy asked.

Foondek raised a hand and shrugged. "I touched his arm and showed him the statue of Deytham. I told him that I could see his pain because I felt it too. In that moment, I saw who he was, and he saw me. After that, after some time, we became friends.

"They deal with grief as we do. Sometimes poorly. They love as easily, and where there once may have been anger, and sadness, Maksim and I built a friendship, and I would call him brother."

Many soft hoots rang out from the crowd.

Maksim put his hand on Foondek's shoulder and performed a short-necked undulation. Foondek and Maksim exchanged smiles as a scattering of chut-chutting floated through the crowd.

Kempok locked eyes with Debra. "Are you still afraid we may kill you?"

Debra nodded, then shrugged, then sighed. "I am. I have always been afraid I might become a meal. I'm very hopeful you do not eat me."

"Afraid for your life?"

"Afraid I would poison you. Some of your people have died because they ate our flesh."

Kempok thumped her tail. "We will not kill you. We will certainly not eat you. It is not our tradition." She stood and turned to address the crowd. "Hear what I'm saying. These creatures are safe here in Botham. They are to be allowed freedom, as if they were Ombax. Treat them as you would a guest. But be sure to teach them to be proper guests. They don't know our ways, and many lives have already been lost because of it. The loss of life must now be ended. Now we shall begin a friendship."

A murmur arose from the crowd. "What about the lightning?"

"They are allowed to use it when they need it." She swung her head to face Debra. "But they should ask permission before they show it."

Debra bobbed her head eagerly, then showed her teeth.

"Foondek, why is she baring her little teeth at me?"

Foondek chut-chutted. "It's how they show pleasure. They use it when they are very happy."

Kempok chut-chutted. "Well, it certainly isn't a threat. Such tiny things." She turned to Bengdoy. "What of your people?"

Bengdoy chutted. "I believe it would be best if we limit contact to your capable hands, Kempok. Until we are able to ensure their safety in other places. Bamthapeem stands as a warning to us all of how badly it can go."

Kempok stood. "Agreed. Now it is time to eat. Our guests may eat our food, but it may not be good for them. The same goes for any food they have brought. Ombax should be warned away."

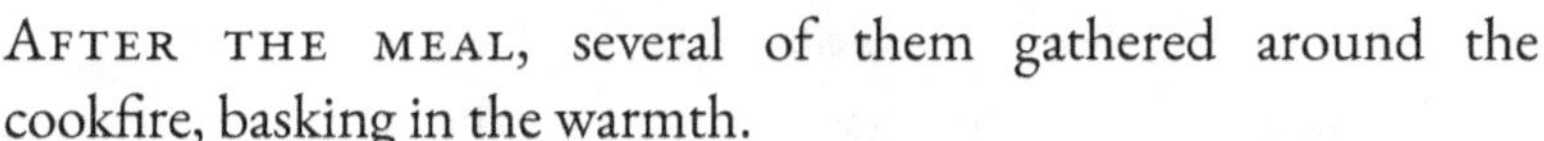

AFTER THE MEAL, several of them gathered around the cookfire, basking in the warmth.

"Are we to bow down to you?" Kempok asked. "Worship you? What do you demand of us? Obedience?"

"No," Maksim said, "not at all. We are not worthy of worship. We are not the sky people in your history. We do have proof that those beings existed. It is how we knew to come here. We found a place where they had been. But we've never seen them. We have no images. Only one suit they wore for environmental protection. Your images are much better than that."

Daksey undulated. "We take great care to preserve them, and to copy them as closely as possible."

Bengdoy huffed. "Let him speak."

Daksey almost huffed, but thought better of it.

"Ages ago," Maksim said, "you destroyed your world. We destroyed ours in our grandfather's time. No, we are not better than you. We survived because we had people living in orbit, on other worlds. And we've learned one interesting trick. We can twist spacetime, jump between the gaps from one place to another. This can take us to other stars. But we are no better than you. We do not make demands. We found your location listed among others. One was our own. We were listed as too primitive to contact. The other location was listed almost the same way. They had listed yours as being worthy of contact, but that was over four thousand years ago. That is why we chose to come here. Nothing more. We wanted to meet you. We hope to learn from you."

Masax swayed. "Perhaps you would come to take our world from us."

Maksim turned his head slightly, then shrugged instead. "We don't have so many people that we would need to. We didn't come as invaders. We came as friends. We came to say hello. You are not alone. And to ask if you knew where the sky people went. You call them, Dapkasamok?"

Bengdoy huffed. "On that count, I can say we do not know. We have no records of them ever returning."

Kempok huffed. "If they came after the war, who would know?"

"Then maybe we can find out," Maksim said. "Maybe we could do it together."

"You would take us with you?" Amthek asked.

"We would teach you what we know," Maksim said. "You could walk among the stars with us."

Kempok flicked her tail. "That would be more than the sky people did. There is no record that they ever taught us anything more than that they existed, and the general direction they came from."

Daksey cast a glance at Bengdoy and was about to speak, but caught her slight shrug and thought better of it. There would be time, and Daksey remembered what part of the Desok Bofoy'bo held the sky map. The location of the star from which Dapkasamok came had been clearly marked.

"We would welcome some of you to come to our home above your world. Foondek has built a place for living, and we can make it larger. He showed us the food you grow to eat, and we'll soon be able to grow animals for you as well."

Bengdoy rocked back and forth. "I would love to see your ship. Perhaps in time, I will be able to leave my duties for the journey."

"There is no hurry."

"Masax," Kempok said, "your pouch-husband and pouchling both lived there. Perhaps you would consider going for a time."

Masax held still. "I don't know if I'm excited, or terrified. Perhaps some of both. I think I would want to wait a while. Let the little one grow into his own skin first. Then, perhaps with another pouch-husband..." She glanced at Amthek. "...it might be the right choice for my family."

Amthek hunched and hooted. "Or two. You might need two more pouch-husbands." He glanced at Daksey.

Masax met Daksey's eyes, and he understood. He chutted to himself. Bongeex might actually envy him. He looked up to the night sky, gazing at the stars. Softly, he said to them, "I am coming."

FOONDEK STOKED HIS POUCH GENTLY. He separated from Masax and the others so that Deypax would hear less noise. He had become restless. He started humming, a slow melodic tune as he walked among the trees of his village. The commotion in his pouch settled.

He spotted Moya'se down the hill. She met his eyes and started climbing.

Foondek chutted. "Ah yes, Moya'se. With every swing of your tail, you fend off insects with your overly fragrant fumes."

Moya'se blinked. She burst into rapid chut-chutting. "I've heard better insults from an ankle-biter. It's good to see you home, Foondek." She tilted her head. "Do you remember how to hunt?"

Foondek chut-chutted. He gently stroked his pouch, encouraging Deypax to peek out. "Come out little one, and meet a hunter."

Moya'se hopped from foot to foot and hooted softly.

Deypax popped his head out. His large eyes looked up at Moya'se.

"He is so beautiful. He looks healthy. Is he healthy? Have you been feeding him well? What did you eat up there?"

Foondek raised his hands. "They have plenty for us to eat. Before they tried to make contact, they gathered plants and soil. I made sure Deypax ate well."

She bent over and gazed at the child. "Kempok told me about Deytham." She looked up at him.

Foondek swayed slightly. "It's new for you. It must be hard."

She huffed and shrugged her shoulders. She stood as tall as she could and put both hands on her hips. "We thought you were both – all three of you were gone. Having you back is so good, and having this little one... still sad, yes. But I'm very happy to see you, Foondek."

Foondek flicked his tail. "If we can now be friends with the visitors, I believe the days to come will become much more interesting."

She snorted. "Better than hunting?"

Foondek shrugged. "Perhaps not for all of us. I've seen how much you enjoyed the hunt. How good you have become at it."

"Seen? Where... the flying machines?"

"They let me watch you. Even help you when you fell into that pit."

She shrank back. "That was you?"

Foondek chutted. "I am proud of you. You did all the right things when they needed to be done. All I did was bring help."

"After that I kept an eye out. I didn't see those things again."

"They are good at hiding. Very quiet. They never meant to be seen. It was only because you were in danger that they allowed me to use them."

Deypax stretched and pulled his head back into the pouch.

"I think he is tired. Time to rest. We can talk later. I'm going up to the house." He stopped and looked toward the tree into which his home was built. "I hope I still have a bed."

Moya'se chuckled. "Masax may have let it get dusty, but she never emptied your rooms."

He undulated. "Thank you, Moya'se."

"Good to have you back, Foondek."

RECEPTION ISSUES

Tuesday, December 17, 3297, 11:31

Since returning to *Endurance*, Debra had given all her attention to getting the restaurant up and running. Ted sat quietly at a table near the front, reviewing automated log entries.

"Al, is the water ready for the noodles, yet?" Debra busied herself at the chopping station. A growing mound of freshly cut vegetables glistened in the light.

The chefbot responded in a deep, pleasant voice, "The temperature is within the required parameters. Would you like to insert the noodles, or shall I?"

"I got it. I want to learn some of this as I go."

The entrance slid open. "Hello. Nice place you have here."

Debra grinned. "Hello, Captain Betsy! Here to eat?"

Betsy smirked. "No, I'm doing a rat inspection. So where are your rats? I want to inspect them."

The chefbot raised one finger. "Small mammals have not been brought to this star system—"

Debra waved her hand. "Drop it, Al. She was joking."

Betsy chuckled. "What's on the menu?"

"I was about to put noodles in the pot."

"What kind?"

"Rice," Debra said. "Want noodle soup?"

Ted smiled at his wife. A flash of light glinted in her eye. The sound of nearby lightning and the impact of the wall was the last he remembered.

A DISEMBODIED VOICE called his name. A familiar voice. Not Debra. What was she saying? His name. She said his name. He struggled to open his eyes.

"Ted, your eyes are open," Dr. Puttkammer said. "Are you with us?"

Ted tried to nod. His head wouldn't move. The ringing in his ears was the loudest thing in the room. He couldn't speak. He tried moving his legs and arms. Nothing worked. He raised his eyebrows.

"We've immobilized most of your body. Just a precaution. You'll be fine. You needed some repairs. Don't try to talk. You had damage to your right leg, the back of your skull, and along your spine. Then there were a bunch of lacerations. A couple were pretty deep. I was in a hurry to stop the bleeding, so I'll let you pick which ones you want to have scars for."

Ted knitted his eyebrows together and strained to look left and right.

She nodded. "Debra is alive. Missing a couple of things, nothing vital. Nothing that can't be replaced. She'll be fine. She's going to take a little more fixing, that's all."

Ted blinked back tears and took a deep breath. He forced himself to relax.

"That's better. Now hold still while I doublecheck our work."

She called over her shoulder, "Shea, are you almost done with that?"

"Nearly complete, Doctor. The bones are stabilized, and none of the nerves were damaged beyond minor abrasions to the epineurium. I'm ready to withdraw the surgeon and seal up his neck."

"Good. When you are done with that, release the upper block and let him talk. Mind the pain. Let me know if you need anything else." She leaned toward Ted. "I'm going to go back and start on Debra. You'll be in the recovery bay shortly. Please be patient."

Ted closed his eyes. The recovery bay. He was still in surgery. She was fine. Got it.

●● ———————————— ●●◉●● ———————————— ●●

SKIP CHECKED the status of the victims. Five dead, seven injured. Betsy. His heart ached. His fist slammed the wall. "Security, have you found who did this?"

"We are running the trace now," Zon said. "There were a lot of deliveries to both the restaurant and the ship over the last few days. The initial scan didn't show anything, so I did a full contact trace, including any system anomalies. That should catch any tampering."

Jake entered the control center and took his position.

"Jake, assemble security teams, get ready to run this bastard down. You're in command here. I'm heading to security."

"But, sir, your place is here. If anyone goes, it should be me."

"I'm doing this myself. You stay here."

"But–"

"That's an order, Jake." He turned and stormed down the passageway.

Skip made the short walk to the security office and thrust himself inside.

Zon busily swiped his displays and examined data trails.

"Anything?"

Zon nodded. "I have the spot where they intercepted the package. There's a three minute delay. Long enough to open it and swap out the contents. I have two points with enough room. Still running back the crew tracers. There. Down to six intersecting possibilities."

"Show me."

Zon dealt out the faces like cards. "Six different people who were in places they could have used to obtain access. Most would have had plenty of time. This one might have been rushed." He pointed to a young woman. "Data Technician Charity Matsuo. She's from Tatislavic Transport."

Skip nodded. "Who was closest?"

Zon pointed to a familiar face. "Anna Ruggiero. She was in the machine shop long enough to have done it. Just one thing. She left with this." He zoomed into a small piece of equipment. "If she made that, she wouldn't have had time to get to the transport line and back."

Skip nodded. "Next?"

"Felicity Varner, a geologist. Asteroid miner." He frowned. "Huh. Look at that. Grade five demolition expert."

"Let's start with her. Where is she now?"

"Mid-level, between the cargo hold. She's headed toward the park."

Skip opened a com channel. "Jake, get a team to mid-level between the park and the cargo holds. Apprehend Felicity Varner."

"On it. Got a team stationed nearby."

"I'm on my way too."

. . .

Nando and Zon caught up with her on the lower level. Skip approached cautiously.

"What are you accusing me of?" Felicity asked.

"No one is accusing you," Zon said. "We are following a couple of trails, and you happen to be at the wrong end of one of them."

She looked at Nando. "Nando, please. Tell him it can't be me."

Nando frowned. "I've talked to you maybe twice in the past year. You gave me the cold shoulder the second time. What makes you think I would know you well enough to think you weren't the culprit?"

"Sure, here in the real world, Nando. You know who I really am, because in the virtual world, I showed you my heart."

"Briana?"

Felicity nodded.

Nando shook his head. "Fine. I can stand by your side. But you still need to be questioned, like anyone else."

She pointed at Skip. "Tell your father to have them leave me alone. You know I didn't bomb anyone."

Nando looked at Skip, then back at her. "Sure, probably not. But they'll figure it out. Just come with us."

"You don't believe me!" She shoved Nando away from her. "I'm innocent. Hear me? Innocent! Onada, I love your son. Please, don't let them break us apart. Delikan is lying. He knows I didn't do this."

Zon glanced at Skip. Skip frowned and nodded.

Zon took her wrist and spun her around. Before he could secure her arms she twisted, sending her heel slamming into his temple, then lashed out and shoved her fist into Skip's throat.

He stumbled backwards as she made for the ladder.

Nando grabbed her shoulder and deftly avoided an elbow, but her next attack hit his abdomen. The two grappled, twisted, and struggled. The blood-soaked front of Nando's uniform was ripped and sliced. She had a knife.

The two spun violently and tumbled to the deck. Skip moved forward and attempted to catch a leg. She moved quickly. He chided himself as the stars blocked his vision on his way to the deck.

He could make out their figures, hear the sound of their flesh, pounding each other. Then a ripping crunch. Her hands shot to Nando's face, thumbs gouged deeply into his eyes. Her chin clamped as she spasmed, then went limp. Nando rolled off her and attempted to stand. He fell forward and stopped moving.

Skip yelled, "Medic!"

•• ——————— ••●•• ——————— ••

LATER THAT AFTERNOON, Skip called Jake and Robert into his office. Robert had brought Brenna with him. Just as well she heard this too. He nodded at his son. "Jake, I'm going to put you on the *Pang Yu*. You'll oversee repairs then take her back to Earth. You can catch the next ship back."

Jake nodded. "Yes sir."

Brenna shook her head. "Skip, I don't think that's the way it should be."

Skip sighed and shook his head. "You just transferred. I didn't want to–"

"No sir. It's my ship, my crew. Sorry Jake, but it's been almost a decade since you were aboard. I know the crew, and I know the ship better than you. The new engine especially. I'm the logical choice to take her home."

Robert lowered his head. "I'm going to have to agree with her. I can manage the engine conversion."

Brenna put her hand on Robert's shoulder. "Then I'll grab the first ship back, if I can."

Skip glanced at Jake who simply nodded. "AutoGov, transfer Brenna Dotseth back to the *Pang Yu*, effective immediately."

"Acknowledged," AutoGov said. "Sub-Commander Dotseth, as the highest ranking functional crew member of the *Pang Yu*, will you be assuming command?"

"Yes," Brenna said. "I assume command."

"Command transferred. Congratulations Captain Dotseth."

Brenna's throat tightened. She closed her eyes to fight back tears.

Robert reached out and placed his hand on the back of her shoulder. She folded into his embrace.

Skip cleared his throat. "Jake, take over the onboarding of supplies for them. Make sure they have everything they need."

Jake nodded sharply. "Aye, sir. I've already transferred some of our spare parts for their bridge repairs."

Skip sighed. "All right. One with it, then."

Jake spun on his heel and headed up toward the docking ring.

Skip nodded at Robert. "Brenna, I know this is hard on you. She was..." Skip's voice cracked.

Brenna slipped out of Robert's embrace, turned, and hugged the old man. "It's okay. I know."

She felt his stiff outer shell melt. He held her for a moment.

"I'll be okay. I'm more worried about you."

Brenna half smiled. "Of course you are. I only hope I'm as good at leading a crew as her."

PIECES GONE MISSING

Thursday, December 19, 3297, 9:28

"We matched her DNA to what we found inside the clean suit," Zon said. "The particulate evidence says the clean suit had been in the service tunnel. She had no business in there. Her attack was pretty brutal. She did not want to be questioned. I feel for Nando, though."

Ted sighed. "Yeah. Must have been tough to hear. Good work, Zon."

"Thanks. Hope you and your wife heal up fast."

Ted smiled. "Thanks. But I figure I can milk this for a couple of weeks, Acting Chief. Have fun. Oh, and look into the sensor maintenance schedule. The report says they were all down for maintenance at the same time along the path she took. Can't be a coincidence."

Zon's jaw dropped. Ted closed the connection and limped back into the recovery room. The medical tech noticed. She frowned. "Is your pain response slow?" Her name floated above her head. *Shea Bakke.*

Ted shook his head. "Nope. Just feels weird. Still healing, I guess. How's my wife?"

Shea nodded toward the next room. "She's doing as well as can be expected. She's awake, if you want to go in. She's still got some juice in her, but the counter agent is already active."

"Thank you." He headed for the next room. Rows of beds with their head to the wall and feet toward the passage lined the short hall.

Debra lay in the first bed to his left. She looked up at him and smiled. "Shay sessy." She frowned. "My libser too pig."

Ted chuckled. "Give it a moment. You'll be fine." He glanced around the room, and spotted Nando. His face swollen, his ribs bandaged and bloody. He was still out.

"Less. Wuss muh lek."

Shea, headed for Nando.

"Ey! Wass mu leg?" Debra pointed to where her right leg should have been.

Ted frowned. "It's not there?"

Shea came back and nodded. "There wasn't much left to salvage. I'm afraid you'll need a new one."

Debra lifted her palms and shook her head. "Ghih?"

Ted could feel the realization like a wave of relief. "She's from Luna. I think she's confused as to why it's not there yet."

Shea nodded. "You two are new here. We haven't had enough time to grow spare tissue for you. You are going to have to make do with a prosthetic for a few weeks while we grow enough to build a new leg."

"See darling? All in good time. Now relax."

Nando started moaning.

Shea turned back to him. "You awake, Nando?"

His hand went to his face. The bandage over his eyes was firmly fixed. "Did I lose my eyes?"

She sighed. "You did. The bandages are holding the new ones in place while the rectus muscles grow attached. They probably feel funny because we shut off the nerves to prevent any twitching."

Nando remained silent for a moment. "Shea?"

"Yes. I'm handling your recovery."

"Oh crap. You didn't make me cross-eyed or anything, did you?"

Ted smirked. "Nando, be nice. She's got plenty of skills. I've seen her in action."

Shea turned to Ted and smiled. "Thank you, Mister Becker, but I think he's worried I might mess him up on purpose. See, we used to see each other, and I terminated the relationship. I was quite angry at the time." She paused. "Maybe a little cross-eyed."

Nando moaned. "I'm so sorry."

Ted chuckled. "Nando took down the one who hurt my wife, killed the others. He's pretty much a hero in my book."

Shea frowned. "I'm sure your new little girlfriend will be quite pleased." She turned away from them both.

"Um, the attacker was his girlfriend. And I think she faked everything."

Shea spun around. "Faked it? She did this?" She stepped closer to Nando. "You idiot."

Nando sighed. "I am. I know. She came after me because of Skip. Figured his son would be good for information. She was right. This whole thing is my fault."

Shea folded her arms. "You aren't going to get any sympathy from me just by admitting yourself to be an idiot. I already knew that."

Nando shook his head. "I don't want your sympathy. I don't deserve it. I let myself be played. I chose a fantasy over reality, a great reality, better than I deserved, and I don't even know why. I... I want to say I'm sorry."

Shea lifted her hand to wipe away a tear.

Ted used his internal controller to capture an image. He captioned it *She cares* and sent it to Nando.

After a moment, Nando continued. "There's no way I can ever make it up to you."

She crossed her arms. "No, there isn't." She wiped another tear.

Debra reached up and took Ted's hand, watching the drama play out.

Nando sighed deeply. "Look, if you ever start to forgive me, maybe I can try an apology. Or two. When you're ready."

"An apology? Two? You are such a damned idiot. After what you did, you should apologize to me every day of every year for the rest of our lives."

Nando opened his mouth to say something, then stopped. Then smiled. "I accept."

Shea blinked. "What?"

"I accept. I'll marry you, and I'll apologize to you every day for the rest of our lives."

Shea's dark skin tone didn't hide her flush. She glanced at Ted and Debra, then signaled the privacy divider. With a swoosh, the opaque curtain hid them from view.

From behind the curtain Shea said, "This is so unprofessional."

"It's all my fault. I am so so–" Nando's voice suddenly became muffled.

Debra giggled. "Is she kissing him?"

"Or suffocating him?" Ted said. "Either way I'm on her side." He cast a long glance at Debra. He inhaled deeply and let the air out slowly. "AutoGov, release my pregnancy safeties."

"Acknowledged. Inhibitor reversed. Regular sperm production will be fully functional within three days."

Debra grinned. "I had to wait fourteen days. No fair." She leaned over and kissed him.

THE HARD RETURN

Thursday, December 19, 3297, 14:13

The look on Robert's face told her exactly what he was thinking. He came in swiftly, and wrapped his arms around tightly.

Brenna held him close. "I wish there had been another way. But it's my duty."

Robert nodded and relaxed his arms enough to bring his face to hers. "We seem to be having a phenomenal run of luck. All bad. I have to stay for the same reason you have to go, and I love you all the more for it."

Brenna smiled. "All this time together and now you drop the L word?"

Robert chuckled. "I wanted to be sure you understood how I felt."

Brenna leaned in and kissed him. She took her time. Tears welled up in her eyes. She leaned back, struggling with the words. "Now you understand how I feel too."

"How soon are you going to leave?"

Brenna sighed. "We're a few days behind schedule as it is.

Maybe another day or two, and I'm probably going to be very busy for it all."

Robert nodded. "I'll arrange for cover. You tell me when and where, I'll be there until the day you leave."

She kissed him again. "How about here, now?"

He giggled. "Might be a touch too public, but sure."

She gave him a lopsided grin. "Your place in fifteen minutes. I'll schedule myself a few hours downtime."

"Got it. See you soon." He slipped out of her arms and headed for the lift.

Brenna took a deep breath and nodded, then watched him disappear. She felt the pangs of loss, already growing in her chest. She shook her head and headed back to the operations center. Time to get everything ready for the trip home.

When she arrived, there were two technicians hard at work repairing one of the damaged consoles. "How soon until we can resume loading?"

"We'll be there in a few more minutes. Just setting the connectors here. Everything else has been repaired and reconnected."

Brenna nodded. "So, I can expect the ship to be ready tonight?"

The techs looked at each other. "Probably. Tomorrow morning at the latest."

She swiped her display and wrote a message to her crew. *Pang Yu will be loaded and ready by tomorrow morning. I want to use the rest of the day to wrap up any lingering business. The current plan is to depart at 0800 on Monday. Be sure to double check all stores in the morning and verify everything is secure for jump, then take the rest of the time off. Muster at 0730 Monday.*

She sent the message, then headed for Robert's apartment.

•• —————————— ••●•• —————————— ••

MEMBERS of both crews filled the park. Ted kept a watchful eye, as Debra stepped onto the platform in the clearing.

"I am Debra Becker," she said. "By now you all know my history. It's no secret. The recent attack was meant for me. My friends paid the price. Again. I came here to get away from it. Seems like I may never escape. So, I'm calling you out, now. Anyone still loyal to Masters and Billings, step forward and say so. All I want is to live in peace. Your corporation doesn't exist anymore, and the people back home are still rebuilding from the war. So many people died on both sides. How many more need to join them?"

Skip stepped onto the platform. "Listen up. There are open berths on the *Pang Yu*. Anyone who wants to go is invited to leave. Staying here to exact revenge will accomplish nothing. If you feel so strongly, go home. Work to rebuild what you love. Find the people you left behind. The rest of us, including the Beckers, are staying here. We've a lot of work to do. An inter-species relationship to build. Fighting among ourselves cannot be tolerated."

Dr. Mukumba stepped forward. "Is that offer open to anyone? No offense to the lady, I have no hard feelings there. But I think my work is done here. My assistants are all quite capable of continuing. I would like to return home. If I may."

Skip nodded. "Anyone else that wants to go, pack up now and board the *Pang Yu*. Dr. Puttkammer will put you into cold sleep for the trip home. The ship leaves tomorrow morning, so decide right now. The offer is first come, first frozen until they are full."

FUTURE PROSPECTS

Mas'eeng Foythey, Second Six, Late High

Bongeex felt the strain in his thighs. His third climb to the airship, and there were still baskets of food to lift and place in the dark belly of the airship. The sunlight seemed too bright as he emerged and headed down to where they were organizing the food. In the distance, Kempok caught his eye and strode toward him with purpose.

Bongeex knew that look. She had that look of determination. Like the clouds gathering for a storm, not something that could be avoided.

"Bongeex," Kempok said. "I have made my choice. I've selected a suitable egg-mother. I believe it will be a good match for you."

He shrunk and undulated slowly. "Yes, Kempok. As I promised, I will comply."

Kempok chut-chutted. "You don't look as pleased as I had hoped. Tell me, what is on your mind?"

Bongeex took a deep breath and exhaled. "I've flown in the sky, felt the wind from high above. I've seen the engine of the most amazing vehicle in the world. And I met an egg-mother that... I find it hard to say the words. Everything about her pleases me. She is intelligent, beautiful, kind, patient, and she taught me new things without any hesitation. So I'm sorry if I cannot be thrilled at the prospect of something less. I gave you my word, and I will keep it. I will always keep my word, Kempok."

Kempok chut-chutted then continued chutting.

Bongeex shrunk further. He hadn't expected that.

Finally, she said, "Bongeex, you poor thing. You know I love you, so I will give you a final say. I will tell you the name of the one I have found. If you tell me that will not suit you, I shall search again." Kempok raised one long finger. "I must warn you, I'm rather proud of this choice."

Bongeex undulated. "Thank you, Kempok. I doubt that I will find a reason to reject her."

"The egg-mother I like will require much manual labor from you, and you will be taken far from this tribe. I ask that you visit from time to time, or at least send word."

Bongeex undulated. "I shall not lose myself. I will send word often and visit when possible."

"Good. Because that airship goes all over Thoxmoyang. No telling where you'll end up."

Bongeex felt his heart stop. He wavered. "What?"

"Maykath Kayfox wishes to marry you, and I like the match. It is my understanding you will be required to perform much manual labor. Working in the engine room, loading cargo and such."

Bongeex bounced from foot to foot.

"So. Do you wish to reject this one? Shall I try again?"

Bongeex leapt forward and wrapped his arms around Kempok's neck. He held her tightly.

"No need to strangle me, I'll find you a better match."

Bongeex released her and chutted. "No need to put yourself out, Mother. I shall make the best of the situation."

Kempok sighed. "I know you will. And eventually, bring me grandchildren. I want to feed them koox."

STORMBRINGER

Saturday, December 21, 3297, 15:15

Radinka took one last look at herself in a blank virtual space. Just a mirrored image of herself for company. She tilted the pirate hat ever so slightly and smiled. "Engage pirate protocols and record."

She paused for a moment to gather her thoughts. "This message is addressed to the one I call Ferdinand. I'm recording this to be delivered after I'm gone. I am fairly certain you were never able to ascertain my identity, but you will be able to narrow down your list of candidates now. I'm sure, given your talents, that if you so choose, you could eventually figure it out."

She spread her arms. "As I said to you before, I have another mission I must attend to. If you have survived, you are now in charge of the group. I won't limit you by attempting to define your mission. I will simply recommend that you keep your head down. Let them become complacent. Listen for the sounds of dissent and carefully recruit a new team. Train, observe and build trust among yourselves. Then, when the time is right, when you can see plainly what needs to be done, you will be in a position to accomplish it."

Radinka sighed. "I never liked cold sleep. It isn't an option that I take lightly. But the ship is going where I need to be. So that is what I shall do. Or rather, have done."

She bowed deeply, with a flourish of her pirate hat. "I wish you luck. End recording and save. Now end program."

Gabriel extracted himself from virtual reality and sighed. "Upon confirmation that the *Pang Yu* has jumped away, set a timer for eight hours, then release the message to the character called Ferdinand in the Tipsy Raven simulation."

"Acknowledged."

"Have all my belongings been packed away on the *Pang Yu*?"

"Affirmative, with the exception noted previously."

Gabriel patted the pouch at his waist. "Very good. Transfer the virtual reality interface to recycling and make sure it's destroyed as soon as possible without drawing attention. Time to get going."

Without even a final look he left his apartment and began his long journey home.

CAPTAIN OF THE PANG YU

Monday, December 23, 3297, 10:25

Captain Brenna Dotseth floated inside the cage that surrounded the Conn, the nerve center of the ship. Safety straps allowed her freedom of movement, while ensuring she wasn't thrown out during maneuvers. An array of displays, mostly virtual, surrounded her. One of them showed a live image of the ring she and Robert had explored. *So many unanswered questions.*

Master Lieutenant Dugan interrupted her thoughts with the announcement she had been anticipating. "Conn Nav, we are at the jump point."

"Nav Conn, aye." Brenna cleared her personal displays and waved the ship wide circuit on. "All hands, prepare for jump. Engineering Conn, report pre-jump status."

"Report pre-jump status, Conn Engineering aye. Stored power at one hundred percent. Heat sink is at one sixty-nine kelvin. Reactor is secured. I have a green board."

"Engineering Conn aye. Navigator, verify your coordinates."

"Verify coordinates, Nav aye. Conn, my coordinates are verified. I have a blue board."

"Nav Conn aye. Ops Conn, report all contacts within one thousand kilometers."

"Report all contacts within one thousand kilometers, Ops aye. Conn Ops, no contacts within range. We are clear to jump."

"Ops Conn aye." Brenna paused, taking one last look at the world below. Far in the distance, the tiny shimmering ring of the *Endurance*. In her heart, she knew Robert was watching. So many unanswered questions. "Engineering Conn, commence the jump."

ECCLESIA ADVENIT

Tuesday, January 21, 3298, 7:59

Skip entered MCC for the start of another quiet watch.

"Congratulations," Kai said.

He smiled. "Thank you, Kai. Lenny did all the fun parts. I'll just be changing diapers."

"Valerie must be very happy."

Skip chuckled. "Oh, you only heard yesterday's news. This morning Ami came up positive too."

"Both of them?"

Skip nodded with a grin. "The Onada clan's next generation is going to be big. Lenny would be almost comically happy." His grin faded a little.

"Did they ever work out the naming?"

Skip nodded. "Lenny backed off. You know, it was his mother's family tradition to take the woman's surname. They convinced him it would be better all-around if the two ladies took his."

Kai frowned. "We going to have a party?"

"It'll probably be this weekend. Big celebration."

"Be sure to record it all. I'm sure Lenny will want to see it when he comes home."

Skip took a deep breath and exhaled slowly. "When he comes home."

Kai touched her ear and turned back to her screen. She swiped the display. "Skip, we detected an incoming jump signature out near Kethday."

"Can you identify it?"

"I've got the sensors tracking it now." She paused, listening intently. "I'm detecting a carrier wave. It's an Allied Industries ship, belonging to..."

"What is it?"

"Sir, it identifies itself as a Mormon Catholic Missionary Ship. Audio coming in now, sir."

"Play it."

"This is Bishop Justin Wells, commanding the *MCMS Saint Xu Guangqi*. I am sending this to the *AEX Endurance*. We have just entered the system and are starting standard operations. We intend to jump as soon as we've completed and should arrive near your orbit shortly after that. Please acknowledge."

"Good grief. Missionaries are knocking on our door."

"Do you think we can feed them to the Ombax?"

Dayexmad Fadmey
(Complete Story, or The End)

NOTES ABOUT THE OMBAX

The Calendar

There are two Ombax Seasons – Mas'eeng (grow large) and Mas'beem (grow small) in the West, and in the East they are called Eef'paath (increase) and Mo'othsey (decrease).

There are eight months total:

1. Bayfod
2. Masassof
3. Foythey
4. Bayok
5. Ethmof
6. Ofbof
7. Kopom
8. Eeth

Each month has four full counts – First, Second, Third, and Last. Each Full Count has eight days, which are simply numbered.

At the end of the eight months there are several days left over.

This is called the Short Count, and in odd numbered years has five days, with six in even years.

An Ombax day is about six hours longer than a human day. It's split into eight sections:
1.Risingday'fox
2.Earlyfeysoy
3.Early Highfey'key
4.Highestothkey
5.Late Highthey'key
6.Latetheydop
7.Settingday'foo'
8.Nightemak

THE SECTION NAMES refer to the position of the sun, and night is the longest section. Exact lengths depend on the time of year. There is a full translation matrix for these section names, however their translated names appear in the story because it just seemed like too much. Same for the numbered days.

The year is numbered as well. Currently it's the year 11162 by their numbering system, which is octal. In decimal, that would be 4722. At this time, it's unclear what the base date is –

either the Sunfire War, their nuclear war which we've dated to around that time, or from the founding of their religion, which is understood to have happened several centuries later.

Omseep, the Ombax Language

I've mapped the most common words of the Ombax language. Typically, larger words are contractions of two or more smaller ones. The apostrophe is used to show a glottal stop, which is a loud pulse emitted by the Ombax throat. It's often, but not always, used to denote a place where two words were joined, and some sounds in the middle have been omitted. For example, Mas'eeng is a combination of mas (grow) and poyeeng (large) with the "poy" dropped. Mas'beem uses the same prefix, with beybeem being the root suffix. Again, dropping the "bey" for a glottal stop.

Some words do not use the stop to indicate missing sounds. The name of the major city, Afothameex, is a combination of asfoyoo' (electric) and thameex (city). Literally, this is Electric City.

ACKNOWLEDGMENTS

I would like to express my sincerest gratitude to Jed Whitton. I asked him if I could get some stellar data with Cartesian coordinates when I first realized where this book was going to go. He answered me promptly, and within hours I had more than 87,000 star systems in my database. His file imported perfectly the very first time. As a software professional, I truly appreciate it.

I want to thank Persephone Grey for her help in editing this book. Her meticulous attention to detail has made this a better story, a better book, and I hope, a better reading experience for you.

The best images I've seen so far of what a Kalpana Two station could look like are done by Bryan Versteeg at *SpaceHabs.com*. I studied his art to fix in my mind what *Endurance* looked like.

Thank you to James Beall for your help in understanding what I needed to have to make the nuclear-powered steam engines work. While far more complicated than I had hoped, it certainly raises plenty of questions that I left unanswered in this story.

Thank you, Isaac Arthur, for your contributions to the local biology. You helped me invent non-human explosive diarrhea. Eventually we need to put this on a trophy for your shelf. In all seriousness, your correspondence as well as your video series were vital to the development of this book, and I'm eternally grateful. Find him at *IsaacArthur.net*.

I also would like to thank Charles E. Gannon for his TRIPS application. It helped me figure out the course the two ships had to take, and was instrumental in determining the final destination star system, which I didn't actually refer to in this book. Check out his website at *CharlesEGannon.com*. Also, read his books! He is one of my inspirations.

The list of other people I want to thank is growing longer by the week. Each is important in their own way, so in *no particular order*, I want to thank Jake Clark, Patrick Dugan, James P. Nettles, John G. Hartness, Christopher Ruocchio, Charles E. Gannon, Christopher Kennedy, Les Gould, Darin Kennedy, Stuart Jaffee, A. J. Hartley, Jody Lynne Nye, Michael Stackpole, J. A. J. Minton, T. Frohock, Dino Hicks, Rob Bignell, and Allen Wold.

A big shout out to all my friends in the BookTube universe. Amy, Andrew, Brian, Cronk, Edward (Gryftkin), Jakob, Sid, Slay, Sebastian, Chance, Deanna, and most especially, John and the entire crowd at *Talking Story*. Thank you for all your support!

For more information on the books I've written, my newsletter, and my small, but very fun community, come to *AutomatedEmpire.com*. You'll find links to all my social media.

THANK YOU TO MY SUPPORTERS!

IndieGoGo Supporters

Jill B. Wood

Natt Jantasto

Landon Crispens

John Chappell

Sheryl W. Homan

Dee Clingenpeel

Aditya Nimmagadda

L. Wayne Camp

Phil Romanus

Tricia Makin

Atit Patel

Dino, Patron Saint of Storytellers

Chris Ritchey

Cliff McDonald

Charlie White

Derby Hilp

Nancy Northcott

Patrick Dugan

Andrew Mattocks

Brandon Whitworth

Christian Glasneck

Sharlin Kay Canton

Edward Myers
Methawee Myers
Robert Laymon
Greg Ivaska
Landon Crispens